SUNSHINE'S SYNDICATE

Sunshine's Syndicate

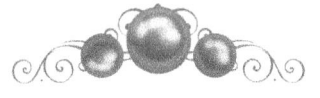

BRITTANY TUCKER

FIRST

FRUIT PRESS

Content Warning: Graphic violence/death on page, alcohol use, suggestive content, character with history of physical abuse, panic attacks, mild language.

Copyright © 2024 by Brittany Tucker

Interior Graphics by B.E. Padgett

Cover by Miblart

All rights reserved.

No part of this book may be reproduced in any form or by any electronic or mechanical means, including information storage and retrieval systems, without written permission from the author, except for the use of brief quotations in a book review.

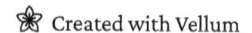

❀ Created with Vellum

*To Samantha Ann Leigh,
This story wouldn't exist without you
and your insistent demands for "MOAR!"
Thank you.*

CARNAGE

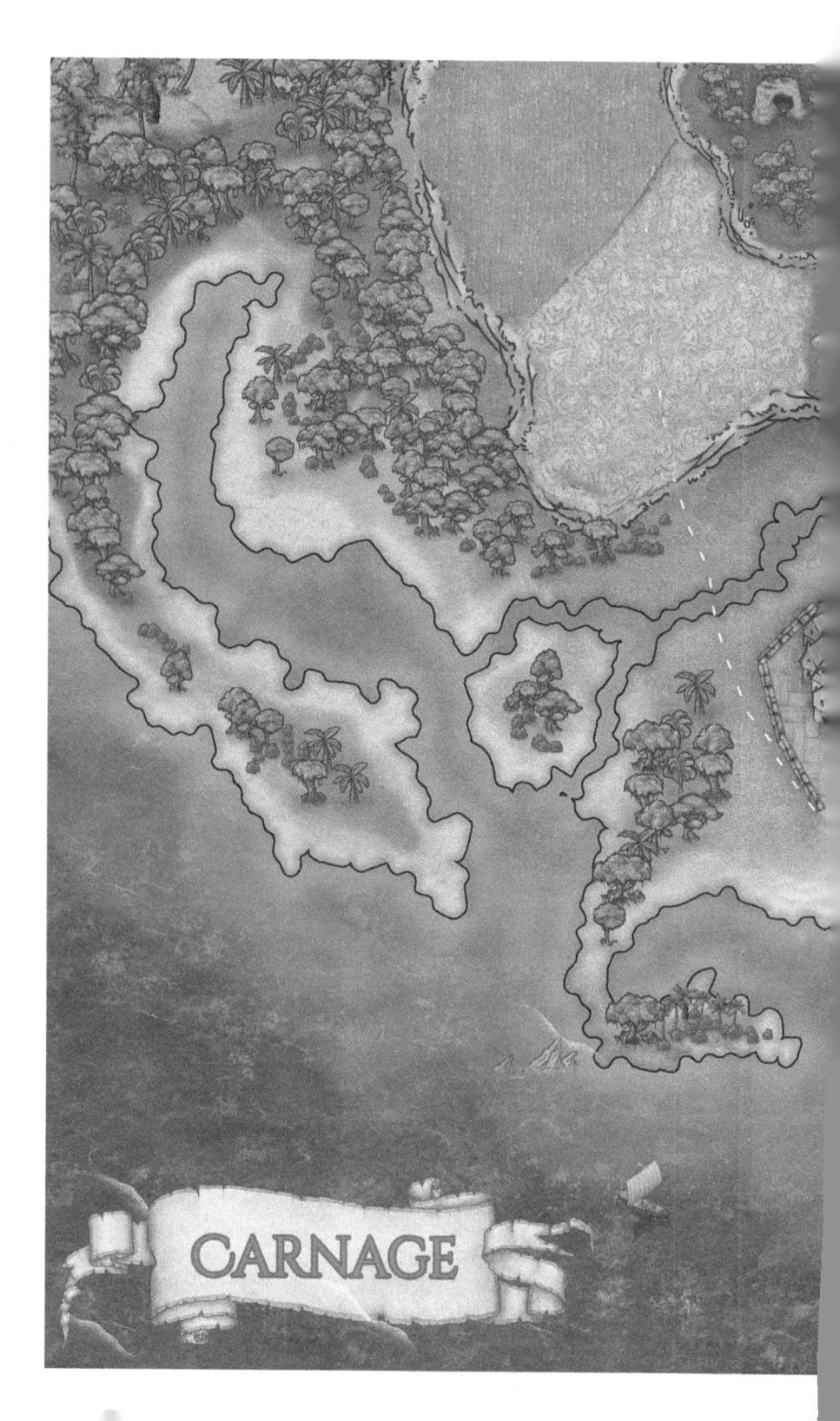

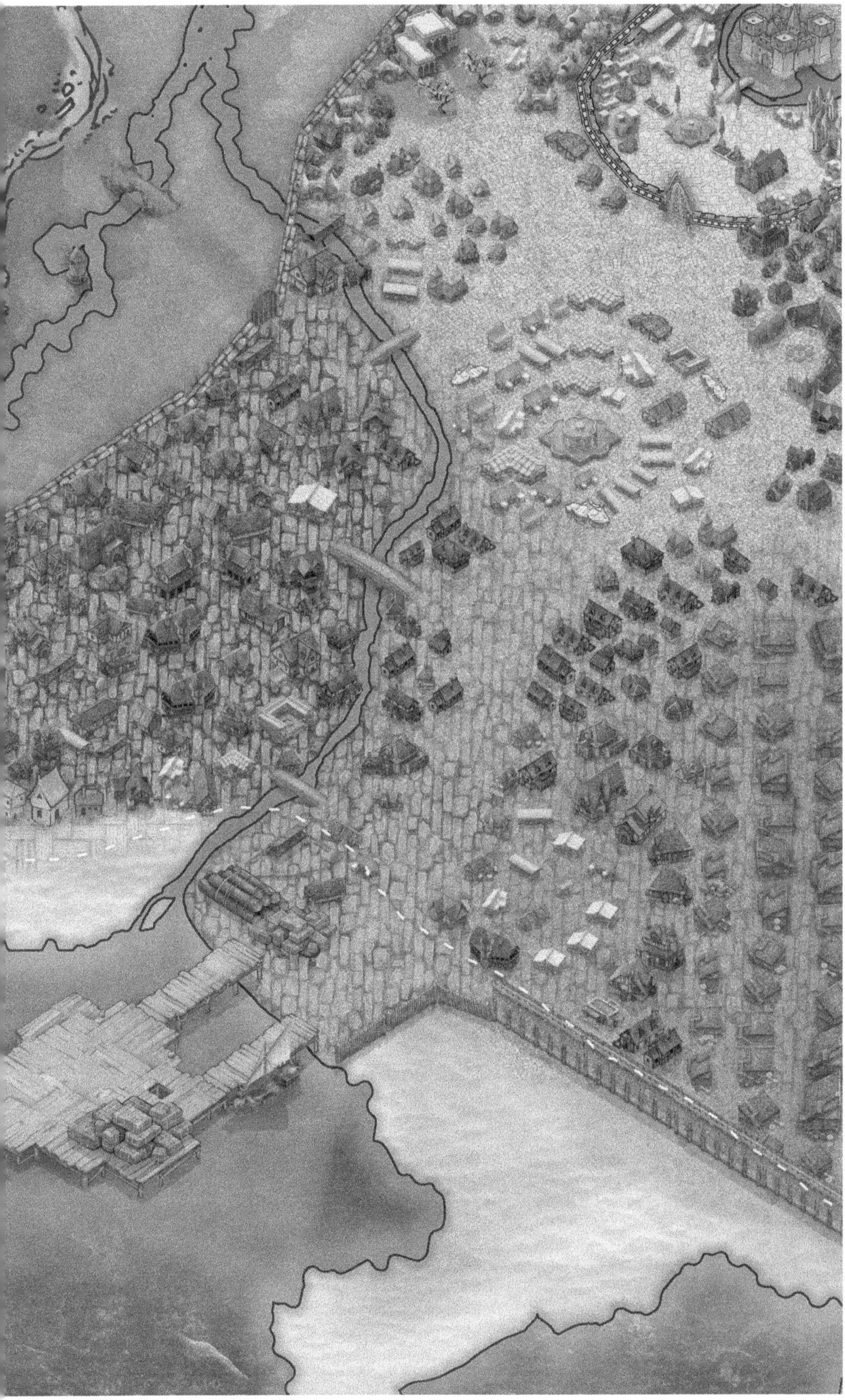

Chapter One

To hell with the Elves—I'm going to steal back Cyclone's bones.

The traitorous thought sent a tidal wave of adrenaline through my already trembling limbs. Goosebumps skittered up my tanned arms, making me shiver.

The growing crowd encircled the opal and barnacle-stained dais where Cyclone's son, Surge, now stood in his place—our reigning prince never to be crowned.

Murmurs. Catty whispering. The noise rubbed at my nerves like sodden wool. I stared at the empty space above the throne and fought to stay present. It would be so easy to let my mind wander away somewhere else. Somewhere lovely and warm. Somewhere that fear didn't linger like the stench of bile.

Cyclone had been legendary—a war hero—the greatest Merfolk king in a millennium.

Now he was dead—his rotted corpse nailed above the Lantern Palace, the conquering Elven emperor's seat of power—and I would bring him home. I owed him that much.

I clenched my fist until the enlistment papers within it

crumpled—my name, Tetra, scrawled across the top in a lazy, arrogant script. *This is stupid—absolutely ridiculous to consider.*

And I was going to do it. Damn it, they all could watch me.

Anxious chatter turned the above-sea chamber into a beehive, snapping me back to attention. I shifted away from the onlookers toward the salt and brine-stained walls to get a better view of the prince.

Surge stepped to the edge of the dais, high above the Merfolk he'd hoped to rule—at least until we were invaded and lost. That was one year ago.

He's nervous.

Surge's bright, crimson fins fluttered on his calves and forearms as he swept back his lengthy, black hair. It was pretty—such a deep color—like the obsidian arrowheads I sometimes dug out of the coral beds. Thousands of scaled bodies watched him open a water-stained scroll.

He'll stop this. I gripped the letter tighter as he cleared his throat and chewed at the skin on the edge of his full lips. The men and women of The Dam held their breath in anticipation.

The Dam—our ancient stone city carved into the side of a cliff—was the cell we were now confined to. Our once stunning metropolis had become a prison.

Surge took a heavy breath and began to speak. "Addressed by the blessed Elven Empire."

A unified *hail* echoed off the rocks.

I crossed my arms over my chest to contain my pounding heart. *He won't let this happen. He'll stop this.*

"Hail." Surge cleared his throat again, a muscle flexing in his jaw. "Our dominion will continue west, across the Tyrr sea. Naval forces must be bolstered and readied in retaliation against the Seafolk sycophants in the waters beyond. Every able-bodied male above fifteen years will be transferred to an established encampment to prepare for war."

Stunned silence.

Surge sucked in a sharp breath, voice cracking as he continued. "All able-bodied females above the age of eighteen, that are not with child, will be transferred to an established encampment to be prepared for war."

Angry voices. Frightened voices. Outraged, wailing voices.

I covered my ears as the shouting threatened to crush my skull.

That was me. At twenty-one, I had no family, no bonded mate, and no one to miss me when I was gone. The letter I carried—my orders to prepare for deployment—weighed down my arm like a millstone.

I would die on the front lines for the man who'd taken everything from me.

Surge's many guards stamped their mighty spears, creating a booming order of silence.

The shouting stopped.

"A census will be taken." Surge's tone rose an octave higher as he continued. "Anyone who refuses to submit to the draft will be declared enemies of the Empire. You will be expected to report by the date listed on your summons." Surge's long fingers shook as he rolled up the scroll. I could have sworn his dark eyes were lined with silver. "Blessed be the name of the Empire."

He's not going to save us. A numbness seeped through my body, my blood. *We're going to war . . . with the wrong people.*

I wasn't a fighter.

I was a collector—a self-proclaimed connoisseur of beautiful treasures and antiques. I would be one of the first to fall.

He's not going to save us. The thought continued to repeat until it had me sprinting from the throne room. I couldn't breathe. The noise, the colors—they ripped through my attempts to stay grounded as a bubbling sob escaped my throat. *No one will miss me.*

The winding, brown rock corridors of The Dam cut into my bare feet. The entire city was crafted from the cliff sides jutting out from Tyrr's far coastline. I'd never lived anywhere but the open ocean until the Elves took over. My parents kept us as outliers, making our living off what we could sell from the sea to the local towns.

But they were dead now, too—skeletons at the bottom of the bay. I was hauled away to The Dam before I could even bury them.

My fingers trembled, breaths ragged, as I unlocked the sea-rotted door to my dorm. It was tight, barely wide enough for me to move in, but at least I had somewhere to sleep, food to eat, and a slim shelf over my salt-water basin where I could set up my remaining trinkets.

A sparse shelter—one of the few comforts Surge could grant to those who'd lost their homes and freedom.

I sunk onto my lumpy mattress, gazing blankly up at my treasures. A ruby hair clip. A silver pocket watch with emerald hands. Dozens of gold coins, predating when the Elves were even a whisper of a threat on the Tyrr coast.

He was supposed to protect us.

Surge had crumpled—the Merfolk had crumpled—when Elf lord Sayzar Ameliatus nailed Cyclone's brutalized body to the tower above the Lantern Palace and crowned himself the new Emperor of Tyrr.

But I will get him back. I didn't know how, but it felt right. Surge needed a push—a shove off the proverbial cliff. We could still take the sea back.

Anxiety seeped into my skin as I glanced up again at my collection. God knew I wasn't meant for war. No, I was meant to open an oddities shop, to brighten people's dreary days by giving them a place to see and buy interesting, fantastical things—to find little escapes from the ordinary wrapped inside a precious trinket—their own little treasures.

Sayzar Ameliatus had taken that future from me.

A small smile cracked my chapped lips. *I will take it back.*

I stood and shoved everything I knew and loved into my woven bag. There was only one person who would help me now—one person who could help me save my pilfered future.

Loach.

I kept my eyes on the ground as I descended the slippery, algae-stained steps to the Bottom. The only area of the city situated below sea level, the Bottom would be the first to flood if The Dam were to breach.

A sprawling, tented market—Seafolk of all kinds could be found here. Selkies, Cecalias, and outlying Merfolk wandered the shadowed places deep below the breathtaking, opalescent splendor of the halls above. Many of Tyrr's unbonded Merwomen made their homes down here, too, where they traded contraband for luxuries and comfort.

I kept my strides long as I moved through the marketplaces, my head low. Several familiar merchants waved at me from their stalls. I waved back with a close-lipped smile. Though I wasn't the only scavenger in The Dam, I was the best. Even as a child—when my parents would sell here—the traders fought over who got the first pick of my haul. I could have made a fortune off the trinkets I collected if the Emperor hadn't locked us away.

"Tetra!" Kevn—a spindly-legged, moss-green-haired

Merman—called to me as I approached the Spoiled Oyster, Loach's tavern. Kevn gave me a quick up-and-down. "I haven't seen you in days. I was starting to worry you'd bailed on us."

"And where would I have gone?" I hadn't decided if it was a problem or not that all the tavern staff knew me. It probably was. I forced myself to smile. "I've just been . . . busy. Is Loach in?"

Kevn scowled, picking at a loose, green scale on his elbow. "Yeah, he's in. Be careful, though, he's cranky as hell."

My smile was genuine this time, more out of relief than anything. If he'd been out, I might not have had the courage to attempt this stupid plan again. "He's always cranky."

Kevn caught my elbow as I tried to pass, anxiety dusting his expression. "Are you okay? Your eyes are all puffy."

My skin crawled at his touch. It wasn't his fault. Flesh just freaked me out. Too squishy yet firm all at the same time. "I'm fine. Promise."

"Okay." He let go. "You know if you need anything, you can always come to me, right? I've got friends, if you know what I mean. We'll take care of you."

"Thank you." I plucked off that loose scale. He hissed. "I will make sure to remember that."

I didn't have the heart to tell him that I didn't want to be taken care of—I wanted to be left alone. The people meant to watch over me were gone.

Kevn's lingering gaze followed me into the Spoiled Oyster.

The tavern was quieter than usual. There were even seats left at the bar. Probably because citizens were still gossiping about the drafts. Several Mermaids leaned against the counter, grinning at the barkeeper, hoping to win a free drink. Chains of pearls and opals fell between their naked breasts, around their slender waists—the current fashion. Clothes were optional when you spent most of your life below the waves.

One of the girls rose a haughty brow at me and my gaze dropped to the soggy floorboards. Her hair and fins were such a splendid, bright pink—dusted in canary yellow. Warm colors were cherished above all others among the Seafolk.

My eyes burned as I brushed my long, teal blue hair into a bun. At least my skin had remained bronzed despite how much less I saw the sun now. The tan looked nice with my cat-yellow eyes, and the golden scales dusted on my nose and cheeks like freckles—the only warmth I had. My fins and scales never shifted beyond ever-boring shades of purples and blues.

The bartender didn't stop me—instead giving a friendly wave—as I trotted down the warped staircase behind the bar. A heavy, wood door sat at the end of the hall on the bottom floor. The stench of cigar smoke wafted from the space between the hinges. I scraped my teeth across my tongue as the stench coated it. Burnt. Ashy. Disgusting.

I raised my fist to knock—

"Don't bother, Tetra," A deep voice grunted as the lock clicked free. Slowly, the door swung open. Loach stared down at me. "I'd know the sound of your elephant gait in my grave."

Loach—one of the last Kraken-humanoid beings in existence.

With a head like a squid, thick tentacles grew around Loach's mouth and chin like a man might wear a mustache and beard. Others called him one of the sea's remaining monsters, but I just knew him as Loach—the arms dealer who sometimes bought my trinkets out of pity.

I pursed my lips. "What's an elephant?"

"Never mind." Loach opened the door wider. Candlelight flickered in his dreary office. "What do you want?"

I rocked from heel to heel. "Can we talk?"

"Sure." Loach rolled his pebbly black eyes as he ushered me inside. "Because I have nothing better to do."

"Oh, good." I grinned as I sat myself at his desk, tucking the length of my short, green shift beneath me. The candles had burned low, leaving the room dim. Stacks of paper, books, and envelopes littered the top, along with empty bottles of ink and snapped pens. A few of the treasures I'd sold him months ago he used as paperweights.

But that was long before I'd gotten my draft.

Loach sighed as he plopped in the spindly wooden chair across from me. One of his tentacles picked up a fresh pen, filling it with ink, before it started taking notes. He glanced at the bag at my hip. "Did you bring something for me? With Surge's announcements, I'm not sure if now is the time."

"You heard?" I squeaked and pushed my crumpled letter toward him. "I'm being drafted."

Bless him. Loach read over my summons, his expression souring before he tossed it back to me. "Damned Elves."

We just stared at each other for a moment. I shifted in my chair.

Loach leaned back and sighed. His milk-white, oily skin gleamed in the low light. "I'm sorry to hear it, kid."

My breath caught in my chest. *Don't cry.* "I can't fight, Loach. I can barely slice an apple."

From beneath his tentacles, Loach smiled sadly. "I know."

"I won't last three months."

"So, you'll die with the rest of them. What's that have to do with me?"

I tucked my fingers under my thighs, breathing in through the nose, out through the mouth. "I'm going to steal Cyclone from the Lantern Palace."

Loach blinked once or twice before breaking out into a deep, rumbling laugh. "You're going to *steal* Cyclone? There's nothing left of him but bones."

I nodded, struggling to hold his gaze. "Bones fit in a bag as easily as gold."

Slowly—ever so slowly—Loach leaned forward, steepling his three-fingered hands over his desk. "And, my dear, how do you plan to do that?"

At least he hasn't chased me out yet. Besides locking the Merfolk in The Dam, the Emperor had created a barrier around his newly conquered city—Carnage—specifically to keep *us* out. To keep the Seafolk utterly dependent on the Elves to trade with the mainland—and there it would remain until the entire coast submitted to his rule.

But Loach could get me in. He had friends and connections everywhere.

I shrugged. "I don't know yet. I'll figure something out, but I need help to get out of The Dam and into Carnage. You can do it. I know you can."

Loach's eyes narrowed. "You think so?"

"Yes. That's what I just said."

Loach scanned over my face before he stood, moving to throw a log into his hearth. As he did so, one of his tentacles rose to brush a small, black box on his cobbled mantle. "Then what? If you succeed? Humor me."

I blinked at him.

"Then what?" Loach growled sharply. "What will you do if you manage to bring Cyclone home?"

"Then I'll lay him at Surge's feet." I let the words pour out, laying bare all my dirty, rebellious thoughts. "Maybe that would be the push he needs to fight back. He has an army—*had*—he just needs to use it."

Loach smiled . . . just a little. "And if he doesn't?"

"Then, at least, I'll have done all I can." I wiped my sweaty palms on my bare thighs. The sprinkling of pale blue and lavender scales over my skin were cool to the touch. "I don't know how to use a weapon, but I'm good at finding things. If any part of Cyclone is left nailed to the palace, I'll find it."

Loach shook his head. "The Elves will peel your shiny skin from your body."

"They'll kill me no matter what I do."

"You're an odd one, Tetra." Loach's tentacle opened that black box and took a small pouch from inside, laying it on my outstretched waiting palm. "You'll try to get through that barrier with or without me, won't you?"

I nodded as I opened the bag. Inside were finely ground pink crystals. My brow rose. "Salt?"

"Filtered from the sea," Loach answered, "the Elves have forbidden salt water within city limits. Makes it easier to control the remaining Seafolk inside." He gestured to the pouch. "You'll die within two days without that. That's enough salt to last about—eh—four weeks."

"I have three until I'm deployed." *He's not going to come.* My heart sank. Loach and I had never been friends, per se, but he'd always been kind. *I don't know why I thought he would.*

My throat burned from repressed tears. *No sad thoughts.* Mama always said worrying never changed anything. I worried anyway, but still, it was a nice thought.

Blowing out a breath, I tucked a loose strand of hair behind my ear before dumping the contents of my bag on Loach's desk—all my treasures, everything I had left. "Is this enough?" Loach gave me a questioning look, so I clarified. "For the salt, I mean?"

Loach let out a low laugh. "Kid, once you cross that threshold, there's nothing you could offer that's worth more than the contents of that pouch."

I perked up, wringing my hands together. "So, you're going to give it to me?"

"Of course not," he scoffed, "I'm coming with you—and

you're going to help me strip the Ameliatus' treasury dry." Loach spat on the moisture-stained floorboards. "The Emperor can rot."

His words settled on me like a thick blanket. *The treasury.*

Ironically, I hated theft, but taking back Cyclone's body didn't *feel* like stealing—it was more like a recovery mission—but robbing the Lantern Palace?

I cringed. "Do I have a choice in that matter?"

Loach's twisted mouth sneered beneath his tentacles. "Do you?"

I smiled flatly. *He's got me there.* "No, I guess not."

Chapter Two

"I didn't expect it to be so . . ." I gestured to the rippling dome of pure energy encapsulating the portside city of Carnage, glimmering in shades of yellows, pinks, and blues. *Kind of like me.* "Colorful?"

Loach snorted, perched beside me on a craggy rock jutting out of the water a few miles offshore. "Says the color-changing woman."

I glanced down at my hip-length hair, now lightened to a bright sky blue. The shade of a Merfolk's color was determined by water temperature to ensure the best camouflage. The waters along the coast were pleasantly warm. It had been years since I'd been this close to shore. I never had a reason to. I'd forgotten what it felt like.

Leaving The Dam wasn't the issue—Surge didn't keep many guards, despite the Emperor's orders—but getting through the barrier was an entirely different game. I hadn't been able to sleep all night thinking about it, and now the fatigue sat on my chest like a boulder.

Loach pointed to a bluff on the far east side of the city.

"The Emperor did a damn good job of keeping Seafolk out, but he underestimated the tenacity of a hungry criminal." He straightened his sodden, heavy coat. Why he chose to swim in full, formal dress was beyond me.

"Some of my associates dug a concealed tunnel through the cliff face. It's a tight squeeze, but I reckon we can get inside if we shimmy."

Even from this distance, I scanned Carnage's high brick-red towers and massive outer walls. It was a fortress. My throat went dry. "And what about the Enforcers?"

It was well known that Sayzar always kept a highly trained group of Elven soldiers around him and the Lantern Palace. I wouldn't stand a chance.

"We avoid them." Loach rolled his eyes as his middle tentacle pulled a skinny knife out of his boot, dropping it into my lap. He winked. "But take this in case we can't."

It took everything I had not to recoil. I lifted it with the tips of my fingers, grimaced, and tossed it in my bag. "Can we go now?"

Loach merely nodded before diving into the water.

I followed. As soon as I fell below the waves, my lungs shifted. Changing to absorb oxygen from the air to the sea. Loach had already swum a reasonable distance ahead. I grinned as the wide, iridescent fins on my calves and forearms flared. I pressed my ankles together, hooking my fins to create a massive, iridescent tail.

One roll of my body sent me shooting forward, cutting through the sea faster than Loach could ever hope to swim. Krakens—though vicious—were a lumbering lot.

Beds of bright, orange coral flashed beneath me, speckling with the greens, blues, and golds of tropical fish. Whitetip sharks wove through the jutting reefs, watching. They were never much of a bother.

I surged past Loach in three powerful strokes, careening for the bluff.

I couldn't stop smiling at the thrill singing through my blood.

This is where I belonged—consumed in the speed and the wildness that only endless leagues of open sea could provide.

And the Emperor was going to destroy this—all of it. He'd already taken away our freedom as punishment for Cyclone's rebellion. Mama and Papa lost their heads when they refused to kneel. I'd been too frightened, too cowardly then, to die beside them.

I winced away the memory. *No bad thoughts.* I couldn't change what's been done, but I could change something now. Now is all I had. *And that has to be enough.*

As we neared the bluff, the deep vibrations of Loach's voice echoed through the water, catching in my pointed ears. I slowed, turning to see him gesture to part of the submerged cliffside. Loach descended, fading into the shadows where the cliff blocked the light.

This is it. My gut twisted as I followed. Once I passed through the barrier, there was no going back. Well, I guess I could, but I'd still be a rebel—an enemy of the Empire, as the Elves liked to call it. I would be an enemy.

Loach brushed his hands over the rock, pulling away thick clumps of moss and seaweed. Beneath, a tunnel opening—about as wide as I was tall—was carved into the bluff.

"Like I said." Loach's words floated to me. "A tight squeeze."

I tried not to let my rising panic show as I watched Loach wiggle his way into the opening, his boots the last thing visible before disappearing entirely into the darkness.

What was I thinking? I held my breath—mainly to keep from hyperventilating—as I squeezed in behind him. The path was instantly dark. Solid rock pressed against my back. Bile rose in my throat as I sidled forward on my forearms. *You're not going to die. Not today.*

Loach's movements created vibrations through the tunnel.

This passage could collapse at any moment. I swallowed my nausea, and the tunnel grew narrower every inch I crawled. *Pretend you're somewhere else.* I finally breathed. In through the nose, out through the mouth. A sharp rock sliced into my knee, but I ignored it even as the coppery tang of blood found its way through the water and into my nostrils. *Pretend you're somewhere else.*

My childhood home flooded my mind. Just a rickety driftwood hut. I could almost smell the lemons Mama plucked from the trees. The path was so tight now that I inched forward on my belly—but I was *not* trapped in a cliffside. The weight on my back was just Papa's heavy wool blanket—the one he'd let me steal when we spent our nights topside. The fibers scratched against my skin—too rough, too heavy. It was going to choke me.

Clawing, clawing. My skin burned where the blanket refused to let me go.

I shrieked as it cut into my arms. No, that was Loach's nails digging into my wrists. I yelped again as he hauled me out of the tunnel, the rock scraping against my scales as my head breached water. I scrambled onto a dry landing and fell to my knees. I sucked in a ragged breath, two, three. *You're alive. You are here, not there.*

Loach pressed his finger over his lips as he pulled a torch from a nearby sconce. With a quick strike of flint, the narrow, rectangular room was bathed in the firelight. "This way."

I placed my hand over my throat, willing my heart to slow as I followed him up a flight of stairs that sat on the far end of the chamber. *I'm safe. I'm safe. I'm safe.* My voice was hoarse as I asked, "Where are we?"

"Beneath Carnage," Loach grunted, his thick clothes leaving a wet trail on the gritty, stone floor. "We should come up into one of the nearby warehouses."

I chewed my thumbnail. It tasted like mud. "Should?"

Loach glared at me, the torch casting an orange glow over his pale skin. "I've never been through here myself. Just my employees."

Even better. "Well, that's comforting."

"Watch it." Another glare. "You're lucky I'm here at all, kid."

"I didn't *force* you to come." I wrapped my arms around myself, fighting the first chills from the frigid air despite the warmth of the waters. "You chose that for yourself."

"I'm aware." Loach slowed, raising the torch to inspect the walls. His tentacles began prodding at every crack and seam, searching. "Trust me, your people's livelihoods aren't the only ones at stake if Surge doesn't rise."

I started picking at the cracks with him, not knowing what else to do. "And here I thought you were just in it for the money."

"That, too." Loach passed me the torch as he knelt. "What happens to men like me when our trade is cut off from the coast's only major city? We go broke." He pulled out his knife and started scraping at a loose brick. "The sea creates its economy, which Sayzar has so foolishly disturbed. Without the materials the Merfolk mine, Carnage will slowly fall apart. Which, again, isn't good for me."

I held back a surprised laugh. "It seems like you're a hero, after all."

He glanced up at me, eyes murderous. "Say that again, and I'll smack that goofy smile off your face."

I grinned, knowing he never would.

He just shook his head and kept at the wall. Eventually, his blade sunk into a space between the stones. Twisting it, the wall clicked, and a slim gap appeared in the rock. Loach shoved his fingers inside and began to pull. Sweat beaded on his temple. "Help me, damn it."

"Oh, sorry." I set the torch carefully on the ground before grabbing hold of the wall. My skin crawled as layers of dust from the ceiling blanketed us. I pulled, nails chipping against the rock, but the gap widened a crack.

"Harder," Loach hissed through gritted teeth.

I braced myself, yanking back with all my might. Just as my fingers were about to slip, the wall slid with a loud crunch, opening a second passage in the tunnel.

Loach bent over, leaning against his thighs, panting. "You're stronger than you look."

"Thanks." I stared down at my battered palms, at the dry coating of dirt caked to them, and swallowed back my revulsion. I hated dry skin. "I guess."

Still breathing heavily, Loach picked up the torch. "Come on."

The new path rose higher and higher until we came to a heavy wood hatch over our heads. Loach pressed it gently. "It's not locked." I wrung my hands as he lifted it an inch, peering through. "It looks like a warehouse to me. It's empty. Let me help you up."

I stepped back. "Why do I have to go first?"

Loach's eyes flashed mischievously. "Because this was your insane idea." He shoved open the hatch and didn't ask before grabbing my waist and practically tossing me into the room above. I landed on my stomach with a loud *oof*.

"Quiet," Loach snapped.

"Warn me next time," I shot back, and he chuckled. I stood,

knee still throbbing from where the stone cut it. I'd never been in a warehouse, but this is what I would have expected. A suffocating number of crates were stacked nearly to the ceiling, half concealed with moth-eaten blankets. Most were intact, but some were broken open, with what looked like furniture peeking out the top. The only door was on the far wall, blocked with more crates. By the layers of dust covering everything, no one had been in here for a couple of weeks, at least.

I whispered to Loach, "I think it's empty."

"Think or know? Specify."

I took another glance around, pursing my lips. "Know. Just get up here."

Loach clamored through the opening in the floor and brushed off his trousers. "This is the place. We'll be safe here for a while. We'll head out at sundown."

Indeed, streams of light leaked through the smudged windows. Sunset wouldn't be for a few hours. I let out a relieved breath, thankful for a chance to rest and calm myself. I picked at the edge of one of the crates. "What is all this?"

"Supplies." Loach scowled as he sat on a box with a low groan. "Product that should have already been sold. None of its mine. The cheaper warehouses are used for commercial use."

I lifted a solid brass ingot out of an opened crate, its lid carved with an artful *B* within a wreath. The metal was surprisingly heavy. "Does Surge buy weapons from you?"

"No. Cyclone used to buy weapons when needed, but no one buys anything anymore, thanks to our new overlords."

"And that's why you agreed to help? To stop them?"

"That . . . and other reasons." Loach dug around until he found a container filled with clothing. He tossed me a small set of work clothes, tall leather boots, and a grey, hooded cloak. "Here, get dressed. People will notice you walking around in just that skimpy dress."

I looked over the garments, crinkling my nose at the musty stench. "Ugh. How dull."

"That's the point."

I folded them over my arm before finding a private corner to change. Despite being men's attire, the tunic and breeches fit well. When raised, the cloak's hood hid the blue of my hair if I didn't jostle it. It was the boots that were a problem. They pinched my fins terribly when laced all the way. I kept them as loose as I could without them falling off.

When I finished, Loach had made two impromptu beds out of dusty, old coats and rolled-up sweaters for pillows. He flopped down on his jacket with a groan, pulling his wide-brimmed hat over his eyes. "We might as well get some shut-eye while we wait. Tonight will be busy."

I brushed a bit of dirt off the coat he laid out for me before I sat, crossing my legs. My eyes stung and my lids were heavy from lack of sleep. "So, what's next?"

"You tell me," Loach chuckled, crossing one ankle over the other. "Did you expect me to plan this whole charade for you?"

"No," I shot back, then paused. *Did I?* I assumed he'd magically know a way into the palace. Anxiety began to bubble up in my chest. I shook my head. *One step at a time.* "Maybe? I don't know, but I don't have any experience with . . . illegal activities. I'd appreciate your input."

"Well." Loach folded his arms behind his head. "There's a tavern on the east side where several of my contacts frequently visit. The Enforcers usually steer clear of it. We'll head there and see about hiring us some muscle. We're going to need it."

I wrapped my coat blanket around my shoulders. My teeth had started to chatter. Air had a way of chilling you to the core that I never could get used to. *I miss the sea already.* "Okay." A thought struck me. "You don't think we'll have to . . . kill anyone, do you?"

Loach lifted his hat just high enough to give me an amused look. "What do you think?"

My stomach lurched. I laid down, adjusting the pillow sweaters. "Goodnight."

Loach just laughed softly. It wasn't long until his breathing grew steady, his sighs turning to heavy snores that whistled between his tentacles.

I curled into a ball, trying to fight the numbness that had begun to spread to my toes. A bright light shone through the window, streaking the cracked stone floor in gold. *It must be around two o'clock.*

I blew on my fingers, trying to regain some feeling. *I don't want to hurt anyone.* It wasn't that I was afraid of violence—I'd seen and been the target of enough—but I didn't enjoy it. It appalled me when I moved into The Dam how many seemed to relish in it. Glorify it. Bring it into their beds.

I'd defend myself to the death, if necessary, and I supposed that's what I was doing now. The Emperor had pushed me into a corner, and I had no choice but to fight back.

Do I have a choice? It didn't feel like it. Wherever I turned, every option came with the potential of torture or decapitation. I scrunched my eyes shut, willing sleep to find me. *I want to live.*

"What makes you happy?" Mama used to ask, her lavender hair braided around her head like a crown.

"*My treasures,*" I'd tell her, bundled in a quilt on her lap as she read to me by candlelight. I had so many trinkets set in perfect lines on every flat surface in our little driftwood hut. They were perfect. *We* were perfect.

"*Treasure can be taken away.*" Mama kissed my forward. "*Learn to love something that lasts forever.*"

I never knew how to answer her.

I drifted off with a hot tear rolling down my cheek.

It only felt like moments later when something hard smacked into my boot. "Get up."

My eyes shot open, and I looked immediately at the window. Outside, the sky had shifted to shades of vibrant purples and orange—sunset.

Another smack to my boot. "Did you hear me, woman? Move."

All feeling left my limbs. That wasn't Loach's voice.

I rolled onto my back just as a cold blade pressed against my throat.

My breath caught. *No, no, no.*

A raven-haired Elf leaned over me, holding a wicked-looking dagger to my neck. His thin lips curled up at the corners. "Ah, I see I finally have your attention."

Blood roared in my ears as I managed to shift far enough to find Loach—now sitting with an auburn Elf in elaborate silver armor pressing a sword to his chest.

Soft fingers—far too soft—stroked my cheek, then twisted into my hair. "Pretty." His pale eyes scanned my face, my golden freckles. My head swam as my breaths came in too shallow. He yanked my head back so hard I yelped, exposing my throat. "We could hear your friend's snoring from three blocks away. You're not supposed to be here, sea-whore."

"How did you get inside the city?" The second Elf's blade pierced the front of Loach's shirt, staining it with blue blood. He grinned. "But you don't have to answer yet. I'm happy to make this last for hours."

They're going to torture us. Cold steel scraped against my skin. This couldn't be over. We hadn't even started.

Loach caught my eye, the look filled with silent commands I couldn't decipher. Slowly—ever so slowly—his tentacle lowered toward his belt. His attention then snapped back to the Elf and he growled, "Maybe if you pulled that damned thing out of my pectoral, I could tell you."

His captor glanced at mine, who nodded.

The auburn-haired Elf took a step back, lowering his sword just low enough that Loach's tentacle quickly yanked at knife from his belt and flicked it deep into the man's throat. Shock passed over the Elf's features before red spittle bubbled over his lips. He collapsed in a mushy heap.

The second Elf screamed in rage, and I scrambled away as he dove for Loach, who rolled away just in time to avoid taking that dagger in the gut.

"Tetra, run!" Loach cried as the Elf wheeled on him, teeth bared.

Run where? I swiveled. A rusted padlock held the main door shut. *The window—we never checked if it was locked.* It sat wide open. That's how they'd gotten in. *Stupid. Stupid.* Even in full armor, they'd been silent.

I ran and sprung onto the sill, pausing just long enough to consider turning back. I couldn't leave him here. I couldn't—

"Just go!" Loach took a punch to the jaw before kicking the Elf into a stack of crates. "I'll find you!"

The Elf's vicious gaze flickered at me, and this time, I did what I was told. My hips nearly got stuck as I leaped out the window. I wiggled then landing on my palms as I hit the cobblestone street outside. Pain jolted all the way up into my shoulders. I rolled end over end before my feet hit the road and I was sprinting down a nearby alley.

I've never run in shoes. It hurt. The boots chaffed my ankles raw in minutes, but I didn't slow. I ran until my legs began to give out—the miles on land passed so slowly. The evening sun blinded me as flashes of green and brown buildings blew past me. I had no idea where I was going. The street was tight—

enough so that as I tried to round a corner, I skidded straight into a solid wall instead.

The air whooshed out of me as I bounced off and my back hit the ground. Something in my spine cracked.

Another warehouse. I desperately tried to suck in a breath. Its olive-green shudders were locked tight, with not a hint of light behind them. Hopefully, that meant it was empty. Why so many abandoned buildings? This must be a shipping district.

Groaning, I turned on my side—which sent me rolling down a small flight of stairs onto the warehouse's dropped patio. My already injured knee smacked on the edge of a step—hard—and I nearly bit through my lip to keep from screaming.

I just laid there—on the bottom of those damn stairs—until my ragged gasps slowed, and the pain in my joints faded to a low throb.

What a great first day. I managed to rise to a sitting position, leaning my aching back against the warehouse door. The sun had gone down, casting blue-tinged shadows over the alley.

I wiped the sweat dripping into my eyes on my sleeve. *How far did I run?* Hopefully, it was far enough to keep me out of trouble because I couldn't walk another step in these hateful boots.

I unlaced them, hissing as blisters popped on my swollen feet. The boots made a loud clunk as I tossed them across the patio.

Well, this sucked.

By the quality of the armor, those Elves had to be working for the Lantern Palace—for Sayzar Ameliatus.

Enforcers. My chest tightened as the word clanged through me. Loach had killed one. Hopefully, he'd managed to kill the other.

I curled around myself, resting my cheek on my battered knee. There was no shouting, no rushed footsteps approaching. Maybe Loach had managed to get away. *He mentioned a tavern on the east side of the city. I'll head that way. That's what he'd do.*

I rocked, wiping my runny nose, then rested against the doorframe. Just a few minutes. Enough time to catch my breath. My lids were still so heavy. My body hurt. I pulled my hood low over my face. Just a moment to clear my head—then I'd make sure Loach was safe.

A few heavy-lidded blinks later, I was fast asleep.

Chapter Three

"Oi!"

I jolted awake with a high-pitched shout.

A coppery skinned Human man stared down at me from atop the staircase, his hard mouth set in a grim line. "Can you shove off? I have work to do."

"S-sorry." It took me two tries to climb to my aching feet. The Human's glower deepened. *He probably thinks I'm drunk.* Thank God, my hood was still up. Now that I looked, I noticed the small, carved sign hanging over the doorway: *Digmen's Deliveries.*

"Nod off somewhere else." He wasn't gentle as he pushed past me. Pulling a brass key out of his pocket, he unlocked the door and slammed it behind him.

I blinked at the place that he'd been, not quite awake. The sun shone brightly overhead, lighting up the alley and revealing that similar shops now open for business. The scent of smoke clung to the air, tickling my throat. I rubbed my face and groaned. *It must be mid-day. I can't believe I slept that long.*

Slowly, I stepped into the alley, every movement sending

shockwaves of pain through my joints. At first, I thought it was from last night's escape, but then the ache spread into my lower back, my chest. *Salt withdrawals.*

Damn it. With a huff, I reached for the bag on my hip—and found my side empty.

My stomach bottomed out. *I don't have my bag.* I hadn't grabbed it when I fled from the Enforcers. Which meant I didn't have any salt. I only had a few hours before the full force of salt sickness would take hold.

Sharks. I ran my trembling fingers through my tangled hair, snagging on the knots. *I can backtrack to the warehouse. Grab my bag.* Even as the thought came, I knew I couldn't. Not if soldiers were hanging around. I couldn't stay here.

There has to be salt somewhere. Wincing, I set off down the street. The shops and manufacturing buildings were all the same shades of green, the color painted straight over stone. Probably mined from one of the many undersea quarries along the Tyrr coast—ones that our people had built and traded from for centuries. Providing half the continent's gold, copper, nickel, and cobalt.

Taking a different route than the night before, the back alleys began to widen, leading to the entrance of a bustling marketplace. A strong breeze blew a strand of hair over my face as I left the alley—pale, blue hair.

Oh no. Quickly, I braided my hair tightly down my back and tugged my hood lower. I checked my reflection in a nearby window. None of the blue was peeking out, but the cloak made it stupidly obvious that I didn't want to be noticed. At least it shadowed my freckles.

I sighed. *This will have to do. I can't shift now.* All Mermaids could temporarily change their appearance—once a hunting tool of our ancestors, tracing back to the ancient Elves—but it would drain up any precious salt reserves I had left in my body.

I couldn't risk it, especially not with the way the achiness was already spreading into my palms.

I'll be fine. This is fine. I marched out of the alley into the crowds, mimicking the steady gate of the people darting around the square.

And it literally was a square—filled with peoples of every shape, size, and color.

Carnage. The trade capital of Tyrr.

A bustling market connected four main roads—north, south, east, and west—but there was no rhyme or reason to how the vendors had set up their stalls. Wagons, carts, and spindly, pitched tents littered the open space between the highways. A family of banana yellow-skinned Imps—two feet tall, at most—hawked off cheap jewelry and poorly woven rugs. A portly Human woman laid out dozens of trays filled with bowls of roasted vegetables and meat pies.

I took it all in, awed despite the nausea building in my throat from all the different scents colliding. My parents had brought me to Carnage once as a child, but I remembered little.

But I *did* remember the Lantern Palace, hovering over the city like a new mother. From the northern side of the square, the palace towered above the buildings beyond. A hazy mirage of ivory columns and spires. Even from here, in the full of day, faelights twinkled along the palace battlements—an invitation. A façade. Hiding the wickedness of the ones that dwelled within.

Now, standing in the center of the chaos—between two arguing shoe polishers—I craned my neck back to get a better view, making my sore spine pop. *Cyclone is up there, somewhere.*

Had he mummified in the heat of summer, or was dust all that remained of the king that had brought the Merfolk to glory?

I choked back the lump growing in my throat. *No bad*

thoughts. I can't think of that now. Loach would stay hunkered down until night fell again if he was alive. Kraken weren't a usual sight in the city—or anywhere.

Shoving my clammy hands in my trouser pockets, I glanced around. The entire afternoon was mine to do with as I pleased. Hiding was the safest option, but...

I needed salt, and I'd never find it sitting around like a stump. Giddy anticipation bubbled inside me as I strode north toward the Lantern Palace.

I wasn't used to being in the direct sun so long... or spending so much time walking. Swimming used different muscles. I was drenched in sweat by the time I reached the palace's outer bailey an hour later—a large plaza that led to a massive curtain wall, enclosing the palace and its inner courtyard away from the common rabble.

A multi-layered fountain—carved to show influences of all the races that called the Tyrr coast home—sat at the courtyard's center. Dozens more merchants lingered about, haggling passersby into buying tourist paraphernalia or over-priced street food.

I hung back, sitting at one of the bench tables outside a seafood restaurant. Vibrant yellow and orange umbrellas sheltered the patio from the sun. Thank God, because it was sweltering out here. I thought it was supposed to be cool in the springtime.

A bead of sweat dripped off my brow, and I brushed it away, swallowing against the unbearable dryness in my throat. *I won't last much longer without salt.* If I was going to find scrapes of salt anywhere it would be here. Even fish out of the trash would help. Hopefully, I'd still be able to walk by nightfall.

My mouth watered as the briny breeze carried over the luscious scent of fried tilapia and boiled crab. I moved to touch my bag again only to find my side empty. *Damn it.* My money was inside it. I slumped in my seat. *The garbage it is.* I just had to wait until the remaining customers cleared off. They probably wouldn't like watching me cram their leftovers down my throat.

At least from here, I had a perfect view of the palace's battlements, of the lines of Enforcers surrounding it. Tall, lean Elves—male and female—wearing that same menacing, silver armor that the men who attacked us wore. Their piercing eyes scanned the crowds from beneath their feathered helms. A glint of light—a reflection of the sun on metal spaulders—revealed more Enforcers atop the palace's spiraling outer towers. Their skin emitted an ethereal glow—visible even from here—another reminder of the superiority and magic of their race.

I guess walking in through the front door isn't an option. I propped my elbows on the chipped redwood table, resting my chin on my palms. The gate leading into the palace's inner court had to be more than ten feet tall, fashioned out of twisted silver and gold painted arches. *I might be able to climb over it.* My gaze flickered again to the Enforcers guarding the walls, hefty crossbows strapped to their backs.

Or not. I leaned back with a sigh, making the bench creak. *Loach was right. We'll need some extra help.* It hadn't occurred until now that I'd need money to *pay* for this help. I chewed the skin along my thumbnail. Maybe they'd agree just from the promise of a portion of whatever we found in the treasury.

Two benches to my left, a pretty Orc woman caught my eye. Her skin was a lovely shade of emerald-green, her eyes a rich chocolate brown. Instead of eating, she just glared at me as she picked her fried trout into tiny, squishy pieces.

My cheeks heated, and I lowered my chin, shifting my freckles from gold to brown. My hair was covered well enough. I winced as a shooting pain split through my side. *Sharks.* Even that tiny bit of magic hit my salt reserves.

The Orc woman started to whistle a simple, robust tune. Breathing heavily, I tried to ignore her despite the death glares she continued to send my direction.

I should have left, but I was so tired. My ankles burned where my boots rubbed against my fresh blisters and the salt ache had spread all the way into my toes.

"Can I get you something, Hun?" I jumped as a male Orc—skin the color of maple bark—slid onto the seat across from me. He was about as thick as a tree, with chipped, yellowed tusks curling out from inside his lower lip. The white apron covering his torso was stained with grease and oil. His thick brows rose. "I noticed you've been out here for a while."

"Sorry." I kept my head down, peeling the table's flaky paint. "I was just enjoying the shade."

"Fair enough." This Orc had the same chocolate brown eyes as the female. "Are you hungry?"

With a small smile, I turned out my pockets, revealing nothing but lint. "I don't have any money. I'll leave if I'm bothering you."

"That's not what I asked." He glanced at my stomach as if he could hear it rumbling. "Are you *hungry?*"

"Um . . . well." The female Orc was still watching. Maybe this male was hers, and she was about to kick my ass for getting too close. But for the salt, it was worth the risk. I kept picking at the red paint. "Yes, please."

"What do you like?" He smiled, revealing more of those vicious tusks. "I've got snapper, swordfish, tuna, oysters, crab—"

"Crab, please," I blurted. "With butter, if it's not too much."

"Not at all." He winked as he rose from the table. "Hang tight. I'll be right back."

Should I make a break for it? If I ran, the female might chase me down, considering the dirty looks she was sending me. *But how can I say no to crab?* Instead, I waited. Arms curled over my chest as I kicked at bits of gravel on the patio. Not ten minutes later, the male Orc returned with two steaming plates, mugs, and a pitcher of ale. He laid the feast on the table, pouring us each a cup of the golden liquid.

"I haven't seen you around here before." He pushed the plate piled high with bright orange crab legs toward me. It took everything I had not to smash my face into them. "My name's Geralt, by the way. I own this place."

"Thank you, Geralt." *Should I make eye contact? Would that be too much?* I swirled a leg into the bowl of hot, melted butter he provided. I took a bite, the shell's crunch the perfect contrast to its soft, rich meat. I did a happy wiggle in my chair and took a sip of ale, the burn of the alcohol harsh against my raw throat. *God, this is good.*

Geralt gave me a strange look before cracking into his own crab. "Are you from Carnage?"

"No." I took another bite. There was nothing in life better than butter. "But that shouldn't surprise you." I gestured with sticky fingers to the crowds out in the courtyard. "There seem to be lots of tourists. New faces must be common."

"They *were*." Geralt chugged down half his ale in one swallow. "Until last summer."

Last summer. "Oh?" I nearly choked. That's when the barrier went up. My limbs grew leaden as I lost my appetite. *He knows, he knows, he knows.* But how could he? I'd muted the scales on my face, and my hair was tucked away. At worst, he thought I was a vagrant.

Geralt's gaze flickered to where I dropped my crab leg, then back to my face. Before he spoke, I swear he gave the female Orc a look. "Do you need somewhere to stay? I have a spare room. It's not much, but it's warm."

I stood—too quickly—and my hips smacked into the table, spilling both our drinks. "N-no, thank you. I should be going."

"There's no rush." Geralt leaned back, wide lips pursing. "Stay. Eat."

"I have somewhere to be." I brushed some crab shell crumbs off my tunic. "Thank you again."

Geralt just nodded.

I turned to leave, pausing just long enough to swipe another crab leg off my plate. Geralt's deep, rumbling laugh tickled my back as I hurried back towards the market.

I'm terrible at this. My strides were too fast. There were so many sounds, so many smells, and colors. It made my temples throb even worse, setting my heart off like a hummingbird in flight. *I miss Loach.* The crab soothed some of the aching in my throat, but I hadn't eaten enough to help the sickness spreading through my body.

A loud, clear bell chimed six o'clock. Dark wouldn't be far off. *It's going to be fine.* I'd head east and see if I could find the inn tavern mentioned. How many could there possibly be? I chuckled. *Probably hundreds knowing my luck.*

I shrugged deeper into my cloak, and dozens of passing shoulders collided with mine as I sidled through the crowds back into the main square. It was embarrassing how long it took me to figure out which direction was east, having to stop more than once to ask for help. *Finally,* I was heading down the main highway toward the correct edge of the city.

More than once, I swore I caught a flash of emerald-green out of the corner of my eye.

Everything is fine. I'm fine. The thought didn't stop the nervous sweat from dripping down my sides.

The main road was wide enough across for three wagons abreast. I didn't like it. I moved to the edge, closer to the shops, to keep out of view. The dryness in my throat spread upward, making my sinuses burn with every breath. My vision swam, the flashes and smears of newly lit streetlights disorienting.

Another flash of green.

I bit back tears as I ducked into a side street to my left. *I'm not going to make it. No bad thoughts. I'll be fine.* I had to be. I had to be.

The street narrowed to a dead end, with nothing but over-filled trash bins to keep me company. I pressed my head against the alley wall, grateful for the sharp coolness of the limestone bricks. *It's fine. It's fine.*

It wasn't fine.

The air rushed out of me as a hard blow punched between my shoulder blades, smashing my face against the wall. *Not this again.* The flat side of a cold blade pressed against the back of my neck. I managed to turn my head enough to get a look at my attacker.

Chocolate brown eyes stared up at me—up, not down. The female Orc only stood as high as my collarbone. She flipped her dagger to the sharp edge, pricking my skin, and gave me a devilish smile. No tusks—but shining, black horns curled out from the top of her head and her straight teeth were pearly white. "Now, now, where do you think you're going, lovely?"

With my eyebrow raised, I managed to gesture back toward the main street. "Um . . . that way?"

She scowled, her full lips the perfect frame for her pronounced, arched nose. "Don't be a smart ass."

"I wasn't."

She yanked back my hood—my pale blue braid spilling over my shoulder—and spun me so my back was to the wall. "Merfolk are forbidden to enter Carnage if you aren't aware."

I wiggled, trying to lessen the pressure of her gloved fist against my chest. "I'm aware."

"Then why are you here?"

"Shopping?"

"Play with me and I'll punch your teeth in."

"Ack." Even the thought made my stomach roll. *What do I do? What do I do?* "I'm . . . looking for someone."

The female Orc just let out a long sigh, pursing her lips, before reeling back and punching me square in the gut.

I doubled over, gasping, as my blasted hurt knee hit the cobblestone. In one swift movement, she had both of my arms behind my back, tying my wrists together with a bit of rope.

Lord, she was strong. Despite her size, lines of heavy muscle showed through her tight, black body suit.

"That wasn't my teeth," I wheezed.

She snorted and pulled the rope tighter.

"Stop!" I wriggled. "I'm trying to find my friend. Well, he's kind of a friend. More of an—"

"Shut up." The Orc yanked me to my feet. "If you don't want to talk to me, you can explain why you're here to the Emperor."

My blood ran cold. *Sayzar Ameliatus.*

She dragged me by the wrists back toward the main street. I stumbled and fell onto my backside. She tried to pull me up, but I refused to budge.

After several attempts to move me, she kicked my thigh and hissed. "Get up!"

"No!" I was bigger than her—weighed more. She couldn't lift me. "I told you. I need to find my friend."

"Who?" She pulled with all her strength, looking like a farm girl trying to drag a stubborn mule. "Another Merfolk?"

"Again, not technically." I ground my teeth as I fought to remain on my bottom. I was *not* going in front of Sayzar. "He's a Kraken. They're not illegal, are they?"

"A Kraken?" She sounded shocked as she released the hold on my binds, sending me flat on my back. "What in the hell kind of business do a Mermaid and a Kraken have in Carnage?"

Why did I say that? In all honesty, I'd never been a good liar. At this point, nothing I said really mattered. She'd let me go or take me to the Emperor. I rolled onto my side and jerked my chin up defiantly. "I'm going to steal back Cyclone."

Surprisingly, she took a step back, brows pinched together. "What?"

"I'm going to take him home, where he belongs," I continued, voice cracking, "so he can be buried with the honor he deserves."

I wouldn't mention my hopes that it would rally Surge to war.

The Orc blew out a sharp breath. "You're making this up."

I let out a high-pitched, nervous laugh. "I wish I was."

Exhaling, she ran a hand through her shoulder-length black hair, smoothing it as she gazed north—as if she could see all the way to the Lantern Palace. She picked at her lip. "Damn it." She yanked me to my feet. This time, I let her. She jerked her chin toward the main street as she cut my binds and untied the ropes. "Follow me. Let's talk—nicely." With that, she turned and strode out of the alley.

Sharks. I followed. Where else did I have to go? I couldn't run with the salt withdrawals this intense. We stepped back onto the main road, and instead of continuing east, she led me across the highway to another off-side street.

I thought about bolting anyway, but instead asked, "Where are we going?"

"Some place safe." She shrugged. "Well, safe-ish."

What's with this place? "What's your name?"

She chewed on her words for a moment before deciding to answer. "Agatha Paine."

I groaned. "That doesn't bode well for me."

For the first time, she smiled at me over her shoulder. "And yours?"

What could it hurt? "Tetra."

"Tetra," she repeated. "This way. It's not far."

I managed to keep my questions to myself—for now—as she led me through the weaving back streets of Carnage. These buildings seemed more residential with their scalloped shudders, overgrown flowerpots, and meager, fenced lawns. I found myself taking in all the details and colors more than I watched where we were going.

Agatha must have noticed because she said softly, "After the Emperor took over, many craftsmen went out of business."

I glanced back. "Why?"

She snorted. "Why do you think? With the ports closed, taxes and prices have shot through the roof. No food or supplies come in unless the Emperor permits it."

I nodded. That lined up with what Loach had said. It seemed it wasn't only criminals and Seafolk that were hurt by closing off the coast—all of Carnage was suffering.

We spent the rest of the walk in silence.

After another fifteen minutes or so, we reached a shoddy black-and-white, three-story building that may have once been an inn. Half the shingles were missing from its steep roof, and the windows were stained opaque from the salt spray rolling in on the breeze.

Agatha pulled a small key from the pouch on her belt and opened the splintered door. "After you."

She's going to stab me. One step inside made me want to turn and sprint for the hills. Not because of the threat of violence in the air but because of the layers and layers of dust caked onto the bare wood floors and sparse furniture. Cobwebs hung from the ceiling, heavy enough to snare a bat. I peeked to the right to see a steep, narrow staircase—leading up—attached to a circular kitchen.

I scrunched my nose. "And this is?"

"You can call it my hideout." Agatha sat at the small table against the far wall, entirely at ease with her dagger strapped to her thigh. She gestured to the seat across from her with the barest curl of her lips. "It's not much, but it's paid for."

Acid burned my already parched throat as I swallowed back bile and brushed off the rickety chair before sitting. The grittiness of the dirt on my palms would send me into a downward spiral on any regular day, but today was anything but normal. Sucking in deep breaths, I wiped my hands off on my trousers, faking a smile. "It's lovely."

"Are you thirsty?" she asked.

I nodded, and she passed me her canteen. I ripped off the cork, guzzling down half the contents before taking a breath. It was warm and stale, tasting of old leather and void of all the salt and minerals my body so desperately desired. Either way, it was heaven.

Agatha watched me, her eyes tracking the water dripping off my chin. "You're salt sick, aren't you?"

"Do you know much of Merfolk?" I wiped my mouth then nodded. "When my friend and I got separated . . . he has the salt."

"I see." Agatha rapped her short, neat nails on the table.

"Are you going to kill me?" I took another drink from the

canteen, keeping my gaze fixed on the window behind her. *Eye contact, no? This is the worst.* "Turn me in?"

"Depends on what you say next." Agatha splayed out her fingers, resting her palms flat—no weapons. "What do you hope to accomplish by retrieving Cyclone's remains?"

This time, I forced myself to hold her gaze, no matter how painful. "I already told you. He belongs to the sea."

"I know what you've told me, but I want the truth," Agatha said, "tell me all of it. Now. Or I swear I'll cut out your eye. Who's your friend?"

"Relax, damn." I ran my tongue along the inside of my teeth. *Sharks.* "His name is Loach. He's an arms dealer who works out of The Dam."

Agatha cursed. "I know him. Not personally, but . . . hell." She scanned me head to toe. "That still doesn't explain why *you're* here?"

I bristled and straightened. "What is that supposed to mean?"

She gave me an apologetic smile. "Hun, it took five minutes of tracking you to tell stealth isn't your niche. Plus, you're too clumsy to be a soldier."

Ouch. I drew a fish in the dust on the table. "Does ambition and a perky attitude count as a skill set?"

Agatha chuckled. "You're an odd one, Tetra."

"So, I've heard."

"Where is he?"

"Loach?" I gave her an exaggerated shrug. "I told you we got separated. He mentioned a tavern on the east side of town. I was headed that way before you so rudely interrupted me."

Agatha watched me, a dozen emotions passing through her gaze. "Do you have any ideas the consequences if you succeed in stealing back Cyclone's bones?"

I raised a finger. "It's not stealing. He doesn't belong to Sayzar."

Agatha actually laughed. "Answer the question."

My voice lowered as my eyes dropped back to my wringing hands. "Yes, I know... war."

A careful inhale. "And you're okay with that?"

"It's going to happen either way," I confessed, "the Emperor is drafting—forcing—my people into a naval army to continue his campaign across the ocean."

A flicker of horror passed over Agatha's features. "You're lying."

"Why would I?"

"And you'd rather start a war between the Merfolk and the Elves than fight for them?"

My parent's faces flashed through my mind. Our driftwood hut. My treasures. My dreams of sharing my collection with the world. I exhaled. "Yes."

We just stared at each other. Or at least I stared at the space between her eyes as she considered me. Agatha seemed to decide something and said, "Come on, Tetra. I know where we'll find your Kraken."

Chapter Four

I shrugged deeper into my cloak as Agatha led me back to the highway. Night had fallen. Powered by Elven magic, street lamps lined each side of the road, bathing it in a warm, friendly light.

Agatha shortened her strides, falling in line beside me as she whispered, "Mermaids can change their appearance, correct?"

I glanced around, feeling the imaginary stares of passing townsfolk. *They can't hear your thoughts, Tetra.* I nodded discreetly. "Yes, but using it will burn through the rest of the salt in my body. I can't risk it."

"I suggest you take the risk." As we rounded a bend, Agatha nodded to the Enforcers monitoring the street from an elaborate booth. "You didn't fool me. You won't fool them."

I swallowed, my throat like broken glass. "How did you guess I was Merfolk, anyway?"

Agatha snorted. "You ate your crab leg in the shell."

Oh. I really was terrible at this.

From the booth, the silver gaze of one of the male Enforcers slid to me. Calculating, suspicious. With my hood up, I was practically screaming that I was up to no good. He rose, stepping out of the booth, and began to move toward us.

Agatha tucked in tighter against my elbow. "Change. *Now.*"

My heart thundered. *No, no, no.* "I-I don't know if I can."

"*Do it.*" She hissed.

I scanned Agatha's features, taking in her dark hair and eyes. Beautiful. Seductive. Everything I wished I could be.

Exhaling, I soaked in the colors, wishing them for myself and *willing* them to be mine. Agony shot through my side—the last of my salt reserves giving out—and an electric buzz ran from my scalp to the tips of my toes.

The Enforcer kept moving—his head cocked and predatory—as he approached.

"Hun, your hair is a *mess!*" Agatha drawled, louder than necessary, as she grabbed my shoulder and spun me to face her, throwing back my hood. "Let me fix it. You can't go to the bar looking like *that.*"

My long braid spilled over my shoulder—now a rich, ebony tangle. It really was a mess. The world wobbled as Agatha began to re-braid it. The Enforcer was blurred—out of focus—but he stopped. He scowled, face half hidden behind his great, feathered helm—seeing now exactly what Agatha wanted him to see—two silly women heading out for a night on the town.

With a huff, he headed back toward the booth. We weren't a threat.

"Stupid meat-head," Agatha exhaled as she tied off the end of my braid, rubbing the strands between her fingers. "I've never seen that in person before. Your skin is darker, too. Even your ears are round."

I'm going to throw up. Gasping, I gripped my stomach as another jolt of pain shot through my side. "We need to keep going."

Agatha took the hint. She retook my elbow, steadying me, and we continued toward the eastern quarter. She kept a quick pace, eyes darting to every face we passed, watching for any sign of interest toward us.

I kept mine trained on her polished, leather half-boots. Usually, I could hold a shift for a day or more without effort, but now, every time my mind began to wander, the shift started to slip. Hints of blue threaded through my black strands. The ache had spread up my jaw and into my skull. I focused on my breathing. *In through the nose, out through the mouth.*

"Almost there," Agatha whispered, "don't die on me."

Raucous laughter rumbled through the cool evening air, mixed with the notes of a jolly fiddle and coated with the scent of booze—a promise of hot food and good company. I tried to glance up to find the source of the fun, but the world was turning sideways.

Don't puke. The ground shifted from cobblestone to worn, stained wood as she dragged me inside a tightly packed, warm building.

This must be the tavern. A wave of relief flooded me, followed by more nausea. I shouldn't have looked up. The stink of unwashed bodies, meat sweats, and cheese that had set out too long forced their way up my nose.

Sharks, here we go. I retched, stumbling, and vomited all over the tavern floor. A deep, harsh voice cursed in disgust. Agatha dragged me to the front counter by the wrist, staining my knees with bile, and plastered on the fakest smile I'd ever seen.

Behind it, a honey-blonde, thin-faced Human woman—perhaps the barkeep—polished a wine glass, shooting Agatha a murderous look as she propped herself against the bar.

Agatha grinned and pointed me out. "Do you have any

rooms available? My friend's had too much fun, if you know what I mean."

The woman's lip curled back in what might have been an attempt at a polite smile and glared at the mess I'd had left for her. "Two silvers."

Agatha's lips set in a hard line as she pulled the coins out of her hip pouch, muttering something about robbery before sliding them across the counter. "Key?"

Another homicidal look. The barkeep tossed her a keyring. "Room 202. Second level. Enjoy your stay."

Agatha crinkled her nose sweetly and crooned. "Thank you." She looped her arm around my waist and dragged me toward the stairs. "Come on. I think you need to lie down."

More strands of blue wove through my braid as the shift continued to slip. Acid burned my tongue. "What about Loach?"

"I'll find him," Agatha said sternly, and I believed her. "Let's get you somewhere safe, and I'll—"

We weren't one flight up before the shout of a familiar voice echoed down the stairway. *"You load of trash!"*

More angry voices followed, accompanied by the sound of shattering glass.

I fell on that same damn knee and croaked. *"Loach."*

Agatha cursed as more grunts and scuffling came from above us. "Are you sure?"

"Positive."

"Hills alive." She helped me lean back against the stairwell. The tavern's dim candlelight shone on her emerald skin as she tucked her hair behind her ears. "Stay here. I'll check it out."

I nodded and rested my head against the wall, trying to stop the spinning.

Agatha took the stairs two at a time.

After a minute of silence—two—the muffled shouts started again.

I can't just sit here and do nothing. I rolled onto all fours and crawled my way up the stairs—one small step at a time. *Loach saved my life. Agatha is helping me.*

In my heart of hearts, I knew these people didn't care about *me*. Whatever they wanted, I was just a means to an end, but they'd still been kind. I couldn't sit here even if all I was good for was a distraction.

When I reached the top, the room door across the hall from me was wide open. Agatha stood in the entry. From between her legs, I could see Loach sprawled out on the floor inside. A male Orc and Human stood over him, armed to the teeth, but their shocked gazes were fixed on Agatha.

Loach's beetle eyes snapped to me as soon as I slid into the hallway.

"Boys." Agatha's entire demeanor changed. Her gloved hand ran up her hip seductively before settling on her waist. "What—may I ask—are you doing?"

"We could ask you the same thing, Paine." The Orc spat, his long beard bobbing against his bare chest. "I suggest you get the hell out of here."

The Human—a short, stubby thing—nodded in agreement.

"Now, that's just rude." Agatha pouted as she sauntered through the doorway. I added the movement to my mental list of behaviors to practice. Her chocolate eyes lingered on Loach. When he finally looked at her, she winked. "I had plans with my friend here. It wouldn't be good for me if you left him in pieces."

"*Friend?*" The Human asked, incredulous. "This beast? Do you have any idea how much the Emperor will pay for Kraken hide?"

Agatha moved closer, the crackling in the burning hearth louder than her footsteps. "You're asking the wrong question, Hun." Her smile turned wicked. "You *should* be asking how much you value your own hide."

The two men exchanged looks.

Agatha's hand hovered over the dagger on her thigh. "One."

The Human whimpered as he tore past her, straight out of the room—tripping over me as he dove down the staircase. The Orc stared blankly after him.

Agatha gripped her dagger's hilt and purred, "Two."

"Three," Loach growled as he slammed his knee straight into the Orc's groin. Mouth agape, a fish out of water, the Orc fell—just as Agatha lunged.

I'd never seen anything like it.

In two swift movements, she twisted behind him and wrapped her arm around the Orc's thick neck. He went limp in her grip as she hit a pressure point, knocking him out cold.

Agatha let him drop unceremoniously as Loach scrambled to his feet.

Red welts—the promise of bruises—shone on his cheekbones. "Who the hell are you, woman?"

Agatha stepped to the side with a smile. "The one who got *her* here alive. Do you have any salt?"

"Bloody hell." Loach glared at her as he thundered past into the hall. My shift failed as he scooped me up in his arms and I groaned as the pain in my stomach shot down my thighs. There was a hint of concern in his voice as he muttered, "Hang in there, kid."

Agatha poked the drooling Orc with the toe of her boot. "We don't want to be here when he wakes up. Follow me."

"Grab those." Loach pointed to several bags in the corner of the room—mine among them—and Agatha swooped them up before leading us to the second floor.

The jostling of Loach's arms made me gag, but I managed, "What happened to the other guard?"

Loach's mouth quirked beneath his tentacle-stache. "Dead in a crate with his friend."

I swallowed. *Dead.* Because of me.

Once we reached the empty next floor, Agatha unlocked room 202 and ushered us inside. This room looked identical to the last—a simple hearth, a twin-sized bed, a stained sofa, and a meager dining table.

Agatha started on the fire as Loach laid me on the bed. He pulled a canteen and that blessed pouch out of his bag and tipped a generous amount of salt into it, giving the canteen a good shake. He passed it to me. "Here. Drink it all."

I nearly sobbed as the warm, salted water coated my tongue, fighting off the rawness in my mouth and esophagus. I didn't come up for air until I drank half the container.

"There you go, much better." Loach patted my head almost affectionately, then wheeled on Agatha. "But *you* haven't answered my question: Who the *hell* are you?"

Agatha struck the tinder, and embers caught in the kindling. "Did you know those men?"

"You first."

She shot him a glare and pointed at me. "I saved her ass. *You* first."

I swished another mouthful of water, letting it coat my teeth, before swallowing. "Her name is Agatha Paine." Agatha's glare shifted to me as I gestured between her and the Kraken. "Loach, meet Agatha. Agatha, meet Loach. Now, please, play nice and quit the posturing."

With a grumble, Loach shut and locked our room door. "Those men are black market traders. This tavern is one of their usual haunts. I was hoping to hire them—" Loach paused, catching himself. "—but they'd decided the bounty on Seafolk was too appealing. Bastards. No loyalty."

The fire was roaring happily now. Hips swaying, Agatha moved to the dining room table and crossed her toned arms over her chest. "You should have known better," she said.

"I did," Loach shot back, "but my options are limited, and I needed to find the kid."

With the salt coursing back into my veins, the spinning in my head began to slow. I managed to sit up on the bed. "Agatha found me first. She could have turned me in, but she didn't."

"Oh, she didn't?" Step by intimidating step, Loach braced against the dining table and sneered down at Agatha. "And why, Miss Paine, would that be?"

She didn't balk beneath his heavy stare. "I would like to know what a petty arms dealer wants with a Mermaid that plans to steal Cyclone's corpse."

Loach cursed and wheeled on me. "You told her?"

"It was either the truth, or she turned me in." I bristled. "I didn't know what else to do."

"Damn it, you should have kept your mouth shut."

"Watch it," Agatha snapped and leaned back in her chair. She smiled at me. "I like her."

"Agatha, Agatha, Agatha . . . where have I heard that name before," Loach muttered as he paced. He froze, holding up a finger. "Not Agatha Paine, the Orc spy turned Elven-controlled bitch?"

My eyes widened.

Agatha sucked on her teeth. "It seems we all have secrets."

I gasped as Loach drew his sword, stepping toward her. Agatha didn't flinch.

"What will the Emperor think when he finds that you've

fraternized with the enemy?" Loach crooned. "Those cowards saw you with us, sweetheart."

Agatha let out a bitter laugh. "Those *cowards* would never say a word against me."

"You sure about that?"

She propped her feet on the table and jerked her chin toward me. "A truth for a truth? What do you gain by helping her reclaim a dead king?"

I took another swig of water before wrapping my arms around my knees.

Loach thought for a moment before exhaling. "Besides humiliating that piece of trash, Sayzar?" Another pause. "I want the treasury. As compensation for all my men that have gone without paychecks for a year, thanks to that bloody barrier."

Agatha grinned. A genuine, true grin. "I was hoping you'd say that."

"Why?" I asked as the fire in my throat finally settled.

"You met my brother, Geralt," she replied warily. "That restaurant is his only source of income to feed his family of seven." A shake of her head. "But now, with the prices skyrocketing . . . the taxes . . . they could be homeless by the end of the season."

My eyes burned. *Geralt*—her brother, not her mate—had been kind enough to give me a free meal despite his hardships. I wanted to hug her, but she'd probably punch me. Instead, I said, "I'm so sorry."

"Sayzar blames the need for the barrier on the Merfolk, but I know that's crap." Agatha's attention shifted to Loach. "The Emperor needs to be stopped."

"We're proposing war." Loach cocked his head menacingly. "War doesn't fend off starvation."

"No," Agatha winced, "but if we can bring the barrier

down, I can take them home—to the mountains—where they'll be cared for by my tribe."

My heart hurt—for her, for her family.

The Orcs of Tyrr had lived in the mountains outside Carnage for centuries, selling lumber to the city in exchange for their needs. By keeping the Merfolk out, the Emperor had kept everyone else out and trapped those who remained inside. He didn't seem to care that he'd disrupted the flow of an entire country as long as his campaign continued.

Agatha stood, squaring her shoulders as she faced me. "Do you really mean to start a war with Sayzar Ameliatus?"

My breath caught as I nodded. "In a roundabout way, yes."

Agatha extended her hand to me, but as I reached to take it, she pulled back, holding my eye with stern ferocity. "Promise me we'll find a way to break the barrier, and I'm in. That is my condition. Do that, and I'll help you take back Cyclone."

I wanted to cry, but I smiled and shook her hand instead. "Welcome to the team, Agatha Paine."

Chapter Five

Agatha dumped a pile of clothes on my head. "Pick something."

I groaned, pulling my covers over my head. They smelled like mothballs and so did the clothes. From the lack of light filtering through the blinds, the sun hadn't risen yet. I sat up and rubbed my eyes. "Now?"

"The less eyes watching us leave, the better." Agatha kicked Loach in the side where he slept on the couch, and he jerked awake with a curse. Her lips quirked as she tossed him some fresh garments, pointing to the adjoining washroom. "Out. We need to change."

Grumbling, Loach rolled off the couch, wiping his face as he slammed the washroom door behind him.

"Where did you get these?" I riffled through tunics, pants, and coats before settling on a plain brown day dress—its hem and sleeves long enough to cover my fins—and a simple pair of leather sandals. My poor, blistered ankles would appreciate the breather.

"The barkeep owes me." Agatha ripped off her black body

suit without hesitation, tossing it in the corner, revealing her muscular abdomen and small, perky breasts. "She has a stash of supplies set aside in case I need them."

It was a struggle to arrange the blankets to strip without exposing myself. Blushing, I glanced down at my own ample bosom. It wasn't like a Mermaid to be self-conscious, but never in my life had I been able to describe myself as *toned*, even in my youth. The soft, rounded curves of my hips and stomach saw to that. Too much butter.

Agatha quickly and efficiently dressed in a fresh, tight pair of leathers and greaves. Her eyes darted over my ears and my hair. "Do you think you'll be able to shift today?"

I nodded, buckling my sandals. "Any suggestions? I don't want to stick out."

"What you did yesterday was fine," she shrugged. "You pull off a Human well."

My brows furrowed. I wasn't sure if that was a compliment or not. Either way, I turned my gaze to the coals in the hearth. The deep, solid blacks—rich and decadent. A buzz moved from my scalp to my toes as I willed the colors to become mine, my now loose hair shifting from pale blue to onyx. It was . . . invigorating.

I ran my fingers over my ears to ensure they were small and round instead of pointed. Beneath my dress, my fins had faded into my skin and no longer glittering with iridescent scales.

"I think I like the blue better." Loach stepped out of the washroom, tucking his button-down shirt into his trousers. "It suits you."

I gave him a small smile. "Thanks?"

Agatha tossed him a fresh coat and a thick scarf. "This should cover your," she grimaced, gesturing to his tentacles, "appendages."

"You like them?" Loach made a show of using those

appendages to lace a curved sword onto his belt. Agatha made a gagging gesture, and he flipped her off—but not without a smirk, I noticed.

"Who was the last to wear this?" Loach sniffed the collar of his new coat. "It stinks of Orc."

"First of all, go to hell," Agatha snarled. "Second, that's cute coming from someone who reeks of dead fish." She turned to me before he could respond. "Are you ready?"

I nodded, and we followed her out of the tavern. The barkeep waved happily as we left, glad to be rid of us.

Thirty minutes later, we were back on the main street, heading toward the market. I pulled the sleeves of my dress down to cover my fingers. The cool air didn't seem to bother Loach and Agatha. They argued back and forth in lowered tones as we walked, utterly unaffected by the morning chill. I couldn't get used to it. At least beneath the waves, the temperature stayed consistent. It didn't change every time there was a damn breeze.

Ignore it. I turned my attention back to the city.

Carnage—now that I could take it in without the salt withdrawals—was homey. Rustic and charming in the way I would expect from a fairy cottage in the forest, half buried in moss. Most of the rooves on this side of the city were red clay tile, and the homes and buildings were made of mud and stone, readily available from the bay.

What would they do now that the Seafolk couldn't trade? Where would they get their supplies?

Besides us, there were very few out and about at this hour. An Imp family of four that I recognized from the market yesterday strolled by us—pushing their heavily ladened cart of trinkets—filled with the familiar shine of fake gold and gems.

Wearing only rags, the youngest's ribs jutted out too far as he grabbed at his mother's sunken arms. Heavy purple shadows discolored the father's bright yellow skin.

It made me . . . hurt. Without thinking, I reached out to stop them. "Excuse me?"

Loach and Agatha froze, hands shifting to the weapons I knew lay beneath their coats.

The male Imp tugged the cart to a stop, glancing up at me with an irritated, suspicious gaze. "Oi?"

Now that I had my bag back, I reached inside and dug out a few copper coins. *These took forever to save.* I rubbed them together and smiled. *Oh well.* "Do you mind if I take a look?"

In an instant, the Imp's eyes brightened. "M'lady, for you, anything, anything! Come, come!"

The children nearly shook with excitement as their mother held them by the wrists. The male unfolded the cart like paper origami I'd once seen a traveler perform. It was impressive.

As I expected, there was more costume jewelry than I'd ever hoped to see in a decade. With a bow, he waved to his collection. "Take your pick. You'll never find the like again! The quality!"

"Tetra," Agatha stepped toward me, but I waved her off.

"May I?" I asked as I knelt beside the cart. The Imp nodded animatedly. That private, happy place in my soul sang as I began to sort through his treasures. There were so many pins —perhaps nickel—painted in cheap gold paint. Corded necklaces with glass pendants posed as rubies, emeralds, and sapphires. There were more gaudy rings than I could count.

I loved them—all of them.

The Imp continued to babble about the legends of each piece—of tales of battle, forbidden love, and bloodlines gone by. Loach took a protective step toward me as the Imp hung some beads around my neck. I ignored him.

A particular bracelet caught my eye. It was simple: braided black leather adorned with a ruby-red chunk of worn sea glass. Pretty.

I rubbed it between my fingers, inspecting it in the dim, early light. "How much?"

The Imp clasped his long fingers together. "One copper."

I gave him two.

With many thanks, he folded up his cart, and the family continued on their way.

Smiling, I tucked the bracelet into my bag and skipped to catch up with the others. It wasn't long before we crossed through the market and were headed toward the west side of Carnage.

Loach shot me a strange look over his shoulder every ten minutes or so.

Finally, I asked. "What?"

His tentacles twitched. "You know the beast probably stole that, right?"

"You're one to talk," I shot back. "How many things have you stolen? Even in the last month?"

Loach shrugged, clearing his throat.

Agatha let out a low laugh and shook her head.

We stepped onto a well-maintained side street—the wealthier end of Carnage by how the road was free of potholes and immaculately clean. Boutiques were the common commodity, filled with overpriced clothes, handbags, and silky slippers—all in the latest fashions.

"So, who is this friend of yours?" Loach asked as we passed a bench filled with well-dressed old women—the snooty sort —some Humans, some Elves. They stared at the scarf over Loach's face with disdain. He stared right back, making one of them huff.

"I never said he was a friend." Agatha shoved her hands into her pockets. Her steps light, confident. "More of an acquaintance?"

Another movement I wrote into my mental list, but her words unsettled me. "Then who is your *acquaintance*? Can we trust him?"

"I wouldn't even call him that, to be honest." Agatha grimaced. "And I make a habit of trusting no one—but if I were a betting girl—I'd put money down that he's the only person in Carnage who hates Sayzar Ameliatus more than we do. Not only that, but his family wove half of the wards in the Lantern Palace."

My eyes widened. "I thought only Elves can create wards?"

"A common misconception." Loach waggled his fingers at the old women in a friendly wave. They squawked, appalled. "Elves are the only race that can weave them *naturally*. Anyone can learn, but it takes a lot of study and a cunning mind."

I chewed on the inside of my cheek. "And you think this person will help us?"

"No idea," Agatha shrugged, "but it's worth a shot."

"And . . . in the case he says no," Loach patted his hip. "I cleaned my blade this morning."

My mouth formed a perfect O. "*Stop it.*"

Agatha laughed. "That won't be necessary. Boot has almost as many criminal contacts as you, Kraken. He's not going to blab."

This time, I clapped my hands over my cheeks. "His name is *Boot?* That's the sweetest thing I've ever heard!"

"I wouldn't go telling him that," Agatha said, leading us toward the side of the street. "He's a Goblin. From what I know, he used to serve in the Lantern Palace before buying out his freedom. Hard as nails, this one. Ah, here we are."

We stopped in front of a small, square shop built into a strip with several others. Behind its large, smudge-free windows were simple, wooden display cases. I stepped closer, peering inside. Atop cream velvet cushions lay some of the most beautiful jewelry I'd ever seen.

Thread-thin, silver chains dripping in true emeralds the size of my thumbnail. An ivory strand of pearls, the color only found on the reaches of the southern seas. Lapis lazuli and diamond hair clips, shaped into orchids.

I wanted to crush my nose against the glass, to take it all in like I might have as a child. Oh, those golden cuffs—stamped with ruby tear-drops—would look so handsome against my tanned skin.

The store itself was crisp and professional—free of the flowers and adornments of the surrounding denizens. There was just pristine glass and a simple, purple-painted sign that read *Fineries.*

I was in love.

A soft bell tinkled when Loach opened the door and held it for us. I nearly squealed as I trotted in behind Agatha. She took in the open showroom, the dozens of display cases as if she expected a hell-hound to come crawling from beneath the sandy, alder floorboards.

"Oh!" My gaze settled on a simple pearl necklace staged on a bust behind a counter, the rope tethered between it and the showroom wore a sign labeled *Employees Only.* This pearl was a dainty petal pink. It was perched in a rose-gold flower so finely detailed that it may have been carved by an angel.

My hand fell over my chest as I held back the tears burning my throat. It looked so much like the one Mama wore, gifted to her by my father when he'd proposed their bonding.

Loach and Agatha made a good show of pretending to scan the jewelry.

"Do you like it?"

I glanced up—well, down—to see a handsome, male Dwarf gazing up at me in expectation from behind the counter. He was a tad younger than me, with soft, brown ringlets falling over his eyes.

I blinked, "Me?"

His smile was genuine as he gestured to the necklace. "Yes, you. I know that sparkle in your eye. It's beautiful, isn't it? It would look even lovelier on you."

Loach let out a sputtering laugh.

I turned to shoot him a glare but met Agatha's eye instead. I didn't have to decipher her look: *This is our chance. Take it.*

God, help me. I smiled back at the Dwarf, tossing my hair over my shoulder. "It's stunning. I'd love to meet its designer. Is he in?"

The Dwarf's eyes became more guarded. "The owner is a busy man. He doesn't do meetings without an appointment, I'm afraid. I'll pass on the compliment, though."

Push it. Make yourself useful. I may not have powerful friends or be able to wield a blade, but Loach and Agatha couldn't do what I could. Mermaids had powers beyond shifting to appeal to our prey—we could also sway them with our voices. Our bodies—the curves and sweet smiles—were just another weapon from the days when my kind ate men alive.

It felt dirty and disgusting, but Cyclone would come home, no matter the cost. My voice dropped to a tenor as my people's old magic coated my tongue, tasting of strawberries.

I'd only used it once, and the memory wasn't pleasant. "I would love to tell him myself." *I'm sorry.* "I promise it would only take a moment."

My allure clawed into him without resistance. The Dwarf's mouth parted, his heated gaze falling to my lips, completely unaware of what I'd just done. "He-he may be in the back."

Lord above. I smiled wide. "Would you call him for me?"

I heard Loach chuckle as the Dwarf stared at me in awe. It wasn't until I raised a brow that he seemed to snap back to attention, running a hand through his curled hair. "Of course. P-please, wait here a moment."

He stepped through a rope behind the counter, swaying slightly.

Agatha patted my shoulder. "Nice work. That's a handy trick."

"Let's hope I don't have to use it again." How many moral codes would I have to break before this was over? "It feels . . . wrong."

"Well, it worked." Agatha snorted. "Sometimes that's what it takes to get work done. At least we won't have to force an audience."

"You didn't say talking to him would be a problem."

"I also never said it wouldn't be."

She had me there.

A Human couple stepped into the shop, drifting toward the engagement rings. Loach leaned against a display case, crossing an ankle over the other, watching them.

Agatha gave me a cheeky grin. "So, what are you going to say to Boot?"

My throat went dry. "What? Why me?"

"Again, this is your idea, kid," Loach whispered as he switched legs, eyes still on the Humans. "I'm not the talker here."

I pushed Agatha's hand away. "What about you?"

She cringed. "Orcs and Goblins don't have the best history. Especially not in Carnage."

I rubbed my face, groaning as the panic set in. My fins brushed against the skirts of my dress as my shift faltered.

"Watch it," Loach growled.

My breaths were coming too fast. I wasn't ready. I'd never met this man—let alone a Goblin—before. How was I going to—

"M-my lady?"

Sharks. I sucked in a ragged breath, double-checking that my shift was in place before I turned to face the Dwarf. Behind the counter, he rubbed his smooth chin, expression still hazy as he grinned. "The owner will see you. Right this way."

"Thank you." I plastered on a fake smile as he lowered the rope between the lobby and the back and ushered me to follow him.

"Call me Ivan." He rested his hand on the small of my back.

My skin crawled, feeling his calloused fingers through my dress. "Thank you, Ivan."

I shot one last pleading look to Loach and Agatha. They waved in unison.

Bastards.

Ivan led me into a narrow hall lit with faelights imbued into the low ceiling. Several doors lay on either side, neatly labeled: *Metalsmithing, Polishing, Beading, Design.*

At the end of the hall lay an intricately carved oak door: *Private.*

I swallowed the lump in my throat as Ivan opened the door, guiding me in with his touch. Inside, a simple desk sat in the center of an oval office. Shelves upon shelves of novels, manuals, maps, and scrolls hung from the plain, paneled walls. A ferocious wolf-skin rug was thrown over the otherwise bare granite floor.

My jaw dropped.

Scattered over the desk, the coffee table, and atop the hearth were pillars of amethyst and rose quartz taller than the Imps in the market. They were *stunning*.

"Sir." Ivan bowed toward the desk, retreating out of the room, but not before taking one last glimpse at my backside. I gave him a sad smile as he left. *I am the worst.*

"Have a seat, girl."

I turned back toward the desk.

A spectacled creature sat in a plush, red velvet armchair, his gnarled fingers steepled over a ledger stained with fresh ink. He waved toward the chair across from him. "Sit."

I tried to control my breathing—*in through the nose, out through the mouth*—as I did as I was bid, tucking my skirts beneath me.

I'd never seen a Goblin.

They haled from caves deep below Tyrr—at least, that's what I'd been told. In the last two hundred years, they'd been kept as slaves after the Elves took the mountains.

This male—Boot—watched me with large, orange eyes like an owl's, partially hidden by thick-framed glasses. His skin was the shade of rust, as craterous as the moon. Everything about his rugged features completely contrasted the sophisticated, tailored, teal suit he wore, a striped tie around his neck.

Those orange eyes gave me a quick once-over. He turned back to his ledger and began scratching some numbers. "Was that necessary?"

My brows pinched. I fidgeted in my wicker chair. "I'm sorry?"

"Enchanting the boy." Boot waved dismissively. "It seems rather excessive."

Oh. I chewed on my tongue. "I didn't—"

"Don't bother lying," Boot sighed without looking up from his papers, voice like gravel. "I've seen the effects of

Merwoman before. Such a primal, bestial gift . . . to influence the carnal desires of men." He met my eyes this time, setting his glasses on the desk. Holding that gaze made my heart sink into my stomach.

He cocked his head and grinned, his teeth jagged, stained, and brutal. "So, what brings you to me, Seductress?"

He's smarter than me. It should be Loach in here. Don't panic. I swallowed. "I-I wanted to praise your work."

"Little liar. How predictable." Boot put on his glasses again, picking up his pen, almost disappointed. "Such is the way of your kind."

His claws were so artfully filed, honed to the sharpest of points—finer than any needle or carving tool. The time they must have taken, the care.

"Beautiful," I whispered, not bothering to hide my stare.

Boot's eyes narrowed. "Pardon?"

"Your nails," I blushed. "You use them to engrave, don't you? Your metalwork is incredible. Using an extension of yourself instead of a blade is ingenious. The pearl necklace you have on display was hand-crafted, wasn't it?"

Boot regarded me more carefully this time. The office felt stuffy. "You have an interest in metal arts?"

"Very much so." Excitement bubbled in my voice. "My parents were collectors. I wanted to open my own shop . . ." I paused. It was silly to say any of this. To even let those forbidden desires out of my heart. My throat tightened. "I apologize for rambling."

Boot's ears were long, crinkled, and bat-like. They wiggled as he said, "Why are you here?"

I'd almost forgotten. "I need your help."

"Help?" Boot practically scoffed. "A Merfolk would call on the aid of a Goblin?"

"Is that wrong?" I asked. *Just say it.* Honesty had worked on

Loach and Agatha. Maybe it would save me now. "I seek to reclaim my king, Cyclone, from the Emperor."

Something like surprise flashed over Boot's features.

"You don't have to tell me how stupid it sounds." I blew out a hard breath, leaning back as I watched the wood in the fire pop. "I know it is—but it's either this or go to war for Sayzar. I'd rather jump off a cliff. I'm laughingstock with a sword."

Boot stood, coming around the desk. He was about chest height to Agatha. His feet were bare and as gnarled as his hands. He stroked his long, pointed chin. "And this brings you to me— why?"

"Wards," I admitted. "I'm told the palace is full of them. I don't know how to get past them, but you do . . . don't you?"

One minute passed. Maybe two.

Boot grinned.

"Sir!" I jumped a mile as Ivan slammed through the office door, his curls sticking to the sweat dripping on his face. "Enforcers—"

"Hell," Boot strode toward the door, paused, then wheeled on me and pointed. "Girl, come. I may need you."

I didn't hesitate to follow him into the hall. Boot's steps were hobbled and slow—an old injury, maybe—but that didn't hinder his ferocity as he marched into the showroom.

Where's Loach and Agatha? I didn't see them. Only the Human couple remained inside the store—backed into the corner—faces coated in fear as they watched the two Elven soldiers waiting at the counter, arms crossed, expressions sour.

Their armor matched the two that attacked us in the warehouse. One male, one female—their luminous eyes scanned over me and Boot in a fraction of a second, analyzing every threat.

They found none.

Beneath their helms, their features were nearly identical. Only the shapes of their bodies damaged the uniformity I imagined the Emperor strived for.

"There you are." The male Enforcer tapped his metal, gloved fingers on the glass counter hard enough to scratch it. "It seems you've been up to no good, cave dirt."

Boot grimaced as we stepped behind the counter. I wasn't sure if it was because of the insult or the scratched glass. "I wouldn't dream of causing inconvenience on your day, Reymar. Where do these accusations come from?"

He knows them personally. My pits were sweating now.

The haziness of my allure had left Ivan by now. He watched the Enforcers with indignant terror.

The female Elf spit as she dropped a solid piece of wood on the counter with a bang. This time, the glass cracked. The Humans slunk out of the shop as Boot let out a silent hiss.

My pulse fell into my ankles. I knew that bit of wood. It was the crate lid I'd seen in the warehouse—engraved with a *B*.

Boot.

No, no, no, no.

Boot looked at the lid curiously. "One of my supply containers. Why would this cause you to ruin my day with your obtrusive presence?"

"Watch your mouth, Goblin." The female Enforcer leaned onto the counter, nothing short of vicious. "Be grateful I haven't already taken your head."

I backed away a step. *Where the hell are Loach and Agatha?*

"Do you know where we found this?" The Elf called Reymar asked.

Boot jerked his chin to Ivan, and the Dwarf quickly retreated into the back. "Humor me."

He's bold. I'd never have the guts to speak to an Enforcer that way. I backed up until my bottom hit the wall. The female Elf's gaze snapped to me, and my eyes dropped to the floor. *I'm no one. Nothing.* Hopefully, she'd believe it.

"This," Reymar tapped the lid. "was found sealing one of *your* crates. Inside were the bodies of two *dead* Enforcers, Goblin."

My hands clapped over my mouth. *We did this.* The Elves that Loach had killed...

Boot remained remarkably calm. "That's dreadful to hear."

"Show some respect," the female Elf hissed.

Boot raised a crooked finger. "Those warehouses have been public property of Carnage since the barrier was raised. Anyone could have shoved those bodies inside."

"*Those bodies?*" Reymar was livid. This wasn't going well. "Those were my kinsmen. Murdered. Like street dogs."

It was so subtle. Boot's eyes flashed to mine, and then he tapped his lips. A request—a question. To me... for aid.

I can't believe I'm going to do this. Using my abilities on an innocent Dwarf was one thing but on an Elven Enforcer?

The Elves were the very center of magic. The ancient, near-immortal ancestors of all of us who could weave it.

Damn it all. I smiled, then. Tasting strawberries on my tongue. Chocolate. My essence wrapped around the male and female, drudging up all their dreams, their desires. Submission, pain—that's what I found—the excitement of a hand gripping their throats at the peak of pleasure.

I became that. *Embodied* it.

Leaning over the counter, I brushed my fingers over Reymar's. "This loss, it's..." I choked back a tear. "Unforgivable. I hope the perpetrators die screaming."

The Enforcers shared a glance. Wary, cautious, but also... dazed.

"Yes." Reymar scrapped the metal nails of his glove painfully into the back of my hand. I didn't flinch. "When I find who's behind this, I will gut them. Twist their intestines into fishing nets and set them out into the bay."

Boot's eyes narrowed.

I gave Reymar a wicked smile. "Good. Long live the Emperor."

He copied my movements, words barely a breath. "Long live the Emperor." Then he plunged his metal fingernail into my wrist.

The female Elf drew her sword and smashed the hilt into the glass counter in rage. "*Sea-bitch.*"

I cried out and tried to pull away, but Reymar's claws sank deeper. Hot blood leaked from my arm. *I've ruined it. I've ruined everything.*

Just like the Enforcer in the warehouse, Reymar whipped out his hand and took a fistful of my hair as his blade pressed against my throat. He repeated, "Long live the *blasted* Emperor."

Despite my nearness to death, those words struck me as odd.

"And let him live in ruin." Loach purred over Reymar's shoulder . . . just before he plunged his sword into the unprotected space between the Elf's neck and shoulder.

Reymar's body convulsed. Enough that I retched, losing control of my shift.

The female stepped back, only to find Agatha's muscled arms wrapping around her neck. "Suck a tit, Elf," Agatha purred, and with one quick twist, the second Enforcer was dead. Her body fell to the floor in a heap, eyes an empty void staring up at the ceiling.

Boot dared to stomp his foot. "Scoundrels! Look at what you've done to my floors!"

"You're welcome." Loach wiped his blade clean on the female Elf's cloak. "Do you have somewhere we can put these before we're noticed?"

Boot grumbled something about a basement before wheeling on me, pointing one of those razor-sharp claws at my throat. "You did this!"

"Me?" I smacked his hand out of my face. "I saved you . . . kind of."

"It doesn't matter who did what." Agatha yanked off the rope separating the lobby from the back. "We need to get the hell out of here before more Enforcers show up."

"You—" Boot shook a finger at her, his cratered cheeks flushing a bright red. "It—does this have anything to do with recovering Cyclone?"

I took Boot's hand, wrapping it in my own. He blinked, stunned that *I* would have the audacity to say, "It has *everything* to do with Cyclone," I pleaded. He looked like he was about to argue, so I added, "The Humans will report what happened. At least come so the Enforcers don't hurt you when they investigate."

Boot hesitated before mumbling several curses under his breath. He wheeled on Loach. "You . . . I've heard of you before, Kraken." Realization dawned on him. "Damn it all, did you kill the other Enforcers?"

Loach placed a three-fingered hand over his chest in feigned offense. "Why would you assume it was me?"

Boot's glare could have turned a volcano into a glacier.

Loach sighed dramatically. "Yes—it was me—but that's beside the point."

Agatha finished dragging the corpses into the back. *Poor Ivan.* She wiped the sweat from her brow. "We're going to ruin the Emperor, Goblin. Hear us out over a cup of coffee?"

A pause.

Sweat dripped down my sides.

To my surprise, Boot laughed, the sound closer to a hyena's cackle. "Fine, but just one, and it better be strong." He turned and shouted down the hallway. "Ivan, clean this up. Put the bodies in the tub. There's lye in the basement."

Chapter Six

Boot wrinkled his nose as Agatha ushered us into her hideout. Those orange eyes scanned over the furniture, the dust coating the floor. He sniffed. "I'm already regretting my decision."

"So am I." Loach yanked off the scarf covering his mouth—freeing his tentacles—as he removed his wide-brimmed hat, exposing his shiny, milky scalp. "This place is disgusting."

Agatha glared at him as she shut and locked the door. "Sleep outside then, calamari."

I patted her shoulder reassuringly. "Don't be rude, Loach. We're lucky Agatha was willing to sacrifice this space for the team."

"Team?" The bluntness of Boot's words brought a chill to my bones. He sat at the table, choosing the chair I'd previously cleaned. "That word implies a level of sophistication, not the stupidity of people that would lead Carnage Enforcers to *my* shop, getting *my* possessions destroyed."

Loach raised his hands. "That was an accident."

Boot cocked his head, accentuating his twisted chin. "Case in point."

I grimaced as I sat on the filthy sofa, clasping my hands over my lap as I cleared my throat. "Agatha, you mentioned coffee?"

She took the hint and gave me a quick nod. "Right. I'll be back."

I shifted toward Boot as she trumped off toward the kitchen. The sounds of glass clinking together echoed as she dug through the cabinets. *God, please let the dishes be clean.* I smiled pleasantly. "I suspect you'll want repayment for the damage to your store?"

"Correct." Boot gestured for me to proceed, his lips curling to expose those jagged teeth. "Plus, compensation for today's lost business."

Loach plopped down on the sofa beside me, kicking up a cloud of dust. "You were a slave in the Lantern Palace?"

Boot let out a low hiss. "Indeed."

"You know the layout?"

"Again, indeed."

"We can talk about that later." I waved away the dust bunnies bouncing in the air as I sighed. I didn't want any more fights. "But you need an explanation. I'm not sure where to begin, honestly."

Boot just waited . . . expectant.

Where better than the beginning? So, I told him everything —starting with the Emperor's confinement of the Merfolk, my drafting, asking for Loach's help, and his conditions.

Agatha returned with four chipped—but hot—mugs of fresh coffee. She sat across from Boot, who watched me with a harsh, discerning expression.

Honesty has gotten you this far. As I cleaned and bandaged the wound on my wrist, I continued talking about meeting Agatha and our rendezvous at the tavern. She shifted uncomfortably, staring down at her dainty hands, as I shared her fears for her brother's family and, finally, what led us to Boot's shop.

When I finished, nervous and tongue-tied, Boot reclined in his chair and narrowed his eyes. He held out his mug to Agatha. "Another cup."

She swiped it from him with a huff but didn't argue.

Boot waited until he'd had another sip of the black coffee Agatha passed him before he answered, regarding me thoughtfully. "The wards in the Lantern Palace are ancient, girl. Older than me. To think I can break the spells of centuries-old magic is foolish."

"You won't have to break them all." Agatha leaned forward onto her elbows. "Just the hold on the Wardstone and the treasury. If the Elves in Carnage are one thing, they're arrogant. They think too well of their militia. I can pick my way through any of their material locks . . . just not the magical ones."

"I can outfit us with supplies and weapons," Loach added. "Once I get in touch with my contacts. I'm owed more than a few favors."

I wanted to mention how well that went for him last time, but I kept my mouth shut.

Boot glanced between them slowly, his gaze falling on me before saying, "It won't work."

The words hit me like a punch to the gut. *I can't fight for Sayzar.* Not after my mother and father, after the cove . . .

Not after everything I'd lost.

"Whether you decide to join us or not, I'm taking Cyclone back." My throat and eyes burned. "I'll lay his bones at Surge's feet or die trying. I won't help conquer more nations."

And there it was—*won't*.

Not *want* or *can't*, but I absolutely refused to serve the Emperor.

I could still see his face—the pin-straight, ruby-red hair,

the chiseled cheekbones offsetting his blue eyes. Why he'd personally come to my precious piece of paradise, I didn't know. My family hadn't been the only ones to call that beachfront cove home.

There were dozens of us—outliers, rejects, and eccentrics. We'd been our own little pod—independent, happy, and loved. We shared the fruits of our labors, leaning on each other to survive. We were almost as perfect as all my treasures.

Then Sayzar Ameliatus came—tall, handsome, and graceful—with the burning sun and a circle of armed soldiers at his back. We hadn't known then that Cyclone had fallen. I often wondered if things would have been different if we had.

Out of the twenty-four, we were all given the same choice—kneel or die.

I was the only one who kneeled.

Hot tears spilled over my cheeks. I was a traitor . . . a coward. *I'm sorry, Mama.* Pinching my eyes shut, I tried to shake the memory away. "I will ruin him if I can. That's a promise."

Loach and Agatha remained silent as Boot drained the last of his coffee. He raised a taloned finger. "If I'm to work with you, I'll require payment."

My shoulders slumped in relief. "Yes." My words were breathless. "Anything. If I can give it, it's yours."

"Madness, all of this." Boot stood and limped toward me. Loach's fingers hovered over his dagger as Boot stopped in front of the sofa, our eyes level. His blackened lips curled back into a smile. "But the Wardstone—it will be mine."

"Impossible." Agatha gaped, instantly on her feet. "It's taller than you are! We'll never be able to move it."

I blinked in surprise. I hadn't realized the Wardstone was that large. It made sense if it was powerful enough to encapsulate an entire city.

"You want my help?" Boot ignored her, leaning in until our noses were practically touching. "You want me to take down the wards? Give me the Wardstone, and I'm yours to command, Tetra the Seductress. What say you?"

"We *can't* move it," Loach shot back. "Not without ten men."

Boot's gaze never left mine. "What say *you*?"

Me.

Me.

This was my decision. To decide what I was willing to sacrifice to make this happen.

I inhaled. Boot smelled like freshly churned soil. "If you take down the wards, we'll find a way to give you the Wardstone."

Loach and Agatha cursed.

Boot grinned, extending a hand. "Shake on it."

I took it. Despite our height difference, his fingers swallowed mine as we shook.

This was happening. *Really* happening. Surge would fight back and re-take the Tyrr coast in his father's name.

"I'm not carrying the thing, damn it," Loach grunted and leaned back against the torn sofa. "I'm too old for that."

"Agreed." Boot stepped back. "We'll need muscle. I have an idea for that." He tapped a sharpened nail to his lips. "But first, there are items I need from my shop: books, research notes, and personal belongings. They'll need to be retrieved without alerting the Enforcers." He sneered a little. "I'm sure they've noticed by now that two more of their friends have gone missing."

"I'll get your stuff," Agatha replied, unfazed. "Make me a list, and it's done."

"Good, good." Boot began to pace, leaving a trail on the dusty floor. "We'll also need a base of operation." He glanced around the room and cringed. "And I assume this space will be it?"

"Unless I decide otherwise," Agatha snapped as she reached for her coat. "Seeing that *some* of us are unappreciative of free room and board," she added.

"It's wonderful," I reassured her—and it was. Dirty and broken, it may be, but I could see it—a place of safety and refuge, a temporary home.

I smiled, feeling some of the giddiness return. "It just needs a little love. I'll take care of that. Do you have a broom?"

"In the closet." Agatha's brow rose, and then she turned to Loach. "Your weapons and supplies?"

"In a private storage facility, out by the bay." He kicked at the sofa's cracked leg. "But again, we'll need some muscle to do what we need without making a parade out of it."

"Let me worry about that." Boot snapped his fingers. "Pen and paper."

Agatha muttered as she dug out an old pen, ink, and a stained scroll. Boot jotted down a few notes before handing her the parchment. He gestured between her and Loach. "You two, take care of this." He pointed at me. "Girl, with me."

With more than a few eye rolls and huffs, they left. Boot spread more scrolls across the shabby table and began to sketch out maps of what I assumed to be the Lantern Palace. With a steady hand, he drew ballrooms, armories, bathhouses, council chambers, and at least sixty separate bedrooms—all from memory.

I was in awe. To have a mind like that . . . I still struggled with my rights and lefts. I grabbed the broom and worked in between watching him as the sunlight sank outside the grimy windows, staining the dirt and dust with orange. As the hours passed, he pulled out a separate parchment and began drawing a blueprint I didn't recognize. It looked like the ruins of a chapel. His sketches moved lower, into levels below the pews and steeples—to familial tombs and underground altars.

I swept and cleaned as he drew, pausing every fifteen minutes to admire his progress. Outside in the overgrown beds, vibrant daffodils bloomed in the spring sun. I clipped a few, arranging them in the vase I'd found beneath the sink. They looked lovely atop the freshly polished coffee table, which perfectly complimented the patterned rug I'd dragged from the closet.

The moon had risen—and I'd just started scrubbing the stairs—when Loach and Agatha finally returned, sweating, arms piled high with canvas bags.

My back ached as I set aside my mop and bucket to help them. At least the first floor was spotless and livable now. Boot didn't glance up when they entered, instead waving toward the kitchen. "Leave those over there."

"You're welcome." Loach slumped down on the sofa as he wiped his damp forehead on his coat. "We got it—all of it. Ivan says hello, by the way."

"And we helped ourselves to your wine." Agatha dropped six more bags on the kitchen counter with a glassy clunk. Boot glared at her. Agatha grinned, then ran her finger over the counter. It came back clean. "It looks nice in here. Good job, Tetra."

"Thank you." I beamed.

She stepped around the table, peering over my shoulder at Boot's sketches. "And *what*, may I ask, were you two doing besides cleaning?"

"Planning," Boot replied, his sleeves stained with ink. "A skill you three seem to lack."

Agatha glanced over the map of the palace, eyes narrowing as she snatched up the unfinished drawing of the chapel. "Where the hell is this?"

"Orcs," Boot spat, trying to snatch it back from her, but Agatha was faster. With her brows scrunched, she passed the map to Loach. "You know this place?"

Loach's beady eyes widened as he scanned over the parchment. "Yeah . . . this looks like the remains of Carnage's original church." As he swapped pages, taking in the drawings of the underground levels, an emotion I'd never seen from Loach before passed over his features . . . fear. "Why—in all that is holy—did you map out the catacombs?"

Boot's returning smile was absolutely feral. "Recruiting our muscle."

Loach gently folded the map and returned it to Agatha, never taking his eyes off Boot. "Ghosts and monsters. That's what you'll find in those crypts, Goblin."

"I know." Boot rolled up his finished drawings. "But let me explain, *Kraken*. My family had served in the Lantern Palace long before the Emperor came to power—back when the first Elves ruled Tyrr." He began digging through the packs Loach and Agatha had dumped on the kitchen floor. "The wards guarding the catacombs are even older. If I can successfully undo them, then maybe . . . maybe . . . we'll have a chance to unweave the connections on the Wardstone."

"What's in the catacombs?" It felt silly to ask. Agatha watched the two men curiously.

"I told you." Loach sprinkled some salt in his water canteen and shook it before taking a sip. "Monsters."

"Monsters with—what did you say we needed?" Boot smiled wickedly. He pulled a heavy tome from his pack and let it fall loudly on the counter. "The strength of ten men? What about ten men in one?"

Patterns and shapes I didn't understand littered the book's pages. Handwritten notes were etched beside them in a strange language.

Agatha sidled beside me by the kitchen counter, tucked her short hair behind her ear, and muttered. "Do you have any idea what they're talking about?"

I shook my head, anxiety rolling in my stomach.

"You're insane." Loach enunciated, deliberately slow. "Insane. He'll kill us all . . . just for the fun of it."

Agatha rolled her eyes and pulled a sack of beef jerky out of her coat pocket. She handed me a strip. "Would either of you care to elaborate?"

"Our new friend is proposing we release a homicidal, lunatic Vampire." Loach rubbed his cheek with a tentacle. Not the most attractive gesture. "If rumors are correct, one that has been entombed for a century for committing unforgivable crimes against the nation."

"One hundred and twenty years," Boot corrected. "And he's a Vampire *Offspring*—a different creature entirely."

"Oh." Loach swiped a piece of Agatha's jerky and threw it at Boot's head. "Pardon me for not distinguishing between a bloodthirsty animal and its spawn."

"Vampires?" Agatha let out a loud, sharp laugh. "Krakens, Mermaids, Goblins, Orcs? What's a dash of spicy seasoning to our mixed entrée of mediocrity?"

"Could he help us?" I took a bite of the jerky. *So deliciously salty*. I hadn't realized how hungry I was. "I mean, would he make a difference?"

Vampires—all I knew were the stories I'd heard as a child. They defied natural law with their strength, otherworldly powers, and general love of brutality. Predators. Murders. Living outside of society in *hives,* picking off folks that strayed too far from their outlying towns and villages.

Sharks. When I was young, the older folk always warned us not to wander too far into the woods, but some children did anyway. They never came back.

Boot nodded. "If we are going to break through the Emperor's forces, take the Wardstone—" He gave Loach a hard look "—*and* make off with the contents of the palace treasury, Jayvin Dyre might make *all* the difference."

Loach rubbed his face. "Damn it all to hell. We have nothing to barter with."

"Freedom? We can offer him that," I blurted, a glitter of hope sparking inside me. Of all people, I knew the appeal of being freed from a cage. "Do you think that would be enough?"

"By nature, an Offspring will want nothing more than to return to its master . . . its creator." Boot picked at his lip. "My guess is that he'd sell whatever's left of his soul to escape that tomb."

Tomb. What would it be like to be locked underground? To never see the sun or feel the wind against your skin? *Horrible enough to beg for death, that's what.*

"Tetra," Loach warned. "This is a terrible idea."

"Everything I've done since I got my draft letter has been a terrible idea." I held his eye for once. *Escape. Freedom.* If I could give someone that, I would. *Even if they're a killer?* I shook the thought away. "When can we leave for the catacombs?"

Oh, Boot's smile was vicious. "As soon as you make the call, Seductress."

Chapter Seven

We'd leave the next evening.

I'd spent the rest of the day cleaning the second floor of the hideout—sweeping, dusting cobwebs, shaking out curtains, and straightening the books filling the small, personal library.

Eventually, Agatha joined me, and we chatted while we worked—about her family back in the mountains, her nieces and nephews, and her transition to living in Carnage. I enjoyed listening to her talk. Her voice had a nice rhythm and was pleasant to the ear.

The third floor held six small bedrooms, all sharing one enormous, fully functioning bathroom. Agatha explained that she'd bought the abandoned hotel when she'd first moved to Carnage, hoping to fix it into a bed and breakfast, which she'd run alongside Geralt's restaurant. After the barrier rose, financial difficulty and Elven domination ended those dreams.

Loach and Boot continued to argue downstairs about the plans to break into the catacomb. More than once, a dish shattering echoed up the stairs, followed by raised voices, and

Agatha would start screaming about them breaking her hard-earned china.

And I kept finding myself... smiling.

I didn't know these people, not really, but this felt right—like a sign that Cyclone approved of what I'd started. That he wanted to go home and to be laid to rest in the house of his forefathers.

By the time we'd finally headed to bed—some later than others—I'd passed out without a fuss in my freshly washed sheets, and for the first time in a year, I didn't dream.

Loach and I went grocery shopping the following morning with Boot's money. He had been unhappy about our lack of funds. Today, I'd shifted into a blonde, green-eyed Human—for the practice—wearing the same brown day dress as yesterday. Loach looked miserable, but by the time we got back to the hideout, it was spotless. Agatha had kept up the work while we were gone.

The others went back to planning as I started on brunch—not because I had to but because I *liked* to. Cooking had always fascinated me. How you could take so many random ingredients, throw them all together, mush them into a pot, and somehow, they'd come out delicious.

I enjoyed laughter around the dinner table—missed it. We'd always had such great feasts back at the cove, made up of the fresh fish and oysters we'd spend the day catching.

Bacon sizzled in Agatha's old, cast-iron pan as Boot rolled out his map of the catacombs onto the table once again, holding it down with his notebook.

"Here." He circled the picture he'd drawn of a broken archway. Beneath the arch, a stairway led straight into the earth. "This is the entrance to the chapel. Thankfully, the door lays within the limits of the barrier." Boot scratched his chin, sipping on the cup of coffee I'd made him. "I imagine the

Emperor did that on purpose. There's more than just Vampires below Carnage. Better to keep the area under watch."

Listening, I used a fork to flip the bacon, the grease hissing and spitting in the pan.

"What else is down there?" Agatha asked. Today, she had chosen a cream blouse and brown trousers, which complimented her emerald skin. "I hadn't realized the chapel was being used as a prison."

"It's not, as far as I'm aware." Boot swirled the contents of his mug. "Jayvin Dyre was sentenced down there before Carnage became a trade central. When Sayzar Ameliatus took over, he knew better than to release him or risk an escape during the power shift, so he sealed off the chapel completely and buried it." He tapped a long nail on the table and huffed. "Some in my clan say a guardian is protecting the lower levels, but I've never seen any mention of it in my research. This guardian is likely no more than more wards or a clever fey trap."

"He's that dangerous?" I scraped the finished bacon on a plate before starting on the eggs. "This Offspring?"

"He's dangerous enough that the Emperor is afraid of him." Loach rubbed his wrinkled forehead. "So that should be enough for you."

"Who put him in there?" I asked.

"Some say he was caught after failing to assassinate Tyrr's previous ruler." Boot chipped in. "Some say his creator locked him in the catacombs because she could no longer control him."

"*She?*" That surprised me. "His creator is female?"

"All Vampires are female," Boot answered. "The true Vampires, at least. They create spawn—or Offspring—from males to breed with, use as protection, and lure in prey, but they're not as powerful. Similar to a queen bee and her drones."

Not as powerful? Sayzar Ameliatus was so terrified of this spawn that he placed a sentry over a *warded* catacomb. What kind of powers did a fully-fledged female Vampire possess?

"He sounds great to me," Agatha chuckled. "When does he start?"

They all looked at me.

Finishing the eggs, I rationed the steaming portions onto four plates. I licked a bit of grease off my thumb as I passed them out. "We'll leave at nightfall."

Agatha's brow rose as she picked up her fork.

I shrugged. "Vampires can't come out during the day, right?"

Boot used his knife to cut his bacon into six equal pieces. "That's. . . it's not that simple, but darkness would be best, correct."

Loach picked up his plate and headed for the stairs. "I'm going back to bed, then. Wake me up when it's time to go."

The night came too quickly.

My breath misted as I exhaled. The weather in Tyrr could be so unpredictable. I bundled deeper into my coat, wearing a fitted, matching navy tunic with trousers beneath. Two heavy canteens hung over my shoulder, filled with blood from the unlucky goat we'd found on the way out to the fields outside Carnage.

I'd never seen farmland—the rows and rows of barley, sprouting corn, and wheat were beautiful in a haunting way.

Rusted tools were laid aside, ready to be used in the morning. By fall, the crops would be gone, and there would be nothing left to replace them unless the Emperor took down the barrier. From what the others told me, he wouldn't do that until he felt the coast was secure, which required using the Merfolk to bring the remaining rebellious Seafolk to heel.

Loach kept beside me as Agatha walked ahead with Boot, her torch casting an orange glow over the dewy pastures, speckled with dandelions and poppies.

"We shouldn't be far." Boot gestured toward a grassy mound ahead. I would have thought it was just a hill, but he said, "That's the entrance to the chapel."

"How were you able to draw out the catacombs?" Agatha's breaths were ragged, wheezing as if the cold air irritated her lungs. "I meant to ask earlier but got distracted by Tetra's cooking."

"It wasn't that bad," I huffed.

Loach chuckled lowly, the sound carrying over the meadow.

The torchlight illuminated Boot's rusty skin. "My grandfather helped design them. He wove most of the wards in the lower sanctum. The Emperor's forebearers commissioned him to seal off the entryways years later."

"Hills alive." Agatha's jaw dropped. "That would make your grandfather over a thousand years old."

"I never said I was young." Boot trotted up the hill with surprising ease, despite his claim. He hovered his torch over the ground, brows furrowed, swaying it back and forth until he paused over a patch of reeds. "Ah, here it is. Dig this up."

The three of us exchanged glances.

"Bloody useless." Loach sank to his knees, cursing as he tore away the tall, browning grass. "All of you."

As the reeds fell away, a rotten, wood hatch started to

appear—warped from the weather, its metal hinges rusted a deep red.

Agatha knelt, cocking her head as she studied the heavy padlock sealing the hatch. "I thought you said there was an arch?"

Boot's lip curled as he lowered his torch over the lock. "Touch it."

A slight hesitation. Agatha reached out and ran her gloved fingers over the metal.

The air... rippled.

I felt it as much as I witnessed it—a warning against my bones—as indigo energy waves spread over the hill.

Loach cursed, backing a step, as a great, stone arch formed—towering sixty feet over us. The hatch was replaced with a narrow, steep staircase heading deep below the ground.

Just like what Boot had drawn.

"The rest of the chapel remains beneath." Boot leaned down as if to touch the first stair, but a second wave of energy repelled him. Strange words and symbols flashed in the air, a silent conversation for anyone who could understand.

My mouth opened in awe. "Wards."

The ancient language of the Elves, capable of all kinds of magic. According to Loach, others could learn it, but it would always be a second language, not ingrained in their cells like it was with Elven kind.

"*Haymer saitus.*" Boot whispered as he traced several shapes over the stairs. "*Dragus mor lenar quid.*"

Another flash of indigo as the spells beneath the arch gave away with a sigh. The sound rippled over the meadow as if relieved to be released from its constant vigilance.

Loach blinked. "What the hell did you say?"

Boot sneered as he stood, brushing dirt off his knees. "I

said. *Open up—now before I hit you with the Kraken.* Ancient Elvish."

"Ha." Loach shot him a look. "Funny."

I wasn't sure if Boot was joking.

Agatha tested the first stair with the toe of her boot—and touched stone. The ward was gone. She took another step, offering me a hand. "Shall we?"

I sucked in a deep breath, tugging my hair out from beneath my jacket—now a darker shade of teal blue from the stream I'd sipped from earlier. It was nice not having to shift for a little while and have that constant drain on my salt stores. Shaking the anxiety out of my limbs, I took her hand and smiled. "Let's do this."

Boot followed behind us as we descended into the chapel, his torch illuminating a well-maintained pathway leading down, down, down until the pale glow of the moon above faded away, leaving us in nothing but torchlight.

The stairway spiraled lower and lower until we reached a second arch—this one mortared together with mud and simple brick.

Loach kept a hand readied over his sword as Boot stepped past us. He trailed a finger over the open air beneath it, murmuring. There were no bursts of energy this time. No symbols.

"This isn't warded." I gripped my chest as Boot stepped through the arch. "This should be the entrance to the chapel."

"No traps? Perfect," Loach groaned as he followed. "They probably weren't worried about us getting much further than this."

I squeezed Agatha's hand as we followed. The narrow tunnel now branched into a larger chamber—a pantheon of ancient marble pillars and intricately carved statues.

"Damn," Agatha whistled, stepping cautiously toward the

nearest statue—a long-haired woman in a billowing gown, her delicate face hidden behind a thin veil. "Who were these people?"

"The old rulers of Tyrr." Boot held up his torch, revealing dozens more statues of equal craftsmanship. Human men and women, Elven males, even a Dwarven woman—fearsome in marble.

It took my breath away. "They're beautiful."

"Yeah, yeah." Loach waved dismissively, wheeling on Boot. "When do we get to the part where monsters try to kill us?"

It was hard to imagine anyone wanting to harm us here. I took in the gold and silver threads snaking through the marble and the forgotten empty fountains. This place had been a sanctuary once—peaceful. *What changed that?*

That was a silly question.

Sayzar did. His whole family line had.

Boot's lips quirked as he nodded toward the chamber's far end. "This way."

Agatha stayed close beside me as we headed deeper into the pantheon. Her steps were light and alert as her eyes scanned every crack and corner hidden in the shadows.

"How much further?" Loach asked after twenty minutes of wandering in the dark.

"It's here." Boot raised his torch to reveal a broad set of double doors inset in the stone walls. Charred portraits of sobbing Elf females were burned into the wood.

He didn't have to touch them—the energy of the wards rippled at our mere presence, creating symbols and words that, even without study, I understood to be a question: *Who are you?*

"A slave," Boot murmured in the Common Tongue, again stroking his nail down the open space before the doorway. "A servant, come to claim another."

Some say his own creator locked him in the catacombs. A flicker of sadness painted my heart. I'd been ready to start a war over the *idea* of being someone's property.

These men had *lived* it—for centuries.

Agatha squeezed my hand again. Maybe she felt the same.

Loach stepped ahead of us protectively as the wards responded with new symbols—upside-down triangles, siphons, and shapes of words that I could only describe as bitter.

My stomach lurched. "What is it saying?"

Boot's gaze flickered to me, eyes narrowed curiously. "It's asking for promised payment."

"What does it want?" Loach snapped. "My retirement? Tell it the Emperor already stole that."

I pulled away from Agatha's grip. Something about the colors, the pain anchored to them...

What if I became that?

What do you want? I whispered in my mind. A warmth licked up my neck as I felt myself begin to shift, my bones aching as they lengthened. *Name your price.*

That heat smiled, shaping my body to who and what it desired. I didn't fight it—this wasn't a power I possessed, but one granted by something far older.

"Hills alive," Agatha cursed, her eyes as wide as saucers. "What did you do?"

Loach stared in horror.

Boot just laughed.

I glanced down at my hands, now belonging to a man. *What the hell?* I reached up and my fingers snagged in ruby-red hair, silkier than the finest gowns. My skin glowed—literally *glowed*.

"The wards want Sayzar." Boot stepped forward, examining my face, which I assumed belonged to the Emperor. "That's its price."

Nausea licked up my throat, threatening to bend me over. *Why him? Why ask for what I cannot give you?*

But I did know.

This church had once been a landmark, a comfort to all who sought sanctuary from it. I knew it in my heart of hearts. Sayzar's line had sealed it away. Like he'd robbed my home from me.

If it's in my power, I will give him to you. I knew I was promising impossible things, but sometimes, even lies brought comfort.

I gasped, my skin on fire as I shifted back into my own body.

The double doors swung open—an invitation. Permission for a promise.

Thank you. I sent the thoughts out to whatever magic may be listening. I swore I felt that warmth brush against my calf.

Loach cleared his throat. "Well . . . that was odd." With a hop, he moved through the doorway. "Shall we? Before it changes its mind?"

None of us hesitated to follow.

The second chamber moved lower into the earth, and it was . . . angrier. The air was almost too stiff to breathe. Violent. Confused. Sad.

I let my fingers trail on the damp, lichen-stained walls, feeling it crust beneath my nails—a small attempt at reassurance. And it was dark—so, so dark. Boot's torch barely made a dent in the infinite blackness before us.

We felt our way down the corridor, warning each other here and there when we caught our toes on a loose cobblestone or bit of rock.

"So," Agatha's whisper vibrated through the stillness. "About those monsters?"

"I'm not sure what sentries were placed here, but like I said, they're probably just wards," Boot admitted as he scanned the ground with his torchlight. "My grandfather was known to exaggerate. That door could have been the worst of it —until we come to the catacombs, at least."

"*The worst?*" The voice that answered was splinters and snapped bones.

My stomach sank as I realized we'd rounded a corner leading into a third chamber. Moonlight streamed through a hole in the ceiling, shining over a statue twice the size of those that decorated the chapel's entrance.

The ground shook as the statue *stood*—reigning to a height of at least twenty feet.

"May God above spare us." Agatha drew her dagger, brushing it against her lips before pressing it to her forehead. "Because we are fu—"

"*Who are you?*" Not a statue, but an enormous beast. It raised its horned head as it inhaled, showing the pinkness coating the inside of its nostrils. Mucus dripped off its speckled muzzle, splattering over hooves the size of our nice, clean coffee table.

"Hmm." Brown eyes—cow eyes—shifted to me. *Bull's eyes.* "Their stinks, I know. Not yours, shining woman."

My scales. I'd forgotten about the ones freckling my face and neck, reflecting in the moonlight. *It doesn't know Merfolk.*

"You son of a bitch." Loach wheeled on Boot, rubbing his hands over his milky face before drawing his sword. "A bloody *Minotaur?*"

"My grandfather left out that detail." Boot backed toward me, gaze flickering to the scattered bones on the floor, then up to the hole in the ceiling. "This explains where the Elves have been sending the prisoners they sentence to death."

To be eaten by a Minotaur. I grabbed Boot's wrist. "You said Jayvin Dyre is strong, right?"

Boot nodded with a swallow.

The Minotaur shook its head, sending dust and bird nests flying from its horns. *How long has it been here?* Decades? A millennium?

"You seek the *Offspring*?" Its words came out in snorts and grunts, spewing more snot from its nose. It scratched curved claws into the floor, cutting out trenches in the stone. "He is *my* prisoner. *Mine.*"

"Tetra." Agatha shook the tension from her arms and gave me a reassuring smile. "Please convince our *muscle* to come out here and help. I didn't stretch enough for this."

"Agreed." Loach moved beside her, his elbow brushing hers. "We'll take care of this. Go get the Vampire, kid."

No, no, no, no. I'd just started to make friends for the first time in my life, and I was about to lose them.

My eardrums felt close to rupturing as the Minotaur roared, shaking the surrounding pillars. Loach kissed his blade and sighed. "I'm here for a good time, not a long time." To my surprise, he nudged Agatha's side. "You ready?"

She grinned. "Do I have a choice?"

They didn't.

Chapter Eight

They're going to die. We're all going to die.

The thoughts repeated over and over as Boot drug me to the left side of the chamber. The dust I inhaled burned my lungs. The Minotaur's bellows shook rocks from the ceiling as we descended another staircase.

"We can't leave them!" I tried to pull away, but Boot was powerful for his size.

"You can't *help* them." Boot hissed as we reached a lower landing. He muttered unrecognizable words over the empty air between us and the dark hallway beyond. The wards protecting it shuddered—a ripple in the air—but they didn't budge. He cursed. "You want to save them, girl? Convince the Offspring to join us." He drew symbols over the open space. Indigo light flared, but that was it.

"What's wrong?" I smacked my hands against my hips, over and over. A crack formed on the stairs between us, making the chipped, stone floor rumble. "Hurry!"

"Quiet." Boot's drawing became more manic as sweat

beading on his horned brow—then the energy on the landing peeled back angrily, a split grape.

"*Now!*" Boot shoved me over the threshold, the wards yanking at my hair and clothes as I fell onto the ground inside. The crash of another pillar falling vibrated up into my shins. I fell to my knees on the other side of threshold.

Then everything went silent.

Completely silent.

I staggered against the wall, breathing heavily. No longer did the world shake. The roars and shouted orders between Loach and Agatha disappeared. It was so quiet. Like I'd teleported to another world that had no care for what lay above it. A film clung to my skin like a thick fog, making my eyelids heavy. The hallway was so smooth and clean. It would be so easy to slump to the floor and fall asleep.

"Go!" Boot's growled, voice muffled, as he splayed his hand over the entry and grit those jagged teeth. I'd almost forgotten he was there. "I have to hold this open. It's not as welcoming as the last one." The ward shuddered, making him groan in pain, but Boot remained standing. "Don't screw this up, girl. *Move.*"

Alone. The air rushed from my lungs. *I'm doing this alone.*

Offspring. Murder. Lunatic.

But my body was so tired. A little nap wouldn't hurt. Just a quick refresher and I'd be alright.

"*Go!*" A wreath of angry energy moved up Boot's arm, and his eyes slammed shut. "*Now.* Be quick."

"Yes," I whispered as I forced myself to stand. Not just for him, but for Loach and Agatha—before they were torn to pieces. "Okay," I breathed, trying to shake away the haze. "Okay . . . this is fine. I'm fine."

I still had those canteens—those precious, full canteens over my shoulder. My ace in the hole. The hallway was illuminated despite not having an obvious source of light. Blue-grey. Misty. Sleepy.

I kept my hand on the wall as I struggled to move, clutching my chest, willing my breaths to slow. The hall ended abruptly, yet the left side of the corridor fazed in and out, semi-translucent. I touched it, and energy rippled off, dancing up my arm curiously.

This isn't a ward. I backed a step, but the energy held firm. It wasn't going to let go. This was something older, much older—and it wanted me to stay.

It's going to kill me. No, it's not. I can do this. I exhaled. *In through the nose, out through the mouth.* There wasn't time to fact-check Elven magic—it was now or never.

I brushed my finger against the false wall, which opened easily, inviting me to enter. There was no resistance, no hint of the magic that separated the hallway from what lay inside.

Breathe. Breathe. No bad thoughts. I pinched my eyes shut and stepped through. When I opened them, I was met with nothing but darkness and stagnant, thick air. A deep hum echoed through the silence, rattling the walls, shaking cobwebs from the low ceiling.

I clutched my throat. As my eyes slowly began to adjust, an orange faelight sputtered to life in the gloom and began moving slowly up and down the aisles of stained ivory. It flickered about as if dancing to music only it could hear. I took a single step forward and the clack of my boot heel could have been the screams of the damned. So loud. The aisles of stone were endless, a maze of faultless, straight lines.

Not stone. I moved—cringing at the noisiness of my own breathing—and brushed my hand over the wall. It was smoother than it should have been. No grit. Soft.

Lord above. My lips parted as my fingernails caught on a flap of leathery, dried flesh. My legs went numb. *Skulls.* Thousands of them. Uncountable. Stacked floor to ceiling, their empty, black eye sockets watching me.

The catacombs. I shouldn't be here. I was of the living, and this place belonged to the dead.

So many. I traced the open hole where the nearest skull's nose should have been. The fear I expected didn't come. My senses were too heavy. That sleepiness still gripped my mind. *Who were these people?*

That little faelight darted closer and twirled around me—almost friendly, teasing—a companion I didn't know I needed. It fluttered down the corridors of bone, stopping occasionally to beckon for me.

Does time pass here? I followed, and the grey haze coating the hall only intensified as we moved deeper below ground. *This isn't so bad.* It was comfortable. Pleasant, even. I ran my fingers over the nearest aisle wall, letting them catch in every crack and crevice. *So many bones.* Thousands and thousands of years of corpses. Were they murderers, thieves, desperate lovers, mothers, fathers, starving children?

Sharks. The warmth of the tears streaming down my cheeks shocked me awake, my pulse pounding in my ears. My breaths were coming too fast. It made my head swim. *This is ugly magic.* I looked up, properly taking in the gloom. *It wants to keep me here.*

The faelight was so far ahead. Without it, I was lost in the dark. The light seemed to sense my hesitation and returned. It fluttered around my ankles and knees before settling just above my shoulder. *Friend, friend, friend, friend. Follow me.*

"No," I said to no one, chasing it away. "This is far enough."

It felt like the faelight frowned at me.

"Hello?" I called awkwardly into the darkness, and my voice echoed through the aisles. *Stay calm. Stay calm.* I sidled left until I felt the bitter cold of the skull wall press into my palms. "Jayvin Dyre? I'm here to talk to you."

The faelight danced around my face, partially blinding me. I swatted it away with a huff. *What if he's not down here?* We hadn't planned for that. Could Vampires die of starvation? Loneliness?

I shifted my foot and felt a crunch. When I glanced down, I was standing on a large foot. "I'm sorry!" I leaped backward with a shriek and hit the wall, raining dozens of skulls over my head, bruising my shoulders and scalp. "I'm sorry, I'm sorry!"

There was no answer. I don't know why I expected one.

My entire body shook as the faelight moved, revealing that the foot I'd crushed wasn't living, but the start of a fully formed skeleton. Bowing forward—one bony arm extended, the other folded behind its back—as if asking for a dance.

The faelight rose, revealing five more skeletons standing together in a circle—their pieces glued together with magic—shaming a kneeling skeleton in the center of them, its fists covering where its ears would have been. The others danced, jeering—tormenting the poor soul on the floor.

There was something . . . artful to them. A story wanting to be told. My fingers shook as I gently traced the inviting one's fleshless palm.

I exhaled, breath forming a mist around my mouth.

"*Impossible.*"

I gasped as cold fingers trailed down my arm, extending it as I curled into the touch. Frigid lips pressed against the hollow of my neck, followed by a slow inhale. A voice—all shattered glass and unheard screams—whispered. "You feel *real*."

I'm dead.

"Don't—" I wheeled, but there was nothing and no one behind me. Only more empty-eyed skulls.

I'm so, so dead.

No . . . I could see it now.

In the darkness where I'd stood—a broad slash of a smile, the outline of a lithe, male figure watching me. I cursed and backed against the aisle of the catacomb, my fingers desperately gripping onto dried bone. *I can't breathe. I can't breathe. I can't breathe.*

Boot . . . Agatha . . . Loach. They were all going to die because of me.

The body faded into the shadows of the faelight.

I took several slow, deep breaths. The silence permeated everything. So still. I could hear the blood pumping through my veins, through the tiny vessels in my ears.

Cool breath tickled my neck. "I can feel your fluttering."

I stiffened with a sharp inhale, staring at the dancing skeletons, counting each of my heartbeats. *Keep it together, Tetra.* I swallowed. "Am I?"

Teeth scraped against my throat. "Keep fluttering. I like it."

Screw it. I slammed my head back—hoping to break a nose—and hit something hard. A muscled shoulder. *Damn, he's tall.* "Wait—"

Too late.

The shadow reached for me at the same time I ducked. When I hit my knees, long fingers caught in my hair.

Then he was gone—only the echo of a wild laugh remained.

I jerked up and stumbled down the nearest corridor. *No, no, no, no.* I was so stupid to think this would work—all of us were. I'd barely managed twelve hours of salt withdrawals. What would over a century without blood do to someone who depended on it?

The faelight turned, bobbing up and down as if in celebration. Watching. Waiting for me to die.

"Listen." I slid the canteens off my shoulder, legs trembling as I stood. "Look, I-I brought you a gift. Blood."

"*Thank you.*" A large, grey hand encircled my throat, slamming my spine into the aisle. I clawed at strong fingers as I fought to bring air to my lungs. The canteens clattered to the floor with a heavy thud, just out of reach.

The faelight illuminated a male face in its soft orange glow. *Sharks.*

Jayvin Dyre was more beautiful than any treasure I'd ever salvaged from the bottom of the sea—more beautiful than of my memories of the cove, more beautiful than the ocean itself. His skin was the color of mourning doves, and the jagged locks falling into his blood-red eyes that of freshly fallen snow. He was a work of art.

"*Please,*" I managed to gasp.

He tangled the fingers of his free hand in my hair and yanked back so hard my neck cracked. I didn't feel it, though— only his sharp teeth sinking into my neck, the sensation of my blood being called to his mouth. The pain was unbearable . . . until it wasn't. It numbed into something pleasant. Calming— just like the magic haunting this place.

Maybe it was a gift. One last kindness before the end. His grip tightened as my body began to relax.

I could stay like this. It would be so easy to let it happen. To just fade away into nothing. Just like he had into the shadows. I wouldn't have to go to war. Wouldn't have to remember the way I'd kneeled. Mama and Papa would find me on the other side and I could beg them to forgive me.

Jayvin sucked against my throat with a sigh, curling his arm around my waist as I slumped against him.

No.

Loach. Agatha. Boot. They'd die if I failed them now.

"Stop!" Lifting my arms felt like slogging through mud. I

slammed my palms into his muscled chest, over and over. Swimming in quicksand would have been easier than fighting the fog covering my mind. "I'm trying to get you out here! Listen!"

Everything stopped. That was almost more frightening.

So slowly, his nose brushed against mine as he pulled away, his ragged breaths smelling of salt and copper—my blood. Jayvin Dyre gazed down at me with bright, ruby eyes, his pupils dilating as he purred, "Say that again."

Vampire Offspring. Slave. Servant. Drone. A perfectly crafted treasure.

A stream of hot blood dripped from the throbbing bite wound on my neck. *Tell the truth. Honesty got you this far.* My entire body trembled as I gripped his biceps to steady myself. God, every part of me hurt. "I-I'll free you in exchange for your help. A favor for a favor."

Jayvin didn't budge. He cocked his head, predatory, scanning my face as if he'd never seen one before. The joints in my fingers ached as I released my grip on his arms, pointing to the canteens I'd dropped. "I-I brought you those. Goat." A nervous giggle escaped my lips. "I didn't know how to get people's blood."

Fingers still woven in my hair, his gaze flickered to the canteens, and his nostrils flared. "Liar."

"I'm not lying. Listen . . . please?" I was grasping at straws . . . and extremely dizzy. "At worst, you'll have to wait a few more minutes before draining me dry. Please?"

I whimpered as Jayvin leaned in—too fast—and his wet tongue traced my collarbone, licking away the blood that had pooled at the base of my throat. The wounds on my neck *burned* as he kissed them gently. This time—when he faced me—his lips were stained red.

He smiled, revealing lengthened canines. "You taste like sunshine."

I blinked. "Thank you?"

Jayvin wheeled and snatched up the canteens, dropping me to the floor. Instead of unscrewing the lid, he just ripped it off and poured the goat blood down his throat without bothering to swallow.

"Am I going to turn into a Vampire?" *Sharks.* I stood rubbed the bite wound on my neck. There was nothing left of it but a raised itchy welt. "I'm not judging, of course. It would just be nice to know."

Jayvin finished the first canteen before tossing it, his face lit up by that lingering faelight. He wiped the blood off his chin, then licked it off the back of his hand as he panted, "No."

I let out another anxious laugh. "That's good, I guess."

Jayvin had just enough time to cover his mouth before he retched and projectile vomited across the aisle, staining the watching skulls red.

"Oh no." I tore a bit of fabric from the hem of my shirt and offered it to him. "Are you okay? Here, take this."

Jayvin lurched backward and slammed into a raised tomb, his luminescent eyes wide and confused. He traced panicked circles on the ground. "You're a ghost?"

"No, I'm Tetra." I straightened, my tunic sleeve speckled in blood. "And I need your help."

Slowly, cautiously, Jayvin picked up the other canteen as he studied me. This time he unscrewed the lid carefully, holding his stomach before taking another shaky swallow. "Talk. Fast."

"Right." *Thank you, Lord.* Exhaling, I rubbed my face and sore neck. "Okay, okay. Give me a second."

His pupils dilated again as he watched the movement, gaze snagging on my pulse. "Faster."

"You've been in here a long time?" I dropped my hands to

my sides and blurted. *Think, think, think.* "One hundred and twenty years?"

Jayvin leaned back against the aisle wall and furrowed his pale brows, eyes unfocused. "One-hundred twenty-seven years, three months, and eighteen days."

"Damn." I chewed my lip. He watched that, too. "Well, I'm not sure how much you've missed, but I'm going to steal back Cyclone's body from the Emperor."

"Hmm." Jayvin sipped the goat's blood as he stared at my throat. It had taken me this long to notice he wore *rags*—a barely stitched-together, brown tunic over equally thread-bare breaches. No shoes. *He must be freezing.*

Focus. Loach. Agatha. I shook my head to focus. I'd almost forgotten about the Minotaur. "Doing that means I have to break into the Lantern Palace. Help me in exchange for your freedom?"

Sadness. True, deep sadness. "You can't give me that."

"I can."

"How?"

"My friend knows how to take down the wards." I chewed my filthy nails. "He's waiting for us now—in the hall. It's a lot to explain, but would you give me a chance to do so?" My mind flashed back to Agatha. "Over a cup of coffee?"

Jayvin's laugh was hoarse—like he hadn't used it in years. Or perhaps he'd used it too often. "I don't know what that is, Sunshine."

Sunshine. The fluttering started again. "Coffee or a chance?"

He noticed. "Either."

"Let me show you?"

I gasped as my back was to the wall again. Towering over me, Jayvin curled his lips back over his red-stained fangs and extended his hand. "Swear it."

My everything hurt. "W-what?"

"*Swear. It.*" He snarled, the sound echoing off the walls of the catacomb. "*SWEAR IT!*"

"*Okay!*" I turned my face away and shook his hand. "Okay, I swear it! If you help me rob the palace, I will free you."

A burning sensation scorched the skin over my forearm, wrist, and down to where our fingers were conjoined. I gaped at the shining, silver band weaving up both our arms, almost to the elbow.

An Elven binding.

My gaze snapped to his gently arched ears before raking over the dim—but definite—glow beneath his skin and eyes.

Sharks. I pulled away, the thread between us burning into a metallic scar. I cursed. "You're half Elf." Or at least he was before becoming an Offspring. No wonder he was so lovely.

"Come." With a low growl, Jayvin grabbed my wrist and dragged me back through the catacombs, the faelight flickered along behind us in excitement.

I stumbled and landed on that damn knee again. "I'm not going anywhere." I scrambled to my feet. He didn't let go. "I already promised. I can walk by myself!"

Jayvin ignored me.

I dug my heels into the floor as we passed the dancing skeletons. This time, he allowed the stop, turning toward me with an irritated expression and hissed. "Why are you so slow?"

"That's rude." I snapped back. He blinked at me. I yanked my hand away and pointed at the skeletons. "Who are they?"

I didn't know why it mattered, but they had a story. I wanted to know it, even if it was from a thousand years ago.

Jayvin's gaze flickered painfully to the kneeling skeleton in the center. "It doesn't matter."

"It does to me."

With a violent shake of his head, Jayvin grabbed my wrist again and led me the rest of the way back to the entrance of the catacombs. I didn't argue. If he squeezed any tighter, he'd snap the bones in my arm.

The faelight bobbed happily behind us. As we reached the door, Jayvin snapped and the light disappeared, the glow of it diving back beneath his skin.

"That was yours?" I asked, but he didn't answer.

As Jayvin reached to touch the translucent space between the catacombs and the grey hall beyond, his chest began to rise and fall in rapid breaths. Something like whimsy colored his features. Dreaminess. When he touched the barrier, it was as solid as a rock. His face fell. "You swore..."

"Yes, I did." I pulled out of his death grip and moved toward the barrier. When I touched it, my hand fell through without resistance. I flexed my fingers, feeling the sparkling energy curling around them. "And I meant it."

Panic—true, genuine fear filled Jayvin's ruby eyes as I stepped through, only an ancient spell separating us now. He leaned against the barrier, shaking as he swallowed and whimpered, "Invite...me...out."

"Invite you—" I'd forgotten about the rules of Vampirism —that they couldn't enter or leave a residence without permission from another. Had his creator really locked him away with such an archaic law?

I glanced up the hallway, still grey-blue and sleepy. Boot would still be holding open the ward unless he'd abandoned me. Loach and Agatha would be battling the Minotaur unless they were already dead. My minutes in the catacombs had felt like hours.

"*Invite. Me. Out.*" I jumped as Jayvin slammed his fist into the barrier. It faltered but didn't fall. His voice turned pleading. "Don't go."

My heart cracked.

His voice broke as he pressed his forehead against the invisible wall. "Sunshine, don't leave me here."

I inhaled and backed a step. Loach said Jayvin was a monster. That he'd rip me to shreds. Lure me into freeing him, then tear us all apart, enjoying every moment of it.

And, damn it—I was going to let him out.

"Jayvin Dyre," I breathed. *Sorry, Loach.* Jayvin nearly sobbed at the sound of his name. "Would you *please* come into the chapel?"

With all his weight rested on the barrier, the energy faltered, and he just... fell through.

Jayvin landed on his hands and knees in the hallway with a loud crack. He sucked in one breath. Two. Trembling, he stroked the stone floor, tracing those strange circles in the dust. When his stunned gaze finally rose to mine, he looked... awake. Not in that dreamy haze anymore. Not angry. Just *scared*.

I took another step back toward the stairs and cleared my throat. "There's a Minotaur up there. It's trying to kill my friends."

Jayvin stood, shaking as he stared at the fresh scrapes on his palms.

God, he's enormous. I was tall for a woman, and he had me by over a foot. Another step back. "They came to get you out. We all did."

I wasn't sure if he heard me. He just kept staring at his palms.

"Jayvin?" Boot was waiting. Loach and Agatha needed us. I hadn't gone into the catacombs for nothing. I stepped forward and touched his arm. "Let's go. *Now*, please."

"It hurts." Jayvin licked the blood off his cuts. "Like they're real."

"They are." This time, I pulled on his elbow. "We need to move."

He didn't resist as I led him up the staircase. Boot was there, atop the landing—his eyes pinched shut, the veins in his face and neck poisoned with that indigo energy. He peeked them open as he heard us approach and released an audible cry of relief.

"God above, Tetra—" Boot glanced up at Jayvin, the blood draining from his cratered skin. "And . . . you. Hurry up!"

Jayvin still didn't argue as I yanked him through the threshold. Boot cried out as he scrambled back and let the ward slam shut with a thunderous snap. As soon as it closed, all the horrors of the room above returned to life. An ancient roar shook the chapel. Somewhere, Agatha screamed words I couldn't make out.

Jayvin still stared at the crusted blood on his palms. The wounds had long closed.

"You!" Boot jumped and grabbed hold of Jayvin's collar and pulled him down to eye level. "You're free because of us. Do you understand?"

Jayvin's blazing red eyes widened as they slowly found Boot's. "Yes."

"I assume you remember how to kill?"

Jayvin's answering smile curved into something feral. "Yes."

"Good." Boot released him, barely coming to Jayvin's waist. The Minotaur roared. "Take care of that, would you?"

"*Te-tra.*" Jayvin sounded out the two syllables in my name as he turned, his gaze snagging on our matching silver scars. "Te-tra, who do you wish to die?"

I've made a huge mistake. My cheeks warmed as I breathed, "The monster upstairs."

Jayvin strode up the staircase, his gait quick and confident.

When we reached the chamber above, what had once been beautiful had been turned to ruins. The carefully sculpted pillars had fallen. White dust filled the air, the last remnants of their existence.

The ground quaked again as the Minotaur came into view —his face, muzzle, and arms stained in dark with blood.

"Tetra!" Loach knelt behind the stump of a pillar, expression so relieved I thought he might puke. He jerked a finger toward the beast. "Help her!"

I knew who he meant.

The Minotaur swung its head, and Agatha tucked and rolled her way across the chamber, dodging its horns. Wounds on her thighs and arms stained her clothes, her hair caked grey with sweat and dust.

"Hills alive!" She noticed us at the same time Loach did. "It's about damn time!"

The Minotaur turned and locked onto Jayvin, red dripping from his nostrils as he inhaled once, twice, then bellowed, "*Offspring.*" The Minotaur's massive footsteps shook the broken chunks of the statues around us. It pointed viscously at him, a death promise. "You've been sentenced. You are *mine.*"

Jayvin craned his head back, throat bobbing, his eyes dilating until they were entirely black. He inhaled, tasting the scent of blood in the air. "You . . . you are going to be a very big skeleton."

My breath caught in my chest.

The Minotaur spat then charged, breath releasing steam and mucus into the sour air. It raised its fists into giant battering rams. Agatha dove behind the pillar beside Loach, barely avoiding getting trampled.

Jayvin moved toward the beast, his long strides eating up the distance between them. At full speed, the Minotaur swung. And Jayvin just . . . leaned out of the way.

It didn't look natural, especially when he casually dodged a second blow. Then a third—leaning back so the swing soared right over his head. Frustration and bewilderment twisted the Minotaur's features. "You?"

"Me." Jayvin's grin was wild—breathtaking. As the Minotaur struck again, he leapt and clung to its arm. The swing's momentum dropped Jayvin onto the beast's shoulders, and he wrapped his legs around its neck.

Jayvin let out a hysterical laugh as he snapped off the Minotaur's horn—its scream ear-shattering and full of agony—before he effortlessly plunged the horn deep into its skull and twisted. The Minotaur's body convulsed before crashing to the ground, sending up a stream of broken rock and marble.

Dead.

Loach and Agatha stepped out from behind the pillar, breathing heavily.

Jayvin howled with manic joy as he yanked back the Minotaur's head by its remaining horn and sunk his fangs into the meaty column of its throat. The blackened veins on Jayvin's jaw and neck—on the exposed muscles of his arms—faded as the Minotaur withered. *Withered.* Like a plant left in the sun without water.

Jayvin sucked in a gasping breath as he pulled away. Rivers of blood spilled down his front, soaking his tunic. Panting, Jayvin's gaze snapped to mine. Those red eyes were so bright, gleeful, and full of life. A warmth spread through me, setting my body on fire. *What the hell did I get myself into?*

Jayvin's ran his tongue over his teeth as he smiled. "*Mine.*"

Chapter Nine

As the dust settled, Loach scratched his head and stared at the giant, drained corpse. He sheathed his sword. "What just happened?"

From the center of the room, Jayvin sat back and gave the Minotaur's head a loving pat. "He died."

"I can see that—" Loach turned to me and jerked a thumb toward our new companion. "And I repeat, what happened? Is he on our side, or no?"

I shrugged, cheeks hot, and brushed off my tunic. "I *think* so?"

Agatha wiped her stained dagger on her pants. "So, this is our muscle, huh?"

Jayvin leaped off the body and strode straight toward Agatha, only stopping when she pulled her knife on him, pressing the curved tip into his gut now that they were only inches apart. She hissed, "Back off, buddy."

Jayvin didn't flinch. He grabbed her dagger by the blade. Blood streamed between his fingers. "Give me this."

She jerked it away, cutting him deeper, and scoffed. "Get your own."

Jayvin didn't seem to notice. He pursed his full lips in frustration then lunged for the knife strapped to her thigh.

Agatha managed to dodge him. "Tetra, get your dog!"

"He's not a dog!" I called back.

"He's a dumbass," Loach muttered, and Boot chuckled.

"Stop it, both of you," I yelled as I tripped over a chunk of pillar while jogging toward them. Just before hitting the ground, Jayvin caught me, cradling my waist. "Um, thank you." I cleared my throat as Jayvin picked some rubble from my hair and smiled. *God save me.* I smoothed down my tangled waves. "You don't need Agatha's knife. We'll . . . I'll find you one."

Jayvin touched my hair again, pouted, and then let out an exaggerated sigh. "Fine." He turned and pointed at Loach. "Who's that?"

"Let's just get topside first, shall we? Then we'll do introductions." Loach was drenched with sweat. He picked up Boot's torch and blew on it, bringing the embers back to life. "This way."

Agatha shot Jayvin a nasty glare, making a show of sheathing her dagger on her hip.

Jayvin glared back but stayed behind me as we ascended the staircase to the upper level. The ground of the chapel's main chamber was cracked—the Minotaur's destruction—but the statues were still in place and unharmed.

A knot in my stomach loosened. What a tragedy it would have been to lose all that history. As we left the chamber and headed back above ground, I could have sworn the statues turned to watch us go. I tried to ignore the shiver trailing down my spine and focused on maintaining my footing on the slick, muddy steps.

As we grew higher, fresh, cold air brushed my face. I groaned in relief. "Finally."

The others were outside catching their breath under the arch when I realized Jayvin hadn't followed. Fear shot through me as I turned, but he was there, ten steps down, staring at the slim slash of the night sky above. He gripped his chest as it shuddered, mouth agape as he tried to suck in air.

He's hyperventilating. "No, no, no." As I trotted back down the stairs, his eyes shifted to mine. They were terrified. "You're fine," I told him and smiled, but the assurance might have been for me. "The wards are gone. You can come out. I swore it."

Jayvin nodded, gasping as he pressed his forehead against the stone wall and managed to take a shaky breath.

"Good. In through the nose, out through the mouth." I sounded way too chipper. He'd probably snap my neck out of annoyance. "That's what my Mama always told me. Just try it."

He did—over and over. After several minutes, his trembling began to settle.

"See?" I said and brushed a bit of dust off his shoulder. "It's going to be okay."

Jayvin pulled away from the wall, eyes still wide, a smear of muck on his brow. Without thinking, I wiped it away with my sleeve. He just watched me. Cautious. That haziness returning to his handsome features.

I managed another nervous smile. "Come outside with me?"

As Jayvin inhaled, he nodded and wobbled. He followed me up the steps until we were above ground, beneath the arch. Boot sat in the grass, rubbing the arm burned by the ward. Agatha bounced from heel to heel, gesturing for us to hurry. Loach shot me a questioning look, but I shook my head and mouthed, *"Don't push it."*

From behind me, Jayvin let out a low gasp. I turned, and his snow-white hair glowed in the moonlight, absorbing it's pearly rays like a stone might the sun's. A thousand emotions passed over his face as he gazed out over the meadow, inhaling the scent of wildflowers and the ocean breeze. Carnage lay like a slumbering giant on the hillside, the Lantern Palace an ivory, hovering sentinel beyond.

My heart ached for him. *One hundred and twenty years, three months, and eighteen days.* I wouldn't have survived. I'd barely managed a year trapped in The Dam.

"We need to get out of here before someone notices," Loach ordered, starting down the mucky, dirt path toward the city. "And someone *will* notice. Trust me."

"I have a plan for that, as well." Boot followed him, still nursing his arm. "Having a Vampire Offspring freed on Carnage will do wonders for keeping the Emperor off our trail."

"If you say so." Agatha's hands hovered over her daggers as she shot another glare at Jayvin. "He was more trouble than he's worth, if you ask me."

"Agatha—" I began, but she didn't hear me. They muttered together as they walked. After all that adrenaline, I wasn't even sure if they were processing what had happened yet. I didn't think I had, either.

The birds chirping to greet the morning fell silent. The moon had grown so low, casting shadows over the meadow and onto the hill's edge. Jayvin tentatively stepped to the shadow's edge, brushing his fingers over the darkness like water.

My mind flashed back to the catacombs—to that smile that faded into the bones, to the body that had formed behind me and brushed a kiss to my neck. The faelight.

My heart nearly stopped. *He's half-Elf.*

Which meant he was capable of magic . . . Vampirism or not.

No, no, no, no. I managed to swallow. "Jayvin?"

Slowly, he glanced at me over his shoulder—and gave me a sweet, apologetic smile.

"Don't." It was my turn to panic. "Don't—"

Jayvin dissolved into the night.

"Stupid, stupid, *stupid.*" Loach slammed open the door of the hideout, making the hinges groan. "Stupid for listening to you lot, stupid for fighting that God-forsaken Minotaur, and stupid for thinking a brain-warped drone could be bargained with." He reached into the cabinet, pulled out a cup, and poured himself an unreasonably large glass of red wine. "Ridiculous, all of it."

"Quit taking your bad attitude out on my stuff." It took a few tries for Agatha to get the door to latch. "Or you can sleep outside."

I stood at the edge of the kitchen, holding back the tears threatening to fall as I wrang my hands. *This is my fault.* I'd seen what he was about to do and did nothing to stop him. Not that I *could* have stopped him. Jayvin was . . . something different.

It had taken two hours to return to Carthage and the hideout—two hours of searching, fighting, and name-calling.

Boot didn't say a word as we entered. He slumped down at the dining room table and cracked open one of his thick notebooks, thumbing through the pages.

Agatha stepped around to pour herself some wine and was kind enough to slide a mug to me. Usually, I would have refused, but I snatched it up and drained half the glass in one swallow. It didn't stop that sinking feeling from returning to my stomach.

For whatever reason—for those brief moments—I thought he'd stay with me. Even worse, I'd liked the idea—to be around someone who knew what it felt like for the air to get trapped in their lungs, to understand what it was like to have your own body betray you.

Loach continued to slam dishes and cabinets. Boot disappeared into his scrolls.

I drained the rest of my wine, the tartness making my jaw clench, and headed to the third floor. I didn't want to be awake anymore. Maybe I should've downed the rest of that bottle so I wouldn't have to think anymore. Loach's shouts echoed up the stairs as I slipped into my borrowed bedroom.

It hit me then that I didn't own anything except for my bag, which I'd just dumped on the rickety chair in the corner. Even the clothes I wore weren't mine. But the bed was bigger than I had in The Dam—wider even than my parents and I shared in the cove.

Last night, I could fully stretch out for the first time in years. Though the pilly blankets were older than I was—the room bare except for a rocking chair and a single trunk—I was grateful for it.

Maybe I shouldn't have drunk that so quickly. Vertigo hit me as I sat on the edge of the bed. My boots made a sucking noise against my ankles when I yanked them off. I cringed at the sound, reaching to touch the still-tender wound on my neck. Healed but sore.

He took my blood. Maybe that's why I felt so out of sorts. It was just an effect of Vampire venom. *That's what it is. Just the venom. That's all.* My racing thoughts had nothing to do with the way his lips had felt on my throat.

The door creaked open as I slid my pants over my hips.

"It's just me." Agatha slipped inside, and I relaxed. She raised a bottle of wine. "Share with me?"

I smiled and nodded, shucking my pants onto the floor. Not even two days ago, this woman held a knife to my throat. Funny how quickly things changed.

I pulled off my tunic, leaving on only the uncomfortable undergarments she'd given me, as Agatha climbed beneath the blankets, wearing a granny-ish, floor-length nightgown. She fluffed up the pillows, and rested against them, before passing me the bottle. "You did well today, Hun."

I grimaced as I took a sip, the sweetness bursting on my tongue, as I turned onto my side. "It doesn't feel like it."

"Loach is just disappointed and angry." Agatha took the bottle back. "He'll calm down."

"He left." *Jayvin*. I wished he was here beside me. I shook the thought away. *It's just the venom.*

"Honestly, I don't blame him." Agatha shrugged and pulled the blankets over her chest. "If I'd spent one hundred years underground, I wouldn't be sticking around either."

"One hundred and twenty-seven." I took the bottle and chugged it this time.

Agatha paused and cocked her head as her fingers brushed the welt on my neck. I shivered. "Hills alive, Tetra. Did he bite you?"

"That," I sighed and rubbed the wound again. *There's no point in lying.* "Yes, but that was before he realized I had the canteens."

"You're lucky you're—" Her eyes widened. "Did . . . how bad did it hurt?"

I licked the wine off my lips—trying to forget the way he'd done the same with my blood. "It didn't—not really."

Agatha covered her mouth as she burst out laughing. "What a night. I'm glad it's over."

I laughed with her, more exasperated than anything, but it lifted some of the heaviness off my heart. We shared the bottle, talking and giggling, before she ran down and got a second. At some point, we drifted off. Agatha slept like a rock, snoring softly the few times I'd woken in the night from dreams of teeth scraping against my skin, halls of skulls and bones, and dancing orange lights.

When I woke again, the pinkish hue of the morning sun shone through the window, my head pounding from too much wine and not enough salt. Agatha was still sound asleep, twisted in the blankets, so I had nothing but the corner covering my chest.

I yanked at the covers and grumbled, "Bed hog."

A raspy voice chuckled.

Shock sapped the feeling from my limbs. A ruby-red gaze watched me—bright and alert. Jayvin Dyre's eyes dilated as he scanned over my exposed thighs and abdomen, every inch of him covered in gore. Perched on the foot of the bed, he smiled, "Good morning, Sunshine."

Chapter Ten

I kicked him square in the jaw.

Jayvin tumbled backward and hit the ground with a loud *oomph*, shaking the room like an earthquake.

Agatha was awake and on him in an instant. She dug her knee into his chest and pressed her dagger to his throat. I hadn't even realized she had it. I grabbed my dirty tunic off the floor and quickly tugged it on.

Jayvin reclined, grinning as he kept his palms up and exposed his throat to her. "Hello, again."

Agatha was quite the spectacle with her weapons and oversized nightgown. "You think creeping on sleeping women is funny?" She nicked his skin, drawing blood. "I've killed men for less."

Jayvin's brow arched in confusion, his gaze flickering to me. "Creeping? Sunshine invited me for something called coffee. I want it."

That's how he got in. My stomach lurched. *Vampires can't enter private residences without permission.* But I'd given him that permission.

"Why?" I winced as Agatha's knife dug deeper. "Why come back?"

Jayvin didn't seem to notice. His eyes never left mine. He smiled, then raised his arm, the light of the sunrise highlighting the silver scars burned into his forearm.

Sharks. I rubbed at my own scars. Beneath my sleeves, I'd forgotten about them. *The Binding.*

Agatha's mouth parted. "Tetra, you have to be joking me—"

"Oi!" Loach burst through the bedroom door, brandishing his sword like a drunk. He swayed as he took in the scene, growing furious when he realized who Agatha had beneath her. "You bastard!" he bellowed, "All that work, and you split faster than a banana in a monkey's paw."

"That was a terrible metaphor." Agatha stepped off Jayvin's chest, digging her heel into his sternum. "But accurate."

Jayvin frowned as he propped himself onto his elbows. "Did you happen to notice the enormous energy ward outside?"

Agatha stepped back and sneered, "So, you can speak in full sentences now?"

"Starving has a way of making the mind addle." Jayvin wrinkled his nose at her, then sat up more. "I'm quite proud that I didn't slaughter you all last night. Celebrations all around."

And we thought two canteens of blood were enough. My grip tightened on the blanket over my lap. That could have gone horribly, horribly wrong.

Boot appeared in the doorway, wearing a more atrocious nightgown than Agatha's. His blurry eyes widened at Jayvin.

Loach lowered his sword—barely. "Tried to escape, did you? Welcome to the present, Offspring. The Emperor has a big, damn barrier around the city. Nobody gets in. Nobody gets out."

"What happened?" *He's soaked.* Every inch of Jayvin was covered in blood, staining his hair and clothing. It was smeared across his face. *Is any of it his?* I chewed my lip. "Are you hurt?"

Jayvin blinked at me. It was the first time I'd seen him look so . . . present. "Pardon?"

I gestured to his clothes. "Are you—do you need bandages?"

"Oh." He tried, and failed, to wipe some of the blood off his chin. "I was . . . feeding."

"On what?" Loach snorted. "A horse?"

Jayvin's eyes widened. "How did you know?"

Agatha paled. "God save us."

"Well, I promised you a cup of coffee, didn't I?" I jumped out of the bed with a nervous, breathy laugh. "Boot, would you help me with breakfast?"

Jayvin's gaze locked onto the slender fins on my calves. Leaning forward, he rubbed the back of his neck with a huff. "I can't figure out what you are. I don't like that."

"I'm Merfolk." I blurted, twisting my hair around my fingers. "A Mermaid."

Too quickly to react, Jayvin rolled forward onto his hands and knees and grabbed my leg.

Agatha's blade was out in a second. "Drop her, leach."

Jayvin ignored her. My heart skipped several beats as he ran his fingertips over the edge of my fin, over iridescent blue and lavender scales surrounding it. *It's just the venom, Tetra.*

His brows pinched together. "How have I not seen your kind before?"

Loach growled, ready to strike at any moment. "There's Merfolk all over Tyrr."

"I'm not from Tyrr." Jayvin shot him a scathing look before

releasing my calf. He was by the door in less than a heartbeat, smiling as Boot stumbled back and cursed.

My skin felt cold without his hand on it.

Jayvin's lips widened into a wild grin. "I promised Sunshine help in return for freedom. What am I helping with?"

"You can help yourself to some personal space, you brute." Boot dusted himself off as he stood. "As well as a bath. You smell like death and entrails."

Loach pushed past them. "Why am I not surprised you're familiar with the scent of innards."

Boot and Loach headed to the kitchen, arguing, and Jayvin slid—*slid*—down the banister after them, cackling like a schoolboy.

Agatha rubbed her face, her ordinarily emerald skin paled to a sage green. "What kind of circus did we just join?"

"I've got no damn idea." I shucked off my dirty tunic in favor of a clean one. "I'm learning just to roll with it. I'll be the juggler."

She let out an exasperated laugh and smoothed her hair. "Fair enough. I'm not a fan of clowns."

By the time we joined the men downstairs, Boot was at his wit's end, nose-deep in porridge preparations. Jayvin had taken a bite or more out of *every* dry grocery we'd bought, with Loach doing his best to keep him out of his cheese stash.

My brow rose, the question rolling off my tongue without permission. "Can Vampires eat?"

Jayvin chewed the chunk of oatbread in his mouth as he

scanned me head to toe. I blushed. He swallowed. "Yes. It's just more of an . . . indulgence."

"Then stop indulging." Loach tore the loaf out of his hand and shoved it back in the cupboard. "You owe us an enormous debt, drone, and work needs to be done."

Drone. Jayvin visibly flinched.

Loach either didn't notice or care. "We've got weapons to move, Emperors to overthrow."

"*Em-per-or.*" Jayvin sounded out the title and popped his lips. "I don't know this word."

"It's like a king." I took the bread Loach had tucked away and started cutting it into slices before slathering it in butter—anything to keep my hands busy. I passed them out as Boot ladled porridge into small, chipped bowls. "Someone who takes over a land and all its people by force." I paused, raising a brow. "Or maybe that's a tyrant. A conqueror? Sayzar is easily all three."

Another wince. "Who was taken by force?"

"Everyone." Agatha started on the coffee, setting the pot over the small stove. "Carnage was home to many, all free to go when and where they wished. Then an Elf legion, led by Sayzar Ameliatus, arrived. He sealed the city, claiming he wouldn't open it until the entire Tyrr coastline submitted to his rule."

"This city was not here when I knew this land." Jayvin's expression turned dreamy again as he leaned against the stairwell. "It was nothing but a port town, with the same name, and a big, ugly fortress. Humans dwelled there. I'd only come the once."

"Well, that's garbage luck." Loach snorted as Agatha passed him a mug of coffee. "One visit to town only to be shoved into a hole for a century."

Everyone froze, watching how Jayvin would react.

The Emperor is afraid of him. He was locked away in a tomb for a reason. He'd taken out a Minotaur in less than a minute. But instead of rage or offense, Jayvin's eyes wandered to where Boot sat at the table, pouring over his notes. "What are those?"

There was an audible exhale of relief.

"Plans." I took another steaming mug from Agatha and shoved it in Jayvin's hand. He jumped at the warmth but let me drag him to the dining area. "We're trying to find the best way to break into the palace."

Jayvin examined his cup thoroughly, and sniffed it, before taking a sip. He gagged. "This is awful. It tastes like chicory root or . . . I don't remember." His eyes became unfocused as he carefully set the mug on the table. "Who or what is Cyclone?"

Everyone looked at me to explain.

I sat beside Boot, fiddling with the edge of his map. "Cyclone was our king. He ruled the Merfolk for two hundred years before the Emperor murdered him." My eyes burned. "His body still hangs over the palace. I will take it back and return it to his son, Surge. I hope that having his father home will inspire him to fight back."

"We all have our reasons for wanting to ruin Sayzar." Boot chimed in as he snatched up Jayvin's discarded coffee. "But we need someone of considerable physical strength to pull this off. Loach, here, is set on taking the treasury, and I'm not leaving without the Wardstone. You're going to be our bodyguard and pack mule."

Jayvin shifted his gaze to Agatha, lips curling up at the edges. "And what do you want, Orc woman?"

She glared as she shoveled a spoonful of plain porridge into her mouth and swallowed. "The barrier down. To get my family back to the mountains."

Jayvin turned his attention back to me. I swore the silver scar between us burned. "I do this, Sunshine, and I'm free?"

Free.

What did that even mean anymore? Either way, I knew in my soul that the bond he'd seared into our flesh would hold me to my promise. I didn't have much of a choice.

My stomach sank as I nodded. "As free as we can make you."

Jayvin's ruby eyes shuddered.

"Yes, yes." Loach rolled up the map of the palace. "You'll be free to return to your master. I'll be free to get back to work. None of this will happen without weapons, armor, and tools—which I have." He gestured to Boot's sketches. "I heard from my contacts that the Enforcers raided my storehouse after I was . . . evicted from Carnage. I'm told they're being kept in their headquarters. If we can retrieve those, this whole insane idea might be possible."

"You honestly think it's all still there?" Agatha leaned against the counter. "It's been a year. The Enforcers have likely used or sold them all off by now."

"Do you have any better ideas?" Loach snapped.

Agatha scowled at him.

"That's what I thought."

Jayvin shoved his bread and butter down his throat, saying past the mouthful. "Then let's go get them."

"Now?" I asked. He paused as he headed for the door. I made a face. "Um . . . shouldn't you change first?"

He tugged at his stained rags and pouted. "This is all I have."

"I've got some extra clothes in a trunk upstairs in the closet." Agatha said, "There might be something in there to fit your brutish frame. Tetra, do you mind?"

I shot her a look that said *why me?*

She just grinned.

"And show him to the tub," Boot added as he laid out his maps. "I refuse to work with that stench."

God, help me. I clasped my hands together and smiled. "Follow me?"

Jayvin nodded, and I was aware of every movement he made as he followed me up the stairs. When we reached the top floor, I opened one of the empty bedrooms, still as neat and tidy as I'd left it. "This can be yours." I gestured to the bathroom down the hall. "The bath is in there. Left for hot, right for cold."

Jayvin looked at me like I'd said the sun was blue. "Left for . . . what?"

One-hundred and twenty-seven years. Lord, he'd never seen indoor plumbing. I rubbed my face and neck. "Ah, here, let me show you."

Jayvin followed me into the bathroom, expression wary. I'd only done a quick cleaning on it. For an average-sized person, the clawfoot tub was big enough to stretch out and soak up to your neck. I tapped the faucet and the two handles above it. "Um, we have plumbing now. The Elves spell the metal when it's made to heat the water as needed." I turned the left spicket and steaming water poured out, filling the tub.

His jaw dropped. Timidly—as if he expected to get bit—he brushed his finger through the stream. He jerked away. "This is . . ." Jayvin's features fell, eyes widening in terror as he stumbled backward into the sink. "Isn't real." He wheeled and pressed his forehead against the mirror, desperately trying to suck air into his lungs as he traced circles on the countertop. "Not real. Not real. *Not real.*"

You feel real. He said something like that before.

"It's alright." I brushed my hand through the steaming water filling the tub. "It's real, I promise, and safe. There are soaps to wash with, too. Look."

Jayvin's skin became impossibly paler as he glanced over his shoulder and took in my hair—loose over my shoulders—

as the temperature shifted it from a dark teal to an icy blue, my scales and fins lightening along with it. He groaned as he slid to the floor, curling up to bring his knees to his chest, and gripped his hair so tightly I thought he might rip it out.

"Sharks, I'm sorry." I slid down beside him. "I change color sometimes. I should have warned you about the hot water."

In response, he let out a small whimper, rocking, but his breathing had slowed a little.

I wanted to touch him, comfort him, but he was as likely to snap my neck as be grateful for the reassurance. I kept my wringing hands in my lap. "Do you need a minute?"

He nodded.

"I'll go find you something clean to wear." I rose slowly. "Just turn the spicket again to turn it off. I'll be right back."

The water was still running as I headed to the closet on the second floor. As Agatha had said, there was a large trunk in the back filled with clothes of all different shapes and sizes. They were dusty and smelling of more mothballs—like everything else in Carnage—but they'd do.

Most of the garments were meant for women. As I rifled through them, I set more than a few dresses aside to try on for myself. Eventually, I found an oversized pair of men's trousers—far too wide for Jayvin—but they were almost long enough. At least there was a belt and a high-necked, black sweater that might fit.

A few minutes later, I stepped back into the room—meaning to leave the clothes on the bed—but Jayvin was sitting on it, dripping wet and completely naked, studying the faded paintings on the walls. He sat cross-legged, concealing his *private* areas, but I got more than a good look at his sculpted chest and torso, at the deep, muscled V below his waistline.

I forgot to tell him about the towels.

I yelped and scrunched my eyes shut. My mind shot back to my mother's lessons all those years ago. *Everything about Vampires and their spawns are crafted to lure in prey. Beauty is as dangerous a weapon as swords and arrows.* "Ah—I'm sorry." I tossed the clothes in the general direction of the bed, hand over my face. "These are for you."

Beside a rumbling laugh, he might have muttered something else to me, but I'd already fled downstairs and into the kitchen. I must have looked as frazzled as I felt because Agatha nearly spurted coffee out of her nose. "Why are you so red?"

"Nothing. No reason." I grabbed a slice of bread and shoved it into my mouth. Loach and Boot were watching me, brows raised. I chewed and swallowed. "He'll be down in a minute." I sat beside them and slapped my palms down on the table. "So, what's the plan for the day?"

Boot made to answer, but Jayvin came down the staircase, tugging at the heavy sweater I'd given him. As expected, the pants were too big, hanging low on his waist—even with the belt—and the sweater barely concealed his abdomen.

He picked at the too-tight sleeves, lips pursed as his damp, clean hair fell over his eyes. "This is itchy."

"But at least you smell better." Boot gestured for him to sit in the empty chair across from him. Jayvin sat, still fidgeting with his clothes. Agatha and Loach took a seat on either side of me.

"Thank you for the room and clothes." Jayvin kept his eyes on the table as he spoke to Agatha. "Your house is luxurious."

"Luxurious?" Agatha bit out a sharp laugh. "If you say so. You know what—that's what this place will be called from now on: The Lux."

"I like it." I smiled. *This is starting to feel like a proper heist.* A group of people around a table pouring over hand-drawn maps. Boot sighed as his sharp talon scrapped over a sketch of the Lantern Palace. "Anyway—first, as our resident Kraken has made aware, we need supplies." His sketch now included the inner court around the palace and the waterway surrounding it. "The palace is near impregnable, but its people aren't."

Loach snorted, and Boot shot him a glare before continuing, "We'll need to survey the location and find an entry point . . . a weak area."

"Before I ran into Agatha, I watched the courtyard entrance for a while," I said. "The Enforcers at the gate rotated every two hours, as did the ones on the battlement, but in a different rotation. I doubt we'll be able to slip through a watch."

Jayvin glanced up from the pills on his sweater. "We can't just break down the front door?"

"Not unless you want to get shot by a crossbow," Loach replied.

"What's a crossbow?"

Loach chuckled. "If we get to my weapons, I'll show you."

Jayvin grinned.

"Inside the cistern, there's a passage that leads out to the waterway." Boot scratched his chin, deep in thought. "As a slave, we used it to flush the sewer system through it."

"We can't get in through there?" I asked.

"We could." Boot's orange eyes shot to me. "But not without someone on the inside to open the passage."

"Then we get someone inside," Agatha said as she stood to wash her mug. "Simple."

"It's not simple." Loach steepled his three-fingered hands. "Even if we get someone inside, if they're spotted, the Enforcers will slaughter them long before they can set foot in the cistern."

"Not if I'm with them." Jayvin's smile exposed his sharp canines. "My entire existence has been crafted and honed for protection." He paused and sighed, chewing the skin on his lip. "But I can't enter a home without an invitation."

"It's not a home," Loach said. "It's a palace."

"It's the Emperor's home," Agatha shot back.

"But if we got one?" I straightened. "An invitation, I mean?"

"I could hide in your shadow." Jayvin's eyes were so vivid. "If I'm attached to someone, any invitation to them extends to me."

Agatha made a face. "That's unsettling."

"But it could work . . ." Boot tapped his pencil on the table. "But first, nothing will happen without Loach's inventory."

Loach reclined in his chair. "That settles it. We head to the headquarters. We'll figure out the rest after we've returned with my goods."

Jayvin knocked into the table as he stood. "Then let's go."

I realized something as I watched him stand. "You don't have any shoes."

He glanced down at his feet. "It doesn't bother me."

"But it may draw attention." Agatha propped her chin on her closed fist. "People may also be suspicious if they see a giant, grey, fanged beast galivanting down the street bare foot." She waved flippantly. "Can Vampires even go out in the sun?"

"Offspring can." Jayvin crossed his arms and rocked. "But it's. . . painful. I'd prefer not to."

"But you said you can hide in shadows?" I'd seen how he'd disappeared into the darkness in the meadows. I knew it was possible. "Can you hide in mine?"

A devilish half-smile spread across Jayvin's face as he faded —dissolving—into the dark outline behind me, the shadow I didn't know I had.

I couldn't see him, but I could *feel* him. A caress at the edge of my mind. A thrilling weight pulling on my shoulders. A shiver rolled down my spine, and I swore he laughed before materializing again beside the table.

"Perfect." Loach stood and adjusted his sword and belt. "You can ride with Tetra on the way to HQ."

A flicker of excitement had me grinning.

"Is Tetra really the best one to go?" Agatha asked and gave me an apologetic look. "What if it comes to blows?"

That silver scar between us burned. I scowled at my arm. *I wasn't imagining things.*

Jayvin snapped a leg off the nearest chair—it no more than a twig off a bush. "Then they'll wish they hadn't."

Agatha's jaw dropped. "Quit breaking my stuff!"

He smirked, ignoring her, as he shoved the jagged wooden slat into his belt. "Sunshine is safe with me."

"Right," Loach said, taking his coat off the counter and shrugging it on. "What he said. Tetra's shifting will be a huge help getting through the Enforcers."

"It's settled, then." Boot rolled up his scrolls. "As long as all goes well, we'll have a full stock here by this evening."

"What about me?" Agatha looked offended. "I'm not going to sit here and polish rocks."

Boot's lips curled into something terrifying. "Oh, I have a use for you, have no fear."

"Right," Loach repeated, gesturing to Jayvin and me. "You two, with me."

After several hours of planning, we stepped out of the hideout—excuse me, The Lux—and Jayvin fused into my shadow. I shuddered as his presence settled against my back. That gravelly voice brushed against my ear, elated as he purred, *"This is going to be fun."*

Chapter Eleven

"What is that?" Jayvin asked from within my shadow for the hundredth time since we left The Lux.

I glanced to where I felt his attention had fallen: a red water pump nestled between two shops on the edge of the street. A couple of older men hung buckets on the hooks, preparing to fill them.

"It's a spicket that attaches to a reservoir beneath the city," I said. One of the men pulled up the pump handle, and water began pouring out. "It's like a well without pails and ropes."

"Interesting," Jayvin mused. *"More Elf magic?"*

Ahead of me, Loach, with tentacles concealed behind a thick scarf, navigated the streets with confident ease. After plenty of salt this morning, I had shifted into a red-haired, freckled Human. So far, it had been an easy walk.

"No," I whispered back to Jayvin. "The pumps are purely engineering."

"Hmm."

Loach shot me a dirty look, probably annoyed that I was

talking to my shadow like a crazy person. I made a face at him, and he chuckled.

The late morning air grew humid as heavy, dark clouds rolled in, smelling of rain and thunder. I shucked off my coat, tossing it over my arm, revealing the sleeveless tunic I wore beneath. I didn't want to arrive at the Enforcer's headquarters soaked in sweat.

Loach had informed me that the headquarters were located a little west of the Lantern Palace, outside the inner courtyard. In addition to serving as an office, the massive, rectangular structure's separate wings also served as a temporary jail and barracks.

"Look there." Loach pointed out a four-story narrow building lined with tiny windows, each with a miniature balcony. "Most of those apartments are rented by the Elves that arrived with the Emperor's party when he took over."

I took in the classy black-and-white tile and the arched doorways leading into the complex. It was grandiose, for sure, but I couldn't imagine living in such a cramped space. My brow rose. "You'd think they'd want to expand? Make homes for themselves along the shore."

Within my shadow, Jayvin brushed against my arm. Maybe he agreed. Maybe he was cramped, too.

"I think that was the original plan," Loach said as we passed, "but the locals weren't happy to share their land with foreigners."

I almost said I didn't blame them, but it felt wrong. Since their race began populating Tyrr, the Elves, and their magic, had done wonders for the quality of life inside the country. Just because Sayzar was a blight didn't mean all Elves were terrible. I kept my head down, gripping the back of Loach's coat to avoid getting lost in the crowds.

I felt that gentle touch again. *"What are you thinking, Sunshine?"*

A pale, marble building came into view—a thin spire rising above it, adorned with the Emperor's flag—a golden, flaming star on a black backdrop. Breathtaking cherry trees lined the front of the headquarters, their dainty, pink petals dusting the manicured lawn below them. Families and couples—mostly Elven—ate lunch on blankets, cuddled in the branch's thick limbs, laughing as their children played on the grass. A public park.

I chewed on the inside of my cheek. "I . . . I think that no matter what I do, someone will get hurt, and I don't like it."

That brush against my shoulder this time was sympathetic. Kind.

Outside of the headquarters, lines of silver-armored Enforcers stood watch, crossbows in hand and heavy swords on their hips.

Loach shot me a sly smile. "Tell the drone that that's a crossbow."

Before I could answer, Jayvin's voice quipped excitedly in my ear. *"What does it do?"*

"It's kind of like a bow and arrow," I whispered as Loach headed toward the far-left side of the building. "But it's a lot more powerful and does the work for you."

"Can I have one?"

I tugged on Loach's elbow. "Jayvin wants to know if he can have a crossbow."

Loach let out a low laugh. "If we survive this, he can have two."

Jayvin was nearly buzzing.

Loach paused beneath the shade of a cherry tree, lifting his wide hat just long enough to wipe the sweat from his shiny, bald head. "Are you ready?"

I raised the wicker basket, plastering on a fake, confident smile. "Born ready."

Loach gave my head a loving pat. "Good. Don't make a muck of this, kid."

"I won't." At least, that's what I'd told myself all morning. I headed for the headquarters' entrance, comforted by Javyin's invisible presence at my back. Despite my efforts to remain calm, my sides had grown damp by the time I reached the top of the stairs. *I should have worn a dress.*

There were no doors outside the building, just an open pantheon—like the chapel—that led to an extravagant, covered sitting area and reception desk. That's where I kept my gaze as I made to head inside, steps long and fast.

Two sharp-tipped spears lowered to form an X in front of me—an Enforcer on each side of the pillar. The one to my right —female by the voice—snarled. "State your business, Human."

At least my shift is working. My lips curled into that sweet smile. I raised my basket. "My *abhorrent* younger brother didn't come home last night." I exhaled and licked my lips as I dropped my head in embarrassment. "If I know him—and I do —he's waiting for me to post his bail. May I pass?"

The two exchanged glances before raising their spears. "Proceed."

"My thanks." I tucked my hair behind my now-rounded ear as I hustled inside. "Long live the Emperor."

"Long live the Emperor." They echoed, resting their fists over their armored chests. It wasn't until we were safely inside that I finally took a full breath.

"*Amateurs.*" Jayvin scoffed. *"They didn't even check the basket. Security has gotten lax since I've been gone."*

I used my hand to cover my grin as I approached the front desk. A stunning Elf woman sat behind it, bent over a stack of papers, her honey-blonde locks pulled into an eloquent coif, accentuating her high cheekbones. Her lips were moving, muttering. She didn't raise her head.

I cleared my throat. "Excuse me?"

Her eyes peeled from the document she read. "She looked me up and down, seething in irritation. "May I *help* you?"

I scrunched my nose as I raised my basket. "It seems my brother needs to be bailed out again. Any chance I can speak to the warden today? I brought payment."

"Go ahead." She returned to her papers with a dismissive wave. "It's the last door to the left, but it sounds like you know that."

"Thank you." I curtsied despite wearing slim breeches. "I'll be quick."

I strode in the direction she'd pointed—across the lobby toward a vast hall on the eastern side.

"Do you really have a brother here?" Jayvin asked against my ear.

"No," I snorted, then lowered my tone. "But as Boot pointed out, Humans breed like rabbits. More than likely, there was a Human or half-breed locked up today. I guess he was right."

Jayvin huffed. *"It's the same with Elves. They'll shove their cocks into anything."*

I held back a laugh as I headed down the hall. It was longer than I expected . . . and empty. "You're half-Elf, right?" I asked through my giggles. "The ears give it away."

Jayvin tensed. *"So, I'm told."*

"You don't know your parentage?"

"No. I . . ."

I waited for him to answer as I read the signs over the doors on either side of the hall: *accounting, city records, employ-*

ment, archives. Nothing that sounded like a place where they'd keep confiscated weapons.

Jayvin's were heavy with sadness as they brushed against my mind. *"My kind don't keep the memories we made before turning. I don't remember my father and mother."*

My steps faltered. "Nothing?"

A pause. *"Not enough to matter."* A second pause as I continued to walk. *"You should check in there, Sunshine."*

I glanced up at the sign above the nearest door: *Evidence.*

This is it. I touched the door handle—locked. I nearly vomited. "Damn it," I whispered, mostly to myself. "What if someone is in there? We can't just force our way in."

"One moment." The slim silhouette of my shadow—barely visible in the overhead faelights—shuddered as Jayvin left my presence. My shoulders felt too light as a dark mist slipped under the door. My heart lurched as a small yelp sounded inside, followed by a quick scuffle.

The door latch clicked and swung open, revealing Jayvin's massive, grinning frame standing in the threshold. "It's empty now."

I peered around him. Another Elf woman—dressed in a tailored, navy dress—lay propped up in the corner, limp. I swallowed back nausea. "Did you . . . kill her?"

"No." Jayvin's brows furrowed as he glanced back at the woman. "Do you want me to?"

"No, no, *no.*" I slipped past him. "That won't be necessary."

This room was small and windowless, stacked floor to ceiling with labeled chests and traveling trunks. Jayvin watched me as he shut and locked the door behind us. I crouched to read over all the labels. "Sharks." I ran my hands over my braid. "I don't see anything about weapons *or* Loach. Do you think they'd keep them somewhere else?"

Jayvin turned slowly to scan the room. Instead of searching

the chests, he ran his hands over the walls and picked at the cheap wood panels. I rocked from heel to heel as he tossed furniture aside to check the spaces behind them. After about two minutes of investigating, Jayvin paused on a cracked panel behind a storage rack.

"Here." Jayvin smiled and traced symbols on the wall. Three triangles this time. I gasped as a ripple of lavender energy warped the wall, twisting it into whirlpool until it disappeared entirely. Beyond lay a staircase leading downward.

"Wow." I let out a shaky laugh and rubbed my cheek. "A hidden doorway?"

"I swear, the laziness of this time." Jayvin shook his head and stepped into the pitch-black corridor, inspecting it before waiving me forward. "It's clear."

Somewhere outside, an explosion shook the building, raining dust on us from the rafters. An alarm began to sound, screeching so loudly I shoved my fingers into my ears.

No, no, no, no. I froze at the sound of running, but the shouting footsteps thundering outside in the hall were heading *away* from the evidence office. I exhaled in relief. "That would be Loach. Right on time."

Jayvin didn't seem bothered. He snapped, and that orange faelight formed, lighting the passage. His jaw clenched so tightly that I thought his teeth might crack. "Let's go."

I followed him into the corridor, grateful for the light. The lower we traveled, the shallower Jayvin's breaths became. He brushed his fingers along the stone wall more than once, drawing those circles before he let his fist drop to his side.

"You know, I got stuck in an underwater cave once . . . when I was ten." I'd almost forgotten about that. It was odd that the memory bubbled up now. "I was convinced there was a sunken chest—from some long-forgotten kingdom—buried inside it."

Jayvin paused just long enough to glance at me over his shoulder, his features devastatingly beautiful in the dim light. He continued down the staircase. "And how did you get out?"

"My father had to fish me out . . . excuse the pun." I moved closer to him, trying to stay in reach of the light. "I was pinned between two rocks. It took him hours to get me out. I lost so many scales. It was awful. When Loach and I snuck into Carnage, we had to squeeze through a tunnel in the cliffside." I let blew out a heavy breath. "I panicked. I realize now it reminded me of then. I couldn't breathe. Loach had to pull me out."

Ahead of me, Jayvin's broad shoulders tensed. "You were trapped again?"

"No," I replied. "Just too scared to move. It was all in my head."

"Hmm." He made to brush his fingers against the wall again, but the space opened into a large cellar. The faelight floated up to the low ceiling, revealing dozens more crates labeled and stacked floor to ceiling. A cart sat beside the stacks, dusty and unused.

Jayvin surveyed the room, a faint smirk quirking his lips. "Looks like the Enforcers have been busy."

"But why the secret room?" I brushed over the labels, searching for anything pointing to Loach. I set the basket I'd brought on the floor, pulling out the burlap sacks stored inside, big enough for us to carry out a decent load of weapons. "It seems a bit . . . much, doesn't it?"

"Not if they're defending against people like us." Jayvin's smile widened into something wild. He lifted a crate—as if it were nothing but a grain sack—and tossed it onto the cart. He continued to pile them—two, three, four and on until the final crate wouldn't fit. That one, he propped onto his shoulder. "This should do. Ready, Sunshine?"

Lord above. I shook my head. "You can't get all that up the stairs."

Jayvin smirked and nodded toward the back of the cellar. "What do you think is on the other side of that wall?"

I could still hear the alarms from here. I made a face. "The safe bet would be more dirt. We're underground, after all."

"Are we?" Jayvin set down the cart, still bracing the crate against his shoulder. "I would say that we're probably —" *Sharks.* He slammed his bare heel into the mortared wall, over and over, until it blew out in an explosive wave of rock and brick. I gasped as it crumbled, revealing a dark alley on the other side. He grinned and pulled down his sweater. "—above the lower streets."

Jayvin didn't wait for me before manhandling the cart through the gap. I grabbed the back, grunting as I helped lift it over a chunk of rubble. Or at least tried to. It weighed a ton.

Thankfully, the alley was empty. Above, sirens still echoed. Citizens ran, shrieking, past the mouth of the alley. I rubbed my face. "How did you know the street was here?"

Jayvin adjusted the crate on his shoulder. "The heartbeats were too close to be underground."

"We're in one of the most populated parts of the city," I said, shaking the nerves out my hands. "We can't just wheel a half-ton of weapons into the square!"

Jayvin tsked, tongue pressed against his teeth. "You have no faith in me, do you, Sunshine?" He, the cart, and the crates dematerialized into my shadow. I gasped, clutching my chest, as the weight of it nearly brought me to my knees. Invisible or not, I could feel him at my back, holding me steady. *"Just walk. I won't let you fall."*

"Yeah, okay." Legs quivering, I straightened before taking

hesitant steps out onto the street, brushing the dust from my hair and clothes. People pushed past me, crying about a terrorist attack on the headquarters. I tried to keep a wide berth, worried they'd somehow feel the cart behind me. As we headed up toward the park, dozens of Enforcers scouted the lawn, searching for the source of the earlier explosion. They were going to be pissed when they found the mess we'd left in their cellar.

I scanned the faces around us for Loach, but the crowd had grown frantic. I whispered to Jayvin, "Do you think he headed back—"

A second explosion went off—sending a shockwave over Carnage. I dropped to the ground, covering my ears as a massive cloud of smoke rose to the sky on the other side of the city—right where Boot's shop was located.

"I knew this would be fun." Jayvin's invisible hands lifted me from under the arms and onto my feet. *"Keep going."*

"What about Loach?" I hissed, ducking as a third explosion went off. "We might be hurt!"

"He can take care of himself." Jayvin exhaled against my ear. *"Damn it, never mind. He's over there."*

I turned to see Loach hitting the pavement—beneath the overhang of a furniture shop—as an Enforcer slammed a fist into his jaw. Loach's scarf fell away, revealing his tentacles. Three of the four Enforcers backed away and shouted, "Kraken!"

"Sharks," I muttered.

"Move!" Jayvin pushed me into a run, my body weighted down by the supplies attached. My thighs and lungs *burned* as I sprinted through the panicked crowd. One of the Enforcers kicked Loach brutally in the side. Once we were within three yards, a soldier turned and pointing at me, growling. "Stay back! This is the business of the Emperor!"

I jerked to a halt, breaths heavy, as Loach groaned—a bruise forming where his face hit the street.

A shiver of excitement rippled up my back as Jayvin materialized beside me. A weight lifted off my shoulders. The shop's awning shaded Jayvin from the sun as his form solidified.

Jayvin's head cocked to the side as he inhaled and grimaced. "Your blood stinks like rot, but it will have to do."

"Vampire." The guard who'd punched Loach backed away, eyes growing wide with horror as he pulled his curved sword from its sheath. "Dear God."

Loach cursed as he crawled toward us. The other guards drew their weapons, bracing as Jayvin pulled the broken chair leg from his belt.

"Stand down!" The Enforcer braced, sweat dripping down his luminous cheeks. "Or face the wrath of the Emperor—"

He never got to finish his sentence. Jayvin was too fast.

I almost felt sorry for them.

As I helped Loach to his feet, Jayvin plunged the chair leg straight through the Enforcer's armored chest with a sickening crunch. He lifted the man high above his head, groaning with pleasure as the blood leaking from the guard's wound streamed directly into his mouth.

The Enforcer's face paled with death as Jayvin shucked him onto the street, licking the blood off his smiling lips as his laugh turned savage. "I do not know this Emperor."

They took a unified step back.

Jayvin moved again, and I scrunched my eyes shut at the sound of snapping bones and screams of agony. The last three guards fell quickly, drained into nothing but husks.

Chapter Twelve

Jayvin tossed a crate of weapons through the front door of The Lux with a loud, wooden crash.

"Careful with those, you bafoon." Loach winced, gripping his side where the Enforcer kicked him. I pulled his arm around my neck to steady him. "Most of that equipment costs more than your life is worth."

Boot peeked out from the living room as Jayvin began unloading the rest of the crates. "So, I take this mission was a success?"

"I wouldn't go that far." Loach groaned as I helped him onto the sofa. "Pretty sure my rib's broken, and we've got a slew of new corpses to add to our body count."

Boot's gaze flicked to the blood staining Jayvin's mouth and neck. "Were you seen?"

"No," I sank onto the sofa beside Loach. He winced. "But we definitely weren't quiet."

From outside, Jayvin cackled.

"Where's Agatha?" I sat up. *Sharks.* "There was an explosion near your shop! Ivan—"

"Is right here." The Dwarf stepped out of the kitchen, drying his hands on a dish towel. He pursed his lips at the sight of me. "At your service, my lady."

"Then . . ." It took a moment to sink in. I wheeled on Boot. "*You* blew up your own shop?"

"It was time for a remodel, anyway." Boot waved. "Our Orc friend should return from demolition duty soon, hopefully with my jewels in hand. In the meantime, I will continue to pay dear Ivan to help with maintenance and preparations here."

"And it's my pleasure." Ivan shot me a glare before heading back into the kitchen. I could have died from embarrassment.

Another crate flew into the living room and broke open as it hit the ground.

"*Be careful,*" Loach said, hobbling toward the door. "I swear, if there's a chip or scratch on anything, you'll pay for it with your hide, drone."

Jayvin just laughed again.

"But why the explosion?" I asked Boot. "The Enforcers will be searching for us now."

Boot raised a clawed finger. "They'll be looking for whoever is responsible for the so-called *attacks*—for what's already happened, not what will happen next." He sat at the dining room table and pulled out his scrolls. "They won't be searching for thieves planning a coup on the palace."

"So, a distraction?" I exhaled.

Boot tapped his smushed-in nose. "Now you're getting it."

Eight are already dead. Because of me.

I started this. Likely, they had families. Husbands and wives waiting for them to come home. Sons and daughters who'd never hug their parents again.

Children like me.

More will die if Sayzar sends us to war. I picked at the tail of my braid, knees bouncing. *And even more will die if Surge starts his own.* Death was everywhere, closing in, and I couldn't stop it. My chest grew tight, weighted down by tear-stained memories. Was I any better than the Emperor now?

Outside, Loach was shouting something about getting rid of the cart.

I need to move. The longer I sat, the more time the anxiety had to build. I jolted up and wiped my sweaty palms on my trousers just as Jayvin brought in the last crate—a flat box nearly as long as he was tall. He dropped it and plopped down, grinning like a child about to open a present.

Get it together, Tetra. I knelt beside him, limbs shaky, and forced a smile. "Do you need a hammer to pry that open?"

"No. I got it." Jayvin dug his fingers into the lid seam and pulled, making the rusted nails screech. As I shifted closer, his nostrils flared, and his entire body went rigid as he slowly released his grip on the wood. When he shifted toward me, those ruby eyes had the terror-filled look of a rabbit waiting for a wolf to pass. "What happened? Why are you upset?"

"Nothing is wrong," I faltered. *Is it that obvious?* "I'm fine."

"Are you angry?"

"Why would I be angry? Again, I'm fine. Promise."

He held my eyes, gaze flickering to my lips and back, before wrenching off the lid. "Liar."

"I'm not lying." My cheeks grew warm. "It's just been a long day. A tiring few days, really. That's all."

"Your heart's fluttering again." Jayvin chucked the lid into the corner, smirking. "It's distracting."

"Oh." I sat down and crossed my legs. "Sorry."

"You don't have to say that so often." He ripped at the paper wrapping inside. "You have nothing to apologize for."

"Sorry—" I paused, and he shot me a wry look. "It's a habit."

"Why?"

I shrugged and rested my chin on my palms.

He scanned my face again before returning to the crate's contents. The last of the wrapping fell away to reveal an *enormous* great sword. Its blade had streaks of oily black through the metal, the handle wrapped with stamped leather. A blue-black sapphire adorned the hilt.

"*Yes.*" Jayvin stood, lifting it with one hand. "This is *mine.*"

"You going to pay for it?" Loach hobbled back into the living room. "That piece cost a fortune."

From top to bottom, the sword came up to Jayvin's shoulder. Stepping back, he twirled it around as easily as a stick. I doubted I'd even be able to get it off the ground.

"Why is it so . . . big?" I asked, and Jayvin snorted. I shot him a glare, and he grinned at me as he continued to play with the blade.

"It was a custom piece," Loach said as he returned to the sofa. "It was an out-of-country order from a monster hunter. I never got to deliver it." He scowled. "I never got paid for it, either. Damascus steel isn't cheap."

"Monster hunters?" I pried open the next crate with a crowbar. Inside were stacks of swords, sheaths, bandoliers, thick weapon belts, and thigh holsters like what Agatha wore. "That sounds like an exciting profession. What kind of creatures do they hunt?"

Jayvin watched Loach warily as he sheathed the great sword.

"Ask our new friend here." Loach reclined, using a box as a footstool. "I'm pretty sure Vampires are on the top of their list."

Jayvin shot him a bitter look but didn't respond. Instead, he leaned over me and dug through the supplies I'd opened. I prayed he couldn't hear my heart racing again.

"Ah, here we go." He grabbed a mess of leather straps and

shook them out before pulling them over his shoulders and buckling them. He attached the great sword to his back with an alarming amount of ease. Where the hilt peered over his shoulder, the blade tip came nearly down to his knees. Jayvin stretched, squatting before jumping high enough for his hair to brush the ceiling. The sword didn't move an inch. "Perfect. I'm ready."

"Don't go through those without me!" Agatha strode into The Lux, bodysuit covered in soot and ash. I nearly crumpled in relief at the sight of her. She tossed two large sacks—presumably the jewels—onto the table, making Boot jump before she pushed Jayvin out of the way to peer into the crates. She paused, noticing the new blood stains and the sword on his back. "What happened?"

Jayvin pried open another box. "Someone died."

"No, really?" Agatha huffed.

"Four someone's," Loach grunted, a bruise purpling his jaw where the Enforcer punched him. "Sounds like we've created quite a fuss between our lot."

"I have to admit, I was surprised when Boot asked if I'd ever used explosives." Agatha slid on an underarm holster that let her strap six small throwing knives on her sides. "But he's right. We need to keep the Enforcers busy, and this is a good start."

"Aha!" Jayvin pulled out a pair of black fighting leathers and matching boots that looked like they'd fit. After finding several more wearable pieces and some armor, Jayvin stripped off his sweater right there in the living room—exposing the hard lines of his torso and where those pants hung dangerously low on his hips.

"*Whoa*, buddy!" Agatha looked away. I hated myself because I didn't. "Change upstairs, not down here!"

"As you wish." Jayvin exposed his canines, slung his clothes over his shoulder, and headed toward the stairs. "Don't touch my sword, Orc."

"Trust me, I wasn't planning on it, *Offspring.*" Agatha shot back and flipped him off. Jayvin returned the gesture.

A giggle escaped my lips.

At the table, Boot shook his head. "Fools, all of you."

It would take days to inventory all the supplies, but now, we had more swords, daggers, and pikes than I could count, as well as steel and leather spaulders, breastplates, bracers, and helms. Boot wrote down the items, and their values, as Loach called them out.

I found a hood and mask, which Jayvin attached to his leathers to conceal his face in case we had to go in the sun. I even found some leathers that were my size.

When the sun began to set, heavy clouds opened to unleash a humid spring rain. Agatha had dozed off on the sofa as Loach and I finished repacking the supplies. He wiped the sweat off his brow, wincing as he rubbed his fresh bruise. "We'll have the drone carry these to the basement." Loach looked around. "Where is he, anyway?"

I glanced up, panic sparking in my chest. *Where* did *Jayvin go?*

Boot picked at the remains of his dinner—plain chicken and vegetables—and sipped red wine as he poured over his notes. Thunder boomed in the clouds, broken only by the thin strips of golden sunset shining through the windows, illuminating the freshly swept stone floor.

Besides that, the only light inside was Jayvin's dancing faelight, ever-present but unobtrusive. It must have heard my thoughts because it fluttered closer, twirling around me before ghosting up the stairs, an invitation to follow. *Friend, friend, friend.*

I stood and stretched. God, my shoulders ached. I let my arms flop to my sides. "I'll go look for him."

Loach just nodded before joining Boot at the table.

As I headed up the stairs, the faelight bobbed up each step, casting dancing shadowed figures on the walls—dancing bodies, laughing bodies, crying bodies. My mind flashed back to the skeletons in the catacombs. So much sadness, so much pain. The light floated to the top floor and into one of the empty bedrooms. The door was ajar, letting in the rumble of pounding rain against the shingled, metal rooftop.

The roof. The faelight floated through the opened window on the far wall. The rain bounced off the sill and drenching the gaudy-mauve carpet below.

It quickly soaked through the thin fabric of my trousers as I slid outside. Despite the mugginess, the raindrops were cold—shifting my hair, scales, and the fins on my bare arms to a darker shade of cobalt blue. After a few slippery steps across the shingles, the rooftop led to an open terrace, probably accessible from one of the many doorways I hadn't yet explored on the third story. Besides some weather-beaten patio furniture, there was also a rotted wooden gazebo and a rusted fire pit. The expanse of the terrace floor was mismatched with coral tiles in a mosaic pattern.

My heart sank, water streaming down my face, when I realized Jayvin was lying in the rain—shirtless, hands folded over his toned stomach.

He looked . . . peaceful, sleeping, his silver-white hair slicked back off his lovely face.

How long has it been since he felt the rain? I stepped back, the ache in my heart threatening to suffocate me. *When did he last hear the roar of thunder or laughter?* Most of all, why did I care so much?

Another step back.

He'd looked so afraid when he thought I'd been upset. Why? Why did I want to hold this man I'd known for only a day—this *Offspring*—who had no loyalty to anyone and anything but his creator? *Because you're a silly little girl who should have stayed in The Dam . . . who should have refused to kneel.*

I shook my head, hair sticking to my face as turned back for the window, my throat on fire as I held back a sob. I'd let them down—let them *all* down. It was foolish to think I could make a difference now. It didn't matter. They were already gone.

Jayvin's voice was hoarse, the comfort I didn't know I needed. "Hello, Sunshine."

I glanced back. His eyes were still closed. "Sorry—" I paused. "I mean, I wasn't trying to bother you."

He didn't answer but stretched his arms down his sides, his fingers tracing those strange circles again.

I don't want to leave. He didn't tell me to go. Loach would be complaining. Agatha would want to chat about the day's events before bed. A little silence, that's all I wanted. It was a full minute before I gathered the courage to sit down beside him. I tore the tie out of the end of my braid. It felt so good to shake my hair out, to be wet. My skin sucked up moisture faster than it could bead off my limbs, and the knots in my shoulders finally began to relax.

A thrill jolted up my elbow as the lightest touch brushed the iridescent fin on my arm. When I looked, Jayvin's brows were furrowed as he stroked the deep violet, and sapphire scales dotting my skin. "Hmm."

I didn't pull away, but my heart was hammering. "*Hmm*, what?"

He closed his eyes again, returning to tracing those circles on the terrace tiles. "It's just . . . interesting."

I had a thousand questions, but I settled on one. "Why do you draw that pattern?"

He sucked in a few deep breaths—in through the nose, out through the mouth—then flexed his fingers. "It's. . . it's a ward-breaking charm. For detecting illusionary magic."

Not real. All the pieces started to click together. "You think this is an illusion?"

His ruby eyes, tinted with frustration, fluttered open and slowly scanned my face as raindrops dripped down his sides. "I can't tell." His jaw clenched as he stared at the sky, the rain beating on his dove-grey skin. "I must have finally lost it. You're just a cruel creation of my mind. I'm still in the catacombs. And these—" Jayvin traced those circles over and over until his nails dug into the rock. His voice cracked. "These damn wards must not be working because I'm either dead or insane. I can't tell which."

"Sharks." I brushed my dripping hair off my face. *What can I say?* I knew what it was like for your mind to lie to you, to be paralyzed by it. "This is real. I know that doesn't help, but it's the truth." Sighing, I curled up and rested my chin on my knees. "I understand, though, to a degree. I still can't believe I'm here. I've got three weeks to pull this off before I'm labeled an enemy of the Empire. It just feels . . . not real. I can't imagine how you're feeling."

I jumped as his fingers brushed my arm again, the dreaminess returning to his handsome features. "You *feel* real. You smell real. Your heart beats as if you see me."

"I *do* see you." My traitorous pulse pounding in my ears. His gaze snapped to my throat as I swallowed. "And maybe that's enough for now. That you see me, and I see you?"

Jayvin turned back to the sky, eyes closing once more as a crack of lightning flashed overhead, splintering the through the clouds in angry, white threads.

I didn't want to go inside. I missed the sea. I wanted to go home and dive to the depths outside our cove. To feel my fins shred through the currents. I was beginning to wonder if Jayvin had fallen asleep when he whispered, "Yes . . . I think that can be more than enough."

"I'm glad." I said as a giddiness spread into my chest. Laying back, I stretched out beside him—savoring the rain. We stayed like that until long after the storm passed.

Chapter Thirteen

A soft knock on my door jolted me awake. I sat up. My blankets were still damp from crawling into bed hours before in my soaking-wet clothes. "Yes?"

"Get dressed." Boot's voice was barely a whisper. "Meet me outside."

I groaned and glanced out the window. It was still dark out. "Why?"

"Just do it, girl." He blew out a frustrated breath. I flopped back onto the bed, listening to his limping gait shuffling down the stairs. *I wonder if Jayvin's awake.* I stared at the ceiling, visually tracing the patterns on the water-stained wooden beams above. Jayvin hadn't said a word when we'd finally left the roof last night. He'd just nudged my elbow, expression flat, and gestured for me to follow. Once inside, he'd entered his new bedroom and shut the door.

Without knowing what else to do, I'd done the same. *Maybe my presence had been an annoyance, after all.* But there had been a comfortable quiet between us. I'd even drifted off, falling in and out of dreams of dark tunnels and broken, bloody bodies.

Wake up. With a shake of my head, I forced myself to climb out of bed, goosebumps spreading up my arms from the chill leaking through the drafty windows. I changed into something dry and warm before heading to the bathroom. After washing my face and combing the knots from my tangled hair, I crept down the stairs on my tiptoes, cringing every time they creaked beneath me. Heaven forbid I wake Loach this early. Agatha would never forgive me for his foul mood.

Boot waited for me just outside the front door, dressed in a fresh maroon suit and silver bowtie. Steam swirled around the coffee mug he sipped. Once I was in arms reach, he passed me a second, full cup and said, "Come."

"Good morning to you, too." I wrapped my stiff fingers around the mug, grateful for the warmth. I blinked up at the sky. The first rays of pink sunrise chased away the last of the stars. "Why the ungodly hour?"

"Should my day be delayed by your late-night dallying?" Boot scanned my face in irritation, taking in the purple shadows beneath my eyes. "It would behoove you to rest. Especially with the work we have yet to do."

I just drank my coffee, wincing as the hot liquid burned the tip of my tongue. Boot started down the alley at a lumbering pace, heading toward the highway. I kept by his side. Keeping pace wasn't tricky with his short strides. "Where are we going?" I asked.

"Do you always ask so many questions?" Boot huffed, his breaths turning to mist. "I have something to show you. That's all you need to know for now."

"Okay, fine." I huddled deeper into my coat. "Lead on, then."

The back alleys were eerily empty—free of the usual

traders and business owners—but what else should I have expected at this time of day? No right-minded person willingly chose to rise before dawn.

Boot held out his arm to stop me once we reached the main road, glancing up and down the street for Enforcers before heading toward the main square. A salt breeze danced over my skin as we crossed the bridge out of the eastern district. High above, the barrier surrounding Carnage glittered gold and green in the morning sun—the ever-present reminder of the city's confinement.

I could like Carnage if it wasn't for that. After finishing the last of my coffee, I tucked the mug into my inner coat pocket. "Boot?"

To my surprise, his rough lips curled into a smile. "More questions?"

"Just one for now, I promise." I smiled back before glancing up again at the barrier. "How did you become a jeweler? I assume you didn't start your trade until after leaving the Emperor's service."

Boot's pinched nose twitched. "Not exactly. My fascination with metals and gems started much earlier than that. How do you think I paid my way out of the palace? It didn't take long for me to gain a reputation for my skilled repairs on the court attendees' overpriced adornments."

"They paid you to fix their jewelry?"

"No." Boot continued his shuffle down the street. "The Elven ladies and lordlings brought me their belongings and commanded me to repair them—and some were happy to chatter as I worked. Even the wealthy get lonely, girl. I'm a good listener."

"And you what?" The pieces started to click together. "You sold their secrets for freedom?"

"Clever girl." Boot's grin turned impish. "Perhaps you can survive Carnage, after all."

And now all those years of work, planning, and scheming were gone—blown to bits. *To rebel against Sayzar,* I reminded myself. Boot had been willing to throw away his life's work for revenge. God only knew what torment he and his family had endured in the Lantern Palace. I couldn't stop myself from asking. "Do you still have relatives in the palace?"

Boot's large eyes darkened. "I am the last of my line, but others still serve. No more questions."

I nodded, happy for the moment to think. They'd all suffered so much—Loach, Agatha, Boot, and Jayvin. Actual, heart-wrenching suffering. It made my choice to escape the Dam in response to the draft seem like a toddler's temper tantrum.

My stomach sank. *That must be what I look like to the others—a child.* We spent the rest of the walk in silence. I knew our destination once we'd reached the city's western side. Plumes of black smoke still polluted the air over the remains of Boot's store. As we turned the corner to the shopping area, the acrid stench of gunpowder burned the inside of my nose. The ornate benches where those stuffy, wealthy women were now buried beneath debris.

My heart sank. Where once Boot's delicately painted sign had hung, labeled *Fineries,* now only a gaping, black hole remained. The entirety of the storefront had dissolved into white dust.

"W-what . . ." My eyes widened. "What kind of bombs did you use? This amount of damage—"

"Is nothing for you to concern yourself with." Boot gave me a pointed look. I had a feeling his skillset expanded beyond simple metalwork. He continued toward the opening in the crumbling wall. "Come along."

I didn't argue. Boot didn't seem bothered as we picked our way through the destruction. Remnants of showcases and displays were strewn everywhere. Some of the rafters still glowed orange with embers. With each step, ash bloomed around us, making breathing difficult.

I paused—taking it all in—as Boot wandered toward the back of the store, toeing through bits of burnt wood and blackened stone. "Is this what you wanted to show me?" I hated the tears stinging my eyes. "The consequences of turning against Sayzar? I'm aware. I didn't need the reminder, thank you."

"Stop being so dramatic." Boot grumbled as he bent over to push aside a stack of half-burnt ledgers. "Here. Help me with this."

It took almost an hour for me to clear away the last of the charred books. Tripping sweat, I wiped my sweaty brow with my sleeve, smearing it with soot. Boot brushed away the remaining ash coating the floor. A small hatch lay beneath. Boot smiled as he drew a series of shapes in the dust. I tried to remember them. A broken triangle. A three-layered hexagon. Something that looked like a sleeping dragon.

A wash of energy swept across the shattered storefront—a pale green color instead of violet. The air around the hatch twisted until in its place was a steep, narrow staircase heading downward.

"Ah." Boot wiped his hands clean on the hem of my coat. "Just where it should be."

I scowled, snatching my garment away, grimacing at the stain his fingers had made. "What's with this city and secret basements?"

"We can be paranoid folk." Boot snorted, wasting no time descending the stairs. They creaked and wobbled with each of his hobbled steps. I kept my arms behind my back, resisting the urge to hold his collar to keep him from falling.

My sandals slid on slick stone as we reached the bottom. It was too dark to see. Boot clapped, and a series of faelights embedded into the ceiling flickered to life.

My jaw dropped.

This wasn't just a personal collection—it was a hoard.

Not only were there more busts adorned in gold and silver chains, but full suits of ceremonial armor lined the walls. Some were scaled with what could have been actual dragon scales. Others were inky black and shimmering like a beetle's shell. There was a diamond headpiece shaped into crystalized elk antlers. An ash wood lute with solid gold filigree. Burlap sacks were tossed about, and several had tipped over, spilling uncut gemstones—garnets, sapphires, topaz, and emeralds—over the floor.

Boot tittered over to a massive oak chest in the corner and began to fiddle with the lock.

"May I ask questions now?" I rubbed my eyes. *Yes, this is real.* "Because I have a lot of them."

Boot stepped to the side, resting his knobby hand on the chest's heavy lid. "You may... once you open this."

My brow rose. "If I... open it?"

"Did I stutter?" Boot rolled his orange eyes. "No more questions. Open it."

This doesn't bode well for me. I watched him warily as I knelt in front of the chest. Boot's face remained stern. The lock was in good shape—polished silver. Not a hint of rust. It was unlatched. Hesitantly, I reached to remove the lock, and a shock of more green energy zapped my fingers.

"*Sharks.*" I hissed as I squeezed my blistered hand between my thighs. "It's warded, you bastard!"

"It is." Boot gave me an amused smile. "Open it."

"I can't." I sat back on my heels, stunned. "Have you lost your mind?"

"Do I look like the drone?" He snapped. "The door in the chapel's inner sanctum responded to you. That magic is ancient. Cryptic. This should be simple for you."

"I—" I'd forgotten about that. My burnt skin was tight as I flexed my fingers. "I didn't do that on purpose."

"Which makes it all the more interesting." Boot stepped forward and drew four simple lines in quick succession. Green energy crackled as the wards fell.

He drew the lines again, in the opposite direction this time. The wards went back up. "Warding—Elven magic—is mathematical." Squatting like this, Boot and I were at eye level. He held my gaze. "Two plus two equals four. It doesn't matter if it's words, shapes, or numbers—it's all the same. If you add one specific element to another, you create the desired result. The more complex the equation, the more complex the magic."

"Loach said only Elves can weave wards naturally." I sucked in a heavy breath. "It takes years of study for everyone else, but you make it sound so simple."

Boot let out a cackling laugh. "Because it *is* that simple. Why do you think it's so difficult? Most can't grasp such a stark concept. Does Jayvin Dyre think before he summons that little light of his? No. He does it. Without a doubt." Boot nudged the corner of the chest with the toe of his custom-made shoe. "Now, open it."

I *did not* want to get shocked again. "I'm not an Elf."

"Yet you share the same ancestors."

"From thousands of years ago," I shot back. "I don't think that counts."

"I have a theory." Boot wasn't giving up. "Just do it."

"Fine." He wasn't going to let me leave without trying. I pinched my lips together. "You're paying to fix my hands."

Boot smiled and took a step back.

He just does it. I'd seen Jayvin summon and dismiss his

faelight several times by now. He barely seemed to register the action. It was just natural. Easy. *Because he's half Elf, you idiot. He was born with magic in his blood.*

But the door in the chapel's sanctuary *did* reach out to me. I felt it—it's pain, it's wants. I doubted a chest in a dank basement wanted much for anything.

It felt silly, but I reached out and drew lines in the air over the wards, exactly like Boot had done. I held my breath. A moment passed, but nothing happened. No flicker of energy. No bright colors or fanfare.

I sat back on my bottom and groaned. "See? Happy now?"

Boot smacked the back of my head, and I yelped. "You're thinking too hard. Do it."

I rubbed my stinging scalp. "I can't!"

"Do it now, or I'll blow these jewels into oblivion."

My eyes grew wide. "Y-you wouldn't."

Boot pulled out a small round object from his coat pocket and grinned. A bomb. "Are you sure?"

"You *are* insane!" Panic had my entire body trembling. All this wealth—you could feed a whole nation for years—but it was more than that. The world would never be able to see these pretty trinkets. Touch them. Cherish them. They'd be gone.

The taste of strawberries coated my tongue as I struck out with my allure, but not at Boot—at the wards. I cringed as a rush of energy danced over my mind. There were no desires, no thoughts, unlike with living beings. Not even the pain and sorrow that emitted from the chapel door.

No. All I felt from it was an endless sense of boredom. Decades in the dark. Untouched. Unappreciated.

Let me see you. I whispered to the boredom. *Let me touch you.*

A sense of anticipation washed over me, tickling my skin with glee. A warm, glowing light rolled off the chest, waves in the sea. The lock fell away on its own, and the lid popped open. With a gasp, I leaned over the edge—expecting valuables beyond count—but the chest was empty. Bare—except for the daintiest porcelain thimble waiting at the bottom.

It opened.

The chest opened, and I felt strangely calm.

Boot shoved me aside and picked up the thimble, turning it over in his palm. Something soft, almost gentle, passed over his features. After a moment, he held it out for me. "It seems I was correct."

I took it. My fingers were trembling. "Why did that work?"

"Because you have a simple mind, Tetra the Seductress." Boot smiled wide, revealing jagged teeth. "And you're as greedy as I am. I knew you'd never let me destroy so much beauty."

"I'm not greedy." I scrambled to my feet, stuffing the thimble in my pocket. "And I'm not stupid."

"I never said you were," Boot shot back. "And you *are* greedy. You see what you want, and you take it. It wasn't an insult."

I blew out a sharp breath. I didn't want to argue. "Was that what you wanted to show me?" An idea struck me, sending a wave of adrenaline surging through my limbs. "D-do you think I'd be able to open the wards in the palace? Like on the treasury?"

"Ha!" Boot let out a barking laugh. "Don't get ahead of yourself, girl. That locking ward was the most elementary I could find on short notice. Plus, I needed that." He nodded to my pocket, where I still rolled the thimble between my fingers. Before I could ask why, he raised a taloned finger as if guessing my thoughts. "No more questions. That's a story for another time."

Boot picked up a delicate gold necklace from the nearest

pile of goods as we walked for the stairs. After a quick inspection, he tossed it to me. "Here. Keep this."

I barely managed to catch it. When I opened my hand, I forgot how to breathe. It was the petal pink pearl centered on a dainty rose-gold flower. The necklace that had reminded me of my mother's. My throat grew impossibly tight as I looked up. "Thank you—"

Boot was already gone.

Chapter Fourteen

Boot and I hurried back to the Lux, arriving just before noon.

"Where the hell have you two been?" Agatha demanded as we stepped inside. She sat cross-legged on the rug in the living area, sharpening her daggers. With a scrunched brow, she took in the black stains on my clothes. "Up a chimney?"

"Almost," I groaned, a cloud of ash escaping my coat as I collapsed on the floor beside her. "I'll be coughing up black sludge for days."

Boot made a beeline for the table. He glanced around the room as he flipped open his notebook. "Where's Loach?"

"At the market," Agatha let out a low chuckle. "The Vampire went with him. Loach said he had to carry the groceries since he's the one eating us out of house and home."

I shifted to face her, brows raised. Now that mid-day had rolled around, the sun was high, shining, and sweltering. "He let Jayvin ride in his shadow?"

"Yes, but he wasn't happy about it." Agatha made a face and lifted a gritty lock of my hair. "But never mind that. You're disgusting and a fire hazard, Tetra. Again, where did you go?"

"Don't trust us, Orc?" Boot sneered but didn't look up from his writing. "Afraid we're going to betray you?"

"Relax, Loafer." Agatha grinned as she slid a whetstone down her blade. "I'm just disappointed to have missed all the fun."

"We went to see what remained of the jewelry shop," I said before Boot had a chance to make a snide comeback. If he wanted Agatha to know about his theories on my supposed abilities, he could do that himself. "It's a mess."

"I could have told you that and saved you the walk." Agatha sheathed her dagger before standing. She rolled her neck and shoulders. "I'm glad you're back, though. I need to head out."

Boot looked up this time, his fingers stained with ink. "To where, may I ask?"

"Don't trust me?" Agatha sneered as she tugged on her black leather coat. "Afraid I'll betray you?"

Boot glowered before returning to his notes, grumbling about sharing a house with imbeciles.

"Can I come?" I rolled forward onto my bottom. "I just need to grab—"

"I love you, Hun, but no." Agatha stopped in the doorway and winked. "You look like you've spent the last three days sleeping in a dumpster. Go take a bath."

"Fine." I rested my chin on my fist, then winced. I'd forgotten about my burnt fingers. "Go have fun without me. I guess I'll stay here and do nothing."

"Oh, I'm sure you'll find *something to* do." Agatha gave Boot and me a curt nod. "I won't be gone long."

And with that, she disappeared into the alley. *She's not wrong about being filthy.* My body had left a ring of ash imprinted on the carpet.

"If you're desperate to fill your time," Boot began. "You can—"

"I'll pass." I hopped to my feet and hurried for the stairs. "I've had enough for today."

I didn't wait to hear his response. After grabbing a clean dress out of my room, I shut myself in the bathroom, letting out a relieved sigh as I clicked the lock into place. Some peace, that's all I wanted. A moment to think and figure out how the hell I'd unlocked that ward.

A heaviness settled on my bones as I twisted on the hot water in the tub. My body ached for it, *craved* it, but it wouldn't be satisfied here. I needed the sea. Salt. Space to move.

At least this is better than nothing. Steam swirled over the balmy bath water, leaving a coat of moisture inside my lungs. Agatha kept a variety of oils, perfumes, and soaps available. As tough as she made herself out to be, she sure liked to smell nice.

I dug a few lavender sprigs out of a clear jug and tossed them into the tub, along with some rosemary. The heady scent spread quickly, clogging my senses with the fragrance of herbs. A layer of dust and soot fell from my clothes as I peeled them off. *Great, now I'm going to have to clean the floor again.* I dumped even more ash out of my boots.

I almost forgot. I gently tugged Boot's thimble and necklace out of my coat pocket. A chill ran across my skin as I clasped the chain around my neck. I looked into the fogged mirror, straightening the pendant as it fell above my breasts. *Just like Mama's.* In my reflection, tears lined my eyes before I shifted my focus onto the thimble. It was solid white except for the blue-painted farm animals dancing around its width.

Why did Boot give this to me? He would never have kept something like this unless it was sentimental. I set it on the sink counter before turning to switch off the hot water. It would go into my bag—with the rest of my treasures—until the day came that he asked for it back. Maybe he never would.

I lowered myself into the tub and hissed at the scalding temperature, my hair and scales shifting to an icy blue from the heat. As I stretched out, the water seeped through my skin and into my muscles, allowing them to relax. I leaned my head against the tub and took a long breath. *Yes, this is definitely better than nothing.* The mix of soaps left a bubbly film over the water. It reminded me of the oily glaze that coated beef stew. My stomach growled. *I'd kill for a nap and a hot meal.* I'd forgotten to eat this morning.

A nap. I could get away with that. Shadows stained the checkered tile floor, seeping through the high, slated window on the far wall of the bathroom. A breeze gently swung the shutters, creating a series of rhythmic thumps I could pretend was music. I let my eyes flutter closed. Just a little peace and quiet, then I'd—

The window rattled as if shaken by a storm and burst open with a violent crash. I screeched as liquid darkness slipped through the glass, pooling onto the damp tiles before forming into the shape of a man. Jayvin stepped out of the shadows, carrying a massive wheel of white cheese. His ruby eyes widened in shock when they found me, but he didn't look away. "Apologies, I—"

I threw a bar of soap at him. He dodged it far too easily. "What the *hell* are you doing in here?"

"*Where'd he go?*" Loach's angry footsteps thundered up the stairs. "*Embezzling my pantry, that's what he's doing. When I get my hands on him—*"

Grinning ear to ear, Jayvin slid to the floor. As I glanced between him and the door, brows raised in question, he pressed a finger over his smiling lips.

Several bedroom doors slammed before Loach tried the bathroom, roughly jiggling the handle. "Open the damn door!"

Thank God, I'd locked it. "I'm *in* here," I yelled, crossing my arms over my chest. I didn't know why I bothered. "Go piss outside!"

"Is the drone in there?" Loach asked and tried the handle again. "When I find him—"

"Why would he be in here?" I snapped. Jayvin bit down on his lip to keep from laughing. "Wasn't he supposed to be with you?"

Loach cursed, then sighed. "Never mind. Forget it."

As his footsteps receded down the hall, I wheeled on Jayvin, sending water sloshing onto the tile floor. "What did you do?"

He proudly nodded to the food in his arms. "The squid said I couldn't eat this all myself. I told him he was too slow to stop me." His gaze slowly flickered to my bare body, then back to my face. "Should I give you some privacy?"

I rolled my eyes, arms still crossed. "It's too late now, isn't it? You might as well climb in with me at this point."

"If you say so." Jayvin replied as he did just that. Fully clothed. Wearing the most roguish, devious grin I'd ever seen in my life.

"Lord Almighty." I curled into a ball before rubbing my palms over my cheeks. They were burning hot. "I was *joking!*"

"Hmm." Jayvin slid down, stretching his long legs on either side of me. The water made his fitted black tunic cling to his toned chest. "Sarcasm isn't one of my strongest points."

"Silly me," I muttered as my stomach growled again. I held my palm out. "Well, if you're going to stay, at least give me some of that. I'm starving."

Jayvin gladly broke off a large chunk of cheese and passed it to me. He took a bite straight off the wheel and cocked his head as he chewed, his snow-white hair falling over his eyes. "Why do you smell like flowers and campfires?"

"Herbs," I corrected as I sank a little deeper, the warmth in my face spreading into my chest. "Because I was digging around in Boot's burnt shop . . . and I put lavender in the tub."

"Why?"

"To get rid of the campfire smell."

"Ah." Jayvin took another bite, saying through a full mouth. "It didn't work."

"Wonderful." I bite into my cheese, the creamy, buttery flavor coating my mouth. I let myself savor it. "Mmm. This would be perfect baked over apples. Maybe with some cinnamon."

Jayvin's nose wrinkled. "Apples with brie?"

"You've never tried it?"

"I can't say that I have."

I took another bite. It really was good. "A shame. You're missing out."

"It seems I've missed out on many things." His expression grew wistful. "So much has changed, Sunshine."

My heart fluttered like it always did when he called me that name. He noticed immediately, his gaze locking onto my throat before it slid to the pearl pendant. With a hint of vexation, he frowned. My pulse took off like a hummingbird as he leaned forward, bubbles clinging to his sleeve as he touched the jewel, fingers brushing against my tanned skin. "Who gave this to you?"

Breathes shallow, I pushed his hand away. "What makes you think it was a gift?"

"Wasn't it?"

"Maybe I bought it for myself."

"Perhaps." Jayvin leaned back. "But it reeks of the Goblin."

"Then why did you ask?" I asked, "If you knew it was Boot's?"

Jayvin didn't answer. We just stared at each other—thoughtful—and for some reason, it didn't bother me. Despite the turn in the conversation, he seemed content. I ate more and took my time chewing before swallowing, my throat dry. *Some wine would make this even better.* "May I ask *you* something?"

Jayvin gave me an expectant look. "If it pleases you."

"When Boot proposed we free you from the chapel—" Jayvin winced. I picked at the edge of my thumb. "—Loach was afraid. He said that you'd kill us all . . . just for fun of it." I paused. *How do I word this?*

Jayvin's eyes never left mine as his full lips slowly curved into a smile, revealing his sharp canines. "And you're wondering why I haven't?"

I nodded. "He also said you've committed unforgivable crimes against Tyrr."

Jayvin rested his knee against mine, sending a chill up my thigh. "In regard to the self-indulgent slaughter, it's a little more complex than that."

"Complex, how?"

"Maybe someday, you'll see." He subconsciously ran his tongue over his teeth. "But I hope not. As for the nation, I didn't have time to commit any crimes before I was entombed, though I'm sure I was blamed for plenty."

The words slipped out. "By whom?"

Jayvin slid his fingers over my calf fin's spine. I did my best not to react. A hint of longing flashed across his features. Longing and sadness. "Why do you ask?"

"Curiosity." I mimicked the devilish smile he'd given me moments before. "Isn't that why you asked about my necklace?"

Jayvin huffed. He seemed almost relieved. "Yes, that's it. Curiousity."

"Now, get out of my bath," I said, riding the last of the confidence in my reserves. "Unless you plan to wash my hair, as well?"

Jayvin let out a rumbling laugh as he stood, his soaked trousers clinging to all the places I'd hoped they wouldn't. "Don't tempt me, Sunshine."

Chapter Fifteen

Boot slammed his coffee mug on the table, splashing the brown liquid over his notes. "I need a projection ring."

Agatha and I exchanged glances, spoons of porridge halfway to our mouths.

She lowered hers. "I need a vacation. So what?"

After several days of sorting, labeling, and repackaging hundreds of pounds of weapons and armor, Loach was finally satisfied that we had enough supplies to continue with the plan. The night's earlier mists had rolled away, leaving the morning sky clear and blindingly bright. Sunlight reflected off Boot's cup as he took a sip, and it shot me straight in the eyes.

"A projection ring." Boot tapped his pen against his stack of papers, splattering them with ink. "I've gone over every scenario I can think of at least three times. We can't get into the palace without one."

"Why not?" Loach hollered from the sofa in the living room. "What use would we have for a gaudy gem that we couldn't do with one of the other many gaudy gems at your disposal?"

"Says the ignorant cephalopod." Boot threw a crumpled ball of paper at him. "Not all precious stones are suited for projecting light . . . or magic."

"The Wardstone in the palace is basically a giant projection ring, right?" Agatha licked the porridge off her spoon. "So, what do we need a little one for?"

Jayvin hadn't come down yet despite being close to ten in the morning. *He's probably just enjoying sleeping on a real bed.* I'd already resisted the urge to check on him at least six times.

In the kitchen, Ivan washed and sorted dishes. I felt guilty for all his work, but more than once—with a death glare—he assured me Boot was paying him well and not to worry.

I stepped around the counter and slid into the seat across from Boot, scanning over his new drawings—an image of a ring with a large, square-cut blue gem on a thick, silver band.

"The gems themselves have no power," Boot clarified as he adjusted his glasses, resting his craterous cheek on his palm. "They only amplify the magic passing through them. I won't be able to get through the wards on the treasury without one."

"Really?" I finished the last of my breakfast. Agatha took my bowl and placed it in the sink, earning a scathing look from Ivan. "You didn't need one to break the wards on the catacombs."

"I didn't *break* the wards on the catacomb, girl. I opened them . . . temporarily, and not without much effort." Boot rapped his nails against his crinkled ear. "Sayzar will have placed much stronger binds on his wealth—the famous greed of the Elves at work."

"Then let's get one." Agatha adjusted the holster holding the daggers against her sides. "It's a big city. It shouldn't be too hard."

"You'd be surprised." Boot gave her an assessing look. "Sayzar may be young for his kind, but he's intelligent. He had most of the projection rings in Carnage confiscated and locked in the treasury when he took control."

"*Most?*" I asked.

"There's an Elf merchant—Laben—who runs a booth inside the inner court's marketplace." Boot leaned forward and folded his gnarled hands. "He's permitted to wear one by the Emperor—to protect his wares."

I swallowed. "And you want to . . . buy it from him?"

"Not buy it." Boot grinned and revealed those jagged teeth. "I want you to steal it."

"Why?" I gestured to the gold bangles he wore around his wrists, pieces from the collection Agatha had retrieved. "You have plenty to pay him with."

"I'm not willing to invest any more into this cause until we have that ring." Boot's gaze moved to Agatha, who stared back coldly. He tossed her a tied scroll. "You understand."

"I do." Agatha stepped away from the counter and tugged on my sleeve. "Let's go, Hun."

"Wait." Loach let out a pained huff as he tried to swing off the sofa, gripping his bruised side. He'd overdone it yesterday with the shopping and sorting. "I'm going with you."

"Stay." I moved and knelt beside him. "Agatha and I can handle it. We'll be fine. Stay here and rest."

"Hell." Loach ran a hand over his milky face. "At least take the drone with you for protection."

"No, I need him." Boot interrupted, then turned to us. "The girls can handle it. Can't you?"

"*Girls.*" Agatha shook her head and pointed at him. "Watch it, Goblin."

"Rest." I patted Loach's arm. "We'll be back soon. Agatha knows what she's doing."

"Here." Agatha slipped off her thigh holster—dagger and all—and knelt, gesturing me to lift my skirts. Heat crept up my neck, but I did as bid. She strapped and tightened the holster around my bare thigh, checking the fit.

"Keep that hidden." She grabbed her coat off the counter and slid it on to conceal the knives on her sides. "It's party time."

We looked so at odds—her in her fighting leathers and me in a long-sleeved, blue day dress. I waved goodbye to Loach, and Boot gave us a few more instructions before I followed her out the door into the alley.

"Can you understand this?" Agatha passed me the scroll Boot had given her—a map of the Lantern Palace's inner court. She pointed to some scribbles in the corner of the paper. "That?"

I read over Boot's scrawling notes. "Southwest corner of the courtyard. That must be where this Laben sets up his stall."

"Fair enough." Agatha rolled up the map and shoved it into her coat pocket. She glanced over my face. "You did a scarily amazing job on your shift today. I still can't believe that's you."

I glanced at my reflection as we passed by a store window. *She's right. This might be my best work.* From Boot's instructions—and a lot of salt—I'd honed my skin into a fair, luminescent glow. My ears long and arched. My waist-length waves were now a gilded, golden blonde, and my eyes a striking blue. The look of Elven nobility, he called it—and the key to gaining passage into the inner court.

"I wish I could shift you." I fluffed my locks. Agatha had such a distinct look—with her short, black hair and lithe figure—she was easily recognizable. "Do you think they'll know you?"

"Probably." She shrugged as we passed through the crowds heading toward the market. "But according to the official record, I'm on the Emperor's payroll."

Vendors unrolled the awnings over their carts, shaking out worn rugs to place over the cobbled street. I waved when I spotted the Imp family I'd bought the bracelet from days ago.

Agatha snapped my arm down. "Don't."

The Imp father gave us a strange look.

He doesn't recognize me. I dropped my eyes to the ground. *Stupid. Mistakes like that will get us killed.* I straightened my shoulders and shook my head. *No bad thoughts, Tetra.*

"We've never talked about that." I elbowed Agatha's side in an attempt to bring the subject back to her. "How did you wind up working for the Emperor?"

She exhaled, never taking her keen gaze off the faces around us, always vigilant. "That . . . that's a long story."

I gestured to the distance between us and the palace, arching a golden brow.

Agatha smiled, her teeth bright white. "You're the worst."

"That's rude. We all know Loach is the worst."

"True." She laughed and let out a sigh. "I was the one who convinced my brother and his family to move to Carnage, remember?"

I just listened, keeping my back as stiff and straight as possible as we walked, strides long, as I mirrored Elven posture.

"He's such an amazing cook." Her brown eyes grew weary. "He loves it. I knew he'd make a name for himself in the city. He'd always taken care of us. Now, he could get the recognition he deserves. Maybe a chance at early retirement." She balled her fists. "Then the barrier went up."

I wanted to reach out and touch her, reassure her, but I kept my hands folded behind my back. "And his wife?"

"She died giving birth to their youngest son." Agatha watched a group of passing Enforcers, hand hovering over the knives beneath her coat. "She used to sell the herbs she grew—the ones she'd brought from our tribe—but now it's just him and the kids."

The silence growing between us told me plenty. "So, you started working for the Emperor to bring in money . . . as a spy?"

"Of sorts." Agatha cleared her throat. "I've never met Sayzar. The captain of his guard finds me, tells me what information they're looking for, and I retrieve it. Simple as that."

"Simple as that," I repeated, turning my gaze back to the road. Maybe Boot was on to something. "If only things were always that simple."

The crowds grew thinner the further we drew from the market and toward the palace. Where the bodies around us before had mainly been Orcs, Imps, and Humans, now Elves were the dominant force. They were all beautiful, all graceful in a way that wasn't . . . natural. I tried to mirror their movement, to *become* one of them.

Agatha steered me right toward the inner courtyard's main gate. "What about you?" she asked, "you were out of sorts after the shenanigans in the headquarters."

I raised a questioning brow.

"After I got back from blowing up Boot's shop," Agatha clarified. "You looked off. Yesterday you were quiet, too. Is something bothering you?"

I ran my tongue over my dry lips. *God, I miss the sea.* "Jayvin asked me that same question after we got the supplies. Apparently, I'm terrible at hiding things."

She smirked a little. "Or he's smarter than I thought."

"It's nothing."

"You're full of crap."

"*Rude,*" I smacked her arm, and she laughed. I chewed the inside of my cheek, thinking. "It's just . . ." *That I'm no better than the dictator that murdered my family?* I shook my head. "It just bothers me how many Enforcers we've killed. I never meant for this to become a slaughter fest."

Agatha gently tugged me behind her, dodging a raucous group of Human men as we passed through the narrow archway out of the main market. "People die all the time, Tetra."

"It doesn't mean I have to *like* it." I snapped. "Or that people *should* die. Especially because of me."

"You haven't hurt anyone."

"Haven't I?" My throat tightened. "Who asked you to break into the palace? To disobey the Emperor?"

"Don't be so narrow-minded as to think this is all about you," Agatha said, giving me a sad smile. "We all *chose* to be here, Hun—even your Offspring."

"He's not *my* anything." I kept my eyes on the growing battlements, on the Enforcers walking the walls. "You make it sound like I own him."

I yelped as Agatha grabbed my arm, earning startled looks from a few passersby. She turned me until my back was to the street and held up my forearm, the bright sun gleaming off the silver scars branded into my skin. "Do you have any idea what this is?"

I jerked my hand away. She left a red mark on my wrist. "An Elven bond."

"An Elven *blood* binding." Agatha's lips turned downwards. "Blood magic. If he breaks the conditions of your agreement, he dies. If you do the same, you die. Tetra, it was stupid to make such a promise. You're stuck with him until you free him."

But how? A blood bind—

Sharks. He'd drank my blood . . . had said it tasted like sunshine. If I failed to bring down the barrier, would he still be bound to our promise? Enslaved to me like he was to his creator? Bile rose in my throat, threatening to bend me over. Not only was I no better than Sayzar, but I'd also taken Jayvin from one set of chains only to lock him into another.

"Hey." Agatha shook my shoulder. "I didn't mean to scare you, it's just—damn it, let's get to the palace. We can finish this conversation later."

I nodded and followed, hand over my throat, willing my pulse to slow. Two silver armored Enforcers watched the opened, gilded gate between Carnage and the Lantern Palace's prestigious inner court.

How can I ever embody that? I shoved the thoughts of Jayvin to the back of my mind. The Enforcers *exuded* power—not only in their stature but in the vicious way they watched for danger, ready to incapacitate a threat in the span of a breath.

Shielded by several remaining merchant stalls, Agatha pulled up her hood, letting her gait sink into her signature swagger. Her lips barely moved as she whispered, "Remember your part?"

"Yes," I muttered back. *I can do this. I have to. It's too late to turn back now.* Taut as a bowstring, I flipped my gold waves over my shoulder, honing my features into that of cool indifference. I fidgeted with the oversized, emerald crusted belt hanging around my waist—a temporary gift from Boot to deepen the façade—and strode for the gate.

"Halt." The male Enforcer to the right of the gate snapped out his arm. "State your business."

I didn't hide an ounce of the annoyance in my glare. "Do I need a reason to be amongst my own people?" With an eye roll, I glanced back to Carnage's market. "I can only deal with the rabble for so long."

The second male Enforcer stepped toward Agatha, sunlight glinting off his polished spear. "Do I know you?"

Agatha kept her chin low, her posture relaxed. "Should you?"

"She's my bodyguard. Not any of your concern." I don't know why I did it, but on impulse, I reached out with my allure—strawberries coating my tongue—and latched onto the second guard. Unlike the Enforcer in Boot's shop, I felt my mental talons break through whatever barrier protected the male's mind.

Behind his helm, his glowing eyes went hazy, sliding from my pout to where the pearl pendant sat against my chest, then lower to where my dress clung to my hips. His scowl morphed into a dreamy smile.

"You're right, it's not." He stepped back, gesturing for us to pass. "Enjoy your time, my lady. Don't forget to stop for a visit on your way out."

His companion blinked at him. "Wait . . . what?"

The enthralled Enforcer shot him a glare. "I vouch for her."

The first Enforcer shook his head in disbelief, but he stepped back. "Whatever. Enjoy your visit, I guess."

"Thank you." I brushed the second Enforcer's shoulder before resting my hand over my chest. "Long live the Emperor."

His eyes devoured me alive as he copied the movement. "Long live the Emperor."

I passed through the gate, heart pounding, Agatha hot on my tail. Not until we were out of sight and earshot did she pull me aside. "Did you just enthrall an *Enforcer?*"

"I'm as surprised as you are." I shook the tension out of my fingers. "The effect won't last long."

"If I had that ability." Agatha wistfully looped her arm through mine. "I would rule the world."

"You can have it." I adjusted my hair. "It's a dirty, primitive trick."

"Sometimes life is about getting dirty," she grinned. "Come on, let's find this Laben, and get out of here. I have no interest in exploring the inner court."

And a court it was—a court of Elves, magic, and marble.

Sayzar Ameliatus had the battlements surrounding the palace built after occupying it. Time and wealthy, bored occupants turned it into a royal district.

My mouth hung open like an idiot as we passed through the pristine, cobbled streets. Streaming banners hung between spiraling towers, fluttering in the soft breeze. Honeysuckle and clematis clung to enormous, white arches, adorned with pink and lavender faelights.

I frowned. "What's with the decorations? Is there going to be a party?"

"If there is, we didn't get an invitation." Agatha made a face. "They don't know what they're missing. I'm a mean juggler."

After a burst of laughter, my interest returned to the city. More multi-level apartment buildings made up the outside of the courtyard. The inner half was dedicated to the arts—tourism—not that they let many inside to enjoy them.

I wonder if that's the Emperor's dream. To open this space to the public once the coast is under control. I slowed to take in a greying, aged Elf trying to halk off generic-looking paintings.

How long did you live as an Elf to hit old age?

Many races—Merfolk, Vampires, Banshees, Centaurs, Nymphs—traced their ancestry back to the ancient Elves. We shared the same traits of long life, unnatural beauty, and magical capabilities. But like Sayzar, modern Elves only recognized purebreds as kin, leaving the rest of us to be seen as lesser life forms. As we entered from the main street into the palace's outer bailey, that's all I saw—pure Elves. Ethereal, glowing, graceful beings at the top of Tyrr's hierarchy. I clung to Agatha. *This is going to be harder than I thought.*

At least, the Lantern Palace was all I expected it to be and more—pure, faultless white stone, pointed, perfectly symmetrical towers spiraling into the sky. Even in the heated noon sun, the glow of snow-white faelights danced through the spires and columns. Unburdened, relaxed—more proof of their master's power. The bailey was black and white tile, polished to a reflective shine.

"Look." Agatha pulled me tighter against her side, pointing upward, the hilts of her throwing knives rubbing against my ribs. "Cyclone. The Wardstone."

No. I craned my head back, sucking in a shaky breath as I took in the pillar towering over the entrance to the palace. It seemed out of place—built in a hurry—but even from here, eighty feet or more below, I could make out the outline of a haggard skeleton, magnificent armor in ruins, and held together with magic. Below it, the Wardstone looked like a jagged, purple rock, emitting brilliant energy waves into the sky.

Only Agatha's hold on my arm kept my knees from hitting the ground.

Breathe. I begged my body, but the air didn't come. My lungs couldn't expand. Agatha pulled me by the elbow, speaking frantically, but I couldn't hear her.

All I could see was Cyclone's hard, bearded face, smiling down at me as I knelt before him. He'd visited our cove once... due to its closeness to Carnage's borders. When Mama and Papa offered to cook supper for his entire guard, he'd provided a meal for all of us instead. Little had he known we'd been on the brink of starvation that season. All we had my parents planned to give to their king.

He's laughed with us, drank with us, bid me to reach for the stars.

And I believed him—that the cosmos was reachable and that I could enjoy every inch of it if I tried.

I'd been twelve years old, amazed by the beauty and power of our hero and ruler.

Then fear and cowardness had me kneeling to the man who'd murdered him . . . who'd murdered my family and everything I loved, my entire future and dreams.

"Tetra." Agatha's voice sounded a thousand miles away, but the impact of her fist between my shoulder blades *hurt*. My shift flickered. Darkness clawed at the edges of my vision, but I managed a desperate inhale. Two, three. By the time I was breathing again, Agatha had gone pale.

"Hills alive, Tetra." She sat me down on a nearby bench. "Do we need to leave? Do you need a doctor?"

"I'm fine." Clutching my chest, I pushed her away. "I . . . I need a minute."

"Okay." Agatha knelt beside me, stroking my hair. "Okay. Take your time."

I hated the way my eyes burned, the tightness in my throat. *You kneeled, Tetra, you kneeled.* I smacked my palms into my temples. "I'm fine. I'm fine."

"I believe you." Agatha smiled gently. "Breathe."

After several minutes and the curious stares of many passing Elves, my heart finally began to slow. I checked to make sure my shift was still in place.

Agatha stood, reaching out to me. "Can you stand?"

I nodded and accepted her hand. She pulled me to my feet. Her arm wrapped around my shoulders, a grounding weight, as she steered me deeper into the district. "If it makes you feel better, we've reached the inner market."

It did and it didn't.

I glanced up, wiping my runny nose, and took in the vast, covered street along the east side of the palace. As we passed below the canopy, a nice reprieve from the day's heat, it took a moment for my eyes to adjust to the dim light in the aisles of merchant stalls on either side and the center of the road.

Where Carnage's primary market had been haphazard and cheaply built, these were handsome and permanent establishments. Faelights danced between the stalls, illuminating the widest assortment of goods I'd ever seen—spices, silken fabrics, caged exotic birds, and trinkets carved in the images of the first Elves.

It was an effort to maintain my shift as I clung to Agatha's side, to pretend that I belonged here. The eyes of several shoppers snagged on us as we passed. My heart began to race. They knew. Somehow, they knew—

"They're staring at me, not you," Agatha said, as if she could read my thoughts. "My kind aren't the favorite species in Carnage."

"Why?" That surprised me. The lower districts were inhabited mainly by Orcs. Hell, Carnage wouldn't be here at all if it weren't for their industry. "That doesn't make sense."

"Doesn't it?" Agatha glared at a well-dressed couple watching us. They turned away. "My people have always been the first to rebel against Elven dominion, when given the chance. It's been over a century since our last revolt. I think they're all waiting for it to happen again."

I blew out a breath. "People just need to mind their own damn business."

Agatha nodded and cleared her throat, a request to let the subject drop. "Southwest corner, correct?"

"Yes." I smiled wide, imagining us in a thrilling conversation, playing the part. "It shouldn't be far."

Agatha led us deeper into the market, and part of me

wished I could spend all day here—to learn the origins of each artifact on display and study the histories of the cultures behind them. The world was so large, and I'd seen so little of it.

"Tetra." The urgency in Agatha's tone made me tense. "Look."

I followed her gaze and this time it landed on a vendor stall that was significantly plainer than the ones around it. Instead of bright tapestries, this one was tented in tan burlap, and only three trays of goods were out for sale. As we grew closer, I realized that the products displayed were gold and silver chained jewelry, dripping in colored diamonds, nearly to the quality of Boot's pieces.

What caught my eyes, though—what caught Agatha's—was the enormous, blue gemmed ring adorning the merchant's left middle finger.

My entire body stiffened. "Laben."

"Looks like it." Agatha threw back her hood, smoothing her hair, as she shot me a wink. "How about you let me handle this one?"

I nodded and focused on the available jewels as she led me to the stall. They must have magical qualities if he was selling so few. The male Elf—I assumed to be Laben—beamed up at us with vibrant, green eyes. His beaked nose a direct contrast to his wispy, receding hairline. "You ladies look like you know quality." Agatha didn't protest as he waved us forward. "Come. You won't find anything that creates the statement my pieces provide. Many were hand-appraised by the Emperor himself."

"I doubt that." Agatha sneered. "Approved by whatever fence you laundered these from, most like."

Laben's mouth fell open.

I pinched Agatha's side. "You'll forgive my bodyguard." *So much for her doing the talking.* I grinned as I picked up the nearest necklace—a pretty ruby pendant on a slim, silver chain. "She lacks the eye for finer metalwork."

"Ah," Laban gave me a flourishing bow. "A true consumer of the arts." As he straightened, he sniffed, glaring at Agatha. "Foolish of me to expect a Mountain whore to understand the more delicate luxuries of life."

Agatha inhaled and shot me a look I knew all too well. *I'm going to hurt him.*

I shook my head, mouthing. *"No."*

"Screw it." Agatha exhaled, curling her lip over her teeth. One moment, her hand was on my elbow. The next, she was pinning Laben's to the table with a loud *clang*. Her chocolate brown eyes lowered to his ring. "Never mind, I do see *something* I like. How much for that stone on your finger?"

"This?" Laben jerked and tried to pull away, but Agatha held tight. "This isn't for sale, I'm afraid."

"I thought you'd say that." Agatha reached under her coat, pulling out a knife and twirling it around her slim fingers before slamming it into the wood between Laben's. "And I was going to make this easy. Painless. Then you had to make those rude comments." She jerked the knife to the side, and it cut into the web of Laben's thumb. He squealed, and she clapped a hand over his mouth.

"Agatha . . ." I warned. Several Elves rushed past, muttering amongst themselves.

She ignored me, smiling instead. "Give me the ring, we leave." She dug the knife deeper into his Laben's skin, and he moaned in pain, tears leaking from his eyes. "Refuse, and I take the finger. You're choice."

"Agatha." I grabbed her elbow this time. The muttering was turning to gasping and shouting. Several shoppers ran from the market. "What are you doing? We need to go."

She cocked her head. "Choose, merchant. I don't have long."

Laben considered her, skin red and splotchy, but then he slowly smiled beneath her palm. "Ignorant Orc."

A blazing, blue light burned through his ring, blinding us. I yelped as Agatha hit the ground, having taken the brunt of it. Fading laughter and thunderous footsteps flew past us, deeper into the market. *He's running.*

I could barely make out Agatha's frame as she winced and scrambled upright, rubbing her eyes. "You're *dead,* Elf!"

I was on my knees as I watched her fuzzy outline fly down the street after him, leaping straight over a pastry cart that had rolled into her path.

Damn it all to hell. I wiped the irritated tears streaming from my eyes, but it only made the fuzziness worse. Finally finding the edge of the booth, I climbed to my feet. "*Sharks —*" A burning pain savaged my arm. The silver bands wrapped around it throbbed—pulsing ribbons of moonlight. *Not now. I can't deal with this now.* Moaning, I yanked my sleeve over my hand to hide the faint glow emitting from the scars.

"*You.*" The voice was stern and angry—an Enforcer.

Sharks. I managed to get to my feet and leaned against the stall. The blurry outline of at least three Enforcers stalked towards me. "You, stop, in the name of the Emperor!"

Hindsight told me I could have talked my way out of it. I could have played the wounded maiden and escaped without a fuss, maybe even with a polite escort and an apology.

Did I do that?

No.

I bolted, tripping over the skirts of my dress, as I hurdled myself down the street, following Laben's path of blood droplets.

"*Stop!*" The drawing of swords followed the command.

The binding on my arm was on *fire* as I sprinted through the maze of innocent shoppers and vendor stalls. *Don't look back.* I knew what I'd see if I did. The sounds of screams and shattered pottery followed me as I ran, ducking and diving between elbows and knees. The shouts had grown fainter as I skidded to a stop between an intersection.

My head span as my breaths came in ragged gasps. Both directions were just rows and rows of vendors, leading deeper into the maze of the covered market.

Where the hell is Agatha? She'd better have gotten the ring for all the trouble she'd put me through.

"*Stop!*" The voices were closer now.

I sprinted down the left-hand path, skirts whipping around my calves. Sellers of clothing and pleasantries gave way to more practical items—weapons, armor—then to metal objects I assumed were devices of torture.

The shouting grew louder. I glanced back to gauge their distance and crashed into something solid—a person. My back hit the ground, forcing all the air from my lungs with a loud *oof.*

"*Yield!*" Spears lowered over my prone body as I rolled onto my stomach, gasping into the dust on the tiles as I tried to suck in a breath. *I'm dead. I'm dead. I'm dead.* The burning in my binding scars shifted from uncomfortable to writhing torment. I couldn't think.

"*Step aside.*" The voice speaking was soft yet held absolute authority.

I glanced over my shoulder, my vision finally clear enough to see an entire entourage of Enforcers backing away from me, their weapons returning to a resting position.

An ivory, thin hand reached for me—an invitation to stand.

I took it, coughing as I climbed to my feet and dusted off

the front of my dress. I could already feel the bruises forming on my knees, elbows, and forearms.

"Are you hurt?" Such a hushed voice. I'd sworn I'd heard it before.

The Enforcers chasing after me came to a skidding halt, falling to a bow.

"No, I don't think so." I glanced up, taking in the face of my rescuer. "Tha—" Every cell of my being turned to ice. Crystal blue eyes stared down at me with concern, framed by a thin face of porcelain white. Lengths of vivid red, pin-straight hair fell over the man's shoulders as he steadied me.

I know you. I hate you. Only survival instinct had me sinking onto one knee—just like I had a year ago, as I did over and over in my nightmares. I bowed my head, choking back the silver lining my eyes. "Hail, Sayzar."

Chapter Sixteen

"Rise." Sayzar Ameliatus stepped back, the picture of elegance in his gold brocade overcoat and matching doublet. "You have nothing to fear from me."

Liar, liar, liar, I wanted to scream, but I choked back my hatred as I rose. I smoothed my hair over my shoulder and straightened my dress, using the time to ensure my shift was still in place.

In one calculated sweep, The Emperor's piercing, blue eyes scanned me head to toe—his smile beautiful and empty. He glanced at his guards, taking in the dust and remaining drawn weapons, then folded his thin arms behind his back. "Why, may I ask, were my Enforcers pursuing you?"

"Ask them." I held his unblinking stare despite the terror rolling in my gut. Adrenaline made my words careless. "I ran because they were chasing me."

With a quick smirk, The Emperor's attention flicked back to his guards. The ones still standing hit their knees in fear. The plumed captain spoke, "There was a disturbance, Sire. She was at the center of it."

The Emperor pursed his lips, thoughtful. "Did you stop to think that maybe this lovely creature was the *victim* of such a disturbance?"

I kept my head down, blood pounding in my ears. *Don't puke, don't puke.*

The captain bowed his head. "No, Sire."

"Ah." In one liquid movement, the Emperor took my sweaty hand and kissed my knuckles. "I apologize for the behavior of my guards, my lady. Walk with me?"

I just blinked at him like an idiot. "Walk . . . with *you?*"

The Emperor's lips curled in amusement. "Who else?"

Around us, peering through the shoulders of his Enforcer entourage, shoppers *oohed* and *aahed* at Sayzar, gossiping to each other in hushed tones.

"What are you doing here?" I blurted. The Emperor rose a perfectly plucked brow. The onlookers gasped. *Get it together, Tetra.* I bowed my head. "What I meant was . . . I'm surprised to see you out and about, Your Majesty. Isn't this dangerous for you?"

"Sayzar," he offered me his elbow, and his smile turned to a grin. "Please, call me Sayzar. And no, my dear, I am in no danger here."

"Sayzar," I repeated. The words choked me like spoiled clams. "Thank you for your help."

"Come." Arm in arm, the Emperor led me deeper into the market at a leisurely stroll, not giving me a chance to refuse his invitation to walk. As soon as he'd taken a step, his Enforcers were on their feet, encircling their monarch in a practiced formation. The nearest one shot me a glare, and I cringed away.

My skin crawled as Sayzar patted my arm. "Pay them no mind. They are at my command and mine alone." He was not as tall as Jayvin, but tall enough that I had to look up to see his face. He scanned mine, and I didn't miss the hungry glimmer in his eyes. "I'm surprised I've not seen you before, my lady. With your beauty, I surely would have noticed."

"This is my first time in the inner district." I suppressed a gag. *I hate him. Pretend it's someone else. Think of something.* Jayvin's face flashed through my mind, making my skin grow warm. The lie rolled quickly off my tongue. "I spend most of my time working my parent's antiquity stall at the outer market." *Parents I would have had if not for you.* I gestured to our surroundings. "As much as I love Carnage, it can't compare to your inner court. The quality and rarity of the items here are outstanding."

Sayzar tugged me closer, glowing eyes brightening further. "You enjoy antiques?"

Keep him talking. Give Agatha time to get the ring. I gave him the most charming smile I could manage. "I enjoy anything that gives me pause. That I must study and piece apart to discover its secrets. Do you understand that feeling, Your Majesty?" The speech sounded great until I tripped over a crack in the tiled floor. *"Damn it all."*

Sayzar burst out into musical laughter as he caught me by the elbow. I didn't have to fake the blush filling my cheeks now. I looked like an idiot.

"I do understand." Sayzar tightened his grip on my arm, almost possessively. "What is your name, my lady?"

Sharks. I glanced around in a panic, looking for something—anything—as a source of inspiration. Behind a row of shelves filled with books, Agatha gaped at us. *Thank God.* She was dusty, with a splatter of blood on her cheek, but she was alive. She patted the breast pocket on her coat—she had the ring. A string of fake pearls caught my attention and my mother's name came to mind. "Jessa—my name is Jessa."

"I'm happy to have met you, Jessa." Sayzar smiled knowingly. "What did you come in search of today?"

I blinked at him.

"Don't give that innocent look." Sayzar chuckled. "You have the feeling of a collector about you. I doubt you came here without a special reason. Perhaps on a hunt?"

Sharks. I glanced away, chewing the inside of my lip. *Honesty has gotten you this far. Here goes nothing.* "Seems I'm a terrible liar." I let out a dramatic sigh. "I've been searching for a projection ring for years. I've often been told that a woman in my position will never own such a thing, but I can't help myself. I *will* have one for my collection."

Sayzar's lips quirked as he led me to the mouth of the market, back towards the streamers and floral arches. "And why a projection ring, Lady Jessa?"

Lady. I was the farthest thing from a lady. "Because they told me no."

"Of course," Sayzar chuckled. "But you seem like someone good at getting what she wants."

Another genuine blush. "I wouldn't say that."

With a gentle grip on my shoulder, Sayzar turned me to face him, his sharp features honed into confident amusement. With a flourish, he pulled an enormous, raw-cut amethyst and gold ring off his index finger. How had I not noticed it before? My eyes widened in genuine awe.

He held it up, making a show of letting the afternoon sun reflect through the crystal. He glanced at me from the corner of his eye as he lifted my hand. "My projection ring. Given to me by my father, and his before him. Tell them the Emperor gave this to you—a woman of *your* position."

"And why would you give such an heirloom to me?" I was shaking when he slid the ring over the tip of my thumb. "That seems almost foolish."

"I've been called a fool before." He paused, his thin mouth widening. "And I'm not gifting this without condition."

Of course. My lips pursed. "As I would expect from someone in *your* position."

The Enforcers surrounding us exchanged nervous glances.

Sayzar burst out in genuine laughter, beaming, as he reached out and gripped my chin. "I have a matter to attend to that cuts our meeting short, but promise me I can see you again, Jessa the collector. Soon."

I choked back the bile rising in my throat, batting my lashes as I gave him a shy smile. "O-of course, Your Majesty."

"Call me Sayzar." He slid the ring down to the base of my thumb. His gaze flickered over my shoulder. "And tell your friend there that she need not worry. You're safe with me."

I glanced back, only catching a glimpse of emerald skin as Agatha slid behind a market stall. I ran my tongue over my lips. Sayzar didn't miss the movement. "She's . . . she's protective, is all."

My entire body—my soul—fought not to recoil as Sayzar leaned in and pressed a wet kiss to my cheek. "I can understand why."

Chapter Seventeen

"Did you get it?" Boot asked in a way of greeting, still reading at the table, as Agatha and I entered The Lux.

"Nice to see you, too." Agatha plopped down on the seat across from him, propping her dusty boots on his scrolls. His glare was vicious. She tossed Laben's projection ring before him like a moldy potato. "And yes. We got two."

Boot's giant, orange eyes widened as he lifted and turned the ring over between his talons. "Stunning," he muttered. Finally, her words sunk in. "Wait—two?"

"You're back." Loach hobbled down the stairs at the sound of our voices and into the kitchen. I thought he might hug me for a moment, but he dropped his arms to his side. "You got it, kid?"

"They retrieved two, apparently." Loach shoved Agatha's feet off the table, ignoring her mischievous grin. "And—before you so rudely interrupted—they were about to explain how."

Something's not right. The thought stopped me as I was about to show them the Emperor's ring. I glanced around, a flicker of fear gripping my chest. "Where's Jayvin?"

He hadn't come down this morning. I'd just assumed he was sleeping, but I could feel it now—the anxiety hanging in the air, thick enough to choke me.

"I have no idea." Loach shrugged, but there was tension behind the movement. "He's not in his room. Haven't seen him."

"You *lost* our Vampire?" Agatha jumped up, knocking over her chair. "He's huge! How could you lose him?"

"Calm down." Loach raised his hands in defense, but that made me hyperventilate worse. "He'll turn up. Let's start with the ring, shall we?"

He's fine. It's fine. He was just loose in the city, is all.

Alone . . . after he'd panicked over running water.

I gripped my throat, willing my pulse to slow. The burning in our bind had been excruciating before I ran into the Emperor. If he was hurt, would I be able to feel it through the connection?

"Tetra." Agatha's voice softened. "It's okay. Show them."

"Yes, sorry." *Breathe. In through the nose, out through the mouth.* I slid the amethyst off my thumb. Boot blinked in absolute astonishment as I passed it to him. Loach leaned over his shoulder to get a better look.

Jayvin will be okay. I lied to myself but gestured with a small amount of pride to the jewel. "A second projection ring—straight from the hand of Sayzar Ameliatus himself."

The two glanced at us, then at each other, eyes as wide as tea saucers. Boot lowered his thick-framed glasses, pinching the bridge of his stunted nose. "Explain, girl."

"I wish you'd seen it!" Agatha grinned and patted me on the back. "Tetra ran—literally ran—straight into the Emperor and his posse. Apparently, dear Sayzar enjoys going for afternoon strolls in the market." She jigged in place, too excited to keep still. "Tetra charmed the hell out of him, and he gave her that. It was brilliant."

"He wants to see me again," I added as a disgusted shiver ran down my back at the memory of his hungered gaze. "He made me promise."

The men just stared at us in stunned silence.

"Well." Boot shoved his chair away from the table with a loud squeak. "You two have exceeded my expectations."

"Expectations?" Agatha's expression soured. "You make it sound like this was a test."

Boot folded his hands over his rounded belly, crooked lips curling into a grin. "My apologies. I had to be sure."

"W-what?" I turned, hoping Loach would say otherwise, but he looked as surprised as we did. Loach burst into a raucous laugh, coughing as he gripped his broken rib. "Boot, you *scoundrel.*"

I leaned against the counter before my knees gave out. *A test. I promised my time to the Emperor . . . for a test.*

Agatha's expression fell into one of eerie calm as she unsheathed one of the knives at her side and twirled it around her fingers. "Elaborate . . . before I peel the skin off your bony arms, Goblin."

Boot held up the rings. "I needed proof you and Tetra could pull off a coup of this size. That I wasn't dumping my energy and gold into a doomed mission. Loach's reputation proceeds him, as does the Offspring's. I know little of either of your abilities."

Agatha sucked in a breath, two. "Are you saying we never needed a projection ring?"

"That's precisely what I'm saying." Boot carefully folded the jewels into a napkin and tucked them into the pocket of his plaid waistcoat. "But now that we have them, we'll put them to good use."

"I hate you," Agatha exhaled, spinning on her heel to head upstairs. "I hate you both. I'm going to take a nap."

Loach laughed again as he headed for the sofa. I wanted to jam my heel into his wounded side, over and over. Instead, I smiled pleasantly at Boot, who'd returned to his notes. "Does this give us an edge? The Emperor wanting to meet me again?" *Can you please tell me that it wasn't all for nothing?*

"Only time will tell," Boot shrugged. "But any bit of information we can glean is beneficial. We know now that he leaves the palace. That may be useful."

"Okay, then." *A test.* I exchanged my fair-haired Elven shift for my dark-haired Human disguise. I was going to hurt someone if I stayed here. "I'm going for a walk."

Loach called from the living room. "To where?"

"To find Jayvin," I shot back. "Seeing that Agatha and I are the only ones capable of getting anything done around here."

It was unsettling to walk the streets of Carnage alone. *I can't believe they let me go.* I'd expected at least Loach to make a fuss about me leaving, especially with all the extra Enforcers on patrol, but he didn't. Maybe I should be asking why I felt like I needed their permission in the first place.

My dry tongue stuck to the roof of my mouth. *Sharks.* I should have mixed up some salt water before I'd left. Maintaining a shift for so long, and using my allure, had made an alarming dent in my reserves.

But the amount of salt I'd used already made me worry about our stores. Between Loach and me, we'd only brought enough for a month. Who knew how long it would take to infiltrate the palace? I shook the tension out of my hands before smoothing my hair. *I can't worry about that now.* It was anyone's guess to where Jayvin had vanished. He couldn't leave the city, but he might have gone hunting on one of the out-skirting farms.

But why not wait until dark? I chewed my lip. *Can he hunt during the day?* Honestly, what did I know about Vampires and their Offspring? *But the pain in our binding.* I brushed the silver scars on my arm. *That can't be a coincidence*

The sweltering sun beat down on me as I wandered toward the docks. It was about three o'clock in the afternoon—early still. Despite, the streets were nearly empty. A salt breeze whipped through the narrow alley, tossing my dark waves over my shoulder and across my face. A bronze-skinned Human woman waved to me as I passed, her stunning features regal despite her homespun gown.

I waved back with a smile. *She has no idea.* It was jarring to spend so much time within my shifts, to become one race after another—a wolf in sheep's clothing. When I was young, the other girls in the cove made bets on who could come up with the most ridiculous disguises. I'd never won, but I was grateful now for the practice their silly games had given me.

The warehouses, shipping offices, blacksmiths, and carpenters' stores gave way to a rounded strip of tourist shops, encasing Carnage's small harbor like a pretty bow on a present. The cheap cement alleys of the warehouse district ended abruptly, replaced by bright orange and yellow bricks covering the wide street between the shops and the beach.

I craned my head back. The barrier was nearly invisible from deep within the city—another trick of the Emperor's magic, perhaps—but it shone in pulsating colors here beside the port. Now that I was close enough, I could see the shapes of wards dancing through the energy field, taunting me. A reminder that both Carnage and I were songbirds trapped within Sayzar's cage.

Salt on the wind called to me. *The beach.* The barrier could keep me out of the sea but couldn't stop me from touching the sand. Three Orc women watched me as I marched across the strip—each with curled horns protruding from their scalps. They chatted outside a quaint outdoor bar and sipped sweet, white wine—their expressions curious but cautious. I paid them no mind. I wasn't the enemy here, no matter what form I wore.

Praise God. I kicked off my sandals and shoved my feet into the cream-colored sand, burying my toes. The barrier had burned a harsh line into the shore just before the waterline. I sat down as close to the waves as I could without touching the shield, the weight in my heart growing heavy enough to drown me.

My body hurts. I winced as I laid back and stretched out, digging my fingers into the sand. The sun beating on my skin dried the dampness forming beneath my lashes.

I couldn't leave—and I didn't *want* to go—not truly. Not until I held Cyclone in my arms. Part of me started to like Carnage and all its odd people and spaces. It reminded me of the cove, of home.

I could see it . . . a little dream forming. One where I survived, where Sayzar's gold paid for a small shop by the beach to sell my trinkets. I'd scour the depths of the sea around Carnage and see what treasures it held. Maybe Jayvin would stay with me—

No, don't think of that. I inhaled a shuddering breath, refusing to let the tears fall. Right now, all I wanted was to *swim*. Every inch of my body craved the ocean, to be enveloped in the current's comforting weight, unable to fall. No tripping, no bumbling. I was graceful in the water. Beautiful, even. Mesmerizing.

I didn't feel beautiful here—I felt clumsy and fragile. Like a burden.

Stop it, Tetra. Thoughts like that didn't help anyone. My eyes fluttered closed, and I focused on the warmth on my cheeks and chest. On every grain of sand digging into my skin—

Something tickled my nose, and I jerked awake. *Sharks.*

The sun was beginning to set, painting smeary streaks of pink and purple across the horizon. As I blinked, a bright light blinded me.

"What the hell—" My head spun as I sat up too quickly—and an orangey light whizzed by my face. *Jayvin's light.* I rubbed the sleep out of my eyes and smiled. "It's you."

The faelight spun around me happily, leaving a trail of glowing sparks in the air. I held out my palm and it settled over it, bobbing gently. I leaned in close enough to feel it's heat against my face. "Do you know where our mutual friend has gone?"

The light floated from my hand, pausing as I stood and shook the sand out of my dress and hair, then it headed back toward the strip. I slipped on my sandals and followed it across the street. Most shops were closing—rolling down their blinds, bringing signs back inside, wiping down windows. How long had I been asleep?

After several blocks, the faelight stopped in front of a modest brown building with potted, pale blue hydrangeas out front, framing a swinging bench. A rectangular sign above it read: *Bookends.*

I raised a brow at the bobbing light. "He's . . . here? You're sure?"

It passed through the glass-paneled door, illuminating the gauzy white curtains behind it.

Here goes nothing. I tested the door handle. Unlocked. I pushed and it swung open. The signature scent of old, worn pages crashed into me, mixed with the lingering smell of leather and chewing tobacco. Six rows of shelves stretched the store from front to back, filled with tomes organized by shape and color. Tiny, purple signs protruded every few feet, labeling different genres.

It's perfect. I grinned. This was another of Carnage's precious treasures to add to my list.

"Can I help you?" To my left, a lean, red-haired Human watched me. He shoved his glasses up his crooked nose with a huff. "I was trying to close."

I swallowed. "Trying?"

He peered around me and pointed to an adjacent room on the right side of the shop, labeled: *Reading*. He sniffed again before hollering. "But it seems we have guests *that refuse to leave!*"

A familiar chuckle echoed back to us.

Jayvin.

The clerk waved irritably. "I can't lock up until he leaves. You might as well waste my time, too."

I gave the clerk a quick curtsy. "I won't be long."

The faelight danced around me before fading into the reading room. I followed. *Why did he come here, of all places?* I kept my steps light as I passed through the doorway into a small lounge. Sagging, well-used blue armchairs lined the wall against the window. A low-lit hearth cast shadows over the sheepskin rug in the center covering the hardwood.

Jayvin sat on the floor with his back to me. Stacks and stacks of books surrounded him—some left open, some dog-eared, others with their pages ripped out and folded into neat piles.

Thank God. A wave of relief made my knees buckle. *He's fine. He's fine.*

I carefully stepped around his mess of books. Jayvin held a thick, archaic tome open on his lap. He'd pulled up the hood and mask attached to his leathers, concealing all but his ruby eyes and the messy strands of white hair falling over them.

I folded my hands behind my back. "Jayvin?"

He didn't look up. Instead, he reached down to trace those circles on the rug. "Sunshine."

"This is real." I moved around the rug and sat down across from him, back to the hearth. "May I ask what you're reading?"

When he finally looked at me, Jayvin's eyes widened in shock. "Pardon?"

"You like to read?" I smiled as I lifted the book nearest to me, skimming through the pages. A written account of Carnage's trade dealings going back sixty years. *Exciting.* I read the cover of another—a historical recounting of the fall of Tyrr's last monarchy.

Jayvin's pupils dilated as he tightly wrapped a strand of my inky-black hair around his finger. I froze as he rasped, "Why are you different?"

"Oh." I'd forgotten he'd only seen me shift the once. I let it fall, and he blinked in surprise as I formed back into my Human disguise. "I can change any way I want to blend in with the Landfolk. Think of it as a form of protection."

"Hmm." Jayvin played with the strand for a moment before clearing his throat. He let the lock fall back against my shoulder and gestured to the books. "I-I was just catching up on the last century. A lot has happened during my time in the catacombs, it seems."

A century. I'd live that long if given the time—longer even.

Don't think of that now. I licked my cracked lips. My throat was so damn dry. I crossed my legs. "Have you learned anything interesting?"

Jayvin yanked down his mask, his full mouth spreading into a grim line. "I've learned plenty. More than I wanted."

I gave him an apologetic smile. "Welcome to the Ameliatus dynasty."

"Indeed." Jayvin let out a breathy laugh before closing the book on his lap and sliding it behind his back. "I see why you want him gone."

"What's that one?" I leaned over to get a better view of the book and gave him a wry smile. "Are you hiding it?"

"No." His entire body tensed. "It's nothing."

"Liar," I grinned, using the same gravelly tone he'd used on me. "Let me see." I reached around and snagged it out of his hand, skin buzzing at our proximity. The thick, blue tome made my wrist ache with its weight. With a nervous laugh, I read the title. "*Seafolk: Facts versus Legends.*"

Color bloomed high on Jayvin's cheekbones. "I know nothing about Merfolk. I hate not knowing."

"I can understand that." I let the pages fall open. They landed on a hand-drawn image of a full Kraken tearing apart a merchant ship. *Loach's ancestors?* "You could have asked. I'll happily tell you whatever you'd like to know." I flipped through a few more pages, pausing at an illustration of a Merman presenting a female with a blue pearl, her expression overflowing with happiness.

I grimaced and snapped the book shut.

Jayvin took it back with a scowl and opened to the same page. "Why does this bother you?"

"It's. . ." *You said you'd answer.* I released a long breath. "It just reminds me of my parents."

His eyes softened. "What happened to them?"

"The Emperor executed them when they refused to submit to his rule." It was surprising how easily the words came out. "I-I miss them. They didn't have any other children. It's just me left."

Jayvin traced the image of the Merfolk, pale brows furrowing. "What does this picture mean?"

"Merfolk marry for life," I said, letting my eyes linger on the pearl the male held. "We don't take unions lightly or copulate outside our race, like Elves and Humans often do. Gifts are traded as permanent reminders of our bonds."

As Jayvin sketched those circles into the carpet, a range of emotions passed over him. "How long were they married before they died?"

"Eighty years. We are also long-lived." I hesitated for a moment, then drew in a deep, determined breath. "Did . . . did something happen earlier today?"

He gave me a look as he picked at the rug. "Why do you ask?"

"*Our* binding." I raised my arm to show the scars. "When Agatha and I went out this afternoon . . . they started to burn."

Jayvin winced. "I apologize."

"If I can't say that, you can't."

"Touché." He almost smiled. "I . . . it was only—"

"May you two please leave?" The clerk called from the front room. "Some of us would like to go *home*."

Sharks. I stood and smoothed my skirts before offering Jayvin my hand. "Come with me?"

His brows scrunched, but he didn't move. "To where?"

"I don't know." I shrugged. "We can go back whenever we want. It's not like we have a curfew."

"*Want.*" Jayvin chewed on the word as he let me pull him up. "Such a dangerous feeling."

Indeed. I tried not to notice all the ways his leathers clung to him as Jayvin snatched his stack of ripped pages off the floor and shoved them into his pocket. He picked up a few more items off the nearest shelf: a leather notebook, some paper weights, and a slender, corked bottle. After tucking them into his coat, he held up a pen and rubbed his thumb over the tip. "Did you know these are much better than a quill? What a great invention."

"So, I've heard," I giggled, and he pocketed the pen. I wasn't about to make a fuss over some supplies when we were about to steal an entire treasury. As we made for the entrance, I caught the clerk's furious glare out of the corner of my eye and muttered, "Thank you."

He flipped us off.

Behind me, Jayvin's dark laugh rumbled up my spine and into my bones. He leaned in, his breath icy against my neck. "Should I remove him for his rudeness?"

I accidentally jerked the bookstore door open, making the glass rattle. I glanced over my shoulder. Jayvin watched the man's throat a little too intently. "No," I replied. "We're not going to *remove* him. He has every right to be angry."

Jayvin reached over my head to hold the door for me. "As you say." He snapped his teeth at clerk, whose skin drained white before he ducked below the counter. "But do let me know if you change your mind."

Jayvin closed the door behind us, as I ducked beneath his elbow. I ran my fingers over my braid and flashed a playful smile. "Is it common to terrorize innocent shop workers where you're from?"

"Where I'm from," Jayvin purred as he gently tapped my

nose. "His ugly head would have been freed from his shoulders for that disrespect."

My smile fell. "Why?"

Jayvin leaned against the doorframe. "Drones—as Loach is so fond of calling us—serve their queens. Protect them. Cherish them. A good servant does not allow another male to disrespect their queen in that manner."

"I see." I swallowed. The sun had fully set. The faelight floated through the shop window and danced around my face. I opened my palm, and it settled there. "It showed me where you were earlier."

Jayvin stared up at the night sky and stars, red eyes as bright as fresh blood. When he snapped, the faelight disappeared, leaving a soft glow beneath Jayvin's skin. "It seems to have done that more than once."

My thoughts ran wild as I wandered toward the beach. "You mean like it did in the catacombs?"

Jayvin nodded and shoved his large hands into his pockets as he followed me down the main strip. "Yes, like in the catacombs."

"Don't you control it?"

"I create it. It does what it wants after that—" Jayvin stopped as his gaze snagged on the ocean beyond the barrier.

And three times, it's led me to you. I thought, and a leaden weight fell on my heart as I followed his gaze out over the sea. Sharks, my joints ached. I needed it. If only I could touch it, even for a moment...

"You're sad again."

I looked up, and Jayvin's expression was terrified—prey in the sites of a predator—like it had been before. His movements were calculated and precise as he took a step back. "Why are you sad?"

I stammered. "I'm... I miss the water, is all. Promise."

His tension didn't lessen as he scanned the beach, settling on a small patch of palm trees outside the barrier's limits. "Do you want to go out there? Would that make you happy?"

"Of course, I do." I was mesmerized by how the rising moon glinted off his silvery-white hair. "But we can't—"

I didn't get to finish my sentence. Jayvin swept me into his arms, and we faded into the night.

Chapter Eighteen

Smoke and shadows clouded my vision as we moved *over* the ground instead of on it. I screamed as I clung to Jayvin's shoulder. In whatever layer of the world he'd brought us, solid objects had become blurry forms of mist—and we were headed straight for the warbling edge of the barrier.

It's going to fry us alive. Turn us into dust. I scrunched my eyes shut, but the pain never came—only a tingling sensation crawled over my skin as we *passed* through it.

Jayvin's grip on me tightened as we lurched to a stop, slamming the weight of space and gravity back onto my body. "Put me down!" I flailed so hard that he dropped me, and I fell onto all fours. *Sharks.* I gripped my stomach and dry heaved. The world was spinning.

Jayvin knelt beside me with an apologetic smile, peering under me to see my face. "Are you alright, Sunshine?"

"I think so." I dug my fingers into the sand. "Please, warn me next time."

Wait... sand.

My gaze shot up.

Only feet away, soft, sparkling waves rippled over the shore. Fringed palm trees swayed above, lulled by the salt breeze. I sat back as my throat tightened. We were out over a narrow sand bank between Carnage and the sea—the city's personal lagoon. Even in the moonlight, the waters were a striking azure blue.

This is where I belonged—like a bird soaring on the wind—and I wanted the ocean so badly, it hurt. *He did this for me. He got me out.* I let my head fall back and sucked in a shuddering breath as a relieved tear escaped my lashes.

"I hoped you'd be happy," Jayvin whispered. I shifted to face him, and sadness riddled those ruby eyes. "Should I take you back?"

"No, no." I wiped my damp cheek and choked out a laugh. "I *am* happy. These are good tears."

Still crouched, Jayvin cocked his head, tense. "Good tears. Please. Thank you. Asking if I'm well. You say so many words that I'd forgotten existed."

I hate her. Whoever his creator was, she deserved a stake through the heart.

Jayvin leaned back warily as I stood, as if he'd detected the shift in my mood.

"Thank you," I said and meant it. "The ocean is to me what I imagine blood is to you."

"I understand," Jayvin nodded as he got to his feet. He gazed over the waves again, brows furrowed. "Then why did you leave it? The Merfolk must have soldiers to fight. Why you, Sunshine?"

"No one volunteered." I shook out my hair as I let my shift fall, the fins on my legs and forearms scraping against the inside of my dress. "I didn't have much of a choice. It's either take Cyclone back or die in the Emperor's army." A thought struck me, and I wheeled on him. "Wait, you can breach the barrier?"

Jayvin dug a hole in the sand with the toe of his boot, a puppy caught chewing on a slipper. "Yes."

My chest tightened. "You could have left the first night you were freed?"

"Yes."

"Then, why did you stay?"

"I considered it . . . leaving." Jayvin's shoulders slumped as he crossed his arms tightly over his chest, eyes fixed on the ground. "I sat on at the barrier's edge for hours, trying to bring myself to do it. I couldn't." He pushed back his sleeve and studied the silver scars on his arm. "Bond or no, it felt like an awful way to repay my debts. I'd still be locked away if it wasn't for you."

He could have left. I couldn't look at him. If I did, I'd cry. With a nod, I stepped forward and let the waves crash over my toes. *Boot was wrong.* Jayvin made a choice. Maybe Offspring weren't as wrapped in their masters as previously thought. That, or Jayvin was a little different—just like me.

Home. That sensation flooded my blood as the salt soaked into my skin. *Come home.* I remembered what Agatha had said . . . that breaking the conditions of the bond meant death. His pretty talk of repaying debts and gratitude could be just that— talk. A young, foolish corner of my heart didn't want to believe that the bond was the only reason he'd remained.

Minutes of silence passed. It could have been hours. It didn't matter. I was free. He was with me. Seaweed tickled my feet as it washed ashore. In this moment, all was well.

Jayvin rocked from heel to heel. "Say something, before I lose my mind completely."

With a low laugh, I glanced over my shoulder and smiled. "Do you swim, Jayvin Dyre?"

His blinked in surprise. "Not in a lifetime."

"Well, unless you plan on sitting alone, I suggest you join me." I pulled my dress over my head and tossed it onto the sand, glad I'd worn the ridiculous Lankfolk undergarments Agatha had found for me.

Jayvin's eyes filled with desire as he took in my every tanned inch and curve. The look didn't frighten me the way it had when coming from Sayzar or the Mermen back home.

Jayvin looked at me like I was something precious—a treasure to be cherished, not just to be used and thrown away.

He held my gaze as he stripped down to his slim-fitting underwear and tossed his clothes beside mine. I scanned over him. *God, he's beautiful.* A grin spread across his face as he melted into the shadows. I gasped as he materialized behind me, releasing a husky laugh as he traced a circle between my shoulder blades. "Tell me this is real, Sunshine."

I arched into the touch. "This is real."

"Good." Jayvin kissed my neck then threw me into the ocean.

I let out a high-pitched shriek as I flew through the air, landing with a splash as the waves enveloped me. From the heat of the day, the warmth of the seas shifted my coloring to an icy blue. My parched throat and the aching in my joints faded as my body returned to life. *Home, home, home.*

Jayvin dove until we were at the same level. He swam well for a Landfolk, though he struggled to stay upright beneath the waves' pull. I grinned back, hair floating around me in a cloud, and hooked my fins together. In a powerful roll of my body, I surged into the depths. The rush of water created by my tail sent him spiraling backward. He released a stream of bubbles, laughing wildly as he kicked his way to the surface.

I savored the currents ripping against me, the weightless thrill of knowing there wasn't anywhere I couldn't go. The sea belonged to me, and I belonged to it. When I glanced back, Jayvin had dived down again, watching me.

The lagoon wasn't deep enough to hurt a Landfolk. Too deep and their ears would pop. I could show him a little of my world.

Jayvin's eyes widened as I sped forward and grabbed his wrist. He allowed me to pull him down to the seabed and gripped my arm as he studied the schools of bright, tropical fish dashing past. With a wide smile, he pointed out a jagged outcropping, his expression lit with childish wonder.

I pointed to the surface and mouthed, "*Do you need air?*"

Jayvin shook his head and swam towards the rocks. Hundreds of thousands of oysters had it glittering like the night sky. Crabs as wide as dinner plates scurried out of the way as I tugged him deeper. I showed him starfish tucked into gaps in the rocks. Clownfish hiding in their anemones. We chased down a barracuda, and it nearly snapped off his finger.

Hours passed before I finally forced him to swim back to shore.

"How can you stay under so long?" I sprawled on the beach and fanned out my hair to dry. "Other Landfolk would have drowned."

Jayvin sat beside me, his lips curling into a crooked half-smile. "My kind can only be killed by our makers, fire, or beheading. I can't drown, as uncomfortable as it is not to breathe."

My mouth fell open. "You just decided not to breathe?"

"And it was worth it."

"What about dismemberment?" I blurted.

Jayvin rose a brow in question.

"If you get your legs cut off . . ." I motioned toward my thighs. "Do you have to lay around like a stump for eternity?"

Jayvin threw his head back, howling in laughter, before he

said, "I'm sure I could learn to waddle." He wiped his eyes before plucking a tiny, pink clam shell out of my hair. He beamed. "Is this yours?"

"You keep it, I insist." I rolled my eyes, enjoying the moisture beading on my bare limbs and torso. "It's a gift, and one of the sea's most precious treasures, you know."

"Hmm." Jayvin huffed as he closed the shell in his palm. "Gift. Another word I'd forgotten."

What did she do to you? I'd known him for such a short time, but I wanted to know everything. Every hurt, every hope—every day of the centuries he'd been alive.

Vampires were known to be tempters, but I supposed mermaids were, too. Our kinds came from the same ancestors, and at one time, mine had hunted men just like his—but instead of fangs and strength, we'd used sweet words and promised pleasure. What did it hurt for fire to play with fire?

Jayvin shifted, and I caught him watching me from the corner of my eye. I rolled onto my stomach. "What is it?"

He quickly glanced away. "Nothing important."

"Well, you have to tell me now. It will drive me crazy if you don't."

"I can't have that," Jayvin said before shooting me another nervous look, his hands wringing in his lap. "In the book I read about the Merfolk," he hesitated, "it said that Merwomen can manipulate minds with magic. Is that true?"

"Oh." My eyes widened. "Yes, but it's not so complex as what Elves are capable of. The manipulation is purely primal."

Jayvin stiffened. "How?"

My cheeks heated as I sat up. "We can sense the wants of others and embody that. We can't force anyone to do anything—only try to persuade them. The effect is only temporary."

He visibly relaxed and shifted to face me, his ruby eyes bright with curiosity as he said, "I see. Try it on me."

"What?" My face was on fire now. "Why?"

"I need to know."

"I'm terrible at it. It would be an awful demonstration."

"I doubt you're terrible at anything." Jayvin smiled mischievously. "Do it."

Lord, save me. I folded my arms, forcing myself to hold his expectant gaze as I took the clamshell back from him and set it between us. I sucked in a deep breath. "I'm going to try and make you pick that up."

He nodded.

A pang of guilt shot through me as the taste of strawberries coated my tongue. My allure brushed against his mind, and I found it waiting. Where I used to be met with disjointed thoughts and impulsive desires, Jayvin's mind was still—coiled up like a serpent ready to strike.

I shouldn't be here. He could kill me. I'd get lost in the deadly silence of his consciousness and never find my way out. As I tried to pull away, a little of that darkness parted, a gentle invitation.

He won't hurt me. And as foolish as it was, I knew it was true. I allowed myself to peer through, to feel what he'd allow me, and was met with pain—pain, pain, pain, fear, and the slightest glimmer of hope.

I grabbed onto that, and instead of secret hungers, I felt the chill of a pink and gold sunrise on a frosted morning, a moonlit walk across the meadow, a blazing fire in a small, quiet room.

But why would a Vampire want such things? They were supposed to be beasts of chaos and death—craving violence—but maybe that's why those thoughts were tucked away so deep. To what he'd become, they were traitorous wants, indeed.

As I left his mind, I became that—became peace, gentleness, and contentment. I was a warm blanket on a cold, autumn night and cobwebs dripping with dew. I smiled and gestured to the shell. "Will you give that to me?"

Jayvin's eyes glazed over, his expression softening pleasantly as his fingers twitched toward the shell. As they hovered over it, his brows furrowed, and he lightly shook his head before grinning at me. "Not good enough."

I let my allure fall and huffed. "I told you I was terrible."

"I wouldn't say that." He picked up the clamshell and gripped it tightly. "That was... interesting."

Yes, it was. I flopped back onto the sand, exhausted. "Truths for truths?"

"Truth?" Jayvin chuckled darkly as he dusted the sand off his legs. "Another one for the list. But you may have a truth, Sunshine."

"Who is she?" *Please, tell me.* "Your creator?"

Jayvin's entire body jerked as if someone struck him. He curled up and rocked as he traced circles in the sand. Minutes passed, and for a moment, I thought he wouldn't answer until he whispered, "Marceline is the Matriarch. She is law."

Marceline. I imbedded the name into my memory. "Law to who?"

"All of her children." Jayvin rested his head against his knees. "She commands, we obey. Our bodies follow her orders whether we want them to or not. We belong to her."

Oh. *Oh.* No wonder he'd asked about the allure.

Slave, drone, spawn. All I'd known until this last year was freedom. I couldn't imagine that level of servitude to anyone. "Did... was she the one that imprisoned you?"

He nodded.

"Why?"

He let out a long, slow breath. "I didn't obey."

I hate her. I hate her. The Emperor didn't seem so different from this Matriarch. *Maybe that's why he didn't leave Carnage—*

perhaps she can't cross the barrier like he can. But if that were true, he'd risked everything by bringing me out here.

"Thank you." I had a thousand more questions but didn't want to push him too far. I sat up and leaned back on my elbows. "Your turn."

Jayvin smirked. More circles. "Drones don't ask questions."

"You do now. This is real, and she's not here." I kept my voice cheerful. "Ask, and I shall answer. Anything."

In the span of a breath, terror, defiance, sorrow, and finally, something like embarrassment passed over Jayvin's beautiful features. "Are you my friend, Tetra?"

I sidled over until I could rest my head on his shoulder. He tensed for only a breath before relaxing into the touch. "Yes, I'm your friend, Jayvin Dyre."

His voice broke on the last words. "Even when she comes for me?"

I didn't enjoy death or the consequences—but if his Matriarch had been here, I'd be willing to die trying to sever her head from her hideous shoulders. "Will she come? Do you think she knows you are free?"

"Yes, she knows. She always knows."

I looped my arm through his. "I am your friend, Jayvin, even when she comes. Especially then."

Ever so slowly, he rested his cheek against my hair and sighed. "Thank you."

I let my eyes close, savoring the closeness of him. *What do I do now?* Agatha needed the barrier down to save her family. Jayvin needed it up to protect himself. No matter what I did, someone was going to get hurt.

Sharks. I sat up as a thought struck me. "Do you still have that bottle, pen, and paper?"

Jayvin nodded to where his jacket lay in the sand. "Yes, why?"

I grinned up at him. "Up for one more swim?"

The sun had long risen by the time we headed back toward The Lux. Tucked into my shadow, Jayvin listened to me chatter as I walked—about the treasures I'd found over the years and all the places I wished to travel.

Every word engrossed him—like he truly cared.

Even better was when he told me about the lands he'd visited across the decades, about the kingdoms he'd helped rise and fall.

What did it say about me that I had to gain the audience of a male that had been trapped in a tomb for over a century to be found interesting?

I decided I didn't care.

My eyes *burned* from lack of sleep as I wandered back into the warehouse district, Jayvin's weight heavy on my shoulders. I yawned, rubbing my eyes, as I rounded a corner and nearly collided with Agatha.

"*Hills alive.*" Instead of her usual bodysuit, she wore a simple violet blouse and dark trousers, her sleek black hair disheveled. She shook me by the shoulders. "Where have you been?" She paused and grimaced. "And why are you wet?"

"I . . . we . . ." I ran my fingers through my damp hair. "Swimming."

"How?" Agatha rubbed her face then dropped her toned arms to her sides. "Never mind. Where's Jayvin? Did you find him?"

Jayvin formed into a dark mist, barely corporeal, beside me.

He smiled and gave her a cheeky wave before disappearing back into my shadow.

I smiled. "Yes, I found him."

"You scared me." Agatha looped her elbow through mine and led me into an alley to our right. The stink of ammonia and feces gave way to a broader, open street. "I woke up from my nap, and Jack and Ass told me you were gone." She shook her head again. "Damned idiots."

Jayvin laughed softly against my ear. *"Tell her I get the joke."*

I snorted, and Agatha shot me a look. "Jayvin thought your joke was funny."

"I'm flattered." Agatha peered behind me and then down to my feet. "Where . . . where does he go when he does that?"

A weight lifted off me as Jayvin's dark form shifted from me to Agatha. She shrieked, trying to claw him off, and then he leaped back to me.

"Don't—" Agatha's entire body shivered. "—*ever* do that again."

Jayvin's cackle was audible.

I covered my mouth to hide my grin, then cleared my throat. "What are Boot and Loach doing now?"

"How do you deal with that?" Agatha brushed her arms and shoulders with an *ack*. "Oh, and *they* are doing what they usually do—making plans and pretending they're the real money makers here." She nudged my elbow. "It shouldn't be long now. A few more kinks to work out, then Cyclone is practically yours."

A knot formed in my stomach. "And if it all goes wrong?"

"Then we figure it out," she replied, stepping before me protectively as the crowds grew denser. "It's going to work out."

I gave her a grateful smile, but it did little to lessen my worries.

The shops and offices had propped open their doors and turned their signs to *open*. This district seemed colorless and void after the brilliance of the inner court. There were no vivid flowers and banners—just bare steel and tar-stained wood.

Ahead, Agatha's strides were long and sure, the exhaustion in my limbs making it hard to keep pace.

"Sunshine?"

I jumped a mile, clapping a hand over my chest. I'd been lost in thought. "Yes?"

Within my shadow, I could feel the warmth of his breath against my neck. *"I think I remembered something last night . . . from before."*

"What?" A thrill shot through me, and I squeaked, "When?"

Agatha glanced back at me, brow raised, and I waved her off and mouthed, *"Not you."*

She rolled her eyes and turned back to the road.

"In the bookstore," Jayvin replied, *"when you sat down, and your hair was black."* There was a pause. *"I thought I was looking at someone else—a woman that maybe I'd known once."*

That leaden feeling returned to my gut. "A lover?"

"No, I don't think so," he mused, *"she felt like family."*

"Incredible," I murmured, keeping step behind Agatha. "Was that the first time a memory has come back?"

I could almost feel his inhale. *"There was only one other time . . . when I bit you—which I apologize for—I saw a red barn beside an old, white house."*

I chewed on the inside of my cheek. "What do you think that means?"

"Your guess is as good as mine. I don't know why this is happening now, after all these years."

I had to know. "How old are you, exactly?"

Another hesitant pause. *"Since I turned, I've lived two-*

hundred and forty-one years."

"Lord." *He's spent more than half of his life in the catacombs.* "And there were never memories before now?"

"No."

"Tetra!" The sharpness of Agatha's voice snapped me back to attention—just as I walked face-first into The Lux's front door.

Jayvin caught me before I hit the ground and pulled us through the doorway. He cried out as the sun shone on his face and neck, blistering his skin. He cursed as he pressed me into his chest. Once in the shade, the burn faded in seconds, his skin returning to a flawless dove grey. "Hell." He gave his head a quick shake. "I forgot how badly that hurts."

It struck me how badly I wanted to brush my fingers along his jaw.

"Damn." Agatha brushed past him into the living room. She raised a brow at him and smirked. "I know the sun will kill full Vampires, but what about you? If you get too irksome, will you turn to dust if I push you outside?"

"No," Jayvin snapped at her as he gently set me down. "I'd just be very, *very* unhappy."

"Interesting." She plopped onto the sofa and kicked off her boots. "I'll remember that."

I moved over and leaned against the countertop. "How about we *don't* kill each other?"

"If you say so," Jayvin drawled as he began to dig through the cupboards, tossing cleaning supplies and dish rags over his shoulder. "I'm starving."

"*Bastard!*" Loach came thundering down the stairs. "Stay out of my cheese!"

Too late.

Jayvin leaped over him, cackling, and sprinted up the staircase with a huge chunk of cheddar in his mouth. Loach cursed as he tore after him.

Agatha flipped open a newspaper. "Idiots."

I couldn't stop laughing.

Boot came down minutes later, scratching his head. "I see you located our muscle."

"I did." I wiped a stray tear out of my eye as I caught my breath. "Where's Ivan?"

"Buying groceries . . . again." Boot shuffled over to the counter and poured himself, Agatha, and me a cup of coffee. "We can't keep enough food in this house."

There was a crash on the floor above, followed by angry growling and curses.

"And Cyclone?" I pursed my lips to keep from smiling. "When will we be ready to break into the palace?"

"Soon, soon." Boot waved as he sipped from his mug. "I'm as eager to destroy the Emperor as you are, girl. Have patience. Everything must be perfect."

Agatha gave me an I-told-you-so look as I sank onto the sofa beside her, passing her a mug. *Fine.* I took a drink of my own, listening to the chaos upstairs as I leaned against her shoulder. *What will a few more days hurt?*

I could wait.

Chapter Nineteen

And the next several days *were* long.

The number of Enforcers on patrol doubled after the supposed attack on their headquarters and the destruction of Boot's jewelry store. That part of our plan may have backfired. When Agatha and I—Jayvin guarding from my shadow—scoped out the palace, we found the inner court locked tight. The gates were closed—only special permissions allowed entrance.

Not only were the Enforcers on edge from the explosions, but word had spread about a breach in the catacombs—mythical killer Jayvin Dyre was loose in Carnage. The searches happened day and night as they investigated private residences and businesses with determined scrutiny.

Boot assured us not to worry. There was always a way, and at least the Enforcers weren't searching for *us*. They hadn't reached The Lux yet, but Loach ensured they'd find nothing of the weapons and armor we now carried or our plans.

They'd never find Jayvin. Not with abilities like his. It made me wonder how those monster hunters ever managed to track down and kill his kind.

This morning, I had slept late, at least until the curtains were yanked back, spilling blinding sunshine into my face. Agatha laughed as I groaned and rolled onto my stomach, burying my head into my pillows.

"Wakey, wakey, Hun." She stripped off my blankets. Goosebumps covered me as the morning chill latched onto my bare skin. "Move your round ass. We've got work to do today."

"Like what?" I curled up into a ball to fight off the chill. "Listen to Boot complain about the price of black powder?"

"He does like to whine, doesn't he?" Agatha snorted and flopped beside me, pulling the blankets over us. "No, but he does have another job for us. He needs—"

We froze as a sharp knock rapped on the front door below—then it opened with a loud squeak. *The Enforcers found us.* I couldn't breathe. We'd been so close. Now they'd tear us apart, and this mission would be over before it started. Why did they open the damn door?

"Agatha?" Jayvin's raspy voice echoed up the stairs. I'd never heard him call her by her name before. "There's a tiny Orc here looking for you."

"What the hell?" Agatha leaped out of my bed and flew down the stairs. I slid on the clean, white blouse and tan breeches I'd laid out and ran after her.

"*Put him down!*" Agatha screeched as I rounded the stairwell into the living room. "What's wrong with you? Put him down!"

Jayvin held a young Orcling upside down by his foot. The poor boy's forest green skin drained of color as he stared horrified into Jayvin's curious, red gaze.

"Fine." Jayvin's lips curled at the edges as he lowered the boy to the ground. "Ruin all of the fun."

With a whimper, the Orcling—maybe nine or ten—scrambled into Agatha's arms. "*Auntie.*"

"Auntie?" I didn't have time to shift. It didn't matter anyway. The boy had already seen me. "Is this one of your nephews?"

"This is Nash." Agatha stroked the boy's dark hair as the blood returned to his cheeks. She knelt and gave him a stern look. "And he's going to tell me what he's doing out here *alone.*"

"Dad sent me." Nash wiped building tears from his round, hazel eyes. "It's the Enforcers."

Geralt. He'd been so kind and fed me when I stumbled upon his restaurant. If anything happened to him, it would be because of me. I hadn't noticed Jayvin was beside me until his elbow brushed into mine. I didn't move away. Neither did he.

Agatha looked like she was going to be sick. "What do you mean the Enforcers?"

"There's a whole pack of them at the restaurant," Nash continued and stood. "They're looking for you."

I clapped my hands over my mouth. *No, no, no, no.*

Agatha glanced back at me, her expression as terrified as I felt.

"You're fluttering." I jumped as Jayvin stroked my forearm, finger catching on the ridge of the fin beneath my sleeve. "They will not hurt either of you, Sunshine. Not while I breathe."

Agatha turned back to her nephew. "Did he say what they wanted?"

"No." Nash shook his head. "Just to find you."

Loach and Boot had joined us in the living room by this time. Loach ran a hand over his oily, white head before sliding on his hat and scowling. "How did the kid know where to find you, Paine?"

Agatha glared at him as she stood and wrapped her arm

around Nash's shoulder. "I told you before—this hotel was a family investment." Without another word, she scooped her holster off the counter and strapped it on—checking the knives on her sides—before sliding on her long, leather coat. "Let's go."

"Go?" Loach growled as he stepped toward her. Dare I say he looked worried. "What if they're here to gut you? You'd be serving yourself up for slaughter."

"I'll take care of it." Agatha shot back. "I'm not leaving my brother to deal with them alone."

"I'll go with you." Jayvin ran his tongue over his sharp teeth. "A lady shouldn't have to sweat. Besides that, I'm hungry."

"You can't go outside." Agatha gestured to the sun shining through the kitchen window. She shuddered. "Besides that, I'm not carrying you."

"Then I'll go, too." I stepped toward her and Nash. "Jayvin can hide with me."

Agatha glanced between us, hesitant, then nodded. Nash watched us, frightened.

"I'm coming, as well." Boot hobbled to the table and picked up his pack. "The Enforcers know me, and I have leverage on more than a few of them." He jerked a sharpened thumbnail at Jayvin. "It may not come to this one's savagery."

"I think you're all insane—" Loach blew out a long breath. "But I can't stop you. I'll stay here and guard the weapons. This might be the Enforcer's way of getting us out before they raid."

I hadn't thought of that.

Agatha took Nash's hand and jerked her chin toward the three of us joining her. "Get what you need. We're leaving."

Less than fifteen minutes later, we stepped out of The Lux. Jayvin shifted into my shadow as we moved onto the street.

Hand in Agatha's, Nash blinked once, twice. "Where did he go?"

I grinned down at him, and as Jayvin's lips brushed against my neck, I said, "Didn't you know Vampires are made of the dark? He could be anywhere."

Nash glanced down at his own shadow and swallowed. "Anywhere?"

"Anywhere," I repeated, and Jayvin chuckled for only me to hear.

"Don't listen to her." Agatha tugged her nephew closer, but a smile tugged at her lips. "That brute hitchhikes like a parasite."

Jayvin huffed. *"Tell her she's the tapeworm."*

"I'm not calling her a tapeworm." I snapped back.

Agatha flipped me off—well, Jayvin off.

Nash paled again. "Should I be scared?"

"Of course not." Agatha patted his shoulder. "The Vampire knows he could never beat me without all his vanishing tricks."

Boot tsked. "Idiots, all of you."

Jayvin bristled from within my shadow, but before he could respond, I let out a nervous laugh. "So, Nash, are you the youngest of your siblings?"

"No." He clung to Agatha's side as we stepped out of the warehouse district. "I'm number four out of six."

"Ah," I said, voice softening. "I never had brothers or sisters. It must be wonderful to have the company."

Nash and Jayvin snorted in unison.

"I, too, have many siblings." Boot mused, folding his gnarled hands behind his back as we walked. "It's not unheard of for Goblin women to have thirty or more children in their lifetimes."

"Lord almighty." Agatha shook her head. "Your poor mother."

"On the contrary," Boot replied. "She was quite happy. The more of us there were, the less work she had to do. A fair trade, in my opinion."

The street widened as we grew closer to the market, the chunky cobblestone transitioning into a smooth, grey pavement. Geralt's restaurant laid on the northern end of it, facing the Lantern Palace.

"Would you return to your tribe?" I asked Agatha as my mind wandered. Out of all of our late-night conversations, somehow, we never discussed that. "Would you go home with your brother, I mean?"

"We're leaving?" Nash's voice rose an octave, colored by a hint of panic. "Dad never said—"

"Tetra is just thinking out loud." Agatha shot me a glare. I clamped my mouth shut. "She didn't mean it."

So, Geralt hadn't told them. If we succeeded in breaking the barrier, he and his children would head back to the mountains. *He must not want to worry them. Maybe they don't know how bad it's gotten.* Isn't that what parents were supposed to do? Protect their children? My stomach sank as I gave Nash an apologetic smile. "Sorry, she's right. I was just curious."

I jumped as a loud, metallic crash came from our right—from a shoddily built hut crammed between two, abandoned store fronts. Tears streamed down a young woman's cheeks as she tried to brush clumps of gooey porridge off her blue, plaid skirts, the pot that held the hot oats on its side by her feet.

A slender, blond man stepped out of their home, his furious gaze locked onto his spilled breakfast. I grabbed her by the collar and slammed her against their hut and raised his hand. "You—"

Jayvin's weight left my shoulders.

"No!" I reached for him as his incorporeal figure darted from the shadows cast by the eaves of nearby rooftops.

Before the blow could land, the woman let out a low shriek as the man's legs were sucked back into the hut. He clawed at the doorway, mouth gaping, as his nails left red stripes on the molding. The woman ran in after him.

I remembered Jayvin's earlier words. *His ugly head would have been freed from his shoulders for that disrespect.* Instinctually, I reached out and grabbed Agatha's elbow, free hand at my throat. "Sharks."

"That bloke's going to die, isn't he?" Agatha asked.

I gave a quick nod.

Agatha swore, glancing between Boot and her nephew. She pointed at the later. "Stay with the Goblin, I'll be right back."

As we sprinted for the hut, the woman's ear-shattering screams poured from the opened windows. "Jayvin, don't—" My shoulder collided with the doorframe as I skidded into the hut, Agatha at my heels.

Too late. The man's legs were bent in unnatural angles. Jayvin had him pinned to the wall, feet suspended from the ground, as he proceeded to snap the man's index finger . . . then his thumb. With Jayvin's hand over his mouth, smothering his screams, only the sobs shaking the man's chest gave away his agony.

The woman watched, expression teetering on fascination as the bones in another finger cracked.

Agatha stopped short. "Hills alive."

Jayvin's vicious, ruby gaze snapped to her, lips curling back over his teeth. "*Leave.*"

"Jayvin, listen." His eyes shifted to me as I took a single step closer, hands raised. "She can tell the guards. He'll get sent to prison. Times have changed, you don't have to kill him."

"Why not?" Jayvin growled, his eyes nearly black. "Let me feed upon him and remove his stain from the earth."

"You can't eat people, either." Agatha's hands hovered over her daggers. After a brief hesitation, she turned to the woman, brows raised. "Unless, of course, you want him to?"

The woman's cheeks flushed pink, her distant gaze returning to Jayvin. "You . . . you're the one that escaped the catacombs?"

"Escaped?" Agatha let out a sharp laugh. "More like *rescued* from."

A wicked rumble escaped Jayvin's throat and I smacked Agatha's arm. Sweat dripped down my sides. *Someone is going to hear us.* "Yes, and we'd appreciate it if you'd not tell anyone we were here."

The man's lips were blue, his eyes bulging from their sockets. Jayvin's attention was fixed on the woman. "Do you want him gone?"

Slowly, oh, so slowly, she nodded.

Jayvin flashed her a fanged smile before sinking his teeth into the man's throat. As the man let out a strangled cry, it didn't take long for his frightened stare to glaze over. His body crumbled, withering like a dead flower as Jayvin drank the last ounces of life from his veins.

And the woman watched, her expression blanketed in awe.

When Jayvin released him, breathing heavily as blood stained his lips, the man's body fell to the floor in a fleshy heap.

Agatha looked like she might vomit.

"They made me marry him, my mother and father." The woman's eyes never left her husband's corpse. "They couldn't afford to feed me anymore, they said."

Jayvin stalked toward me—not angrily, almost nervous—

as he wiped the blood from his mouth. His gaze fell to the floor as he reached my elbow. "Sunshine, I—"

I reached out and brushed my fingers over his cheek. "You don't need to apologize."

Jayvin's eyes grew wide, but he didn't pull away.

"Well, I'll apologize. Sorry about that." Agatha knelt beside the woman, pulling several gold pieces from her coin purse, and shoving them into her palm. "Promise you won't go back to your folks, alright?"

The woman nodded again as she clasped the gold against her chest.

Agatha's eyes brightened. "Actually, we changed our minds." She pointed at Jayvin. "Go tell everyone what *he* did. Loudly."

I stiffened. "Ag, you can't—"

Agatha grinned at me. "It would be a shame if the Enforcers left my brother's shop to investigate a Vampire attack, wouldn't it?"

Brilliant. I grinned back. "Yes, it would be."

The back door of Geralt's restaurant swung open before we could knock. Sweat dripped down his bark-brown skin, staining the neck of his thick, burgundy tunic. "Sister."

He wrapped Agatha in a tight hug, then knelt and scanned over Nash. He sighed in relief as he cupped his son's chin. "No troubles?"

"None," Nash said, then paused, glancing back at me. "Except for him."

Geralt's eyes flickered at me, and then he slowly smiled. "She's a *she*, kid. And a lovely one at that."

As I blushed, Jayvin formed in the shadow of the doorway, towering over Geralt despite the Orc male's bulky frame, and smiled wide enough to show his teeth. "He meant *me*."

Geralt hit the corner of the door as he leaped back and cursed. "Is that—"

"Yes, he's who you think he is." Agatha threw up her hands. "And, yes, he's with us. Calm down and be quiet."

"Hills alive, Ag." Geralt ran a hand through his dark hair before his gaze fell to Boot. He blinked. "And who are you?"

"The mastermind of this operation." Boot pushed past him and scanned the restaurant's back room. "Where are the Enforcers?"

"Waiting out on the patio." Geralt ushered us inside. Panic tightened his features as he turned to his sister. "They started banging on my door hours ago, looking for you. They won't tell me what this is about and refuse to leave."

We entered behind him into what looked like a giant pantry. Rows and rows of shelves lined the walls, stacked with bags of flour, cans, pots, and cooking utensils. To the left sat a small desk meant for sharpening knives.

Jayvin paused in the doorway, expression fixed in frustration. "May I come in?"

I paused and blinked. *I forgot about that.*

"Yes?" Geralt scratched his chin, eyeing him nervously. "Please, come in."

Jayvin smiled slightly before slinking inside to stand by my elbow.

"It's probably just another contract." Agatha tucked her hair behind her ears and pulled her coat tightly around her to conceal her knives. "Nothing to worry about."

"*Orc?*" An Elvish male voice echoed through the restaurant. "*Report.*"

Geralt winced. "I can only stall them so long."

"I'll talk to them." Agatha hopped from one foot to the other and blew a sharp breath. "I won't be long."

"How about I speak to them?" Boot pushed his glasses higher on the bridge of his squashed nose. "They've yet to inform me who's responsible for destroying my shop, you know."

"What about us?" I held my throat. Jayvin stepped closer to my side, keen on every movement I made. "What if they come back here?"

"Just stay." Agatha wrenched open the door separating the back from the dining room. "Wait for me."

"*Ah.*" A velvety soft voice—so full of arrogance—crooned. "It seems I'm not the only one you like to keep waiting."

My heart nearly stopped. Between the door's cracks, I made out a sheet of pin-straight, burning red hair and glowing, ivory skin. A long, lean Elf propped himself against the bar and folded his thin fingers onto the counter. The Emperor noted every ounce of fear rippling through Agatha's lithe body. "I have a job for you, Miss Paine."

Chapter Twenty

Agatha's knee cracked sharply against the tiled floor as she knelt, head bowed. "Hail, Sayzar."

Jayvin yanked me out of the way, our backs pressed to the wall. I held my breath.

The Emperor ordered in a bored tone, "Rise."

Agatha's boots scraped as she stood, a slight quiver hidden by the firmness of her voice. "I did not expect to see you here . . . personally. I would have dressed better, Your Majesty."

"Damn it." Boot shut the door between the restaurant and pantry. He wheeled on Geralt, jerking a thumb at me and Jayvin. "If he catches them, we're done."

"Here." Geralt moved to the edge of the room and lifted a dusty, patched rug off the floor. Beneath laid a trapdoor. He raised the hatch and gestured for us to climb through. "I use this for my valuables. Get in."

Jayvin went as still as death, his chest rising and falling in quick stutters.

I scoffed. "Again, what's with Carnage and hidden basements?"

"I can ward it for silence." Boot pushed me forward. "As long as you don't act stupid, he'll never know you're there."

I broke out in chills, Agatha and the Emperor's conversation a steady rumble on the other side of the wall.

"How did you know where to find me?"

"There's little I don't see within the walls of my city, Miss Paine. Especially those at my beck and call."

"Then you've already discovered the culprit behind the attack on the Enforcer headquarters?"

There was a pause. "*Bold of you to assume I'd answer, or even entertain, such questioning from staff.*"

"*I'm not staff.*"

"*Aren't you?*"

Give us time, Agatha. Jayvin grabbed my wrist as I moved toward the hatch, his ruby eyes wide with horror. "Please," he muttered, gaze shifting to the hole in the floor. "I can't—"

"You can blend in Boot's shadow?" I swallowed, hating the fear I saw in him. "I can go in alone."

"No," Boot cut in. "Do you think Sayzar Ameliatus became Emperor by being fooled by his own kind's magic? Wards are detected differently. I can protect you with them." He pointed at Jayvin, then to the floor, before hissing at me. "We don't have time for this. Both of you get in now, or you'll never get your king back, girl."

A tremor rolled down Jayvin's body, a bead of sweat breaking above his brow, but he nodded and obeyed. I dropped down, and my feet hit compact soil, the only light in the small stone chamber leaking through the gaps in the floor above. A second soft *thud* sounded beside me as Jayvin followed.

A scape and the dragging of fabric told me Geralt had replaced the carpet over the trap door. Boot murmured a few words, and a rush of violet energy rippled over the hatch. I startled as the Emperor began to speak again. He sounded as if he was only inches away. "I grow bored of this. Shall I get to the point?"

Whatever ward Boot had used not only silenced us but amplified their conversation.

Jayvin curled up beside me, arms wrapped around his knees, and began to rock.

I jumped as Agatha spoke, "As much as I've loved our small talk, Your Majesty, I couldn't agree more."

The Emperor's laugh was soft—too soft. "You're an insolent thing, aren't you?"

"Just direct," Agatha shot back, then hesitated. "What's the job?"

Pressed close, the trembling that had begun in Jayvin's limbs shook my own. "Are you angry with me?"

Chair legs squeaked against the tile above—the Emperor standing. "I need you to locate someone for me . . . with haste."

My heart plummeted. *He's looking for me.* Slowly, Jayvin's words caught up with me, and I turned and frowned. "Angry? Why would I be angry with you?"

Jayvin's trembling had turned into full-on tremors. "I killed him after you told me no." His breaths were coming too fast. "*She'd* get so angry when I didn't listen."

Above, the Emperor continued. "Your beautiful friend . . . Jessa." He said the name I'd given him like it was a delicacy. "Bring her to me."

"I don't know a Jessa," Agatha replied.

"Don't lie, Miss Paine, it's not polite." I could hear the smile in the Emperor's voice. "I recognized you in the market from the descriptions my guards have given me. You were escorting her."

Agatha's tone rose a pitch. "Fine. What do you want with her?"

"Only to speak, to make her an offer. She promised me a visit, after all."

Stupid. A projection ring wasn't worth being in debt to Sayzar Ameliatus. *And Boot didn't need the ring.* Maybe I'd been wrong about violence—I was going to let Agatha kill them both.

"*Tetra.*"

My blood turned to ice as I glanced over my shoulder.

Jayvin ground his teeth as he pressed his forehead to his knees. "*Tetra.*"

No, no, no, no. I scooted closer, touching his arm. "I'm here. What's happening?"

Barely a whisper, his voice was terror incarnate as he spoke in time with his rocking. "*He. Locked. Us. In.*"

He'd been locked away again . . . below ground. Just like he'd been in the catacombs.

"It's okay." I swallowed past my dry throat and gripped his elbow. It wasn't okay. "They'll let us out when the Emperor leaves. You'll see."

"I can't go," Jayvin moaned as his rocking became faster. "Not unless he says so. They're going to leave me. *They're going to leave.*"

"You're getting out of here." My voice cracked. "It's fine. We're fine. I promise."

"*No.*" Jayvin clenched his eyes shut and smashed his palms against his temples. "They'll leave. *You'll leave.*" He let out a shuddering gasp, clawing bloody trails down his cheeks with his fingernails. "*She left.*"

His creator. The Matriarch. She left him in a tomb to rot, and now he thought I'd do the same. "Jayvin." I wiped away some of the blood on his face with my sleeve. The deep gouges had already healed into faded lines. "Jayvin, listen to me. I'm not going to leave you here."

He shook his head violently. *"She left."* He lurched backward—hard—and a loud crack rumbled through the building as his spine hit the foundation. *"She left."*

Boot had said that Offspring had no loyalty but to their creators. If she didn't want him, what did he have left? I knew what it was like to be alone, for no one to care if you lived or died.

Throat tight, I did the only thing I could think of—what my mother always had done for me. I grabbed him and pressed his face into my neck, rocking with him as I wrapped my arms around his shoulders, matching his rhythm. His cold sweat chilled my skin, but I squeezed tighter. The sound he made in response was half a sob, half a moan.

"Shh, shh, shh." He shuddered again as I ran my fingers through his wild, silky locks. Footsteps creaked above us. "You are my friend. I won't leave you."

He gripped my thighs—tight—and I realized he was tracing those circles on me with his thumb.

"This is real," I muttered into his hair. "I see you."

Jayvin inhaled sharply, held it, and then slowly blew out the breath.

"Yes, good." I smiled, stroking his damp cheek. "In through the nose, out through the mouth."

Above, the door between the restaurant's main lobby and the backroom swung open, creaking as it scraped against the room above us.

"Ah." The Emperor's voice lowered to a purr. "Now, is it you causing such a stir?"

Sharks. He must have felt the vibrations when Jayvin hit the wall.

"I told you," Agatha exhaled. "It's nothing to worry about."

"Nothing to worry about?" Boot's taloned toes made a scratching sound as he walked. "I think I'm plenty to worry about." There was a pause. Maybe he bowed. "What a pleasure to finally meet our most glorious ruler. Hail, Sayzar."

"A Goblin hiding in an Orc's pantry?" The Emperor chuckled darkly. "How typical. Even in Carnage, your kind leaches off the backs of their betters to survive. You should be scrubbing my stairs, cave-scum."

Bastard. I grit my teeth. That was the first time I'd heard him say anything less than courteous. *But that's because he'd been talking to me. He thinks I'm an Elf.* His kind—not one of the creatures that served his meals and cleaned his damned sheets.

Jayvin pressed his face harder against my neck, continuing to breathe, breathe, breathe.

I squeezed him tighter.

"How astute of you to see the hardships of my people." I'd never know how Boot managed to keep his tone so even. "But I wouldn't have had to set up shop here if your men could do their jobs. Two attacks in one day." Boot tsked. "That's sloppy work from your Enforcers, Your Majesty. I would be making staff changes."

"Quite." The Emperor's words came out as a bite. "Yours must have been the store that was destroyed?"

"Again," Boot replied. "Another brilliant observation."

"You'll forgive my friend's *rudeness.*" Agatha chimed in. "You know how Goblins can be."

Where's Geralt? Perhaps he went out to keep the Enforcers distracted.

Jayvin's body finally began to relax, melting against mine in a limp exhaustion I knew all too well. When my mother used to hold me, I'd often fall asleep in her arms after the waves of terror and panic had passed.

As the conversation continued above, I leaned back to see Jayvin's face, my fingers knotted into his hair. He'd already been watching me, his eyes so tired as they slowly scanned my face. My stomach tightened as his gaze lowered to my mouth and stayed there, visually tracing the curves of my lips, unabashed, as a flicker of desire joined the weariness.

I may have stopped breathing—and all the reasons I knew it was wrong didn't stop me from leaning in and barely brushing my lips against his, the cool bite of his skin a shock against the heat of mine.

Jayvin's every muscle went taut.

"I'm sorry." I jolted back. "I didn't ask, I shouldn't have—"

I gasped as Jayvin straddled me, pressing my back against the wall as he held my face in his hands. A hint of mania threaded through the smile that exposed his canines. "I told you not to say that."

"Oh, sorry—again." Nerves had me fumbling with the hem of his shirt. My fingers brushed against the hard planes of his torso. It took everything I had not to let them trail lower. I broke out into giggles. "Bold of you to tell me what to do."

Jayvin pushed closer, eyes dilated, as he pressed gentle kisses along my jaw. I shivered. "And what *should* I do, Sunshine? What do you want?"

What do I want? Now, *my* breaths were coming too fast. I gripped his waistband, unsure what else to do with my hands. "I . . . I want you to do what you want for once."

"Thank God." Those beautiful, cold lips crashed into mine as his thumbs brushed against my cheeks, sending a ripple of heat down my spine.

It had been so long since I'd been touched, and even then, I hadn't enjoyed it. It had been an expectation—a transaction in exchange for companionship and the barest of comforts. Something I'd done to survive.

This was different.

I *wanted* this.

I kissed him back, and he sighed as his fingers curled

tightly into my hair. He tugged my head back, and I exhaled as he brushed his mouth over the space between my throat and jaw. He let out a breathy laugh as his teeth scraped against my jugular. "You're fluttering again," he said.

"Yes." I held back a moan as he bit down, not hard enough to break the skin, but enough to drive me insane. If I had to beg him to draw blood, I would—

"I expect her by tomorrow, Miss Paine." The restaurant door slammed shut.

Damn it. My blood went cold.

That's right—the Emperor was here, or was, and he was looking for *me*.

Jayvin pulled me into a sitting position, smoothed my hair over my shoulder, and faster than a heartbeat, he moved to the other side of the cellar.

"He's gone." Agatha's heavy footsteps approached the trap door. "It's safe."

Jayvin gave me a sheepish smile and pressed his finger over his lips.

My body was molten. Forget Boot. Agatha was dead to me now, too.

The hatch swung open, and she peered inside, gaze flickering over the sheen of sweat on Jayvin's skin and the guilty look I imagined I wore. "What the hell happened—" Her eyes widened, and she shook her head in disgust. "I'm sorry, Jayvin. Boot's an ass. The Emperor and his goonies are gone now. You can come out."

Across the chamber, Jayvin made a noise—his eyes filled with panic—as Agatha offered to pull me up. I shifted and grinned at him, reaching out to take his hand. "You heard her. Come on."

His returning smile was the sun glinting on gold. His limbs trembled as he climbed out behind me. Above ground, Jayvin took a shallow breath, sweat breaking on his brow. He wobbled, and I rushed forward and put an arm around his waist to steady him. "You're free." I squeezed him as hard as I could manage. "You're here, not there. This is real."

He pressed his face into my hair and breathed, breathed, breathed.

"We don't have time for this, drone." Boot sat at the worn desk across the room, scratching deep gouges into the wood with his sharp nails. The door between the dining and pantry remained open. There were no signs of Sayzar or his Enforcers. "Be grateful the Enforcers were drawn away when they were, and the Emperor wasn't in a worse mood. Something about a Vampire attack not far from here."

"And should I lock you up in the palace?" I snapped, and Boot's orange eyes narrowed. He knew what it was like to live in a cage. He, out of anyone, should understand. "Would you like to be enslaved again and serve the Emperor his meals?" When he didn't answer, I continued. "No? I didn't think so. How about you keep your mouth shut and have some decency."

Boot grinned, revealing jagged teeth. "Nice to see you growing some claws, girl."

"*Sunshine,*" Jayvin muttered as he twisted my braid around his fingers. I leaned into his touch—just as Geralt burst through the backdoor and locked it behind him.

He scanned over his sister, breathing heavily. "You're okay?"

"Fine." Agatha smoothed back her hair and exhaled. "But we're in a world of trouble."

This is all my fault. I backed a step, heart sinking, only to bump into Jayvin's chest. He gripped my shoulders and brushed his nose along the point of my ear—almost predatory —as he traced a finger down my spine.

He's going to kill me. One way, or another. I suppressed a shiver and focused on Agatha as I said, "He wants Jessa?"

She nodded, quickly noting Jayvin's hand lingering on my back. "Yes . . . tomorrow, at a bistro in the inner court. He didn't give me any leverage on the time."

"Did he say what he wanted?"

"No." Her lips pursed. "But even his best intentions can't be good."

Geralt sat across from Boot and rubbed his temples. "The Emperor is throwing a ball at the palace in the coming weeks. A celebration of his complete control of the Tyrr coast." He scratched the dark stubble on his bark-brown chin. "Maybe he means to invite you."

"He hasn't taken control of Tyrr yet," I added. "That's a little presumptuous, isn't it?"

"A ball?" Boot straightened and adjusted his glasses. "I haven't heard any news of such a thing."

"It's private," Geralt replied. "Inner court only. I only know because I was one of the chefs asked to cater." A smug smile spread on his face. "Apparently his men have grown fond of my fried tilapia."

That explained the banners and flowered arches. He *was* preparing for a party.

Boot jumped down and began to pace, hands folded behind his back. "If that's true . . . this could work to our advantage."

In any world, I couldn't see how the Emperor pursuing me could be a *good* thing. I crossed my arms. "How?"

Boot's gaze shot to Jayvin, to his proximity to me. "Because if the Offspring is attached to your shadow when you're invited . . ."

Of course. My jaw dropped. "Then Jayvin is invited, as well."

"And we have our strongest player securely inside the ring," Agatha said. "Tetra can keep the Emperor distracted while Jayvin gets the rest of us in through the sewers and takes the treasury. This is the break we needed."

It could work. If I could play my part and get the Emperor to invite me to the ball, we could really make this happen, and soon. Cyclone could go home.

"Tomorrow?" I glanced between them—my crew. "We get this invitation, and the palace is ours?"

"It sounds like we've got some shopping to do." Agatha smiled wide as she rubbed her gloved hands together in excitement. "The Emperor isn't going to seduce himself."

Chapter Twenty-One

"I look ridiculous." I tugged at the puffed sleeves of my gauzy, new gown. "Sayzar will take one look and throw me onto the street."

"No, he won't. Quit fussing." Agatha smacked my hand down. "You look great. Exactly what the Emperor will expect—luscious, sweet, and maybe a tiny bit promiscuous."

After an entire evening picking through high-end boutiques and tailors, Agatha found the perfect dress.

At least, in her opinion.

I hated it.

The crimson bodice hugged me tightly from the waist up, exposing my sides, as the neckline fell low below my breasts, almost to my navel. The skirts were loose and airy, but unfortunately, so were the sleeves. Cut out across the shoulders, they fell in puffy waves until they bunched into cuffs at my wrists.

As the sun began to go down on another day, I was about to have dinner with Sayzar Ameliatus.

"If you say so." This fabric felt like barnacles scraping against my skin. "I look like a prostitute."

"Like I said," Agatha winked. "Exactly what the Emperor wants."

"The dress is rather silly," Jayvin whispered in amusement from my shadow. *"But you are lovely, Sunshine."*

I brushed a strand of golden blonde hair behind my pointed ear. I was Jessa now and couldn't let the act slip, even for a moment. I whispered back, "Thank you."

His weight leaning on me was comforting as Agatha and I walked towards the inner court. Sayzar had given her the address of the upscale restaurant where he planned for us to meet, just outside the Lantern Palace.

Instinct had me bringing my bag with me, along with my few remaining trinkets. If Sayzar expected a collector, I'd give him one. I twisted the amethyst projection ring on my thumb—a little piece of him on me, an illusion of my admiration. If I could pretend for that long.

"Ugh." Trying to shake the anxiety out of my fingers, I whispered to Jayvin. "Talk to me. Distract me."

He fidgeted in my shadow. *"What . . . what do you want to hear?"*

"I don't know—*sharks.*" I tripped over my own foot and nearly hit the pavement. Agatha laughed. As I straightened, I blew out a frustrated breath and continued, "Let's see . . . What do you like to do?"

"What do I like to do?" he repeated.

"You must have hobbies," I pondered. "Or *had* hobbies before . . . you know."

"The Matriarch didn't allow such indulgences."

"Humor me?"

"Hmm." It took several minutes for him to respond. *"I like . . . games."*

"Games?" Well, that was a start. Agatha rolled her eyes at me. I waved her off. "What kind?"

His voice perked up. *"In the catacombs, I used to see how many skulls I could pull out of the walls before they all fell. Then I'd stack them again. It kept me busy."*

"That sounds . . ." I chewed my lip. "That sounds awful, to be honest. We'll have to find you some better games to play."

Jayvin chuckled. *"Indeed."*

"Tetra." Agatha turned and nudged my elbow. "We're here."

Two guards were posted outside the gate to the inner court. Before they could lower their spears, Agatha waved a slip of paper stamped with the Emperor's seal in their face—our day pass.

"Enjoy your stay," they said in unison and bowed. We brushed by them with little more than a nod and spent the rest of the walk in silence. In only days, the decorations covering the inner court had tripled. In addition to the flowers, banners, and streamers, there were now jugglers, stage acts throwing swords in the air, clowns, and droves of attendees to cheer them on. Giant jungle cats sat dejected in iron cages. Overexcited dogs barked, nipping at children's heels.

A grand, marble stature—in the Emperor's likeness—was raised over the fountain in the courtyard's center. Fresh and polished, crows and starlings perched along its outstretched arms, bits of sticks and fluff sticking out over his stone crown where they'd begun to build their nests.

"Lord above." Jayvin's breath ticked the hollow of my neck. *"And I thought Mother was vain."*

"Mother?" I replied, fingers finding the rose-gold and pink pearl pendant hanging between my breasts. "You mean the Matriarch?"

"Yes," he sighed, *"but she prefers her power plays to be less . . .*

artful? Once, she nailed the heads of an entire village along the walls of her bathing room and let them rot until they were nothing but skulls."

"Yuck." I ignored Agatha's annoyed glances. "I'm... that's horrifying."

"It wasn't the worst she'd done." I felt him shrug. *"But I'll never forget the smell. It made a terrible mess—I think we're here."*

I glanced up just as Agatha looped her arm through mine. No less than twenty Enforcers stood guard outside a quaint, oak-paneled bistro with a covered patio. They blocked the view within, and they drew their weapons as we approached. Within my shadow, Jayvin let out a low, rumbling growl.

"I'm here on order of the Emperor." Agatha raised the sealed note. "Let us pass, you blockheads."

The nearest Enforcer snatched the paper, luminous skin reddening as he read over the letter. Reluctantly, he stepped to the side, and the others did the same. He lowered into a quick bow. "Proceed."

Agatha scrunched her face as he stepped aside. "Thank you ever so much."

The Enforcer scowled. "His Majesty expects you within."

"You're going to get us killed," I whispered to her as we passed through the arched front doors. "Tormenting them like that."

"If that's how I go," she grinned and patted my elbow, "it would have been worth it."

The bistro's interior was extravagant. I'd never seen anything like it. Not only was the furniture in the dining room made of Elven Blackwood—only found in one forest in the world—but the crystal glassware was so pristine that it scattered bits of rainbow over the equally polished glass walls and ceiling.

They must have been expecting us. As soon as we entered, the hostess—a shorter, black-haired Elf in a pressed suit—directed us toward the outdoor patio.

"Hills alive." Agatha whistled as she scanned the indoor dining area, ribbons of multi-colored light reflecting off her emerald skin. "Do you think they're compensating for something?"

Within my shadow, Jayvin snorted. *"Tell her that was funny."*

I smirked. "Jayvin said that was funny."

"At least someone appreciates my humor." Arm and arm, we stepped out onto the patio. Agatha's jaw dropped in awe. "Never mind. They're *definitely* compensating."

My heart stuttered as I took in the massive willow tree sprouting out the center of the yard, shading the entire courtyard. Pastel yellow and blue faelights wove through the branches, dancing and bobbing to the soft violin music playing from somewhere amongst the leaves—more Elven magic. All the tables were that same stunning blackwood, twisted and curved into elaborate designs, same as the dining chairs.

The Emperor sat at a two-person table beneath the willow, twirling a butter knife between his thin fingers. His striking red hair fell in flawless satin sheets around his face, smoother than the finest silk.

"I can't do this," I whispered to Agatha. "Damn it, Ag, I'm going to puke."

"Get it together." She leaned in and muttered under her breath. "It's do or die now, Hun. There's no going back."

Jayvin growled, loud enough for Agatha to hear. *"I'm not going to let Sunshine die."*

"Nobody asked you, brute."

"Shut up, both of you." I plastered on a fake smile as Sayzar cocked his chin towards us. "Or I'll puke on you on purpose."

He stood as we approached. "And here I thought you'd be late, Miss Paine."

Agatha fell to one knee. "Hail, Sayzar."

I knelt beside her and swallowed back the bile rising in my throat. The Emperor gestured for us to rise. "I appreciate the courtesies, but they aren't necessary here." Sayzar's vivid, blue eyes were locked onto me as I rose, scanning over my gown, over the strips where my now glowing, porcelain skin was exposed. When he smiled, it looked almost genuine. "It's so good to see you again, Lady Jessa."

Agatha quickly kissed my cheek. "I'll be right outside."

I was so thankful Jayvin was with me, especially as the Emperor took my hand and led me to the table, pulling out a chair for me—a perfect gentleman.

I tucked my skirts beneath me as I sat. He took a seat across from me. This time, his gaze flickered to the ring on my thumb, and the corners of his lips curled upwards. "I'm glad to see you wearing my ring. It looks better on you than me, I'm afraid."

With the faelights dancing above, my shadow was long and well-defined behind me—plenty of room for Jayvin to move. Despite the space, he whispered, *"Do women really enjoy all this peacocking? If so, I'm more out of touch than I thought."*

I ignored him and gave Sayzar a wide, sweet smile. "Don't lie, Your Majesty. You have to say that."

Sayzar chuckled and leaned back, crossing his long legs. "I missed that wit. I'm so glad Miss Paine brought you my invitation."

"An invitation?" My golden brow rose. I wasn't sure where my sudden boldness was coming from. Probably stress. "I felt more like a demand to me."

A handsome, well-dressed waiter filled our crystal glasses with sparkling white wine. Sayzar smirked before taking a sip. "I never meant to seem forward."

"Yes, you did."

That genuine smile returned, his teeth perfectly straight. "You see straight through me, don't you?"

"I'm good at reading people." *That's a fat lie.* Sweat dripped down my side as I raised my glass to my lips. "Especially when they're interesting."

"I can't smell any poison," Jayvin murmured against my ear. *"It's safe."*

"This place is stunning." I took a sip of wine, the bubbles biting against my tongue. *Pretend he didn't kill them. Pretend you didn't kneel.* "It's a work of art."

"If only you could see inside the palace." Sayzar leaned forward, steepling his long fingers. "It makes this establishment look like a back-alley slum."

Remember why you're here. We need that invitation. I brushed my blonde waves over my shoulder and mimicked his movements. "And why did you *invite* me here, Your Majesty? Surely not for my wit."

"Just Sayzar," he corrected, swirling the contents of his glass. "You promised me another meeting, did you not?"

"I did."

"I tend to be impatient." Sayzar shook his head and took another sip. "To the dismay of my advisors."

"You don't take me as one that needs advisors."

"I've been known not to listen to them as often as I should."

"So, I've heard." I cocked my head as I dropped my hands onto the table. *Remember why you're here.* "Either way, I'm glad to see you again, too, *Sayzar.*"

The Emperor's eyes flickered to my breasts before returning to my face. His attention then turned to the bag slung over my shoulder. "And what did you bring, Lady Jessa?"

"Just Jessa." He tensed as I reached inside. I grinned. "Don't worry, I don't have any weapons, I promise."

"*You should*," Jayvin grumbled. "*I can tell you at least six places I'd like to stab this preening bastard.*"

I was going to kick him if we survived this.

Inside my bag, my fingers brushed over the red, sea-glass bracelet I'd bought from the Imp family, and I paused. *No, I can't give him that.* My once expansive collection had dwindled to a few select items. Just the thought of sharing this treasure with *him* made me want to throw up. *Remember what he did. He has to believe I'm on his side.*

"I brought you a gift." I latched onto a golden coin and set it on the table between us.

Sayzar's brows furrowed as he cocked his head. I couldn't tell if he was disappointed or confused.

"This." I turned it over so he could see the face printed on the opposite side—the image of a bearded Merman in an opulent crown. *I'm sorry. I'm sorry.* "Is from the first set of coins ever stamped with the head of the Merking, Cyclone."

Sayzar's eyes widened as he lifted the coin to inspect it.

I hate myself. I want to die. I'll get it back. I sat back and smiled. "Your victory over the Merfolk has changed this from modern currency to a historical relic, tripling its value. You have the appreciation of collectors everywhere."

That same waiter returned with plates of fluffy, green salads. As he set them in front of us, Sayzar began to laugh—genuinely laugh—as he turned the coin over in his fingers. "Jessa, you truly are special, aren't you?"

"Depends on who you ask." I took a bite of my salad to give myself time to think. How was I supposed to get through an entire dinner like this, let alone get an invitation into the palace?

As I chewed, Sayzar reached out and stroked the back of my

hand, tracing circles over the outside of my wrist. "Did you know that I'll be hosting a ball at the palace in one week?"

"He's checking for illusion wards," Jayvin warned.

"Oh?" My chest tightened. *Thank God my shift isn't a ward.* "Well, that explains the festivities outside."

Sayzar's lips curled again, and he kissed the palm of my hand as his fingers trailed higher on my arm. "I'd hoped they'd impress you."

I could sense—let alone see—the ripple in the darkness behind me. Jayvin snarled, the sound rumbling down my back into my core. My skin flushed as I stomped on my shadow.

Jayvin yelped and swore.

"Are you alright?" Sayzar leaned over, scowling as he nodded to my feet.

"Just a rock in my shoes." I kicked off my sandals, tucking a foot beneath me while I brushed his calf with the other. *Just kill me. It would be less humiliating.* I grinned. "Much better."

He must have thought the blush was for him because he smiled. "I invited you here to ask if you'd be at my side during the ball. It would be my greatest honor."

"Would it be?" My heart was racing now. I braced my elbows against the table, giving him a full view of the swell of my full breasts over my low neckline. "And what is the occasion for such an extravagant event, may I ask?"

Mischief filled Jayvin's voice. *"That wasn't nice, Sunshine."*

Sayzar ran his fingers through my golden waves. A tremor ran through me that had nothing to do with lust. His heated gaze finally rose to my lips. "Something that I've been planning for quite some time."

My brow rose as I sipped my wine.

Sayzar's smile grew wicked. "My complete dominion of the Tyrr coast."

Geralt had said as much.

"Bold." I circled the rim of my glass. "I thought the Merfolk on the far side of the sea have yet to submit?"

That's why he drafted us in the first place—to fight a war against our own kind. There were only a few rebelling outlying colonies left. If Sayzar crushed them and Surge didn't stand up and fight, no one would be left to threaten the Emperor's reign.

Sayzar glanced up from where he stroked the inside of my elbow, his eyes ablaze.

This was the Emperor—this look. Hate, bitterness, rage, and years and years of poisoned ambition stared back at me. "Tell me you accept my invitation."

"Breathe, Sunshine."

I faked a smile. "I accept."

"I'm so glad to hear it." Just like that, the malice disappeared from his features. Sayzar picked at his salad. "Because I want you to be there when I achieve complete control. When the entirety of the Tyrr sea submits to my rule."

"Breathe, Sunshine, breathe."

I swallowed, forcing a hint of awe in my voice, taking his free hand. "Tell me how."

Sayzar speared a piece of red lettuce. "My Enforcers may suspect otherwise, but I know those loyal to Cyclone must be behind these attacks on *my* city. They've tested my patience too long, and I tire of Surge's games." His lips curled into an arrogant, satisfied smile. "So, I am going to put the Merfolk under his rule to the sword—each and everyone."

Chapter Twenty-Two

"Sunshine? Tetra, breathe!"

My elbow slid off the table as my vision went black. Invisible hands slipped beneath my arms and caught me before my face collided with the table. *"Tetra, breath!"*

"Jessa?" The Emperor grabbed my shoulder, expression more annoyed than concerned. "Are you well?"

He's going to kill us all. There would be nothing to go home to but bones. I sucked in a shuddering breath, my head spinning as the darkness receded. My throat was suffocatingly tight, my eyes burning with the beginnings of tears. *I have to keep it together. Just a little longer.*

"I'm fine." I hid behind my cloth napkin, inhaling again. "I-I just haven't eaten enough today. I apologize."

"Say it." The sorrow in Jayvin's voice almost sent me spiraling again. *"Say the word and he's dead."*

Sayzar knelt beside me and slowly lowered my hand, smiling as he stroked my cheek. "You should have said so. I would have called the main course first." He signaled to the waiter, who swooped back into the restaurant, presumably for our food.

My entire body shook as Sayzar returned to his seat, brows still pinched in concern. "I apologize." He reached across the table for my hand. "I should have kept war talk far from the dinner table."

Would Jayvin really kill for me? I fought to keep my expression pleasant. *I can't believe I'm even thinking that.*

Yes, I could. How much easier would it be if the Emperor died here and now? I wouldn't make it out alive with all the Enforcers present, but at least my people would be safe.

What about Agatha? Jayvin? I can't do that to them.

"You have nothing to apologize for." I took a sip of my wine, tempted to drain the glass. "One should always feel free to speak of their passions."

"I agree." Sayzar stroked the inside of my wrist again. "With Tyrr under my dominion, imagine the possibilities. Carnage could become the new capital city. It would be filled with life, music, and art. Open to all willing to live within the parameters of peace."

Peace? I watched him as the waiter laid out heaping plates of blackened salmon, fish eggs, and whipped potatoes swimming in butter. My mouth began to salivate at the rich smell. *God, the fish looks so good.* I needed the salt. Shifting like this always made such a drain on my reserves. Taking that first forkful felt traitorous, but I was hungry.

Pepper, lemon, and blessed salt danced over my tongue. I sighed, reclining my head, allowing myself to savor the flavor.

Jayvin's faint growls brought me back to attention.

Sayzar watched me, mouth slightly parted, as his gaze traced my neck and collarbones. I set down my fork. *I'm going to need a bath.* "It's wonderful, thank you."

Sayzar's grip on my wrist tightened painfully, his breaths

quickening. "Carnage will see you at my side, Jessa. They will assume we are more than just friends."

"They will." The salmon almost came back up. *My entire people, put to the sword.* It hurt to smile. "Let them talk."

"I don't wish it to be simply *talk*," Sayzar sighed. "When you are with me, I want you to be mine."

Now, I was going to vomit. I covered his hand with mine, making my skin crawl. "But we've only just met."

"I know what I want when I see it." The gleam in the Emperor's gaze made my blood turn. "And so do you. Be mine. Say you will."

My eyes burned with repressed tears, but I gave him my most seductive smile. *This is all my fault.* "I will."

Sayzar's answering smile was the same one I saw in my nightmares. "Good."

After dinner, he asked me to dance with him.

The rest of the evening was a blur of colors, rich flavors, and the disgust of his skin touching mine. Whether minutes or hours passed, it didn't matter. I'd never be able to rid myself of the feeling of *him*.

"*I did this,*" I sobbed as I stumbled into The Lux in the early morning hours—Jayvin and Agatha behind me. I just wanted my bed. To wash Sayzar's perfumed scent off my body and clothes. To get the sensation of his fingers off my skin.

I can't breathe. I dropped to the floor and pressed my forehead against the cold stone, gripping my scalp as I wept. "He's going to kill them because of *me*."

Loach's gruff voice entered the living room. He stopped abruptly at the sight of me. "What the hell happened?"

"The Emperor happened," Agatha shot back. "He's going to commit genocide on the Merfolk."

"Lord above," Loach whispered back. The sofa whined as he slumped into it. He took off his hat and rested it on his lap, dazed. "How much time do we have?"

"*No.*" As a fresh wave of sobs escaped me, Jayvin swept me into his arms and cradled me against his chest. I didn't fight it. I pressed into him to hide my pathetic tears.

Yes . . . Jayvin could touch every place Sayzar had—my arms, my waist, the insides of my thighs, and chase away his filth. I buried my face into Jayvin's chest, greedily inhaling the scent of leather, blood, and ice.

"Were we exposed?" Boot asked anxiously as he entered. "Wha—"

"Quiet," Jayvin hissed at him before nodding to Agatha. "Tell them once she's gone."

"Of course," she replied, but Jayvin had already turned for the staircase. The narrow stairs creaked under his weight. His thumbs traced comforting circles in my back as I clung to him, my body shifting into full-blown tremors that made my teeth clack together.

"*Shh,*" Jayvin murmured into my hair. "We'll save them, Sunshine."

"How?" The words could barely escape my strangled throat. "They're all going to die, and there's nothing I can do to stop it."

"Isn't there?" Jayvin stepped into my bedroom and closed the door behind use. "You won't quit fighting. Neither will I. Not until the breath has left your lungs." He pulled back the blankets and lowered me into my bed, kneeling beside it as he tugged them back over my shoulders.

Maybe it was the stress of it all, but I giggled. "That doesn't count. You don't have to breathe."

Jayvin's laugh was so pure and musical as he stroked my hair. He snapped, and his faelight came to life. "I think you're stronger than you give yourself credit for."

I wanted to kiss him again, to take away all his fears and pain, to let him chase away mine. A tear finally broke through my defenses and fell into my pillow.

Before I could wipe my eyes, Jayvin brushed it away, tilting his head as he studied the moisture on his fingertip. His lips pursed and he dropped his hand back onto the mattress. "In the bookstore, when you asked me what happened to cause our bind to burn . . . I'd woken in my room, and the windows were covered." He swallowed. "I forgot where I was and thought I was back in the catacombs. I panicked and ran like a damned coward."

All that pain . . . that had been his terror.

Jayvin rolled back the sleeve of his leathers, exposing the silver scars on his arm—our bind. "I felt you today . . . when the Emperor told you his plans. It hurt. I should have killed him when I had the chance. Forgive me."

And Jayvin would have. For me.

"I see you," I whispered and traced the scars. "And you see me."

He stroked the hollow of my throat. "I do."

He understood—if no one else did—what it was like for fear to take control. When the panic made it impossible to string two words together. The overwhelming shame when others realized you weren't normal. He knew.

"I do see you, Sunshine." Jayvin rested his chin on his folded hands. "I hate the dark. It terrifies me, and I'm doomed to it for however many centuries I have left to live." His lips quirked up. "There—my pity party for the evening."

My chest tightened into an unbearable ache. "I'm sorry."

His brow rose mischievously.

Grinning, I made to swat him, then paused, squeezing his hand instead. "I'm sorry you've lived so long trapped in the dark."

He squeezed back. "I'm sorry about your people."

His faelight bobbed around us, casting an orange glow over the walls and his dove grey skin. Without it, my bedroom would be pitch black—no different from the catacombs. I licked my dry lips. Holding that shift for so long had drained the salt from me. "Are you afraid now?"

He smiled sweetly. "Yes. Always."

"Me, too." *Screw it.* I didn't want to be alone. I scooted over and pulled back the blankets. "Stay with me?"

Jayvin's ruby eyes widened.

"Not like that," I added, my cheeks heating. *God, I sound so stupid.* "Just sleeping."

A thousand emotions passed over his face before smiled and gently tapped my nose. "One moment, please."

As he left the bedroom, Agatha, Boot, and Loach's hushed voices echoed up the stairs. Would they leave me now that this wasn't just about Cyclone? That there was more than a treasury at stake? Gold would never be worth their lives, neither was winning a war. I should have realized that from the start. I had nothing else to offer them.

Minutes later, Jayvin returned in a simple sweater and loose cotton pants. I didn't have much time to admire him before he climbed into bed beside me. He snapped, and his faelight disappeared into his skin.

As I pulled up the blankets, he hesitantly pressed his face into my neck, inhaling deeply. I rested my head against his, wrapping my arms around him. "Do you want to sleep now?" I felt him smile against my throat. "Or do you want to talk about your rocks? That makes you happy."

"Agates and jasper are gemstones, not rocks." I feigned offense as I ran my fingers through his snow-white hair. "It's a common misconception."

"I'm sure it is." Cautiously, he wove his arms around my waist and shifted closer, drawing those circles on my lower back as he let out a long, shaky breath.

"This is real." I sighed and rested my head on top of his. "I promise."

He nodded tightly in response but relaxed all the same. We laid like that for several minutes as I hummed a tune my mother used to sing me, tracing the curved arches of his ears, the line of his jaw, and his perfect, straight nose.

I felt safe. He made me feel safe, both inside and out. I wasn't sure if I should tell him that, but at that moment, having him here made me happier than all the rocks and treasures I'd ever owned.

"Sunshine?" Jayvin's voice was hoarse.

"Yes?" I trailed my finger down his throat.

He hesitated. "I . . . thank you."

I opened my mouth to respond, but he was already fast asleep, curled against me, his breaths soft and, for the first time, calm.

Chapter Twenty-Three

I woke alone.

The blankets on the side where he had slept were still warm. He hadn't been gone long. Rubbing my eyes, I sat up, my muscles stiff and sore from the tension of yesterday, but I had slept better than I had in years. *I'm going to put them to the sword. Each and every one.* A shiver ran through me as I climbed out of bed, still wearing that revealing red gown. Outside the window, the sky clung to the last indigo veils of night.

As I exited onto the roof, I kept my steps light, not wanting to wake the others. Just as I expected, Jayvin was there—still in his night clothes, his pale skin aglow with the pink and orange glimmers that accompanied dawn hovering just below the horizon. So still, he could have been a statue—a flawless work of marble and patience. With the softness of his expression, he looked to be a guardian—not a monster. Beautiful, not frightening.

His faelight noticed me before he did, whizzing around my face in greeting. Jayvin glanced over and gave me a crooked smile as I approached. "Good morning, Sunshine."

I wrapped my arms around myself to fight off the chill. "May I sit with you?"

He made a face.

My brow rose. "What?"

"It's. . ." He shook his head and patted the space beside him. "You always surprise me. Of course, you can."

"I'm not that stealthy." I shot him a cheeky smile and sat, tucking my legs beneath me. *I should have brought a blanket.* "Loach says I sound like an elephant when I walk."

"What's an elephant?" Jayvin asked.

I shrugged.

"Hmm." Tense, he cocked his head and scanned over my face. Whatever he found in it seemed to satisfy him because he let out a slow breath. "And that's not what I meant."

"What did you mean, then?"

He absently brushed his finger down my arm, lingering on the violet scales around my elbow. "You are . . . kind. Thoughtful. Polite. It makes me pause."

I stared down at my folded hands. "Thank you."

"See." Jayvin turned back to the sun growing higher in the sky, the light not yet close enough to burn him. "Even now."

I scooted closer, trying to absorb what little warmth I could from his cool skin. "Do you come up here every morning?"

He nodded. "I never want to miss another sunrise."

After so long in the dark, I didn't blame him. I watched his faelight dance, casting shadows on the mosaic tile. Somehow, they split, becoming half a dozen dancing figures. One of the figures crumpled as the others skipped around it, laughing.

Just like in the catacombs. I frowned and chased the mocking figures away. "Why do they do that?"

Jayvin chewed his lip. He'd been watching them, too. "It's . . . a lot to explain."

The faelight settled on my outstretched hands and the

shadows disappeared. "I saw the skeletons before. They'd been dancing, also. Did you place them that way?"

"My siblings watched her force me into the tomb." Jayvin exhaled as he picked at his torn cuticles. "Sometimes, when I sleep, I still hear them laughing. Mother laughed, too."

"She's created other Offspring?" Of course, she had. I don't know why that hadn't occurred to me until now. "Only males?"

"No." His nailbed began to bleed. "She has daughters. My sisters."

"Do you love them?"

"*Love* is a strong word," Jayvin snorted. "The Goblin is more affectionate than they ever were, but I am bound to them. Not all of them were terrible. Some even tried at times to be decent."

"How does it all work?" I twisted the length of my teal hair. "Boot made it sound like Offspring were mindless. Completely consumed by their creator."

"It's blood magic," he replied, watching my fingers play in my tangled waves. "And when we turn, we become our creator's property. Her venom inside us gives her control of our minds and body. Vampires operate on law, ownership, and territory. So yes, weaker minds can become consumed. Some of us retain a sense of self, often to our maker's dismay."

"Like you?"

Jayvin gave me a quick, crooked grin before his face fell. "I don't like killing people that don't deserve it." He chewed his lip. "Unfortunately, my *condition* takes that choice away from me most days. It's strange, though. No matter how long I've been away—after all this time—I can still *feel* her. Every time I turn, I expect to see Mother there, watching. Waiting for me to break. To come crawling back and beg her for forgiveness."

"Like a spider in a web." I curled up to rest my chin on my knees. I picked at my skirt hem. "Would you?"

Jayvin blinked. "Would I what?"

"Go back?"

He opened and closed his mouth, conflicted, before whispering. "I . . . I don't know if that choice belongs to me."

"It should be." His response brought a thought back to mind. I inhaled and said, "This is off the subject, but I wanted to apologize to you for the other day."

His gaze snapped to mine. "For what?"

Why does he have to make me say it aloud? I groaned and hid my face in my flimsy gown. "I should have asked before . . . you know." I tugged at the thread I'd pulled loose on my hem. "In Geralt's pantry."

Jayvin's body relaxed. "You already apologized for that."

"Not properly."

His brow arched coyly. "Do you think I didn't like it?"

"No." God, my skin was on fire. "I don't know—"

Warmth jolted through me as he lifted my chin toward him, his bright, red eyes lit with pure amusement. "You're funny."

"That doesn't make me feel better." I tried to look away, but he held firm.

"You're funny," Jayvin repeated and let out a husky laugh. "And colorful, and sweet, and everything I'd forgotten that matters." My stomach tightened as Jayvin leaned in and brushed his nose against my jaw with a sigh. His lips hovered over mine, his voice on the edge of reverence. "May I kiss you, Sunshine?"

"Yes," I said, too quickly, as my heart thundered against my ribs. "Please."

"Thank you," he murmured. My head spun as I forgot how

to breathe, but before he could, the door to the rooftop slammed open.

"For Heaven's sake," Loach shouted. We jumped and turned. Dare I say, he blushed. "Knock that off. Come downstairs, the both of you. We have an Emperor to overthrow."

Jayvin snarled at him, the sound making my stomach tighten further. Loach flipped him off before heading back inside.

"I guess we should see what he wants," Jayvin grumbled as he stood and brushed the dust off his soft pants. He gave me a hand up, then stepped back and scanned me head to toe, grinning. "Though, it may have been your dress that made the squid so bashful."

"Oh." I glanced down. Nearly all my back and sides were exposed. *I'm going to burn this thing.* I crossed my arms over my chest to cover it, my skin growing hot. "I should probably change first."

"Don't go through the trouble for my sake." Jayvin offered me his elbow, and I took it. "I'm not so easily flustered."

"You're terrible." I swatted his arm as we crossed the patio, and he broke out into his musical laugh. I could listen to it forever. Jayvin opened the door for me, bowing with a sweep of his arm. It was my turn to blush. I performed a rather ungraceful curtsy. "Thank you, Jay."

Jayvin froze, still bent at the waist, his expression stunned. He blinked. "W-what did you call me?"

"Jay?" I replied. His eyes dilated wildly he watched me step awkwardly through the doorway. *Tetra, why do you always ruin everything?* I curled in on myself. "It slipped off my tongue. I won't call you that again."

"No, it's not that." His hands trembled as he followed me inside and closed the door behind us. "It's. . . I think someone's called me that before."

"I imagine so." I fought to hold back self-conscious tears. "It's a common nickname."

"No, you don't understand." He shook his head violently, his silver-white hair falling into his eyes. "I mean *before*."

"Oh?" *Oh.* I gasped and grabbed his hand. "Like a memory? From when?"

"Possibly." He glanced down at our conjoined fingers, smiling slightly. "And I don't know."

"It's something." I brushed my thumb against his as the excitement chased away my nerves. "Maybe there *is* a way to get your memories back."

"I shouldn't be having them at all." His brows furrowed as he chewed the skin on his lip. He glanced down the hall. "I need to think. I'll wait for you in the kitchen."

I nodded and let go before slipping into my room. *Maybe who he was is still in there.* Perhaps a Vampire queen's venom doesn't destroy one's memory, but merely blankets it.

I scanned over my private space. My clothes were scattered all over the floor, the armchair, the vanity. My hairbrush lay inches from my boots, and pairs of dirty socks were shoved under my bed. *It's starting to look like my bedroom back at the cove.*

Mine. My possessions. My past. My identity—something Jayvin had never had.

At home, I'd been with people who cared about me and had allowed me to be myself. I glanced around—at the peeling wallpaper, the water stains in the worn, mauve carpet, and the inch of dust clinging to the armoire. Maybe—maybe this could be a home now.

For both of us.

I'd felt the inkling of it before, but now it felt like I was leaving a mark on this place and the people within it. It almost felt like I mattered.

And someone that mattered wouldn't let the Emperor take everything from them—not again. Not her home. Not her friends. Not Jayvin...

Don't think about that. I dressed quickly into a clean sundress, brushed my hair, then headed downstairs.

Jayvin was in the kitchen, as promised. As his eyes flickered over me, I didn't miss the desire hidden behind them before his gaze returned respectfully to the ground. The others were gathered around Boot's Spot—which the dining table had been lovingly re-named—waiting for us.

Loach cleared his throat. "Now that we're all present."

I joined them at the table, trying to ignore him. Jayvin sat beside me, grinning impishly at Loach as he reached over and pulled my chair closer before he casually rested his arm around my shoulders.

Loach glared at him, the look heavy with fatherly disdain.

Men. I glared at them both. "If you two are done?"

Agatha bit down on her lip to keep from laughing.

I straightened, inhaling as I shifted to face Boot. "Sayzar has to be stopped. If I have do it myself, I understand. Saving my people wasn't part of our bargain. I don't expect you to continue honoring it."

Boot—wearing his pressed, teal suit and checkered tie—tapped his pen against his temple. "Well, I'm glad we're all on the same page. While you both were *preoccupied*—"

I rubbed my face and groaned. Jayvin flashed a wicked smile.

"—some of us were already coming up with a change of plans." Boot laid out a fresh piece of parchment. "Nothing has changed except our preparations."

"Nothing has changed?" I replied, aghast, despite the relief latching onto my bones. "Everything's changed. If we don't stop him in time, he'll kill all the Merfolk in The Dam."

"When did he say this would happen?" Purple shadows hung beneath Boot's large eyes. *He must have been up all night.* "A timeline would be more helpful than your mewling."

Jayvin bristled.

"He said he wanted me—Jessa—to be there," I recalled, brows pinched. "So, I imagine he plans to give the order at the ball."

"As I expected." Boot nodded. "Sayzar's proud. He'll want an audience."

"Then we stop him before he gives the order," Agatha said, chewing on a piece of toast. "It shouldn't be too hard."

"Easier said than done." Loach's tentacle pointed to a location on Boot's map—the dungeons. "Especially when we're trying to rob him of his gold and the Wardstone. Plus, we still need a way into the inner court. Our plan depends on the rest of us getting in—and out—of the sewers."

That is a problem. None of this mattered if we couldn't get Loach and Boot into the palace. A thought struck me. "Agatha, do you still have that day pass?"

"I think so," Agatha said. She lifted her coat from where she'd thrown it on the sofa and dug through the pockets. She yanked out a crumpled piece of parchment. "Aha!"

"Let me see." She passed me the paper, and I scanned over it. It had our names and the date when the Emperor requested us to meet at the bistro last night. I handed it to Boot. "He gave us another pass. Agatha will be allowed to escort me to the palace—that's her in. Do you think there's a way we can alter this old one into something you and Loach could use?"

Boot read over the paper, then shot Agatha an irritated look. "The Emperor gave you this?"

She nodded and scowled. "Don't use that sassy tone with me. How did you think we got inside yesterday?"

"This would have been nice to know about *last night*." Boot mumbled something along the lines of damn, bloody Orcs. He traced a series of shapes over the parchment, which shone with violet and lavender light. Wards. The words twisted on the parchment, becoming something else entirely. "The ignorant fool." He cackled. "Arrogance always has a way of coming back to bite you."

Agatha glanced over my shoulder as he passed it back to me. The lettering on the document had completely changed—now inviting him and Loach into the inner court on the day of the ball on the pretense of being maintenance workers.

"Incredible," I said in disbelief. "That easily?"

"We have a way in." Jayvin scratched his nails on the table. "But that doesn't stop the Emperor from giving the orders for his Enforcers to kill."

"Agreed." Boot traced a circle around the city on his map. "That part will have to wait until the barrier falls."

"The barrier will fall when we take the Wardstone." Agatha finished off her toast, dusting the crumbs off her blouse. "Won't that be too late?"

"No." Boot rolled his eyes, as if it were obvious. "Because by that time, we'll have turned not only the citizens of Carnage, but also the Enforcers, against him. There will be no one left to give the order, leaving the city vulnerable for Surge to take once Tetra brings him back his father's body."

"How? How do you make an entire city turn against their leader?" I asked.

"We're not." Boot pointed a sharpened talon at Jayvin, who raised a brow. "He is."

Chapter Twenty-Four

"You sure we can pull this off?" I wiped my sweaty palms on my dress. I should have worn pants. "I mean, without one of us facing a slow, horrible death?"

"You asked me that ten minutes ago." Boot waddled up the street ahead of me. He pulled out a brass pocket watch. "Excuse me, eight minutes ago."

"Sorry, I'm nervous."

"Obviously."

"Aren't you?" At this late hour, the main highway leading to the east quarter was still crowded with citizens heading to the taverns to drink their troubles away. A few lingering street merchants were slowly packing away their products. I swallowed. "I mean, what if he gets hurt?"

Boot knew exactly what *he* I was referring to.

He exhaled irritably as he tucked his watch back into his pocket. "You seem to be ignorantly—or purposefully—unaware of the damage Jayvin Dyre is capable of." This time, he reached up and patted my elbow, the kindest expression I'd ever seen from him. "He should be the least of your concerns. Trust me."

I didn't respond, afraid I'd start crying if I did. This was all well beyond my area of expertise, but I knew my part and was shifted into my human form, ready to play it.

Relax. I repeated, over and over. Boot was right. Jayvin—and Loach and Agatha, for that matter—hadn't survived this long by being amateurs. They knew what they were doing, even if I didn't. Despite all the reassurances, my anxiety continued to grow the closer we got to the east side.

A few Enforcers patrolled the edges of the highway, watching for any unwanted drunken behavior. More sat in their little booths along the roadside, staring blankly into the crowds with drooping eyes.

"Fools." Boot nodded toward a guard who had fallen asleep propped on his elbow. "Sayzar would flay them living if he caught them sleeping on the job."

"Maybe that's *why* they're so tired," I replied. The Enforcer slid off and smacked his face on the booth counter. "They're raiding and patrolling day and night with the threat of a Vampire loose, let alone possible terrorists. They're exhausted."

"Which will make this evening go all the better for us." Boot adjusted his tie. "Just be ready to react at a moment's notice and always expect the unexpected."

I was tempted to mock his sage wisdom, but I nodded instead. Oddly enough, I *did* trust Boot. He could be callous, but he was honest. I'd take honesty over having smoke blown up my ass any day.

We were near the end of the main road and about to turn onto the narrower streets leading toward the revelry when a deafening crack of thunder fell over the street. A ploom of smoke erupted over the rooftops, blanketing the street in grey.

My ears rang as I covered my head and fell to my knees. *Not thunder.*

A bomb.

The screaming started before the shockwaves had finished tearing down the street. The seabirds resting on the streetlamps screeched and took off as a second bomb went off—then a third. A massive cloud of dust and rubble barreled through the alleys and toward the highway. By then, an enormous crowd stampeded in the opposite direction, climbing over each other to escape the chaos.

"Boot?" I couldn't see through the haze. As I tried to stand, a knee hit me between the shoulder blades, and I fell to the ground again. I gasped—trying to force air into my lungs—but ended up with a mouthful of dirt. Fleeing, frightened bodies knocked into me, but I managed to sidle back against the alley wall and clamor upright.

"Boot?" I coughed up a wad of dust. There was no way I could find him in this mess. Past the grey cloud, hundreds of people ran onto the highway—just like we'd planned.

He'll be okay. I sprinted after them. *No bad thoughts. They're all going to be okay.*

Enforcers boomed orders over the panicked shrieking as the street grew too packed for anyone to move. *In through the nose, out through the mouth,* I repeated to myself over and over as I pushed through the crowds.

There are too many people. We can't control this. I stumbled as the stampede came to an abrupt halt—the silence falling over the street more deafening than the bombs. Only the Enforcers were moving, racing for the mouth of the highway, shouting back and forth to each other.

Keep moving. No one stopped me as I used the opportunity to make my way to the front. As I broke through the last row of terror-stricken civilians, the Enforcers fell in line—creating a phalanx.

My lungs *burned* as I skid to a halt—nearly colliding with the butts of their spears. As my gaze rose over their linked shoulders, I think my heart forgot how to beat.

Jayvin stood at the mouth of the highway—his enormous great sword strapped to his back—blocking the entrance into the market district. The blood smeared over his pale face dripped off his chin as he smiled, revealing his vicious fangs. Only when he took a step forward, his head titled in that predatory way of his, did the body beside him become visible.

Jayvin dragged Loach behind him—masked and covered in gore—by the arm like a child might a doll. His brilliant red eyes scanned over the Enforcers, filled with a very different hunger than what they usually held for me.

"Is this all?" Jayvin pouted as he tossed Loach's limp body before them like a sack. "I'm bored. I'd hoped there would be more of you."

"*HALT.*" The Enforcers shouted and locked their shields alongside their spears. "*Yield, in the name of the Emperor!*"

As Jayvin took another step forward, the crowd took a unified step back.

When I glanced around, the eyes of the horrified faces behind me were round with fear.

"Where *is* your Emperor?" Jayvin licked some of the still vibrant blood off his lips. "I'm here for him, after all. I have business to finish."

Some instinctual part of me wanted to be afraid—and maybe I should have listened to it—but when it came to Jayvin, good sense had left me when he'd first sunk his teeth into my neck.

A voice shouted over the crowd. *"It's the killer of Carnage!"*

A second. *"He set off the bombs!"*

A third. *"This is revenge for the catacombs!"*

A murmur broke out behind me, a rippling wave of panic moving through the people.

"Stand down, Offspring!" The Enforcer captain in the center rapped his spear against his shield. "Or we'll be forced to put you down."

Jayvin pointed at Loach, lifeless on the pavement. "Every day that your beloved Emperor doesn't submit to me, I will be delivering another corpse," He crooned, peering up from beneath his long lashes. "Hopefully, there will be enough left of them for you to identify."

"*STAND DOWN!*" The sunset's final rays stretched shadows over the paved street. Sweat dripped out from beneath the captain's plumed helm. "We will destroy you, drone!"

Jayvin's smile grew manic as he brushed the toe of his boot across the nearest shadow. Even the Enforcers gasped as he dissolved into the darkness, only to materialize inches from their barricade.

Jayvin leaned in, gentle as a lover, and whispered into the captain's pointed ear, "You can surely try."

The captain barely managed a whimper before Jayvin slammed a fist into the man's throat. The captain crumpled, breaking the phalanx. The ranks of Enforcers tumbled into chaos. Three of them fell before the crowd realized what was happening, followed by the echo of Jayvin's laughter.

Behind the soldiers, Loach was gone—leaving only a puddle of pig's blood behind, collected from the poor beast Jayvin had for breakfast this morning.

The shrieking returned as the crowd scattered in every direction, sending up another cloud of dust. I was supposed to run with them, to shift into many forms and spread the seeds of doubt among the people.

But I couldn't look away . . . not from him. Time slowed as the Enforcers converged on their new enemy—a unified and powerful force—but it didn't matter. Jayvin was better.

He'd taken down four more guards before he bothered to draw his massive sword. The nearest Enforcer surged forward, preparing to plunge his spear through Jayvin's heart, but he wasn't fast enough. Jayvin spun left, using the weight of his sword as momentum to spiral and slice the Enforcer's head clean off his shoulders.

I flinched but remained rooted in place. Non-lethal blows—that's what we'd discussed this morning. That was our plan. I watched as something in him snapped, and my friend changed into what I'd been warned about from the start—a monster.

Jayvin's grin grew wider, his laughter shifting to something purely savage as he cleaved another Enforcer in half. He snapped the next man's spine over his knee. Another's throat he ripped out with his teeth, soaking himself in a fresh coating of red.

Screaming. So much screaming.

Not from the crowds this time, but from the men waiting in line to die.

The stories I'd been told hadn't lied. Jayvin was a catastrophe, the terror we were taught to fear in the night—and he was killing purely for fun. They were the wheat, and Jayvin was the sickle.

And he was magnificent.

Another body fell in pieces. A head torn from its body like a child's toy. Jayvin skewered through two soldiers at once, twisting and swinging his sword to fling their limp bodies like projectiles into the remaining men that fought to hold the line.

I wanted to be closer, to touch him—to study his technique and the nearly liquid way in which he moved. I hadn't realized I'd moved closer until a taloned hand gripped my elbow, digging into my flushed skin. "You stupid girl."

"I want to see—" I tried to jerk away, but Boot was stronger. He yanked me down until his scrunched nose was in my face. His round, orange eyes were locked on Jayvin, a bead of sweat dripping down his cratered skin. "Bloodlust."

Two more Enforcers fell, but Jayvin's wicked laughter drowned out their screams.

I blinked. "What?"

"Bloodlust." Boot was already dragging me away from the highway. "Welcome to the reality of Vampires, Tetra the Temptress."

More shrieks. There weren't many Enforcers left in the unit.

Boot swallowed as he glanced back, quickening his pace. "The boy will kill us all and not know who and what he's done until the madness subsides."

Sharks. I wanted to be afraid—should be afraid—but again, the feeling wouldn't come. Instead, I asked, "Agatha? Loach?"

"They're fine." Boot's limp grew jerky the deeper we moved into the back alleys. "It seems our Orc friend has the knack for explosives. Loach is still whining about his ruined coat."

That sounded about right. Boot's talons were cutting into my wrist. I slowed. "Wait, what about Jay?"

Boot's bat-like ear twitched. "What about him?"

"We're going to leave him like that?" I skid to a halt. Boot recoiled. "If what you said is true, we can't just let him massacre half the city! He'd never forgive himself."

"I'm sure he's used to it by now." Boot yanked on my arm again. "I'd hoped he would have better control, but I should have known better. There's nothing we can do to stop him, girl."

Like hell, there wasn't.

"Please, forgive me for this." I jerked out of his grip and kicked Boot square in the gut. He doubled over, wheezing, before he hit the ground. He may have called for me, but I was already sprinting back down the alley.

My mouth was a desert with all the dust choking me. If I survived this, I'd be coughing up grit for days. I swerved between citizens crowding the narrow streets, bent over, and gasping for breath. Some leaned against the wall, tears staining their dirt-coated faces.

The closer I got to the highway, the quieter it became. There were no sirens, no more screaming. *He'll be okay. He has to be.* I wouldn't allow myself to believe anything else.

The moon lingered overhead as I ran out onto the main road, clutching my chest as I slowed. White light shone through gaps in the clouds, reflecting off the streams of garnet blood staining the pavement, flowing toward the drainage channels in narrow, jagged rivers.

He'd piled the bodies into one large mound.

Even now, Jayvin looked so beautiful sitting upon his throne of corpses—gripping his hair and dripping with red—as he rocked, his shoulders rising and falling as he sucked in ragged breaths.

No, no, no, no. As I stepped forward, I slipped in a puddle of blood and his head snapped up, his usually ruby eyes were dilated entirely black. Voices cried out from the other side of the highway. Someone shouting for help.

He can't stay here. I managed a smile. "Jay?"

As he slid down to the street, Jayvin inhaled, graceful as a cat.

"We need to go home," I whispered. Slowly, I crept closer and stretched out my hand as if approaching a cornered animal. "Come with me. I see you." I gasped as he jumped shadows—flitting in and out of the moonlight—until our chests nearly touched.

A little color returned to his eyes as he sighed and pressed his forehead against mine. "I-I see you, Sunshine."

"Good." I intertwined my fingers with his. They were sticky with cooling blood. "We can go for a swim until you feel better. Will you take me to the beach?"

"Yes," he exhaled, and some of *him* returned to his voice. "Yes. Let's do that. Right now."

"STOP!"

"No!" I spun around just as another squad of Enforcers charged down the street, wielding spears.

Just like that, my Jayvin was gone.

His gaze snapped up to his new prey, eyes dilating, and the darkness and hunger returned as he let out a vicious snarl.

"Stay back!" I called and squeezed Jayvin's forearm. *He can't stay here. He can't kill every guard in Carnage.* And he would. I couldn't allow him to have that on his conscience . . . or mine.

The Enforcers recoiled, skidding to a halt, expressions twisted in horror as they took in the state of their fallen comrades.

The moment of hesitation was all I needed. I took my chance—as stupid as it was.

"Jay." I slid my finger into his mouth and sliced it open on his sharpened canine. "Jay, *look at me.*"

His lips closed over the wound before I could pull away, sucking at the warmth pouring out of my skin, but he looked at me. His eyes widened—as black as the furthest depths of the sea.

I held back a scream as I yanked my finger from his mouth, tearing the wound open further. His gaze snapped to the red droplets that splattered to the ground.

I don't have to make it far. I smiled, wiping my blood onto my chest and throat, staining me in the scent. *Just far enough that he won't hurt anyone else.* "If you catch me, you can have me—all to yourself."

Jayvin's cruel, returning smile told me he planned to do just that. My death would be slow and savored.

I back one step, two—then sprinted off the highway and didn't look back.

Chapter Twenty-Five

The Enforcers continued to scream useless orders for us to stop. I just hoped they'd be too stunned by the slaughter to follow. How long until word reached Sayzar of what happened? Hell, he probably knew already.

I wasn't delusional. Beneath the waves, I could eat away miles in minutes. I could surge to the depths faster and farther than most Merfolk could ever dream. But on land? I was a joke.

I let my shift drop, needing every ounce of salt in my body ready to burn.

The only reason I hadn't been caught yet was because Jayvin wanted me to get away. This was a cat-and-mouse game, and I was being hunted.

He did say he likes games.

More than once, I slipped and hit the ground as I barreled into the eastern district, shredding the skin on my palms and knees. The highway broke into a rounded courtyard, surrounded by inns and taverns catering to every kind of creature Carnage called home. More clean roads branched off the main strip. I imagined they lead to the seedier parts of town.

Sharks. I slowed just enough to get my bearings. *If I head further out, I'll just get lost. The others will need to find me.*

If there'd be anything left to find.

I just hoped Jayvin would be able to forgive himself.

Around me, all the blinds and shutters were closed, the doors barred with chairs and tables. The shop owners probably heard the chaos and locked up. A smart decision.

The courtyard was a ghost town. There was nowhere to run.

"Te-tra." Jayvin's voice reverberated from the alley, accompanied by a baleful laugh and the sound of metal scraping against stone—his sword. *"Tetra, dear, are you hiding from me?"*

Hide.

I slowed, each breath gritting through my lungs as if they were coated in sand. Where could I hide? I couldn't get inside a building without breaking a window or kicking in a door. Not that it mattered. He'd find me no matter where I ran. I forced myself to breathe, breathe, breathe. No matter how badly it hurt. *But if I play his game, it might slow him down and give us enough time for the bloodlust to pass.*

I didn't imagine what would happen if this went wrong. I spun, searching for something—anything. A wooden chair lay outside the butcher's shop to my right. *I guess I'm breaking the window.*

His voiced was getting closer. *"Te-traaa."*

Agatha was right. It was do-or-die now.

"Come find me, Jay!" I sang back and clenched my eyes shut as I shattered the window with the chair. Shards of glass exploded, slicing the delicate fins on my forearms before clattering to the paneled floor inside the shop. *Don't scream. Don't scream.* Adrenaline had my teeth chattering as I scrambled over the sill. The skirts of my dress caught. *Sharks.* As I yanked them free, a jagged bit of glass sliced into the inside of my thigh. I bit down on my lip to keep from crying out. My blood dripped down the window, as bright and vivid as Jayvin's eyes should be.

"*Sunshine, where are you?*" Heavy bootsteps approached the butcher shop. He wanted me to hear him coming, for me to panic. "*I miss you. Come back to me.*"

Hide, hide, hide, hide. I scanned the area. There wasn't much to work with. Only a bench seat and a dying, potted lemon tree decorated the lobby. The cabinets behind the front counter were too small for me to fit. Stacks of receipts and invoices littered the space by the till. *Here goes nothing*, I thought as I tossed them across the floor, hoping to muffle the sound of my movement as I crept to the far end of the store.

The bootsteps grew louder.

Stupid. I should have kept running. I held my breath as I slipped through the chipped door at the back of the shop. *Please, be an exit.*

But of course, it led exactly where I prayed it wouldn't—a chilled work room.

An enormous wood table sat at the back of the room, stained with years of blood and salt scrub. Sides of cattle hung from iron hooks screwed into the ceiling. More countertops lined the walls, filled with cutlery meant for dismembering flesh.

In through the nose, out through the mouth. I lifted the nearest butcher knife—the blade itself longer than my hand—and waited.

I probably looked rather silly standing in the center of a bunch of dead, dangling cows. I fought the smile threatening my lips, my hands shaking as I held the knife against my chest. *I just need a little more time.* He'd already been coming out of this bloodlust when I'd found him. If the Enforcers hadn't ruined it, we'd be back at The Lux by now. I swore under my breath. *Just a little more time.*

I tensed as a muffled thud echoed from the front room, followed by the crunch of boot heels on glass. My heart pounded so hard I could feel it in my ankles, in the wounds dripping blood down my thighs.

The footsteps paused outside the door.

I gripped my knife tightly and held my breath.

Jayvin purred as the doorknob twisted, "Tetra, your fluttering drives me mad. Why won't you make it stop?"

Black spots clouded my vision from lack of air, but I refused to answer.

"Don't be scared." The door opened a crack, his towering, dark frame blocking out the light pouring in from the street lamps outside. "Remember, this is just a game."

I stepped back and noticed too late the shadow cast by the open door, the darkness stretching across the floor and over my sandaled feet. I looked down, and the shadows started to move. *Sharks.*

Jayvin grinned as he emerged from the darkness and lunged, a flawless and calculated predator.

What he didn't expect was when I rushed *toward* him. His dark eyes widened as I wrapped my arm around his neck and held tight as the force of his body slammed us into the back counter, sending knives and empty, stained pails scattering over the floor. I cried out as lightning pain shot down my spine and into my hips, but I didn't let go.

Jayvin pulled back, lips parted, as he glanced down in bewilderment where I'd lodged the butcher knife into his stomach.

I'm alive. I'm alive. Breathing heavily, I leaned in and whispered into his ear. "Got you." When his stunned gaze returned to mine, I grinned back. "First blood. I win."

"T-that wasn't the rules." A sliver of the red returned to his irises. "I catch you. I have you. That's the game."

Vampires operate on ownership and property.

"And I caught you first." I let go of the knife, and he backed away a step. "You fell right into my trap. Now, you're *mine.*"

One breath. Two.

"Clever, clever, Sunshine." Jayvin's face lit up with a mix of amusement and delighted reverence. He winced as he slowly pulled the knife from his abdomen, examining the bloodied blade as he smiled. "That *hurt.*"

I swallowed. "It won't kill you."

Jayvin huffed a laugh. He moved again, too fast for me to react, and grabbed my waist before slamming my back against the wall. My bruised body shrieked against the pain splintering my limbs.

Jayvin's breaths were ragged as he pinned my arms against my sides. "What do you plan to do to me, Sunshine?" He sounded nearly frightened. "As you said, I'm *yours.*"

Now what? I hadn't thought I'd get this far. Nervously, I ran my tongue over my chapped lips, and his heated gaze locked onto my mouth. I sucked in a breath. "What would you like me to do?"

"Hmm." Jayvin gripped the shoulders of my dress, weaving his fingers into the thin fabric as if he meant to rip it in half. More red returned to his eyes, but the mania remained. "That's not how this works." His voice rose, frantic. "Would you have me on my knees? Should I leave this city in ruins? Will you make me cleave this world in two, if only to have a taste of you?"

My breath caught. "I-I want you to look at me."

He did—and I nearly folded.

"I want you to say it again . . . you're mine. If only for today." I clarified as my stomach twisted into knots. I didn't want to command anything from him, but if this was what he needed to come back to me, I'd do it. "Say it."

"*Te-tra.*" Jayvin trembled as he pressed a series of kisses along my collarbone and moaned. "I am *yours.*"

"Good." I lifted my chin and let his mouth move to my neck. *I could die like this.* "No more killing today. Do you understand?"

He nodded, teeth scraping against my throat as his fingers trailed down my dress's neckline.

"G-good. Thank you." I wrapped my arms around his neck and squeezed. "Now, what I'd really like is a hug."

"*Sunshine.*" Jayvin's voice cracked, and his knees gave out as he lifted me onto his lap. We hit the floor, but I didn't let go. I coiled my legs around his waist, and he buried his face into my neck before he wept, and wept, and wept.

Chapter Twenty-Six

Jayvin had to carry me back to The Lux. My back was too sore, my wounds too fresh, to make it far on my own. He said nothing, but I knew the guilt was eating away at him. He hadn't been in control—and I didn't blame him at all—but that didn't stop the weariness from draining at his features. Making his lovely dove-grey skin look even sallower.

I rested my head against his shoulder and fidgeted with the buttons on his leather jacket. I should have made myself walk to spare him the effort, but I was happy right where I was.

"What are you thinking about?" Jayvin asked, voice hoarse. His eyes were still puffy from tears. He didn't tell me what caused such a surge of emotion, but he would when he was ready . . . or he wouldn't. I wasn't going to press it. We were only a few blocks away from The Lux. By the moon, it was close to three in the morning.

"That I'm grateful I don't have to walk." When he flinched, I added with a coy smile, "You have no idea what blisters these sandals give me."

His eyes—back to a stunning red—flickered to me, then

back to the road. At least his lips curved upwards. "Your poor, dainty feet."

"You might have to rub them for me."

"As you wish."

"I was joking." I sat up as much as I could, resting my arm over his shoulder. "Lord, I wouldn't make you do that."

"I would, though." Relief washed over me when he finally smiled, although I knew it was a mask for the emotions simmering underneath. "I'm at your service for the rest of the evening, and it would be a wonderful excuse to touch you."

Heat flooded my face and neck. "You're touching me right now."

"I know." He kissed the top of my head. "And I'm enjoying it."

I opened my mouth to respond but closed it when Loach came striding around the corner, still dressed in his blood-stained coat. If Krakens had ears, his would-be smoking right now.

"*You.*" He pointed to Jayvin, then his infuriated gaze dropped to me. "What happened to her? What did you do?"

"I'm fine." I tried to wiggle out of Jayvin's grasp, but he was too strong. Gently, he lowered me to a standing position, keeping a hand resting on my stiff lower back. I yanked off my shoes. "I'm fine, Loach. My feet are just killing me."

Loach grabbed the front of Jayvin's shirt and I thought he would punch him, but Jayvin didn't fight, didn't try to defend himself. "You could have gotten us all killed today," Loach growled, one of his tentacles moving to the dagger on his hip. "Pull a stunt like that again, and I will personally remove your blackened heart and display it on my damned shelf. Got it?"

Jayvin dropped his chin. "Understood."

Loach released him and exhaled. "If you think I'm pissed, wait until Agatha gets a hold of you."

Jayvin's eyes widened, but I shot Loach a glare. "If Agatha is angry, she can take it out on me. I'm the one that went back."

"You can tell that to her," Loach said, turning around and heading back the way he had come. "Come on. We've been waiting for hours. It's time to recap."

I tried to hide my soreness as we followed him the last block back to The Lux. Candlelight flickered from the opened doorway, spilling gold onto the darkened streets. As we approached, I heard a gasp from inside, and Agatha appeared in the doorway.

Sharks. Tears stained her cheeks as she strode toward us, her swollen eyes still spilling tears. I braced myself, ready to fight for Jayvin, but he wasn't her target.

Agatha slapped me squarely across the face.

I recoiled, and Jayvin's enraged growl echoed through the alley. He began to move to defend me, but I yanked him back by the elbow. As I straightened, Agatha let out a sob, hugging me with the grip like a vice. "You're a lunatic. I thought you were dead."

Despite the pain radiating through my cheek, I hugged her back.

"I finally made a friend." Agatha stepped back, wiping her nose on her sleeve. "And she goes and tries to get herself killed. Why? Over a bloody Vampire."

I managed a sly smile. "Nice pun."

"Don't make me slap you again." Her mouth fell open when she took in the blood soaking my dress and my hair. "A-are you okay?"

"Oh, I'm fine." Jayvin and I probably looked like we'd just fought in a war. I wouldn't tell her that most of the blood on me belonged to the dead soldiers. "I'm sorry I scared you." I smoothed her frazzled hair. "We're fine."

"We're more than fine," Boot said, standing in the doorway, picking at his sharp talons. "Carnage is in an uproar. My sources say the Enforcers are terrified. By the morning, the entire city will beg the Emperor to respond to the drone's threat."

Agatha glanced over her shoulder at him. "You have sources?"

He scowled at her.

Jayvin's words were barely audible. "You're not going to make me leave?"

Boot turned and waved us inside—and that was that.

Visible relief passed over Jayvin's features, and I didn't miss the way his knees buckled as we moved to follow Loach inside. In the kitchen, Ivan nodded to us, and I smiled back. Two bowls of beef stew and a fresh, hot loaf of bread sat on the counter—just prepared.

My eyes burned. "You stayed up to make us dinner?"

"I couldn't let you go hungry." The dwarf's eyes twinkled. Maybe he'd finally forgiven me. "It was no trouble."

I knelt and pulled him into a hug. Hell, everyone was going to get a hug. "Thank you."

He awkwardly patted my shoulder. "You're welcome. But if you don't mind, I'm going to lie down now."

I backed away, wiping my eyes. "Of course."

With a smile, he headed upstairs. I set the stew and bread on the table and gestured for Jayvin to join me. He was as taut as a bowstring as he sat and began to eat, every movement slow and precise. His attention bounced between the four of us, on edge.

"To the plan or not, we're in a good place." Boot sat beside me, picking up a mug of cold coffee. "We've weakened Sayzar's forces, making our infiltration all the easier."

"I disagree," Loach sighed, rubbing his face as he leaned against the counter. "Ameliatus is going to be on high alert.

We're never going to get anywhere close to the palace, forged pass or not."

"And his Enforcer's attention will be focused on protecting *him*." Agatha pinched off a chunk of my bread. "They won't be worried about the treasury . . . or the Wardstone."

"Or Cyclone," I added. "If I can keep him distracted, he won't notice anything's missing until the barrier falls."

"About that." Jayvin set down his spoon. I was just glad he was talking. "Should the barrier fall so early?"

We stared at him in shock.

"Consider it," he added, licking his lips. "If we break it too soon, the Emperor will be able to bring in outside reinforcements. It will take time for me to remove the entire contents of the treasury. Is there a way to keep the wards up until everyone had left the palace?"

He wasn't wrong. I looked to Boot, who rubbed his chin as he thought. "Perhaps." He sipped his coffee. "But it would require one of us staying inside. The barrier can't survive without the Wardstone."

I fiddled with the Emperor's projection ring, still on my thumb. "Can a smaller stone hold it temporarily?"

Boot's gaze dropped to the ring. Slowly, his cracked mouth spread into a grin. "One of such royal quality? It may support the amount of magic sustaining the barrier for about ten minutes before it shatters."

I shifted in my chair to face Jayvin. "Is that enough time to do what you need?"

Jayvin tapped his spoon on the edge of his bowl. "I'll make it work."

"Then we keep the barrier up." Boot nodded, folding his hands over his lap. "I can ward the ring to power the barrier as soon as it falters—then we'll have, at most, minutes to get our marks before the barrier falls permanently. The rest will continue as planned."

Jayvin stood up quickly and placed his bowl in the sink. "I'm tired," he said before headed up the stairs.

My heart sank. *What's wrong?* Did he think I was upset over the injuries? They were minor. *Or he wants nothing to do with you because you claimed him.* The thought, mixed with exhaustion, had me nearly bursting into tears.

"I think we all need some sleep." Agatha undid her bandolier and tossed it onto the counter. "I'm going to bed."

"Me, too." I bid goodnight to the others and followed her. The stairs creaked beneath us as Agatha glanced over her shoulder at me, her emerald skin sallow, and whispered, "Are you sure you're okay?"

"Fine." I replied. It sounded fake. "Just wore out."

Agatha stopped, and I collided with her back. Her chocolate eyes hardened. "How are you alive, Tetra? I've seen the work of Vampires before. A long, long time ago. You should be a husk."

I should have been kinder, but weariness made me snap as we stepped onto the second floor. "Jayvin isn't a mindless animal."

"Are you trying to convince me?" Agatha scowled. "Or yourself? Just . . . be careful. You're young."

Agatha closed herself in her room before I could ask what she meant.

I stood in the hallway, shaking from frustration and a lack of salt. Instead of going down to mix up some salt water, like I should have, I stormed into my own room.

When I flicked on the light, I cursed and clutched my chest as I nearly fell back onto my ass.

Jayvin sat cross-legged at the end of my bed, rocking as he

gripped his hair. He glanced up, his eyes so tired, and gave me a weak smile. "Did I scare you?"

"Just surprised me." I shut the door behind me and leaned against it. He watched me, still hyper focused on every breath or movement I made.

I chewed my lip. "Are . . . are you okay?"

His face fell. "I almost killed you, Sunshine."

"But you didn't." *So, it is guilt.* "And I beg to differ. I had you with that butcher knife."

He winced and rubbed his stomach. "That did hurt."

"I'm not angry, if that's why you're worried." I tugged off my blood stained dress—he'd already seen me in my skivvies—and slipped on a clean night gown, his gaze dragging down my curves as I did so. Cautiously, I stepped past him to lie back against my pillows. "So, please, don't be angry at yourself."

Jayvin shifted on the bed to face me. He'd changed into his night clothes. "It's not that, though that worry *had* crossed my mind more than once." He sucked on his teeth. "I disobeyed. Loach, Agatha—hell, even the Goblin—they haven't done anything about it. I don't understand."

I rolled on my side. Sharks, my back hurt. "What do you mean?"

"I expected them to beat me." The words spilled out of him. Jayvin started picking at his nails again, rocking. "To chain me up, to humiliate me—or worse—to pretend I don't exist." He shook his head as he traced those circles on the blankets. "I don't know how to act. I don't know what to expect anymore—"

"This is real." I sat up and lifted his chin, nearly breaking at the terror I found waiting for me. "And for tonight . . ." I could reassure him all I wanted, but fear wasn't rational. I knew that all too well. "You are mine, and no one will hurt you."

"Yes." He exhaled and melted into my touch. "Until the sun comes up."

"That's right." I brushed my hair behind my ear and cursed as pain shot through my finger. I'd forgotten about the deep gouge his fang had torn into it. My lips pursed as it began to bleed again. "I guess I should go find a bandage."

"I—" Jayvin took my hand, eyes dilating slightly as he inspected the wound. "I can fix this for you . . . if you'd like."

"Really?" I was breathless. "Show me."

He arched a brow as he stroked my finger—asking permission.

I nodded.

Jayvin beamed before he gently sucked my finger into his mouth. I gasped as my wound *burned*, but as he pulled it out, placing a few kisses onto my wrist, I watched my opened skin begin to knit closed. Seconds later, all that remained was an itchy, pink line.

I gaped at the place the tear used to be. "How?"

Jayvin dared to look embarrassed. "Offspring venom not only . . . sedates our victims but heals the injuries they sustain. It wouldn't do for them to perish before we can bring them back for our creators to feed upon."

I thought back to the catacomb, to the peace I felt with his fangs in my throat, and how the bite marks had closed moments after he'd released me. I didn't have to fake my wonder. "That's incredible. Is that how you can heal so quickly?"

Jayvin nodded, a dusting of pink coloring his sharp cheekbones. "Yes. We're not much help to our masters dead." He lifted my wrist to inspect the cuts and scrapes covering it. "May I fix these?"

My heart was thundering again, but I nodded. Jayvin scooted closer, his venom an oily sheen on his lips, as he kissed each slice on my arms one by one. Fascinated, he stretched out my opalescent fins as he watched his venom weave the torn webbing back together.

Jayvin grinned from ear to ear as he pushed me back into my pillows and examined the parts of me revealed by my flimsy sundress. "Did I get them all?"

I swallowed, throat dry. "I think so."

"Liar," he purred as his finger trailed up my legs, breath catching, as he hitched my dress up high enough to leave my tanned thighs exposed.

It took all my waning self-control not to writhe as he traced around the deep gash on my inner thigh. Touch had never been something I found pleasant—too sticky and hot—but with him . . .

My skin yearned for him instead of wanting to shrink away. I imagined the sensation in quiet moments, or when I was drifting off to sleep, wondering if he'd ever feel the same. Or if I was naive and childish for thinking that maybe, just maybe, he did.

Jayvin's eyes dilated like a cat. "Seems like I missed one."

"It doesn't hurt—" I let out a squeak as he spread my thighs and slowly ran his tongue over the wound. Fire was not a strong enough word for what I felt as my skin knit closed. The venom went deeper this time, mending all the damaged flesh below the surface.

Jayvin leaned back with a smug smile. He tried so hard and failed not to let his gaze wander further beneath my dress. "There, much better."

I wanted him. I shouldn't. Everyone would hear. I didn't care.

Jayvin traced circles on the inside of my knee. "I'm at your command tonight, Sunshine, lest you forget."

I hadn't—but I wouldn't have him like this. Not when he was under my control, as temporary as it was.

My stomach flipped as he crawled over me—his hips settling between mine—but as he leaned in to kiss my neck, I pressed my hand against his chest and stammered, "Have you ever played cards?"

The puzzled expression on his face was comical. "Have I . . . what?"

"Cards?" I replied, as my heart slammed against my ribs. "Like poker?"

Jayvin sat back and blinked. "No, I haven't."

"If you like games, this will blow your mind." I squeezed his elbow as I slid off the bed. "Wait here."

He just watched, completely bewildered, as I darted out of the room. Once in the hall, I burst into Agatha's quarters. She lay sprawled out on her bed, dead asleep, wearing one of her hideous nightgowns.

"Wake up." I jumped onto the mattress and shook her shoulder. "I need you!"

"Why?" She shot up and reached for her dagger. "What's wrong?"

"I need your help to teach Jayvin how to play poker." I grimaced as her expression soured. "Please. Right now? I'll owe you."

She set her blade back on the nightstand. "Have you lost your marbles?"

"We can rest when we're dead, right?" I bounced and smacked her blankets. "*Please?*"

"Fine, fine, hold on." Rubbing her eyes, she got up and dug out her deck of cards. Poor Jayvin looked twice as alarmed when she followed me back into my room. I grinned at him as I plopped on the floor in front of my still lit hearth—courtesy of

Ivan—and patted the space beside me. "Take a seat. Be ready to be amazed."

He did as he was bid, watching Agatha warily.

As Agatha dealt the cards, Loach peered through my opened door, looking groggy. "What the hell is going on?" His expression brightened as soon as his gaze fell onto the deck in her hand. "Deal me in! I can't sleep, anyway. You clowns are in for it."

Boot joined us before the first round was done—our laughter woke him—and God bless him, even Ivan got in on the fun.

Jayvin picked up on the intricacies of the game faster than anyone had the right to, and I would have slayed a thousand stars if it meant I could continue to watch the pure thrill and joy on his face as his fear faded away, and he bluffed and conned his way into owning half of Loach's cheese stash.

If it were in my power, I would never let Jayvin fall asleep another night thinking that he was only valued for his services. He was my friend—*our* friend. Even his Matriarch couldn't change that fact.

We had days until the ball. Everything we'd planned would soon come to a head. It didn't matter. Sayzar Ameliatus could never take this memory from me—the feeling of being home again.

Of having a family again.

Chapter Twenty-Seven

We were so close.

Jayvin—with Loach's help—had kept his promise to the people of Carnage. The pig bodies—after being shredded up and partially dressed in ripped clothing—looked convincing as far as fake murder victims go.

Agatha had set off a few more bombs. Boot hobbled through the streets, loudly airing his grievances about the Emperor's cowardice to anyone who would listen.

The Enforcers were more alert than ever, but also more exhausted.

This was starting to feel possible. In a matter of days, Cyclone would be home and put to rest where he belonged. Hopefully, it would be enough to convince Surge to fight back—or at least stall the Emperor's orders to execute those he'd moved into the war camps.

So, we waited, planned, prepared, but most of all, we played cards—Jayvin's new hobby.

He'd been out when I'd gone to bed that night. I tried not to worry. It must have been close to dawn when the shake of my shoulder jolted me awake.

"Sunshine?" Jayvin leaned over me, grinning ear to ear. Water dripped from his white hair down his face. "Wake up!"

I sat up and wiped the drool off my face, thankful I'd worn a nightgown for once. "Why are you so wet?"

Jayvin shook his head, splattering me with droplets. I licked off the one that landed on my lips. Sea water. He grabbed my wrists and nearly yanked me out of bed. "Get up. I have a surprise for you."

"Surprise?" That woke me quickly. Beaming, I tucked my tangled hair behind my pointed ears, then rubbed the sleep from my eyes. "What kind of surprise?"

Jayvin pressed his finger over his lips and gestured for me to follow.

I hurried to the bathroom and changed into the crumpled pink dress I had thrown in the corner. I grabbed my bag, tossing it over my shoulder, before following him out.

Maybe it was the excitement, but Jayvin didn't hesitate to grab my hand and nearly drag me down the stairs. I did my best to keep up. The kitchen had been tidied since I'd gone to bed, bless Ivan. As usual, Boot's maps and plans were strewn across the table. As we strode for the door, a breeze tumbled through the window, sending one of his papers flying.

"Wait!" Jayvin paused as I picked up Boot's scrolls and tucked them neatly in the coffee cabinet. He'd find them there. "This, too." I slid Sayzar's projection ring off my thumb and laid it on the stack. I shut the cabinet and gave Jayvin an apologetic smile. "Boot planned to ward that this morning. I'll leave it here. Just in case he's up before we get back."

He nodded and grinned again as I entwined my fingers with his. Outside, the full moon sat on the western horizon, the sky lightening from the deepest black to azure. I had to jog to keep up with Jayvin's long strides as he led me down the alley, past the warehouse district, and towards the harbor.

I looked up, taking in the first threads of magenta light peaking over the mountains east. "Is it safe for you to be out? I don't want you to get burned. Someone might see you."

Jayvin glanced at me over his broad shoulder. "Don't worry, Sunshine. I can hide in your shadow if the need arises."

I gave him that and didn't argue as he led me out of the warehouse alleys into the slender strips of shops and bars encircling the beach. As we crossed over the plaza, I tilted my head back and groaned as a fresh, salt breeze enveloped me, promising comfort and the renewal of my body.

When I opened my eyes, Jayvin was watching me—his expression something close to devastation. Anxiety twisted my stomach. "What is it? What's wrong?"

"Nothing's wrong." Jayvin wandered onto the beach and plopped down on the sand. I sat beside him. He couldn't hold my eye as he murmured, "It's just . . . you are—" His brows furrowed in frustration as the first hint of sunrise broke over the mountains outside Carnage, setting the sky ablaze with pinks, oranges, and gold.

Jayvin swallowed and pointed. "You are that. Beyond beauty. Something only God could create." He smiled a little. "I sometimes imagine He took his time with you, knowing exactly what it would take to wake me from my hell." He shifted towards me and gestured to his stomach. "It makes me feel . . . fluttery here."

"Butterflies." My throat tightened, and the edges of my eyes burned as I glanced up at the sunrise. Warm colors—all the shades a Mermaid would be cherished and coveted for.

They may wear warmth, but to him, I was warmth.

"Butterflies." Jayvin's smiled turned dreamy as he turned back to the sky. "That's a good word for it."

It hurt to breathe—and for a moment, I didn't want to believe him. I wanted to believe he was saying what he thought would get him what he wanted, a common trait among men. But if that were the case, he could have had me ages ago. Whenever he'd wanted. He tore my inner shields to pieces and if he'd pushed, I would have caved to him in the catacombs.

"Is this your surprise?" I hated the way my words cracked. "Because if so, it's wonderful."

Jayvin snapped back to attention. "Oh, no, it isn't. Apologies, I got distracted." He stood, not bothering to brush the sand from his breeches. I let him pull me up. He held out his arms for me. "May I?"

Smiling, I nodded, and he swept me up and pressed me against his chest as we dissolved into shadow. The fear didn't hit me this time as he passed us through the barrier. He set me down on the sand in our little lagoon, our favorite swimming spot. Thousands of oyster shells littered the beach, glistening like black beetles in the sand. My brows rose. "Did you do this?"

"Look," Jayvin said, his voice near bursting as he ushered me forward. A single shell, lined with abalone, had been set apart from the others. He picked something small and sky-blue out of it. "It took me all night, but I finally found one."

"Found what?" I asked, even though I already knew—and my heart was falling apart because of it.

"I took notes." Jayvin reached into his coat pocket and pulling out a crumpled piece of paper. He smoothed it out. "The book I read about your people said that blue pearls were treasured above all others."

"That's right." My knees wobbled, and I let my bag drop off my shoulder. "They are priceless. The rarest of all colors."

Jayvin waved me forward, and as I approached and glanced

over the oyster shells, *hundreds* of peals shone in the sand. Whites, pinks, yellows, greys—and everyone tossed aside.

I sat, and Jayvin sat across from me—his smile like the crescent moon—and on his palm sat a perfectly round blue pearl, as vibrant as the sea it was conceived in.

"Take it," Jayvin said, breathless. My fingers trembled as I lifted the tiny gem, the Merfolk's most coveted treasure. "It's a gift."

My voice cracked. "How?"

"I noticed the oysters the first time we went swimming." Jayvin tucked his hand under his armpits, rocking—but this time in excitement instead of fear. "Do you like it?"

"It's . . ." Flawless, stunning, the find of a century. I ran a hand through my loose waves. My voice cracked.. "It's absolutely perfect. I don't know what to say."

Jayvin's rocking slowed. "I don't expect you to say anything. I just wanted to thank you."

It was hard to tear my eyes away from the pearl. "F-for what?"

"For the greatest weeks of my life." Jayvin rolled up his coat sleeve, sorrow filling his features as he glanced over the silver scars on his arm—the ones we shared.

He chewed his lip. "After we stop the Emperor and the barrier falls, there will be nothing stopping Mother from dragging me home." He sucked in a shuddering breath and closed my fingers over the pearl. "She can take away my short-lived freedom, but she can't erase the memories I've made here—not again. This time I've spent with you . . . it was worth every hour I spent in the that tomb."

He knew. He understood.

It wasn't until tears dripped off my chin, and onto my lap, that I realized I was crying. Until now, my mind had done an excellent job shutting out what would happen when our bargain was fulfilled. A part of me just assumed he would stay —that we could continue laughing and playing games day and night—but he was *hers,* not mine.

Mine. I clutched the pearl to my chest as the air whooshed out of my lungs.

"I didn't want to make you sad, Sunshine." Jayvin scooted closer, smile falling as he wiped my damp cheeks. "This was supposed to be a happy surprise."

"Jay." I sucked in a ragged breath. *Can it really be this simple?* "She can't hurt you anymore."

"She will." Jayvin furrowed his brows, then shook his head. "She owns me. She does what she wants. It's alright. I can live with it."

Vampires operate on ownership and property. I blinked once, twice, and then scrambled back for my bag. Jayvin watched me, confused, as I dug frantically through its contents. "But what if she didn't?"

An anguished smile. "But she does."

"But what if she didn't?" *There it is.* I pulled out the red sea-glass bracelet I'd bought from those Imps weeks ago. I raised it over my head, and the wisps of sun peeking through the palms set it aglow.

Jayvin's eyes never left my face. "I'd say it's unkind for you to tease me with such traitorous thoughts."

"Merfolk mate for life, I told you that." I fingered the bracelet. I was going to throw up. "It's a binding, magical law gifted by our shared Elven ancestors—just like our bargain. Above the reach of kings and emperors. Above the laws of Vampires. Each belongs to the other, and to no one else, and may never be separated."

Jayvin went unnaturally still. "Sunshine—"

"In the binding ceremony," I said, rolling the pearl between my palms. "We exchange gifts." When I looked up, tears poured down his pale cheeks. I showed him the bracelet. "Will you accept this? You will be mine, and I will be yours, and you can be free? I won't make you stay if you don't want to. You'll be able to go anywhere you want."

He moaned, tracing those circles in his hair. I pulled his hands away, kissing each of his palms. "This is real, Jay. You don't have to go back unless you want to."

"*Unless I want to.*" Jayvin almost sounded angry as he held my gaze. "You'd be bound to me forever, Tetra."

"That's okay. I don't mind."

"No, it's not," Jayvin replied. I opened my mouth to protest, but he stopped me. Those stunning ruby eyes dilated he brushed his fingers along my cheekbone. "Because I won't leave, Sunshine. All I've wanted since I first saw you—tripping over those ridiculous skeletons—is for you to love me. When I heard your voice, I decided it didn't matter if you were real or not. I would follow you anywhere—even if only to listen to you talk about your rocks. For that reason alone, it would be best if Mother took me back."

He paused and exhaled. "Because I'll never stop loving you, Sunshine, and I'd rather endure her torment for a millennium than watch you give your love to someone else."

I stared at him and just breathed, breathed, breathed.

Finally, I just shook my head and laughed. "You exquisite, blind fool." I'd never witnessed a binding ceremony before. I didn't expect the explosion of light and heat, searing golden scars over the silver ones we already wore as I reached forward and tied the bracelet to his wrist.

Jayvin glanced numbly over the golden marks before his gaze slowly lifted to mine.

It took me back to Mama and Papa, to the golden bands they wore around their wrists.

"I've loved you from the first time you tried to kill me,

Jay." I burst out laughing and wiped my eyes on the corner of my dress. "I'm yours. I've always been yours."

Jayvin's mouth parted as his eyes fell to my lips, his pupils dilating. "Say that again."

"I'm *yours*." He trembled as I crawled onto his lap and kissed his jaw. "And you are *mine*."

"*Mine*." Jayvin's lips crashed into mine as he lifted me by the hips and carried me off the beach, laying me down beneath the palm trees. My fingers found their way beneath his shirt, tracing his hard stomach and chest as he pressed his teeth into my throat and rumbled, "*Mine*."

"Yes," I gasped, and I was. I always had been. "And I always will be. *She* can't touch you anymore."

Jayvin moaned as his mouth moved back to mine, and I opened to let him taste me. He stripped me of my dress and undergarments, the brisk morning air chilling my heated skin.

This—I wanted this.

I wanted *him*.

He chuckled softly as I removed his jacket and pulled his shirt over his head. I raised a brow.

"Apologies." He kissed down my neck, across my collarbone... lower. "This is just different."

"Good or bad, different?" As he continued, I pressed a series of gentle kisses to his lower lip.

"Good." Jayvin gripped my hair and pulled my head back to expose my neck. "Drones aren't allowed to be anywhere but... beneath." I gasped as he bit down on my throat, almost hard enough to break the skin. His chest rumbled as he murmured, "I think I like it up here."

"Only one way?" I breathed, and he nodded. *I'm going to kill her one day. And I'm going to enjoy it.* I scoffed. "How very dull of her."

Jayvin's breath caught as I twisted until my back was to him.

"Sunshine." Jayvin kissed up my spine, his mouth lingering on the space between my neck and shoulder. He sat back, gently wrapping his fingers around my throat as he ground me up and against him, his voice a rumbling command. "Say. It. Again."

"I'm *yours*." I cried out as he sunk his teeth into my skin. My entire body went liquid. Despite his hold, I let my head fall back against his shoulder, melting into him, as his free hand moved to my hip, lower.

"You're mine," I breathed, the warmth of his venom spreading into my veins. "Let's try something new, Jayvin Dyre."

Jayvin growled in agreement before making me his forever.

Chapter Twenty-Eight

Thank the Lord for the shade of the palm trees because we didn't leave in time to beat the sun—or for hours after that. I'd have happily stayed there all day, letting Jayvin continue to show *me* new things until the night came again.

But unfortunately, we had an Emperor to overthrow and thousands of lives to save.

Sitting cross-legged in the shadows, only half-dressed, Jayvin watched with raised brows as I picked each and every pearl out of the sand and shoved them into my bag. "If I'd known they were worth anything, I'd have made a nice pile for you," he said coyly. "What do you plan to do with them all?"

"Sell them, of course." I glanced up and had to squint as I smiled at him. The sun reflecting off the sand was blinding. "Traveling is expensive."

Jayvin grinned—full of pure joy and excitement—because that's what we'd do if we survived the next few nights. When we weren't exploring each other, we'd talked about the parts of the world we wanted to explore, and all the wonders we'd never been able to see. I'd collect new treasures along the way. He asked, "Is that so?"

"As the voice of non-experience, I should think so." I stepped off the beach and curled up in his lap. He pressed three kisses to my neck before wrapping his arms around me. I shook my bag, rattling the pearls inside it. "With housing, food, supplies, and all."

"We could just sleep outside." Jayvin glanced up at the sky, at the sunlight streaming through the leaves. "I'd like that."

"What about when it rains?" I closed my eyes as he traced circles on my back. *He's still afraid this isn't real.*

"I'll build you a house."

"Every time we stop?"

"If you wanted me to." He laid his cheek against my hair. "It can't be that hard."

"Says the voice of non-experience." I giggled. "How about we buy a tent?"

"That sounds lovely." Jayvin's tracing moved to my shoulders as he stared over the crystal clear, blue waters. He sighed. "We have to go back now, don't we?"

"Yes." I didn't want to go either, but at the same time, I wanted to get this over with. We *all* deserved to move on with our lives. With a huff, I stood and offered him my hand. "Let's not keep the others waiting longer than they already have."

"I forgot." Jayvin's eyes brightened as he let me help him up. "Loach and I planned to play for the rest of his cheese this afternoon. He's teaching me the Eight Game Mix, and thinks he'll win—" As he turned, alarm and confusion fell over his features, making my stomach lurch.

Gently, Jayvin faced me toward the city. "Are they anyone you know?"

Eight enforcers stood on the beach inside the barrier. The man I presumed to be the new captain, with his violet, plumed helm, held up a small object. The barrier parted, creating an opening large enough to let the three men on the far side through. But those men didn't pass through, at least not immediately. They stared at us, expressions filled with shock, rage, and betrayal. They were Merfolk.

Not just any Merfolk—it was Surge and two of his highest-ranking guards.

He saw me.

The Dam's prince flared his striking red fins, his onyx hair falling in sopping, tangled waves to his waist, as he stepped toward our lagoon.

Worst of all, he'd seen Jayvin. Even creatures below the sea feared Vampires and their spawn. The Enforcers followed his gaze, and they landed on us. Shouting muffled orders, they drew their weapons, pointing as they rushed toward the open gap in the barrier.

I jumped as Jayvin gripped my shoulders, covering us both in darkness. "Hold on."

As he lifted me into his arms, Jayvin shadow shot past the barrier, using the stretching shade of the palms onto the beach inside. The world shifted into haze and warbling lines, but as we hit the end of the shade, the ground became solid again— the effect so jarring that I fell to my knees. The cries of the guards became deafening without the shield between us.

Jayvin was still in my shadow, but I was corporeal —exposed.

"*I can't hide you in the sun.*" Jayvin hissed in my ear. "*Run. Find somewhere dark to hide. I'm with you.*"

As I stood, Surge and his guards passed through the barrier —eyes fixed on where I'd landed in the sand. The Enforcers flanked them, not to harm them, but to aid them—in capturing me.

Jayvin nudged me in the back—hard. *"Tetra, run!"*

Sharks. I fell once as I sprinted off the beach, past the plaza shops, and into the warehouse district. Only their thundering footsteps and orders to yield told me they had followed.

Why is Surge here, why is Surge here, why is Surge here? I didn't have time to think about it. I wove through Humans and Orcs, each opening their businesses for the day. They cursed as I barreled past, only to fall silent at the sound of the approaching Enforcers.

"You sure you can't hide me?" A Human woman with a wheelbarrow swerved in front of me, but with a shriek, I managed to dive over it. My lungs were on *fire,* but I ate up the ground beneath me faster than ever. "You hid that cart of weapons in the sun when we broke into the headquarters!"

"*That was an inanimate object.*" Jayvin sounded strained. "*Living beings are completely different. I have you, Sunshine, don't stop.*"

I realized then that it was his arms beneath mine, the push of his body, that had me moving so swiftly. I ran until I had no idea where I was going. I sucked in gasping breaths as I surveyed my surroundings—a small courtyard leading to more private businesses.

The Enforcers were still shouting a few blocks back. They'd catch up with us before Surge—he wasn't used to land. With all the stress they'd been under, I didn't doubt for a moment that the Enforcers would kill me without pause or question. Not only that, but they'd seen me without my shift—with Jayvin.

My shift—

Jayvin must have had the same idea. "*Disguise yourself. Now!*"

Out of instinct, I shifted into my dark-haired Human form, slowing to a walk to blend into the crowd. I kept my head down, falling in sync with a group of young Human women heading toward the local bathhouse.

Sweat dripped down my temples as the pack of Enforcers burst into the courtyard. They jerked around—glowing eyes bright—as they searched for any sign of us.

"*Good. Just stay calm.*" Jayvin whispered. "*You can do this.*"

They didn't even glance my way as I passed with the Human group. I let my shoulders relax, letting my hips sway, mimicking the movement of the women around me. It wasn't until Surge entered the courtyard that my heart dropped to my ankles. He may not have been tall, but he was intimidating. Only wearing short, slim swimwear—his heavily muscled, olive chest and thighs were exposed, speckled in red scales. His guards flanked him in perfect unison as he strode toward the Enforcers. "Where is she?"

"We lost her," the captain admitted, still scanning the courtyard. "You know how these sea bitches are, they're crafty."

Surge's full lips curled back over his teeth. "Say that again, and I'll—" He froze as his intense gaze landed on me.

No, no, no, no. I kept my eyes on the ground, but it didn't matter—he saw straight through my shift.

"Stop." Surge stepped forward, hand outstretched. "Wait—"

The Enforcers poured in, locked onto me like a bloodhound.

"*RUN!*" Jayvin had my legs moving before I willed them to. I toppled over half the Humans in the group as I tore into the nearest alley. *Where can I go?* I couldn't lead them to the hide-out. Geralt's restaurant was too far. I'd never make it.

The grey warehouses were a blur as I thundered past—a twisting maze of stacked, square buildings. My eyes widened. *The warehouse.*

"Where are you going?" Jayvin asked as I skidded onto a narrow side street.

Where is it? I slowed to a stop, my teal hair sticking to my sweaty face, and I spotted it—the warehouse that Loach and I stayed in when we'd first come to Carnage.

"There!" I slammed into the warehouse door, expecting it to open, only to be knocked back onto my ass. Locked.

"No, no, no, no—" I couldn't breathe. They were coming. I couldn't breathe.

Jayvin tensed within my shadow. *"Sunshine—"*

"Hello, pretty." My heart nearly stopped as three more Enforcers emerged from around the corner. They weren't out of breath or coated in sweat. They'd been waiting.

The nearest—a short, brown-haired Elf—sneered. "We thought you might come back here."

"Don't—" Was all I could manage before they surged forward, aimed to stab through my chest in a unified attack. I threw up my hands as a shadow mass formed before me. Jayvin braced against the warehouse's wall, facing me, as three swords plunged through his back. The blades stopped inches from my face, and he grunted as they them pulled free, spilling hot blood down his abdomen. Jayvin's face—his lovely face—blistered as the sun savaged every exposed piece of his skin.

"No!" I shrieked, reaching for him, but Jayvin was already moving.

With a pained grimace, Jayvin turned to face the Enforcers. As the light burned his flesh away, he exposed his fangs and snarled, "She is *mine.*"

The brown-haired Elf raised his bloody sword as the others backed away, fear-stricken. *As they should be.* Jayvin was a force of nature. The Elf's gloved hand trembled as he pointed and stammered, "Stand down, spawn, or we'll—"

He was already dead.

With an open throat, he fell as Jayvin converged on the others. He ripped their tongues out before tearing the limbs from their bodies, leaving the remaining stumps of their torsos to twitch and bleed out on the cobblestone. Jayvin lifted the last Enforcer and sunk his teeth into his neck, draining it to a withered husk.

Jayvin let the body fall as he stumbled back into the shadows of the warehouse's roof. As I watched, his ravaged skin returned to its usual dove grey, flawless and free of burns. He groaned, shaking as he braced his hands against his knees. "That really hurt."

"You're going to be okay, right?" I fought back a wave of nausea as I crawled to him and lifted his shirt. The red-smeared, gaping wounds on his stomach had already closed. I was going to throw up. "Please, tell me you're not going to die."

Jayvin let out a weak laugh as he sank to the ground. "No, Sunshine, I'm not going to die. I just need a minute." He looked over what he'd done to the Enforcers with disgust, blood dripping off his chin. "I'm sorry you had to see that—*again*."

Outside, shouting and more footsteps passed the warehouse in a rush.

"Don't be." *They lost us.* I exhaled, slumping against Jayvin's shoulder. Every inch of my body ached. "I'd be dead if it weren't for you." I listened, but the sounds of the Enforcers outside had long faded away. "What should we do now?"

"Find the others." He held his stomach as he stood. "If they'd known to search for you here, they may have already found The Lux."

"But Surge." I shook my head. "I have no idea what's happening..."

Jayvin pressed a bloody kiss to my forehead and laughed. "Welcome to my world."

Chapter Twenty-Nine

The Lux's door sat ajar, hanging crooked on its hinges.

I held my breath as I stepped inside, the tears I tried to hold spilling over my cheeks. Trampled papers littered the floor, mingled with shards of broken dish ware—Agatha's precious china. The sofa had been torn open, and the stuffing inside had been removed. The cabinets hung open—all but one.

My hand shook as I opened the remaining coffee cabinet. Boot's maps and the Emperor's projection ring were still inside. I took a shaky breath and slipped it onto my thumb. "Boot didn't even get a chance to ward it." I choked back a sob as I tucked the maps into my bag. "They're dead. They're dead—"

Jayvin cocked his head as he inhaled. "They're not here."

"Captured, then?"

"I don't think so." Despite his size, his steps were so light as he jogged up the stairs. I followed. Our rooms had been tossed, my clothes scattered across the landing, along with the rest of our belongings. A half-dried blood splatter stained the door to the balcony. Jayvin touched it, bringing his red-smeared fingers to his nose and inhaled. He scowled. "Agatha."

"*No.*" Jayvin caught me as I crumpled, holding me against his chest as I wept. They were dead or dying somewhere—because of me. Because I'd been foolish enough to think I could make a difference. Now Surge was here. Everything was falling apart and—

"Tetra?" The voice was just a slip of a thing—words on the wind, coming from down the hall. I dashed into Boot's room, and Ivan was there, huddled beneath a blood-soaked blanket. Sweat dripped from his thick brows and into his eyes as he glanced up at us and smiled. "You're alright."

Not a question.

Jayvin searched the room as I fell on my knees beside the Dwarf. "Oh, Ivan." I peeled back the blanket, revealing a deep stab wound in his side.

"It's safe." Jayvin crouched beside me and scanned over Ivan. His face fell. "I can try to heal you. It will just take some time—"

"No, no." Ivan cleared his throat before smiling at me, his teeth coated with red. "That's time you don't have. I was almost gone, but your voice brought me back. I always liked your voice, Tetra."

"Let him help—" I reached to open his tunic.

Ivan weakly grabbed my wrist, nodding to Jayvin. "The Emperor knows he's here." He sucked in a gurgling breath. "He tracked him somehow. The others got away. I made sure of that."

Of course, he did. Ivan had always served Boot without question.

Fury, pain, but mostly deep, deep sorrow passed over Jayvin's features. "You're a true warrior. It's too late to find anything for the pain." He chewed his lip until it bled. "But I can give you an honorable death, if that's what you'd prefer?"

I wanted to crumble again, to fall to pieces, but later—right now, I needed to be strong.

With an agonized moan, Ivan rolled onto his back and nodded.

Jayvin looked at me. "Do you have a knife with you?"

"I don't—" But I did. My fingers trembled as I rummaged through my bag and closed my hand around the cheap dagger Loach had given me weeks ago outside the barrier. It felt like a lifetime ago. I pulled it out and handed it to him. "Here."

"Thank you." Jayvin pressed his hand to the Dwarf's sternum. "For your sacrifice."

Ivan sighed, closing his eyes—almost blissful—as Jayvin sunk the blade straight into his heart. One moment, Ivan was there. The next he was gone.

Jayvin wiped the dagger clean on his trousers, then pressed it into Ivan's limp hand, folding it over his chest.

I stared at the body that had once been my friend. At least, he'd been a friend to me. In truth, I'd hardly paid attention to him as he diligently ensured we were fed and had everything we needed, purely out of his loyalty to Boot.

I clenched my fists on my lap. "Sayzar is going to pay."

Jayvin's ruby filled with desire. "You should let me teach you the way of the blade, Sunshine. You'd be a spectacle to behold."

"Best that you don't." I stood, feet buzzing from falling asleep. Jayvin stood with me. I stroked his cheek. "The spectacle would be me cutting myself in two."

He just kissed me, laughing weakly against my lips, before taking a step back. His eyes darkened as he looked over Ivan's body and repeated, "Sayzar will pay."

Jayvin tracked Agatha's blood trail to her brother's restaurant. It was a predictable move, one that the Enforcers would expect, but maybe they didn't have a choice.

The back door was locked but popped open quickly when Jayvin rammed his shoulder into it. We could have knocked, but what if there were more guards inside?

As the door swung open, Geralt cried out as he drew a chipped machete—the blood draining from his face when he realized who was standing on the other side. He exhaled, bracing against his knees. "Did you have to break it?"

Jayvin's brow rose. "I didn't. Can I come in?"

Geralt nodded, and Jayvin slammed the door back onto its hinges before locking it behind us. "See? All better."

"Where are they?" I wrapped Geralt in a hug. "Tell me they're alive."

Geralt awkwardly patted my shoulder. "They're well . . . enough. Follow me upstairs."

I hadn't realized his restaurant had an upstairs. He led us through his black and white tiled dining room, the sign on the front door switched to *Closed*. On the far side, down a narrow hallway, was a ladder leading up to what looked like an attic.

"Up you go." Geralt ushered us forward, but Jayvin stopped me so he could climb up first. After a moment, he reached down and helped me up the ladder. Once I'd reached the top, I was immediately hit by the sharp smell of astringents and gauze. The attic was low-ceilinged and low-lit, with a two-person bed in the far right corner and not much else.

Loach sat on a stool, carefully rewrapping a wound on

Agatha's thigh. From the bed, her eyes widened as she took us in, filling with tears. "Damn it, woman, where have you been?"

Loach jerked toward us, and Agatha hissed as his elbow smacked into her leg. "Tetra—"

"How convenient." Boot hobbled out of the shadows, pointing a taloned finger at us. Jayvin snarled. Boot ignored him, his expression twisted with rage. "How nice of you two to return from playing house *after* the damage has already been done."

I swatted his hand out of my face. "You think we did this?"

"Boot—" Agatha began, but he shushed her before turning back to me.

"I heard you lovebirds leave this morning." Jayvin tensed as Boot stepped closer. "Not an hour later, the Enforcers arrived. What am I supposed to think?"

"Ivan said they tracked us." Jayvin's voice was low and deadly. "Do you have any ideas in that regard? And be careful, Goblin. Another unkind word to my wife, and I may remove your head from your shoulders."

Boot's cratered rusty skin paled, orange eyes falling to the matching golden scars on our arms. "Lord above. You're bonded."

"Could they have tracked us." The rickety stool squeaked as Loach stood. "Boot? Could the Emperor have tracked us?"

Boot's gaze then rose Sayzar's ring on my thumb. "Oh no."

"Oh no, what?" I blurted.

He gestured for the ring, and I handed it to him. Speaking in a low voice, Boot drew symbols in the air over the jewel, his brows furrowing as a wave of violet magic responded, revealing its own symbols. He cursed as he chucked the ring into the corner. "It has a tracking ward. *Damn it.*"

I lost feeling in my legs. *He's been following us since the begin-*

ning. Somehow, he'd known . . . from that very first meeting he'd known.

Geralt watched us, bark-brown skin speckled with sweat.

Boot roared in frustration, ripping at his tailored suit. "Ivan?"

Jayvin's chin dropped. "Gone."

Boot dropped to the floor, sighing as he rested his face in his hands. "Then we're done."

"Not exactly." Agatha tried to stand, but Loach held her down. Instead of snapping at him, she gave him a grateful smile before continuing, "There might be a chance. What if Sayzar's tracking *Jessa*, not us?"

"Either way, we're finished." Boot glared at the ring still in the corner. "The Emperor knows where we are."

Jayvin strode to where the ring sat on the floor, staring at it momentarily before crushing it beneath his heel, shooting shards of amethyst in every direction. "Now he doesn't."

"Surge is here," I whispered. Loach looked like he was about to pass out.

"Cyclone's son?" Agatha asked, wincing as she scooted up higher against her pillows.

"Yes," I nodded, "Which means that either he's onto Sayzar's plan, or . . ."

Agatha's eyes widened, her cracked lips parting. "Or the Emperor invited him to the ball. He's going give the order to execute the Merfolk in front of him."

"My thoughts exactly." I don't know what switch had flipped to make me sound so calm. Maybe it was Jayvin and Ivan's blood still crusted beneath my nails. I gave Boot a stern look. "Tomorrow, we take back Cyclone's bones."

"And the ring?" Boot shot back. "We cannot hold the barrier up long enough to keep out the Enforcers."

"We'll figure it out." He opened his mouth to argue, but I

cut him off. "We're taking his treasury. We're taking the Wardstone. My people aren't toys for Sayzar to play with."

An approving growl rumbled in Jayvin's chest as he stepped forward and kissed my shoulder.

Something struck me. I glanced around. "Loach, where's the salt?"

"Also, gone." Loach tossed his hat on the bed. "I lost it in the chaos."

Damn it. I sucked in a shaky breath. "Jay can sneak us out to the ocean in the morning. Then we'll have twenty-four hours to take the palace before the salt sickness takes us." I caught Loach and Agatha's eyes. "You still in?"

"We're in," they said in unison.

I stepped forward and leaned over the bed, taking the extent of Agatha's wound. I scrunched my nose. "Jayvin can fix that, you know."

Agatha shot him a suspicious look. "How?"

With a laugh, Jayvin grinned from ear to ear. "Venom."

"Hell, no." Agatha shifted further back into the pillows. "I don't want your teeth anywhere near my thighs, brute. I'll survive."

We all burst into laughter. It felt good to laugh.

Chapter Thirty

I couldn't sleep. Not when, by this time next evening, I'd either be on my way back to the Dam with Cyclone's remains or in the hands of the Emperor.

So, I just laid in the double bed beside Agatha, listening to her restless tossing and turning. Apparently, she'd taken an Enforcer's knife in the leg before returning the favor to his skull. There had only been two—a foolish mistake—but with Agatha wounded, Ivan had held the guards at bay as Loach and Boot got her to safety.

Ivan knew he'd die, but he'd fought for them anyway.

Just like I'll fight for my people—whether they know it or not. I rolled onto my back, staring at the dark ceiling. Actually, I hoped the Merfolk find out what Sayzar had planned or how close they'd come to dying. Maybe it would help them to fight that much harder.

You say that as if you've already won. It was more likely my body would join Cyclone's by tomorrow. I rubbed my face, suppressing a groan. *No bad thoughts.*

An orange flicker of light made me wince—Jayvin's

faelight. It floated up the ladder, moving across the floor before bobbing beside my pillow.

Agatha whimpered, pulling the sheer blankets over her head, but she didn't wake.

I held out my hand, and the light settled on my finger like a bird. "Is he outside?"

The faelight darted back down the latter. I rose, not bothering to put a coat over my long-sleeved nightgown. The late spring night had been humid—especially in an attic—and my skin was slick with sweat. Despite my best efforts, I cringed as the floorboards creaked beneath my bare feet. Agatha and I slept upstairs with Geralt's children, their little bedrolls scattered throughout the room. None of them stirred. Orcs must be heavy sleepers. The men had slept downstairs.

Even with the lack of sleep, my body tingled with excess adrenaline. I should be sleeping—I wanted to sleep—but I couldn't. I crept down the hallway and into the restaurant's pantry. Loach and Boot were curled on their bed mats, snoring loudly. Geralt had fallen asleep with his head on his desk. His neck and back would be hurting when he woke. An empty bed mat lay by the far wall, but Jayvin wasn't on it.

The faelight passed through the back door instead of slipping through the cracked window. I twisted the doorknob so slowly it was painful, biting down on my lip as I slipped through out into the alley.

As I expected, the street was empty. The faelight whizzed upwards onto the roof. I glanced up—and of course—Jayvin was there, watching the sunrise. He scowled as the faelight danced around his head before he noticed me below. He smiled down at me. "You should be sleeping."

I smiled back up at him. "So should you."

"Touché." Jayvin leaned over and dropped a rope ladder off the roof. "Here."

The rope scratched my feet as I climbed. Once I'd risen a few feet, Jayvin leaned over and pulled me up the rest of the way before he set me on his lap. I let out a sharp breath as I brushed my hair back off my damp forehead. "Why would Geralt have a rope ladder on his roof?"

Jayvin shrugged. "It was already here when I climbed up."

My brow rose. "You didn't use it?"

He snorted. "Um, no."

"Vampires." I laid my head against his chest as he gently stroked down my arms, over the scales and delicate fins on my forearms. Sighing, I closed my eyes. "Are you afraid? For tomorrow, I mean."

"No, and yes." Jayvin's fingers moved to my calves before trailing up my thighs. "I don't fear my part, only that you'll be alone with that conceited Elf bastard for so long."

I burst out laughing. "You're an Elf!"

"Half," he clarified. "And that's more than enough."

"Well, you got all the good parts." I pinched Jayvin's bicep when he chortled. I picked at the fabric of his thick, black sweater. The thought came to me again. "There's nothing you remember of them? Your family?"

Jayvin exhaled, resting his chin on the top of my head. "I've shared all my memories from before with you. There is information I've recovered over the years, but it isn't much. Mother let slip a snippet or two about the region I'm from and that I'd already been trained in combat before she turned me."

"I don't imagine the Matriarch liked you digging into the past."

"No, she didn't." He swallowed roughly. "But I dug anyway, which was the start of my downfall."

"What did you find that made her turn on you?" I leaned back to see his lovely face. "Before she locked you away?"

Jayvin's ruby gaze flickered to mine, and I didn't miss the

pain behind it. "I found out that she lied. To me. To all of us. After that . . ." He pursed his lips. "I couldn't look at her the same anymore. All the grandeur and mysticism she'd built herself on was a lie. I'd just been too closely bound to her to see it before." Jayvin straightened and lifted me by the waist until I straddled him. "And you? What of your family?"

How little I had shared with him didn't occur to me until now. We talked about so many things, but the cove hadn't been one of them. I rested my cheek against his shoulder as he rubbed my back, and I sighed. "I lived in a pod. There were twenty-four of us in all. We claimed a small cove, only about one hundred miles from Carnage. My mother and father had built a tiny driftwood cabin that we shared." I clenched my fists into his sweater. "They loved me, even though I was different. Even though I was loud, emotional, and didn't play well with the other children."

Jayvin listened thoughtfully.

The tears started flowing once more, and perhaps finally, the truth of it all. "They loved me, but when Sayzar came, they chose to die rather than submit. I was terrified. I thought that if one of us knelt, he would spare us, but I was wrong." A lump formed in my throat. "They abandoned me here alone. They should have chosen me. They should have *lived*."

And there it was—my horrible, selfish truth. I resented them for choosing to die, for forcing me to sell away all their keepsakes, to pretend to care for Mermen who only wanted my body. Whose touch repulsed me—just so I wouldn't have to be lonely and starving for a night.

"We will live, Sunshine." Jayvin murmured into my hair as he tugged me closer. "I choose you. I've had enough of merely existing. Even if it were just me and you for eternity, that would be enough.

"Yes, yes, you're right," I said as I kissed his neck and wiped my face. "That is enough."

And it was.

Jayvin shivered and gripped my arms as my lips brushed against his throat. "Careful with that."

"With what?" I craned back to see his face. His pupils had dilated. I grinned as he shifted his hips beneath me. "You mean this?" With a chuckle, I scraped my teeth across his jugular as he'd done to me so many times.

He moaned, arching into the touch. "*Tetra.*"

"Vampires and throats." I pushed him down and his eyes grew hazy. I pulled my hair over my shoulder and kissed his jaw once, twice, before whispering into his ear. "Remember, you're mine."

Jayvin gasped as I bit down on his neck. It must have felt so silly to him with my ordinary teeth. Before the embarrassment could sink in, he flipped me onto my back and yanked up my nightgown, sending goosebumps over my bare thighs.

My heart thundered as Jayvin pinned me below him, his fingers trailing to dangerous places as he rumbled against my throat. "*Mine.*"

Chapter Thirty-One

"I can't believe you're still doing this." I clung to Agatha's arm as she limped beside me, her wounded thigh tightly bandaged beneath her thick trousers. "You should have let Jayvin heal you. You can't run, you can't—"

"Stop worrying about my part." Agatha was good at hiding her pain, but I knew better. She was miserable. "If you lose focus with Sayzar, we're screwed."

I bit my tongue to keep from arguing further. She was right. I had a part to play.

Jayvin felt giddy in my shadow. *"It's almost show time, Sunshine."*

"At least one of us is having fun," I whispered, chewing at my thumbnail.

Agatha swatted my finger out of my mouth. Jayvin pressed a comforting kiss to the back of my neck. I sucked in a deep breath and held it. *In through the nose, out through the mouth.* I exhaled.

It felt dirty to be disguised as Jessa again. The top half of my golden waves were braided into an intricate pattern and pinned with pearl hairpins—courtesy of Boot.

As were all the jewels I wore. An emerald pendant hung between my breasts—one of the few pieces he'd saved after the raid—showcased perfectly by the low-cut, sea-foam green gown I wore. It sparkled in the white and cream glow of the faelights filling the inner courtyard. The guards had been expecting us, which made our trek through the gate and toward the palace unexpectedly simple.

"Your brother?" I asked.

"Is ready." Agatha glanced back, as if she could see all the way to his restaurant. "He and the kids will run as soon as the barrier falls and wait for me just outside the city limits."

I swallowed. "And then what?"

"Then I'll take them home . . . to the mountains," Agatha said in a rush. "It's a long walk. They'll need protection."

I knew it was selfish, but I didn't want her to go. I tightened my grip on her arm, resting my head on her shoulder.

Despite the soft music floating over the square and all the beautiful flowers and streamers, the heaviness of anxiety coated the inner court. Agatha was on edge. Every few moments, she glanced over her shoulder, lips pursed. "Something's off."

"Why?" Fear sunk like lead in my gut. "What is it?"

"Nothing visible, and that bothers me," she said, looking up at the floating lanterns filled with faelights that gave the palace its name. Her emerald skin looked stunning beneath their orangey glow. "But you'd think the Emperor would have his guards escort you instead of me, considering you're his date, and all."

"Maybe he trusts you?" I replied.

Agatha's thin brow rose. "That's funny. I doubt he trusts his own mother."

"I'm just saying you successfully brought me to dinner with him once already." I shrugged, trying to hide my nerves. "At least, he knows you're competent."

"Tetra, if we die—"

"Stop, stop." I pulled away and shook the anxiety out of my fingers. "Don't say that. I'm going to throw up."

"Yuck." Agatha braced against me and grinned as we made our way up the palace steps. "But if you're going to puke on anyone, make sure it's him."

I chuckled and then covered my mouth when an Enforcer by the doors gave us a funny look. I shifted my attention ahead as we approached the palace's massive, wooden double doors. They were hand-carved with images of Elven grandeur and embedded with flecks of silver and gold.

The magic of the Elves. There was so much good Sayzar Ameliatus could do—that *all* his people could do for Tyrr. My mind flashed to Jayvin's magic. Even being only half Elven, the abilities born into him—his lights, ability to ward, and his shadow-walking—were extraordinary. *Maybe it won't always be like this. Maybe things can change. People can change.*

But they wouldn't tonight.

Agatha tugged deeper into her knee-length coat.

Two Enforcers—wearing armor so elaborately detailed it must be ceremonial—raised their spears to let us pass. I watched them from the corner of my eye as we stepped through the doorway. They didn't have the slightest interest in us or bother to check us for weapons.

The entryway expanded into a three-leveled ballroom, all coral-hued marble and gold-coated bars twisted into the shapes of trees, branches, and flowers. I sucked in a sharp breath, hand over my throat. It was ... painting worthy.

Wide, rounded staircases sat on each side of the room, leading to the third floor. The spaces were backed with male and female Elves, in all shapes and colors, sipping wine and picking at platters of roasted meats and sweet fruit served on platters by Goblin servants.

I wonder if they're Boot's kin. His family had been forced to serve in this palace for centuries. It was time for them to be freed.

The middle level encircled the lower, holding six *massive* dining tables—three on each side—covered in blue-green cloth. On the lower level, the guests danced, draped in clothing of quality I'd never experienced. At the center of the room, a platform had been built. Atop it, something tall and rectangular lay hidden beneath a sheet of glittering, black fabric—a new statue, I'd guess.

I scanned the room frantically for any sign of Surge and his guards—nothing. I breathed out a sigh of relief.

"This is similar to Mother's castle." Jayvin mused. *"Too big to be useful and terribly gaudy."*

I snorted. "I didn't know you had an interest in interior design."

"Maybe it will become another new hobby." Jayvin brushed his fingers over the bare skin on my back. *"It's time for me to go, Sunshine. Be careful. I have no plans on living without you."*

"You, too." A wave of dizziness hit me. I forgot to breathe again. Movement rippled across my shadow, bouncing from me to all the little dark places over the ballroom before disappearing out of sight.

Agatha leaned in as if fixing a strand of my hair and whispered, "Is Jayvin gone?"

"Yes," I whispered back as she preened over my waves. "It's started."

This was it. There was no going back.

By this time, Loach and Boot would be entering through

the sewers and into the dungeon. Jayvin would be waiting for them.

Sharks. I smoothed the silken skirts of my dress as I followed Agatha deeper into the ballroom. *The Emperor is going to take one look at me and toss me out on my ass.* I'd underestimated the wealth Sayzar had accumulated for himself. Even in Boot's gems, I looked like alley trash compared to the rest of his guests.

What could be in the vault if this is what the palace's main hall looks like? I fiddled with the blue-stoned, silver ring I wore. The thought of Jayvin being able to move so much treasure in so little time seemed impossible, but he had assured me it was. *Just focus on your part, Tetra. That's all you can do.*

"Ah, there you are."

A shiver ran down my spine. I turned and found the Emperor smiling at me, his gaze trailing up and down my gown. Damn. I'd been worried about my own looks. As beautiful as they were, Sayzar's guests looked like slobs compared to him.

His cream and sage green doublet perfectly contrasted his vivid red hair. A matching sage cape was pinned to his shoulder with an emerald brooch the size of my fist. He stepped forward and took my hand before kissing my knuckles. "I was starting to worry you wouldn't come."

"Don't be silly," I blurted, then blushed when he raised a brow. I cleared my throat. "Pardon, I meant I'd never dream of such a thing."

Sayzar shook his head and laughed. "You never fail to surprise me, Lady Jessa." His smile faltered as his attention shifted to Agatha. "Thank you, once again, for escorting her to me safely."

"Hail." Agatha sank into a bow, not letting a hint of pain

show through her façade. She smiled at me as she stood, a glimmer of fear behind her eyes. "Call if you need anything."

Sayzar wrapped his arm around me and squeezed. I suppressed a shudder. "She will want for nothing with me. Enjoy the party, Miss Paine."

Agatha just nodded, giving him another quick bow before turning and disappearing into the sea of Elves. *No, no, no, no.* I didn't want her to go. I didn't want to be alone, especially not with *him*.

Sayzar stepped back, lifting our now conjoined hands to twirl me, eyes brightening at how the gown clung to my every curve. "Darling, you look absolutely *ravishing*."

Darling. I could have laughed. Instead, I feigned another blush as I fiddled with my pendant. "As do you. And here, I thought your guests looked grand."

Sayzar tilted his head, letting his fingers trail down the chain on my necklace, brushing the skin above my breasts before lifting the emerald. He shifted it, allowing the ballroom's low lights to glimmer through its facets. "What a delight to see we match." He nodded to his own broach. "Two of a kind, we are."

I rolled my eyes and moved to his side, looping my elbow through his. "It's almost like you planned it," I said.

"You caught me." Sayzar chuckled as he led us toward the left-wing staircase. I hoped he wasn't serious. His gaze flickered to my thumb as he rested his hand over mine. "Would that you'd worn my ring, though."

Sharks. Of course, he'd notice that. I checked for eavesdroppers before I leaned into him. "I couldn't let them get too jealous, could I? I already have your arm. How much more could they bear?"

"You have a point." It was an effort to match the grace of

his steps. "But I've never been one to shy away from the envy of others."

"You enjoy making people jealous?" I teased, lifting my gown high enough not to trip over the train. "How very emperor-like of you."

Sayzar let out an honest laugh as we reached the top of the staircase. "Why should I hide my accomplishments to spare the feelings of others?" He wrapped his arm around my waist as the eyes of every guest on the floor snapped to us. My skin heated in embarrassment as he pressed a silken kiss to my cheek. "Let them watch."

"Is that what I am?" I twisted, our mouths now inches apart. *I wish Jay were here.* The mental image of Jayvin tearing the Emperor apart had me smiling. "An accomplishment?"

My entire body fought to recoil as his lips brushed against the corner of my mouth. "You, darling, are my *greatest* accomplishment."

Someone in the crowd greeted him, reaching to shake Sayzar's hand, and I could have cried with relief. I wanted to scrub my face with soap and boiling water. Sayzar passed me sparkling wine as he introduced me to a portly man who approached us—apparently the palace treasurer.

It continued on like for far too long. He kept me close, ensuring every guest could view the Emperor's new plaything. I gave them all mindless, pretty smiles—making up stories of my ancestry and antique collections on the spot.

I was on my second glass of wine as we headed back down the stairs to the main floor. My skin felt flushed, and my legs were wobbly when we reached the bottom. I jumped when Sayzar suddenly turned to face me, stepping in close. His warm breath smelled of berry wine. "What did you think of those men and women? Speak honestly."

I blinked at him. Was this a trick question? I cleared my

throat again, smoothing my dress as I thought. Sayzar's eyes never left my face. *Honesty has gotten you this far.* Glancing back toward the guests, I shrugged. "I think they're after any advantage your power and wealth could give them, and they're willing to grovel for it."

Sayzar laced his hands behind his back, that cruel smile forming. "You are as wise as you are beautiful." He offered his elbow, and I took it. We continued down the lower level to join the dancers. The couples twirled together in sync with the music. By the size and absurd puffiness of their gowns, it was amazing that the women could dance, at all.

"You see them?" Sayzar nodded to a small group of well-dressed men loitering at the edge of the ballroom, drinking and laughing amongst themselves. I nodded. He continued, "If I left your side, even for a moment, they'd converge on you like wolves to a bleating calf."

The men's eyes flickered in our direction, and one of them shot me a quick smile. I nodded, clinging to Sayzar's arm. "Why would they do that?"

"Because now that we've been seen together," Sayzar took my hand and placed my other on his shoulder, "A dance with you could attract the attention of a wealthy patron, if not solely for being associated with me."

Arrogant bastard. "But I, myself, am no one of importance." I let Sayzar pull me into a slow dance, a jolt of energy shut up my finger and into my arm. I gasped as Laben's projection ring began to glow.

The Wardstone was down.

Sayzar gave a smug smile as his grip tightened, tugging me closer. He probably thought my gasp was for him. "That's the point I'm trying to make."

I must have frowned because he laughed, "I worded that poorly. I meant that power and influence don't come from your birth, status, or the depths of your coffers." He shot the men a scathing look, and they cowered behind a banister. Sayzar spun me, sending my hair spiraling like a golden cloud. His fingers spread over the small of my back as he brought me back to him. "Power, Jessa, comes from what you're willing to do to achieve it."

The drop in his tone set me on edge. Laben's projection ring continued to glow, and I spun it until the jewel faced my palm. I swallowed, raising a brow. "You mean like the way they prey on innocent women?"

"Precisely." He lifted my arms to rest them on his neck, linking both of his behind my back. "Many atrocities have been done in the name of ambition."

The music slowed with our steps. The faelights dancing along the ceiling drifted down until they sat only feet above the platform in the room's center, still draped in black fabric. As I watched, Sayzar leaned in and whispered in my ear, "Did you really think I wouldn't recognize you?"

My blood turned to ice. *No. He's lying. There's no way.* Slowly, I turned my gaze back to his. "Excuse me?"

Sayzar's expression was pure, poisoned satisfaction. He continued to sway me to the solemn tune of the piano. Almost lovingly, he traced my collarbone. "For an entire year, I've dreamt of your eyes—of the absolute horror that filled them when the heads of your family fell. Even better was the way you screamed."

My lips parted, and it felt like the air was squeezed from my lungs.

Sayzar spun me, my back now facing the platform. "Since then, you—my dear—have been my greatest inspiration." His eyes brightened into mania. "I thought to myself, if the deaths of so few could make you bow, what would the deaths of thousands accomplish? Even if one in ten bowed, that would be enough to take the entirety of Tyrr."

A tear escaped down my cheek as specks of black invaded my vision.

"So, you see, *Jessa*." Sayzar brushed away my tear. "All of this—the extermination of Cyclone's entire kingdom—is because of you."

"*No*." A sob escaped me as I tried to back away, but he clamped down on my wrist like a vice.

"And this," Sayzar lifted my hand to inspect the projection ring I wore. "After the wards on the catacombs were breached—and that monster freed—I suspected my Wardstone was the target." Sayzar mumbled a few words over Laban's ring, and it crumbled into dust. A violent flash of violet energy cracked through the palace, inciting several screams, as the barrier fell. "What I didn't suspect was for you and your friends to take the bait so easily. See, if I'd just killed your people—without the illusion of reason—my *own* people may have turned against me."

The dancing stopped. Sayzar backed me against the platform's edge and drew a series of symbols in the air. The sheet of dark fabric fell away to reveal the object atop the platform.

An enormous, glass fish tank.

"Don't—" My knees buckled, but Sayzar caught me and spun me until my back was pressed against his chest. He gestured to the central doorway, his voice wicked and clear as he cried, "My esteemed guests!"

Surge stood in the entry, flanked by his guards, and his dark eyes locked onto me—and they were devastated.

My vision blackened, but Sayzar didn't let me fall. "My proof to you, Prince of the Tyrr seas." Sayzar called over the stunned crowd's wild chatter. "That even your own people mean to betray you. This creature was the first. She won't be the last."

"No—" I tried to scream, but Sayzar's arm tightened around my throat, choking me.

Surge's intense gaze flickered between me and the Emperor, guarded. "This proves nothing. She is one woman."

"A woman who offered me your head in exchange for your kingdom." Sayzar crooned. Surge flinched. "And seeing that you cannot control your own people, I am declining your appeal for self-governance. I, myself, will bring the Merfolk of Tyrr to heel."

They had an arrangement. Fresh tears burned my eyes. No wonder the Dam had stayed untouched for so long. Surge had plans of his own—and I had ruined them because I had been foolish enough to think I'd known better.

Sayzar had made me into his pawn.

The two elaborately armored guards emerged from behind the crowd, their cruel, laughing gazes leering over me.

Sayzar nodded toward the tank. "Throw her in. She'll be tonight's entertainment."

Chapter Thirty-Two

The Enforcers shoved me into the tank, and my shift fell as I hit the water.

It was *boiling*.

I screamed as I went under and it scalded every inch of my skin red. My hair and scales changed to pure white. The shock made me inhale, inviting the inferno into my lungs.

The glass blurred the faces gathering around the tank. The Emperor's guests laughed and made lude gestures as they watched me struggle to breathe. They knew—the entire evening, they'd known—and couldn't wait to watch Sayzar make a fool of me.

"You're going to kill her!" Surge rushed toward the tank, but the Enforcers blocked him. Surge snarled in response. "Get her out!"

Being Merfolk was the only reason I wasn't dead already—our kind being incredibly resilient to water temperatures. Maybe it was pity that made Surge want to spare me. Perhaps he just wanted to question me himself and inflict an even worse kind of pain.

"I don't think I will." Sayzar stepped onto the platform, his demure façade forgotten. He placed his hand on the glass and grinned—he knew he'd won. "She's quite lovely, isn't she?" Sayzar's eyes trailed down my body. "I think I'll keep her as compensation for all the trouble your people have caused."

I couldn't breathe. My throat, lungs—even the insides of my nose—*burned*.

"We've done *nothing*." Surge's onyx hair swayed as he moved toward Sayzar. Again, the Enforcers blocked him. "Would you condemn an entire city for the actions of one stupid girl?"

Stupid girl. That's exactly what I was. Sayzar was right—all of this was because of me, but that didn't mean I still couldn't stop it. *"Surge!"* I pounded my fists on the glass. *"Stop him! He'll kill us all!"*

Surge didn't glance in my direction, his eyes locked on the Emperor.

He can't hear me. I looked up. A glimmer of lavender energy surrounded the tank. *It's warded.* That also must be how the water was staying so damn hot. The top was too high for me to climb out.

"That's exactly what I'm going to do." Sayzar's cruel smile widened as he stepped off the platform. Surge's eyes widened. "And when the last axe falls, you and your people will have become a beautiful example for the rest of Tyrr. The Seafolk will submit to me, or they will not exist at all."

The Merfolk guards drew their weapons at the same time as the Enforcers. Surge's entire body began to tremble. "You're lying. This is a bluff."

"Ask your friend here if I bluff." Sayzar turned and pressed his palm against the tank. "And if she doesn't know the answer to that yet, she will soon enough—"

"TETRA, MOVE."

A loud *bang* cracked through the water as I pushed off the glass, away from Sayzar, just as a crossbow bolt punched through both sides of the tank—straight into the Emperor's shoulder. Guests screamed, scrambling away, as boiling water sprayed from the cracks in the glass. Sayzar cried out in agony as he fell to his knees.

I wheeled, looking to the third floor, just in time to watch Agatha load a second bolt in her crossbow. Grinning at me, she jerked her head to the left. I moved, and she shot another round through the glass. The tank shattered—sending a second wave of water over the fleeing crowd.

Shrieking, blistered bodies in expensive, sodden fabrics tripped over each other as they barreled toward the palace entry. They were met by a wall of Enforcers streaming into the palace—spears and shields readied for battle.

Shards of glass punched into my limbs as I hit the ballroom floor. I retched, for once thankful to expel all the water out of my lungs. The clang of steel against steel had me stumbling to my feet, gasping.

Surge and his guards fell upon the Emperor and his Enforcers. Sayzar grimaced as he blocked an attack, gripping his wounded shoulder. Behind me was another loud crack, and another Enforcer fell—only feet from me—with one of Agatha's bolts through his neck.

"Tetra, go!" Agatha had her crossbow propped on the railing, raining down on the Emperor's men from above. "Plan C. You need to get Cyclone!"

My voice was completely raw. "We didn't make a plan C!"

"I just did." She put another bolt through another Enforcer's thigh, sending him to the ground. "Go!"

Thank God I wore sandals, not heels. I tore across the ballroom toward the hallway I knew lay on the eastern side. Boot had made us study maps of the palace until we could recite the entire building layout from memory.

Sharks. My foot snagged in the skirts of my gown, and I fell, landing on my hip. Groaning, I rolled onto my side and cursed. The body of a fallen Enforcer lay within arm's reach. "Sorry." I cringed as I drew the knife from his belt. "I need this." The skirt of my gown came off in two swipes of the blade, my legs now free from the thigh down.

"You!" Thundering footsteps and the sound of my prince's voice made my limbs locked into place as I rose. Surge strode toward me, his dark eyes wild, his bare chest and three-pronged sword splattered with blood. Without slowing, he pointed his weapon at me. "How could you betray us your own people? If you understood everything I've fought for—"

I flinched as Surge was knocked to the ground with a loud *ooph,* Agatha straddled over his back. She'd jumped off the damn balcony. Pressing tip of her dagger to the back of Surge's neck, Agatha twisted to face me as she took a fistful of his hair. "Go! I'll hold them off."

I stepped back. Sweat dripped down her temple. Blood had seeped through the bandage on her thigh. I couldn't leave her like this. "But—"

"Go!" Agatha cried as Surge writhed beneath her. He swore viciously as she smacked him on the back of the head with the hilt of her blade. "Go now!"

Someone was screaming near the entry. I stretched into a sprint, entering the side hallway. It was narrower than the maps made it look, built from dark stone, the only light coming from the goat-horn sconces mounted to the walls. An ache flowered from my chest out into my arms, down into my fingers—salt withdrawals.

Every part of me hurt, but I couldn't slow down. If Surge

was killed, if Sayzar wasn't stopped—this would all be for nothing.

Cyclone could wait. He was dead, but his son—my prince—was alive. For now, at least.

I needed Jayvin.

The hallway split, and I barreled down the path to the right, leading into a servant's quarters.

Bingo.

"Wobbly shelf, wobbly shelf, wobbly shelf." I shoved items onto the floor, searching for a switch behind them. There were *dozens* of shelves on the far wall of the quarters, filled with cleaning, cooking, and sewing supplies. Pots and clay jars clattered as I yanked on every shelf, sweat dripping down my sides. "Wobbly shelf, wobbly—here!"

A panel in the wall sprung open—just where Boot said it would, leading to the corridors the Goblin servants used to maneuver through the palace unseen. If only I had Goblin dark vision. I clung to the damp stone wall, feeling my way through the corridor, heading upward. The path twisted, jutting off in several directions, but I recited, over and over, the directions Boot had burned into my mind. *Faster, faster.* Jogging blindly was treacherous, but I did it anyway.

My breath came out in a mist, and my toes were frozen before I finally found an exit. Light flickered on the other side of the false panel, but I couldn't make out any voices. I popped the wall out and peeked inside before entering a massive library. Its floor-to-ceiling shelves were overflowing with dusty tomes, cracked scrolls, and worn, leather-bound notebooks.

Not a library, an archive. The treasury was close.

"West staircase, west staircase, watch the missing step." I sprinted up the stairs to my left—nearly killing myself on that damn missing step. My breaths were ragged, my muscles on fire by the time I reached the top, but I didn't slow. I wished I'd had time to pick through all these books and stories. I couldn't imagine the history hidden in their pages. *If—when—Sayzar falls, I will come back. I'll have time to read them.*

Past the landing lay another long hallway—bare except for a plain, wooden door at the end. There were no other ways in or out.

The rusted knob scraping against my palm made my skin crawl, but at least it wasn't locked. I slipped inside, turning my back to the room within as I carefully shut the door behind me, twisting the deadbolt into place.

An ache spread into my throat and my jaw, sucking the moisture from me. Holding Jessa's shift had drained all my salt reserves.

"Well, well."

My heart nearly burst out of my chest as I spun, raising my stolen dagger.

Two Enforcers stepped away from a rounded steel door across from me, smiling as they drew their swords. "Sayzar thought you may come for the Wardstone," the nearer one said. "It looks like he was right."

"Put the knife down, sweetheart," the second Enforcer crooned. "It's not going to do you any good."

No, it's not. I couldn't fight them. More than likely I'd hurt myself. But I wasn't defenseless. I had magic of my own.

I lowered the weapon and closed my eyes, sucking in a steadying breath before I let the taste of strawberries coat my tongue. Maybe it was the adrenaline—or because I was in so much pain—but when I struck out with my allure, it punched straight through their mental shields—a hot knife through butter. They didn't even have a chance to resist.

The men's eyes dulled into blissful pleasure, watching me with expectant expressions.

I straightened, hand over my still hammering heart. "Lower your weapons."

They did, smiling happily at the chance to serve me.

"Open that." I inclined my head toward the door behind them as I fixed my hair. "Now."

They jumped at the order, giddy with excitement. The first one that spoke drew a few symbols over the steel, unlocking a ward. They pulled it open and bowed. I paused as I passed through the doorway, giving them both a seductive smile. "Stand guard. None of the Emperor's staff may enter, understand?"

They nodded pleasantly, and as I entered the next room, they locked the door behind me.

I let out a sigh of relief. That could have been a nightmare.

The treasury was exactly as Boot had described it. A giant square, the far side opened into a balcony. A towering pillar, holding Cyclone's bones sat in the center, overlooking Carnage. Dozens of muddy footprints stained the awful purple carpet. To my left, the vault lay open—its unadorned golden door held ajar by Jayvin's great sword speared into the floor.

The Wardstone was still there—a massive, raw cut crystal set atop a dais. A faint shimmer of energy still glowed in the center, but its powering effects had long since ceased.

Where are they? I crept forward, trembling, to peek inside the vault. It was empty.

I blinked numbly as I stepped out onto the balcony. Without the barrier, the sky was pitch black, flecked with lovely stars. Hopefully, Geralt and his children would get out before the reinforcements stormed the city.

My legs nearly gave out as I glanced up to the top of the pillar.

Cyclone wasn't there.

I was going to hyperventilate. *But I'd seen him before?* That first time we'd come to the inner court, I'd seen the outline of his tormented body hanging from this very pillar.

I backed a step, the beginnings of panic taking hold. I needed to leave, I needed Jayvin, I needed—

"You still surprise me, Jessa." I whimpered as Sayzar approached from behind me, brushing his blood-stained fingers over the fins on my arm. "One, that you truly believed I'd let a rotting corpse mar the beauty of my palace. Second, that you thought I'd let you go. In case you've forgotten, you belong to me now."

I inclined my chin toward him. "Tetra."

"Pardon?"

"My name is Tetra." I let out a shaky breath. "Jessa was my mother. You murdered her and my father. You stole my life away, my future."

"Yes, yes, don't be so droll." Sayzar folded his hands behind his back as he stepped around to face me. Somehow, he'd gotten the bolt out of his shoulder—leaving a gaping puncture wound. His pretty cream tunic now stained red. "Such is the price of power. How many lives have you and your party taken in its pursuit?"

"The vault was already empty, wasn't it?"

"Emptied of gold." Sayzar's lips spread into an ugly smile. "But filled with plenty of my soldiers, ready to remove the heads of your partners."

"You don't own me." *They're fine. They'll be fine. Jayvin is with them.* I grit my teeth, holding his amused gaze. "Nor are my people yours to destroy."

"Ah, but you *are* mine." Sayzar leaned in, tracing the glittering scales on my collarbone. "You kneeled, remember."

I flinched.

A dark breeze swept over the balcony, settling on my

shoulder before brushing where I held the knife against my thigh.

"And you've belonged to me every day since." Sayzar's smile widened. "When all of Tyrr has fallen beneath my banner, you will be my pretty trophy. A living reminder of my greatest accomplishment that I can use whenever I wish."

I stared at him as my brows slowly rose. "You think so?"

Sayzar's breath hitched as that breeze crawled out of my shadow, and Jayvin materialized from the darkness. Blood soaked him, dripping from his hands and exposed fangs as he pressed my knife to the Emperor's throat. His growl was so deep, I could feel it in my bones. "Think again."

Chapter Thirty-Three

The wave of pure terror that fell over the Emperor's face was something of beauty. I wished I could have framed it.

Jayvin's blood-stained lips widened into a feral smile as he tightened his grip on the blade until it drew a shallow red line across the Emperor's ivory skin. "On your word, Sunshine."

Sayzar swallowed, panicked, gaze shifting to me.

I sucked in a breath. *In through the nose, out through the mouth.* Jayvin's eyes were nearly black. He was barely in control. I needed to be careful. I blew out that breath. "Where's Cyclone?"

Sayzar just blinked at me. He wouldn't dare move. Jayvin towered over him by a more than a foot. "Really? That's what you're concerned about now?"

"Yes." I flicked my gaze to Jayvin, and he let the knife cut deep enough to release a weak stream of blood. "Where did you put him?"

I'd seen the body hanging on the palace. Cyclone was here somewhere.

"May I ask a question first?" Sayzar hissed, shifting enough to look at Jayvin. His expression had grown surprisingly calm. "Where are the soldiers I had readied to dispatch you?"

Jayvin laughed. Slowly. Deadly. "They're all over your fancy courtyard. Pieces here, pieces there. Your citizens aren't too happy about it. I think they hoped you'd submit by now."

Sayzar's skin paled, but he kept his voice rigid. "I see."

"Where's Cyclone?" I took a cautious step closer. If I moved too quickly, Jayvin might slit his throat before I was ready. I needed Sayzar alive a bit longer. "We don't have all night."

This time, Sayzar just smiled at me. "You idiotic child. Like I said, did you really think I'd keep a corpse inside my palace?" His smile widened into a grin. "I burned him. The same day I removed his disgusting head."

The world began to spin. I wasn't sure if I was still standing. "B-but I saw him . . . hanging over the balcony."

"You saw what I wanted you to see." Sayzar licked his lips. "What I wanted all of Carnage to see. I happen to excel at illusionary wards."

"I'm aware."

I knew that gravelly voice anywhere.

Boot and Loach strode toward us, gazes flickering between the three of us. They were alive—coated in muck and filth—but alive.

Loach smiled at me from beneath his tentacles, an actual smile. "You alright, kiddo?"

I grinned back. "Yeah, you?"

Loach grunted, nodding toward the Emperor. "I'll be better when this asshole tells us what he did with all the gold."

"Agreed." I turned to Boot. "The Wardstone?"

"As been disabled for now." Boot moved in front of Sayzar, head cocked as he studied him. Jayvin trembled with anticipation as Boot adjusted his glasses. "I've waited a long time for this moment."

Sayzar's brow rose. "Ah. And I assume you're going to tell me why?"

"I cleaned your chamber pots, you know." Boot yanked the brooch off Sayzar's shoulder. "Eight months ago. Before I finally bought out my indenture." The Goblin tucked the emerald into his pocket. "You need to eat more fiber, Your Majesty."

As Jayvin chuckled darkly, Sayzar's expression turned murderous. "I've grown bored of this. Are you lot going to kill me or not? I don't have all night."

"Where's the gold?" Loach drew his sword and inspected the blade. "If you don't want to answer, that's fine. I'm happy to make this take a while."

"Fools." Sayzar let out a sharp laugh. "You have no time. The barrier is down. My palace will soon be swarming with my outside armies."

"Not exactly." Loach jerked his chin toward Jayvin. "Would you like to show him, drone?"

"Gladly." Keeping the knife pinned against his throat, Jayvin spun the Emperor and shoved him toward the edge of the balcony, his smile wicked. "Take a look."

A thrill ran through me as I stepped up beside them. Lights. Hundreds and hundreds of lights poured in from the beach, spreading into Carnage. Men and women carrying torches—the torches we'd readied there last night.

Sayzar couldn't hide his confusion. His men should be coming from the east.

I patted Sayzar's wounded shoulder, and he hissed. "I have a friend named Kevn that works at Loach's tavern. Turns out that he knows a lot of people who don't like you. One letter, with a time and a place, and they were happy to help destroy you."

"My people—" Sayzar began.

"Hate you," Boot interrupted smugly. "Thanks to our resident Vampire. I'm not sure they, or your Enforcers, will support your genocide after you've left them to fend for themselves."

"Clever." Sayzar clapped. "Very clever, I must admit. Except the public's approval is only a fickle boon. I can and will execute your wretched people. The orders are already in place. You can't stop them." He smiled, seeing the horror falling over me. "Your efforts to save your race were admirable but useless."

"Is that true?"

We all turned, the Emperor still in Jayvin's grip.

Agatha stood in the doorway to the treasury, a loaded crossbow pointed at Surge's head. She smirked. "I told you, Prince. He's a lying bastard."

Surge shot her an admiring look. "You planned this, didn't you? The timing is impeccable."

Agatha shrugged. "We do our best."

Jayvin's eyes narrowed into slits. "Why didn't I get a crossbow?"

You can do this. No bad thoughts. I couldn't hide my sorrow as I stepped toward Surge. "I'm sorry. I-I tried to bring him home. I thought . . . I thought it would make things better."

"I heard." Surge glanced at Agatha, and she released him. "And you're braver than I. Thank you. You shouldn't have had to be in this position." Hate-filled his dark eyes as they locked on Sayzar. "Now, we still have filth to tend to."

"There." Sayzar leaned into Jayvin's blade, smiling as blood streamed down his neck. "It's all out in the open. All of our treacheries, all of our failures. Now that I have you all together —" Sayzar's hands fell to his sides, tracing odd shapes against his thighs.

It took one too many heartbeats for me to grasp what he'd done.

A burst of lavender energy exploded across the balcony.

It wasn't until my back hit the ground, near the vault, that I realized I'd been airborne. The rest of us were scattered. Loach and Boot along the far wall. Agatha and Surge were thrown against the door.

Sayzar brushed the wetness off his neck and straightened his tunic. "That's better."

My ears rang as I struggled to draw air into my lungs.

"Finally." Jayvin pulled himself over the edge of the balcony, grinning wildly. His eyes had gone completely black. "Finally. Let's have some *fun*."

Sayzar smiled, hands folded behind his back. "I thought you'd never ask."

Jayvin moved too fast to track. One moment, he was hanging from the balcony. The next, he drove his knife toward the Emperor's skull.

Sayzar traced wards in the air, creating a protective shield of energy. When Jayvin collided with the ward, his body slowed until he was violently flung across the balcony. He hit the back wall—hard—leaving a massive indent in the rock. Jayvin burst out laughing as he rolled onto his back. "I hate Elves."

"An ironic statement." Sayzar traced several more wards as he strode toward him and picked up Loach's sword. "Let's see if you live up to the legends, Killer of Carnage."

The rest of us had begun to get to our feet, but an enormous weight crushed us back to the floor—another ward.

I'm so stupid. He'd given up so quickly. Sayzar Ameliatus hadn't become the conqueror of Tyrr by being weak. I could barely breathe with the ward's energy on my back.

But Jayvin could still move, and he dodged just in time to avoid the savage swing of Sayzar's blade. Jayvin rolled onto his feet, wiping at a trickle of blood that leaking from a gash on his brow. "I would enjoy nothing more."

Sayzar was on him in an instant, striking like a viper. Jayvin blocked and parried, sweeping the Emperor's feet from beneath him before turning on the offensive. Sayzar's back never hit the floor. He twisted, managing to land in a crouch. Jayvin wheeled, slamming his heel straight into Sayzar's jaw, sending him crashing into the vault's steel door.

With a hiss, Sayzar flipped backward onto his feet, his straight, red hair tangled around his face and neck. "Not bad." He touched the bruise forming on his swollen jawline. "But you should have struck to kill."

Jayvin bounced from foot to foot and pouted. His eyes were black. "Already? But we just started."

"Finish this, drone," Loach growled, fighting to lift his head. "Kill him!"

Jayvin's eyes flashed to mine, seeking approval. With gritted teeth, I nodded. It was time for Sayzar to die.

It wasn't until Jayvin lunged that I realized I'd only ever seen him play at fighting. Killing the Minotaur had been a game. Killing the Enforcers had been a game. This . . . this was death. Only centuries of training kept Sayzar alive as Jayvin disappeared, only to rematerialize with his hands on either side of Sayzar's jaw, moments from snapping his neck, his expression void of all emotion. Instead of fighting it, Sayzar twisted as Jayvin did. Spiraling in his grasp until his back was against Jayvin's chest.

Snarling in rage, Jayvin sank his teeth into Sayzar's neck. The Emperor screamed as he pulled free of Jayvin's grasp—tearing away a large chunk of flesh from his throat in the process.

Sayzar backed a step, blood pumping from the hole in his neck. He clamped his palm over it, his skin taking on a green tinge. Violet light shimmered in the air as Sayzar signed another ward over his ruined skin. The bleeding slowed but didn't stop.

Jayvin spat out a mouthful of Sayzar's blood as he strode toward the Emperor. "Sunshine will never shed another tear because of you."

"No." Sayzar stumbled to his feet, his chest heaving. "Her tears will only be for you." With a grunt of pain, he raised his hand and traced a series of shapes.

Jayvin's eyes widened as strands of light bound him, yanking him into the air before slamming him onto the ground so hard the balcony shook.

Jayvin fought and screamed in rage, but the ward held.

"No!" I shrieked, barely able to take in air. "Stop!"

"That's much better." Sayzar's breaths were ragged as he picked up his sword and tested the blade on his thumb, smiling as it drew blood. "We've met before, Jayvin Dyre." Sayzar hobbled towards him, twirling the sword. "Not that you'd remember."

Some red had returned to Jayvin's eyes as Sayzar leaned over him and crooned, "You were still a filthy half-breed, then. I visited your village and paid quite a sum to have the Vampire Matriarch slaughtered."

No, no, no, no.

Jayvin's breaths were coming too fast. He clawed at the ugly, purple carpet as if imagining he was tearing the Emperor's face. He couldn't move.

Sayzar patted his cheek. "Who was that I spoke to? Oh yes, your Human uncle. He assured me you were the best of the best—a true monster hunter." He pulled Jayvin's lip back to inspect his fangs. Jayvin snapped at him and barely missed taking off the finger.

Sayzar clucked his tongue. "Apparently, he was wrong. Too

bad it had to end like it did. Thankfully, when I took over Carnage, your Matriarch requested that I leave you where you were. I was happy to oblige. I didn't need a filthy spawn gallivanting about. She never found out that it was I who sent you to kill her in the first place."

My lips parted. *She'd made sure Jayvin stayed in the catacombs. Sayzar knew.*

The weight of the ward caused my spine to pop as I shifted. Despite their struggles, the others hadn't budged. We were stuck.

Sayzar raised his sword and rested it against Jayvin's throat. "Hopefully, she'll be pacified by your head in a box. I don't need the Matriarch as an enemy."

My kind can only be killed by our makers, fire, or beheading.

Sayzar was going to kill him. Jayvin was going to die.

My entire world narrowed to those two men—the one I loved and the one I hated.

As Sayzar raised his sword, Jayvin turned his head far enough to smile at me, his eyes returning to that stunning ruby red as he mouthed, *"I love you, Sunshine."*

Rage—endless, unending rage exploded through me as the taste of strawberries coated my tongue. I saw my mother's face —my father's—muttering those exact words as the executioner's axe fell. I felt Jayvin's chest pressed against my back, the way our bodies connected, the way he tasted.

The Emperor had taken everything from me.

My allure struck and shattered Sayzar's shields, plunging deep into his mind's black, poisoned recesses. I grabbed hold, twisting it until the strawberry flavor in my mouth shifted into a sickly, sweet rot.

I could feel him, in my mind, struggling to remain in control, but I sunk my claws deeper.

The sword clattered to the ground as Sayzar dropped to his knees.

"Do you think you can do it?" Sayzar's voice whispered at the edge of my mind. *"Are you a killer, Jessa?"*

My lips curved into a smile. *"My name is Tetra."*

As Sayzar's ward broke, Jayvin lunged and pinned him to the Emperor's limp body to the ground, using his legs to trap his arms to his sides. That savage hunger returned to Jayvin's eyes as he made to tear out Sayzar's throat—

With the ward gone, the weight on my back lifted and I rose. "No."

Jayvin froze, his lips spreading into a feral grin as I lifted the dropped sword. Sayzar's dazed blue eyes followed me as I leaned down and whispered, my lips brushing against his pointed ear. "You will never take anything from me again."

I let my allure drop, allowing just enough recognition to fill Sayzar's features. His smile was genuine when he said, "You've never failed to surprise me."

I didn't expect how cleanly a blade could cut through a man's neck until I swung. There was no resistance . . . only Sayzar Ameliatus' head rolling on the floor at my feet.

My eyes met Jayvin's, our chests rising and falling in sync.

The Emperor was dead.

Chapter Thirty-Four

I just breathed and breathed and breathed.

Sayzar's empty eyes stared up at me, the hot blood leaking from his neck pooling around my toes.

Jayvin sat back, his stunned gaze flickering between the Emperor and me, and filling with a heat that I knew if we'd been alone, he'd have taken me right then and there. "Sunshine?"

I took a step back, two, and the sword clattered to the ground.

"Hills alive, Tetra." Agatha entire body trembled as she got to her knees. "Where have you been hiding *that?*"

"Leave her alone," Loach grunted as he stood. "Or she might cut us all to ribbons."

"T-That's not funny." My hands were shaking so badly I couldn't flex my fingers. "I—"

But Jayvin was there—and I burst into tears as his lips crashed into mine. I shuddered as his fingers twisted into my hair. He lifted me and I wrapped my legs around his waist, pulling him closer as I kissed him back.

He was alive. I was alive.

Sayzar Ameliatus wasn't.

"You did this all for my father?" When Surge got to his feet, he walked to the balcony and stared out over Carnage. He shook his head. "I believed that bastard. I believed that one of my own had betrayed me."

Both out of breath, Jayvin set me down and I kept an arm around his waist to steady myself. "There wasn't a reason not to believe him."

"Wasn't there?" Surge huffed, leaning against the railing. "Wasn't Sayzar being my father's killer enough? I was weak. That's all there is to it."

"You're damn right, you were. You see those men?" Loach moved beside him and gestured to the city below, where hundreds of Merfolk now surrounded the Lantern Palace. They had their orders—round up the remaining Enforcers still loyal to Sayzar. Surge could take care of them after that. Loach lifted his hat to wipe the sweat off his milky forehead. "Those are *my* men, not yours. And now—with that bloody vault empty—they're going to skin me alive when they realize I can't pay them."

I glanced back to the vault, refusing to let my gaze fall on Sayzar's butchered body. Loach had bet everything on that gold, and now he was going to leave empty-handed.

"About that." Boot scratched at his crooked chin as he hobbled over to the vault. His usually pristine suit was soaked with mud. He stepped inside the vault's massive chamber, lit only by three dancing faelights. Boot tapped a sharp talon on the inner wall. "Did Sayzar not say that he excelled at illusionary wards?"

We nodded in unison.

Boot grinned from ear to pointy ear. "Jayvin Dyre, would you like to do the honors?"

It can't be. My heart thundered against my ribs as Jayvin stepped into the vault, wide-eyed and uncertain. He glanced to Boot, who gave him an assuring nod. Jayvin blew out a sharp breath, then began to trace those circles on the wall, over and over. Brilliant, lavender energy bloomed in the chamber until it covered us like a warm, tingling blanket.

Anti-illusionary charms.

As the energy dispersed over the balcony, the ward over the trove peeled away like a sheet. With the faelights hovering above, the vault *shone* with gems of every kind—gold, silver, platinum bars, and jewelry in the likes I'd never seen.

It took my breath away—so many treasures—locked away where no one would ever see them. Jayvin bent over and picked a gold coin off the floor, turning it over in his palm before tossing it to Loach. "Better?"

Loach caught it and grinned as he moved to the edge of the horde. Hands on his hips, he let out a gruff laugh. "Much better. This will cover what the Emperor cost me in work."

Next, Jayvin passed me a stunning, uncut ruby the size of an apple. "What do you think, Sunshine?"

I took it and turned, pressing it into Agatha's hand. She stared down at the jewel in awe. I grinned. "Do you think that'll be enough to keep Geralt and the kids fed?" I picked up a second ruby and laid it in her other hand. "And this to finally turn The Lux into a proper bed and breakfast?"

Silver tears lined Agatha's eyes, and she sucked in a shaky breath. "Yeah, I think it might be."

I turned to Boot. "And enough to pay off the indentures of all the Goblins still in the palace?"

"Yes." Boot shot me a crooked smile. "Most definitely."

"And there is more than enough to repair Carnage and the Dam." Surge rubbed his face and sighed. "But before that, we still must determine who will lead Carnage in the Emperor's stead. We can't leave the people here leaderless."

"Not you?" I'd always assumed that Surge would take control of the city. "Who better than our new king?"

Surge smiled a little as he dropped his hands to his sides. "I appreciate your faith in me, Tetra, but I don't belong here." He gestured around him. "My father may have enjoyed ruling land and sea, but I'd rather not. Tyrr's oceans are enough." He made a face. "Besides, the insects up here are horrid. I don't know how the Landfolk endure."

I burst out into a nervous laugh, rubbing the golden scars on my arm.

"Sunshine, look!" Jayvin jogged out of the vault, using his jacket as a satchel to carry out a load of treasure. With his sleeves rolled to the elbows, his golden binds were exposed. "Loach says this will be enough for a tent."

Before I could answer, Surge's gaze flickered between the permanent marks on our arms, eyes widening as the pieces clicked together. "You bound yourself to a Vampire?"

Jayvin tensed, expression turning predatory as he locked onto Surge and stepped toward me. I straightened, smoothing my hair over my shoulder. *Honesty has gotten you this far.* "Yes, I did. *We* did."

"You must know that's forbidden?" Surge shook his head then gestured to Jayvin. "I imagine it is for you, as well?"

Relaxing slightly, Jayvin nodded stiffly. "Punishable by death."

"Well, there's nothing to be done about it. A bond is a bond." Surge shot a quick, longing look toward Agatha. "I always found that to be an archaic law, anyway. You have my blessings."

"Thank you." An idea struck me. I would cry in relief later. I turned to Boot. "Do you still have Sayzar's brooch?"

"Yes," Boot grumbled, digging it out of his pocket before reluctantly passing it to me. "You can't have it."

"I wasn't planning on keeping it." I used the ripped hem of my dress to wipe away some of the blood staining the jewel. I smiled at Surge. "I know the perfect person to rule Tyrr."

Surge's brow rose. "Oh?"

Everyone stopped to listen.

"Yes." I undid the pin on the back of the brooch. "This man loves Carnage more than any I've met. He was willing to risk everything to preserve it, and his family has been part of its history for nearly a thousand years." I turned pinned the emerald on Boot's shoulder. His orange owl eyes widened in shock. I knelt, taking his knobbly hand. "There would be no freedom without you. How does running a city sound?"

Boot just stared at our conjoined fingers, lost in thought. Finally, he sighed. "It sounds like . . ." He looked over each of us, over the vault, over Surge. "It sounds like you all need to get your asses to work. I'd like to sleep on a feather bed before the night's over."

Chapter Thirty-Five

It had been six days since the Emperor's fall. Six days of chaos, bribery, and a lot of smooth-talking on Boot's part. Loach was beside him, overseeing the renewal of trade between the city and the rest of Tyrr.

After Sayzar and the barrier, the citizens of Carnage were more than happy to have a Goblin, one of their own, giving orders. Especially after he reopened the ports and put a hold on tax payments for the next five years so the people could recover.

Boot still hadn't told me why he had me keep that thimble. I hoped one day he'd be willing to share its story.

Geralt's restaurant quickly became Surge's new favorite, and he'd been generous enough to restock my and Loach's salt supply. After some shared words, he kissed Agatha's knuckles before returning to the sea. I didn't miss the blush staining her emerald-green skin as he waded out into the water.

Ivan was given a proper funeral—honored for his bravery.

Deep below the city, Carnage's chapel looked exactly as it did when we left it—smashed into a ruin by the Minotaur. The wards beneath the arch fell away as I approached. They remembered me. Maybe, all this time, they'd hoped I'd come back.

The firelight from my torch flickered writhing shadows across the damp, stone corridors as I descended into the lower sanctum. I shivered as drop of frigid water splattered on my cheek. *I should have worn a sweater.* My footsteps echoed throughout the chamber, reverberating over the dust and cobwebs clinging to the statues that remained standing—the previous rulers of Tyrr.

I clutched a braided lock of vivid red hair to my chest. Light rippled off the portraits of sobbing Elves as I approached the inset double doors that separated the sanctum from the catacombs below.

A warmth brushed my neck, drawing me closer. I raised my torch and a ripple of violet energy shimmered over the door. I sucked in a breath, two, and stepped closer.

A gravelly voice whispered, "It's waiting for you."

I shrieked and my torch clattered to the ground. I wheeled, clutching my throat, and found Jayvin smiling at me with raised brows from the shadows.

"*Sharks.*" I braced against my knees. "You scared me. I think my heart stopped."

"Apologies," Jayvin laughed and snapped his fingers, releasing his faelight. Despite the softness of his features, a sheen of nervous sweat coated Jayvin's skin, his breaths coming too fast and shallow. "I didn't mean to."

"You didn't have to come." I straightened. The last place in the world he wanted to be was here. I took his hand and smiled. "The Minotaur is dead, remember?"

"Yes, it's dead." Jayvin moved cautiously toward the door. As the faelight illuminated his ruby-eyes, they became hazed over and distant. "But the wards are calling for you. Why?"

"Because I made a promise." A fresh wave of heat enveloped me as I showed him the lock of Sayzar's hair. "It allowed me to find you in exchange for the Emperor. It deserves to know he's dead."

Jayvin brushed his fingers down my spine, tracing circles on my lower back. "This is one of the many things that makes you special, Sunshine. Most would have never come back."

"A life for a life." Violet energy surged as I gently placed the lock of hair before the door. "Without it, I wouldn't have you."

As Jayvin tried to answer, waves of light exploded through the chapel. I cried out, slamming my eyes shut as it blinded me. I felt Jayvin's arms wrap around me, pressing me into his chest.

The heat of the waves passed, and my entire body shook as I opened my eyes. Jayvin had pinned me to the wall, shielding me—shadowed from the piercing light above—but now he stared up at the ceiling, mouth parted in awe.

Wait. Light above? I looked up, and if it wasn't for his steady grip, I would have fallen to my knees.

There was sky above us—patches of blue visible through the gaps in the chapel ceiling. A chilled breeze danced over the tears falling down my cheeks as it chased away centuries of death and sorrow.

"The wards are gone," Jayvin whispered. "Sayzar didn't bury the chapel . . . he put an illusion over it."

An illusion. He'd hidden the church away for centuries, and now it was free.

Just like Jayvin.

Just like me.

Jayvin pulled me on his lap as he slid to the dusty marble ground, silver lining his eyes as he watched a puff of clouds roll by. His throat bobbed. "You did it, Tetra."

I let out a shaky breath. "We did it."

He kissed my forehead as I snuggled into him and traced those circles onto his chest.

Jayvin let out a rumbling laugh and tugged me closer. "This is real, Sunshine."

"I was just checking." I kissed his collarbone. "Somedays, I'm not so sure."

"Hmm." Jayvin's fingers trailed down my back, slow and teasing. "Neither am I, but I'm happy to live in any reality with you in it—real or not. I see you."

And he did. He was the only one who ever had. I still missed the cove—to have nothing between me and the open sea—but those days were fading into happy memories instead of cutting me like jagged knives. I was ready to let the past go and finally let my parents rest.

But there was one thing that still haunted the edge of my mind, that relentlessly tugged at the corners of my dreams. "Jay?"

Jayvin's strokes had turned more indulgent as he brushed my loose waves aside to kiss my neck. "Yes?"

"What Sayzar said about before . . ." I sighed, trying not to be distracted by his lips on my skin. "About you having an uncle and a village."

Jayvin went still and repeated, "Yes?"

"We can do whatever we want now." I leaned my head back so he could get better access to my throat. "Do you want to find them, or what may be left of them? Whatever you need, I'm with you."

"I know you are." Jayvin let his canines scrape against my jugular, and I shuddered. "But for now, I just want to live . . . with you. Maybe one day, we can find the truth—together—but all that matters to me now is us."

My body went liquid as his lips hovered over mine. "And how should we live, Jayvin Dyre?"

"Right now?" Jayvin's cool breath against my skin set me on fire as he laughed, "Maybe we get that tent. Maybe we open a trinket shop for you." This time, Jayvin laid back and pulled me on top of him, his hands trailing down my sides. His gaze heated as he played with the straps of my sleeveless dress, his attention then turning to the rose-gold flower pendant hanging above my breasts, the petal pink pearl now replaced with the vibrant blue one he'd gifted me. "Maybe we explore every inch of this damned world just because we can. There's no one left to stop us."

"I like the sound of that." I leaned down and kissed him until our breaths turned ragged. I lifted his chin, and he sighed happily as I trailed kisses down his throat. "To hell with emperors and matriarchs. They don't own us anymore. You are mine, and I am yours. That is enough."

"Yes," Jayvin breathed. "That is more than enough."

Acknowledgments

First and foremost, praise Jesus. The glory and gratitude belong always to You.

To my husband, Corey Tucker: Thank you for being such an active part of this story. Thank you for always being the person I can count on to tell me if something sucks or not. Also, I'd like everyone to know that you named Boot.

To Samantha: Jayvin and Tetra wouldn't exist without you. You've never given up on me. Even when I'm an anxious, blubbery mess (which is all the time). There are so many Easter eggs in this story that only you and I will get. Oh, and please finish Ranch. I'm begging you. I need it.

To Hailey Renee: You are literally a God send. You've always understood the deeper pains I've hidden inside my characters. You are a magical human. I am so grateful to have you on my team!

Thank you, B.E. Padgett: You're my rock. Enough said.

Note From The Author

Congratulations! If you made it this far, you have my absolute gratitude! The process of starting a novel and taking it all the way to publication is a whirlwind, and I can't thank you enough for riding it with me!

If you loved or hated it, it would be a huge blessing to me if you left an honest review on Amazon or Goodreads! Reviews, for better or worse, significantly help to get stories into the hands of new readers. We, the authors, depend on you!

Either way, thank you for taking the time to read one of my brain babies! You're amazing. Just know that.

Love,
    Brittany

Also by Brittany Tucker

A Dowry of Snails and Mud

Noah's Not So Super Summer

The Revenant Series:
The Calamities of Camden Callahan

About the Author

Brittany Tucker lives on an island off the coast of Washington state with her husband, daughter, a menagerie of furry and scaled children, and her imagination. She prefers generic cereal, collects tattoos and action figures, and was in the top 5% on the planet for ships sunk in *Assassin's Creed III*.

Brittany also likes to write books from time to time. (Kidding, all the time.)